THE
SHADOW
KEY

T0190544

Also by Susan Stokes-Chapman

Pandora

THE
SHADOW
KEY

A Novel in

FOUR BRANCHES

SUSAN STOKES-CHAPMAN

HARPER PERENNIAL

NEW YORK • LONDON • TORONTO • SYDNEY • NEW DELHI • AUCKLAND

HARPER ● PERENNIAL

A hardcover edition of this book was published in the United Kingdom in 2024 by Harvill Secker.

HarperCollins books may be purchased for educational, business, or sales promotional use. For information, please email the Special Markets Department at SPsales@harpercollins.com.

FIRST U.S. EDITION

Library of Congress Cataloging-in-Publication Data

Names: Stokes-Chapman, Susan, 1985- author.
Title: The shadow key : a novel in four branches / Susan Stokes-Chapman.
Description: First U.S. edition. | New York : Harper Perennial, 2024. | Identifiers: LCCN 2024012530 | ISBN 9780063392427 (trade paperback) | ISBN 9780063396227 (hardback) | ISBN 9780063392441 (e-book)
Subjects: LCGFT: Gothic fiction. | Detective and mystery fiction. | Novels.
Classification: LCC PR6119.T668 S53 2024 | DDC 823/.92—dc23/eng/20240329
LC record available at https://lccn.loc.gov/2024012530

ISBN 978-0-06-339242-7 (pbk.)
ISBN 978-0-06-339622-7 (library edition)

24 25 26 27 28 LBC 5 4 3 2 1

Dros Gymru

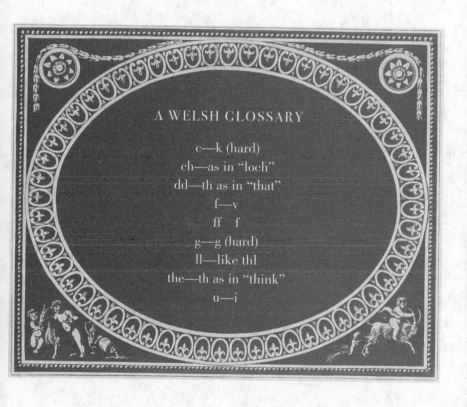

A WELSH GLOSSARY

c—k (hard)

ch—as in "loch"

dd—th as in "that"

f—v

ff   f

g—g (hard)

ll—like thl

the—th as in "think"

u—i

Gall pechod mawr ddyfod trwy ddrws bychan
A great sin can enter through a small door

WELSH PROVERB

He wakes to the unmistakable smell of sulfur and a room as black as pitch.

What woke him, he cannot rightly say. There is a chill to the room that can only be accounted for by the cold Welsh stone, stone which retains little heat even with a fire burning fierce in the grate. There is the screech of a barn owl, a sound that has always soothed him despite its harsh hunter's cry. There too has been the sound of running water from the stream abutting the gatehouse, its watery chime a boon to his tired mind rather than a banc.

And, of course, that smell of sulfur.

It comes and goes. He has tried to account for it, consulted Plas Helyg's gardener about the matter. Fungus in the water he was advised, a consequence of the stream being so close to the wall, compounded by a lack of natural light on account of the crowding trees. Or, perhaps, the smell comes from the mines up on the nearby hill. If the wind blows a certain way, such things might be possible. In any case (he was told) it is no cause for concern, and so the smell is something he has grown accustomed to. It is not so very bad, after all.

Still. Something is different this night. He tries to place the anomaly, stares wide-eyed into the dark, but soon it is no good. With a

1

groan he swings his legs out of bed and in the dark his gnarled toes feel for the slippers on the rug, pushing the soft pumps onto his feet, first one, then the other. It takes him a moment to stand, to accustom himself to the stiffness in his joints. He almost changes his mind, almost sinks back down on the feather mattress, but now he has exerted himself it seems futile to have wasted the accomplishment, and so he forces himself to the window, pulls the curtains apart on their rings.

There is no moon. The trees that surround the house, unfathomable.

He sees nothing.

Only when the old man moves to turn away does he apprehend what is out of place, what it was that must (*must*) have woken him, for there is nothing else to account for it. Beneath the familiar sounds of rural night, the running water of the stream, like an undercurrent, he hears it:

Whispering.

With shaking fingers he twists the window latch, pushes the pane up into its casement, leans out, strains to listen. Frowns.

It is no louder. He thought perhaps it was the wind whispering through the willows up at the mansion or those nearby at the family vault; perhaps, even, the lull of the sea across the valley a mere two miles away. It happens, sometimes, on a clear night.

Yet.

He begins to lower the sash, wonders if his hearing has started to fail him, if his body has found one more damnable way to bow to its advancing years. He has diagnosed it in others. The "bewitched ear." Common, in older folk . . . But what is this? Fingertips pressing onto the glass, he peers down.

Nothing wrong with his eyes.

A light—a lone red orb—has appeared between the trees.

No. Not an orb. A small dancing flame; a candle, he is sure. As he

2

watches, the flame begins a slow trajectory toward the gatehouse and he strains into the darkness, tries to discern a body connected to the candle but perceives none. All he can see is that one single suspended light.

"Who goes there?"

There is no answer, no variation to the candle's movement, no pause to those infernal whisperings. The red light (such an odd color for a flame) bobs along on its journey before it disappears, cut off by the wall below.

Gone.

His sister often speaks of the *tolaeth*, supernatural warnings of death or some other approaching of a calamity. Corpse candles, these. Well, he has never set any store in them, not in any of the local superstitions. He is a man of science, has no patience for silly delusions. Candle it may be, but no corpse about it to be sure. What a notion, he thinks grimly, slamming the window shut. Enaid always did have a fertile imagination.

The old man turns from the window, spends some minutes attempting to quicken the tinderbox. Village folk, he thinks now, descending the stairs with his own candle aloft, and more than one. Though his hearing is very good (and he is convinced now that age has not thwarted him in this instance after all) he did not hear a single voice and no man, no sane one at least, would whisper to themselves outside, alone. It will be those pesky miner's children—led by Cai, probably—sneaking about the woods, carrying naked flames at that! Troublesome whelps. He will soon see them off.

On the bottom step he stops abruptly. The whispering is louder here, he realises. The wretches, then, have got into the house! But how, when he bolted the door, latched the windows fast and firm?

Concentrate, he thinks. Use reason. Where does the sound come from? The red light went to the right of the gatehouse, did it not? The

3

old man raises his candle in its holder, grips the hoop tightly with one arthritic finger, crosses the hall into his sitting room. Nothing, no one, but the whispering is louder now and so he continues round, through the open door into his library . . .

. . . and almost drops the candle on the floor.

A flickering light emits from the bookshelves on the far wall. He shakes his head, rubs his eyes with his free hand, looks again. He must be hallucinating. His bookshelves have no means to glow!

Cautiously he crosses the room, is shocked to discover on the approach that his bookshelves do *not* glow, but there is instead a wide opening within them, the way beyond lit by thick pillar candles in ornamental sconces. For a moment he stares, perturbed. After all these long years how could he not have known there was a door here? It was rumoured, of course, in old Cadwalladr's day, that Plas Helyg and its grounds were a haunt for smugglers. Village gossip, he always thought, a tale to thrill and shock. And yet, here, a tunnel!

He pulls the door open wider, the heavy wood creaking on its hinges.

Before him lies a stone passage, at the end a set of spiral stairs leading downward, and cautiously the old man descends on creaking knees. The iron banister is cool to the touch; he grips it tight, heart pinching in his chest. When he reaches the bottom he is greeted by a rush of air, smells the dankness of earth and wet stone. All of a sudden he is suspended with indecision—he wishes neither to go on nor to retreat. But! He has come too far to turn back now and before him is another, longer passage, lined with torches attached to ornate braziers, crusted with age.

The old man continues on.

Halfway down (or is it up?) he stops. Listens. The echoed whispering is much louder here. Drawn now to its strange cadence he begins to move forward again, uses the flat of his free hand to touch the rough

4

damp walls, hard-knuckled fingers reading crevices in the stone as if he were blind, his worn slippers scuffing on the dirt floor. The smell of sulfur catches at his throat and as the old man coughs he sees his breath pool in the air before him.

How far underground is he? To where does the passage lead? And the whisperings! They come not from village children at all, but someone else, *something* else, and in the wake of that knowledge he finds that he is trembling. But as if an invisible thread has attached itself to his spine, that whispering—seductive yet frightening in its strangeness—pulls him to the end of the passage, and taking a deep and rattling breath, the old man enters the cavernous room beyond. . . .

Meirionydd
Summer 1783

BRANCH I.

There are hells everywhere,
Both under the mountains, hills, and rocks,
And under the plains and valleys.

EMANUEL SWEDENBORG
Heaven and its Wonders and Hell: From
Things Heard and Seen (1758)

CHAPTER ONE

The journey from London had been pleasant enough, to begin with.

The many coachmen who conveyed him made easy and timely progress—the roads were good, the weather altogether fine, and on their approach to the Welsh border the landscape began to take on a new face. Henry Talbot watched as rugged mountains rose in the distance, as previously flat fields started to slope gently upward, chequered black and white with grazing sheep and cattle. Even the air—though the journey by that time had been almost exclusively along open roads and the towns were miles behind—smelt different: fresher, sweeter, with hints of flora and sharp fir. For a brief moment Henry had let himself feel something akin to optimism instead of the bitterness that has dogged him since leaving the capital, but then his progression across the border and thence into the valleys took a decidedly downward turn; the temperature dropped as the horses ambled into dense woodland, the roads within them tight and winding, the chaise rocking from side to side almost continually for twenty miles. At the mountain he heard called Dinas, Henry was required to exchange the luxury of that enclosed vehicle for a pony and cart led by a gruff driver who did not seem to speak any English. By the time they had ascended an incomprehensibly steep hill to then descend along a very bad and stony dirt track (at which point heavy rainfall made itself most keenly known) Henry's mood was sober, the experience having dampened any pleasure he might have taken from the scenery of this wild and desolate country he must now call home.

Until that moment there had been in Henry a sense of denial, as if he were merely playing out a part; until that moment he let himself believe that his journey was a temporary one, to be considered an excursion only, from which he would return in due course. But as the cart's wheels clattered over those uneven roads littered with slate shards and jagged pebbles there was no denying it any longer: his old life is over. His new one must begin.

With a sigh Henry turns up his collar. The sun has finally made its appearance but the lateness of the day has tempered the May air with a touch of cold. Still, this next stage of the journey is picturesque; the vale they travel through now is watered by what Henry assumes is the estuary which widens as the cart advances, its sides bounded by hills and lush woodland. On the curve of another tree-lined bend he catches the scent of brine.

At length they reach the outskirts of a town called Abermaw where the driver stops at the bottom of a sharp incline of shale-rock. Two labourers climb aboard, settle themselves down in the straw next to Henry's trunk strapped into the back of the cart. He looks over his shoulder, doffs his hat, proffers a smile.

"Good afternoon."

Both men stare stonily back. Henry's smile slips. His tone had been friendly; there was no need at all for them to look at him like that and turn so pointedly away. A discord of whispers begins between the two men, and in confusion Henry twists back to face front.

The cart rumbles on. The road angles itself on an unsteady turn; a gull cries high in the arch of a sharp breeze. As the sea hoves into view—an undulating sheet of iron-gray shot with jade—Henry grips the handles of his portmanteau even tighter, takes a grudging kind of pleasure from the sound of waves, the quaint fishing boats bobbing along the horizon.

It is the first time he has ever seen the sea.

Further down at the harbor stand much larger boats, all at various stages of construction. Fascinated, Henry watches as they pass what looks to be the beginnings of a brigantine with its wooden skeleton only half complete, three men at its belly with hammer and nail. Further down the quay he spies a line of smaller boats being loaded with crates, an empty wagon waiting on the sand, and Henry turns to the driver with interest.

"What do you export? Slate? I heard there were mines nearby."

Henry's driver—an older man with a heavily lined face beneath a coarse hay-colored beard—glances at him. He sniffs, says nothing. Henry reaches into his coat, extracts the Welsh dictionary he was obliged to purchase in an obscure bookshop on the fringes of Piccadilly a week before his departure, and thumbs through the pages. "*Llechen?*" he tries, tripping over the word for slate, but still the Welshman does not answer. Behind them one of the laborers snorts, and the cart trundles by—the moment with it. They emerge once more onto open road, leave Abermaw behind them. Henry returns the dictionary to his pocket with a sigh.

He has pored over that dictionary, felt duty-bound to attempt to at least *try* to accept what fate has dealt him. He knows he will be at a loss in this rugged land without speaking the language, but it is damnably difficult; he does not understand the clauses or the grammar, and to his ear the sounds are guttural, hard to adapt to. Henry suspects too that he is mispronouncing everything, applying the incorrect word to the situation, and it angers him, this weakness. He, who was respected for his intellect in London by his colleagues at Guy's and Bow Street alike. He, who could speak to a room full of medical students with eloquence and finesse! Henry sought positions in other places of course, both in London and beyond, but without recommendation no one would deign grant him an interview.

Instead, he has had to come here.

Henry thinks of the letter nestled at the bottom of his trunk, folded and refolded so many times it has grown limp. *My dear sir* (it started), *it has come to my attention that you are without position under circumstances most unfortunate. To ease such misfortune, it would be my greatest pleasure to offer you the vacant post of physician in Penhelyg, Meirionydd.*

It was signed, *I am, &c, Lord Tresilian.*

Intrigued, Henry had located Penhelyg on a map purchased from the same bookseller who later sold him the dictionary, and was disappointed to find it a small and inconsequential mining village in Wales with no large towns or cities to be found that were not over fifty miles away—an isolated place by the sea, quite far removed from anything he had ever known before. Many thoughts jumbled in his head at that moment as he examined the disc of wax that had sealed the letter, its strange curling symbol set within a crimson circle. Who was Lord Tresilian, and how did he come to know of what happened in London? It was something Henry puzzled over for an inordinately long time, yet in the end he could only be grateful for the opportunity. After all, it was blatantly apparent no other was forthcoming.

"Will we reach Penhelyg soon?" he asks the driver now in an effort to distract himself, and though Henry did not expect an answer one comes all the same.

The words are in heavily accented English, but he can at least understand when the driver says, "We'll be there soon enough."

"You *do* comprehend me!" Henry exclaims, but the Welshman only keeps his gaze fixed fast ahead.

And so they proceed in silence for some time more through shifting yellow sands until, eventually, the road veers away from the shoreline, rises upward, inland. Henry watches the slanting rays of the setting sun turn that grey sea into a single thread of gleaming gold before he loses sight of it altogether around a moss-banked bend. Every few miles they pass through desolate-looking hamlets before moving into deeply shaded woodland, and he smells in the chill air (he wraps his rain-damp coat tight about him) the earthy scent of bracken. Above him there is a sharp cry; he looks up, spies the silhouette of an owl soaring high on the hunt.

Dusk has settled now, the sun lost in a cradle of mauve. Henry looks about him, tries to discern anything more than the strange shadows of country, but the dirt track is steadily darkening like ink spilt upon the soil. In the distance there is the low chattering of birds, the eerie hush of trees, of nocturne come to draw the evening slowly in. Henry swallows. He is used to flame-lit streets and noisy tavern din, not this strange almost-quiet, and he is just about to ask again when they might expect to reach his destination when the woodland parts and the driver instructs the pony to slow.

They stop outside a long line of narrow stone houses. The wheels of the cart have scarce ceased the last turn on their spokes when the two laborers—who have not stopped their pointed muttering since leaving Abermaw—jump down.

"Penhelyg," the driver announces.

Henry stares.

So . . . small. So meagre! He looks at the cramped unlit cottages, their doors daubed strangely with a stripe of flaking white paint, each and every one. The only thing that softens their harsh facade is a bank of willow trees set behind them, lithe branches bending gently over the slate roofs. Is he truly to live here in this barren backwater? Has he really left London for *this*?

"Which is mine?" Henry asks, weak at the thought of it, but the driver cocks his head in the direction of the trees.

15

"Further on," that man says, "up in the woods. But you're not going there yet."

Henry looks at the driver in surprise. "I'm not?"

"*Nag wyt*. Tresilian's orders."

As they were speaking, the two laborers had opened the door to the furthest cottage. Now at the entryway they turn, peer unfriendly-like at Henry before slamming the door. The noise echoes dully into the growing night, and Henry frowns deeply at the strip of ungainly white paint.

"Have I offended them?"

There comes no answer, only a grunt, a flick of leather on flank. "*Ymlaen a chdi*."

The pony walks on, takes the cart up onto a path that disappears between crowding trees; Henry must press the soles of his feet into the cart's foothold to brace himself against the incline, squints into the dark. Another owl (or perhaps the same one) utters a bleak cry to the cooling air, and Henry shifts uncomfortably on the hard bench. His back has begun to stiffen with cold, a painful clamp at his spine. He smells dank earth, rotting fungi, and tiredly he presses the portmanteau to his chest. How much farther? His eyes have adjusted to the darkness now, but it has made little difference; the farther up the cart goes the deeper that darkness stretches, the trees an impenetrable blanket, tar-black. Somewhere, far back into the woodland, there is the sound of running water. At one point they pass a sharp fork in the road but the cart does not slow its course until, finally, a dim light appears through the spindled branches of the trees. The driver flicks the reins again, clears his throat.

"That's Plas Helyg," he says, and Henry peers into the gloom.

Ahead is a towering set of gates, the wrought-iron metalwork twisted into an obscure pattern of which Henry cannot make out the details; beyond them, down a wide gravel drive, there stands an imposing stone house. On their approach someone pulls open the gates, and as the pony ambles through them Henry has the uncanny notion that their ancient bars appear to sigh. He cranes his neck, stares upward. Too dark to see it properly, he can deduce only that this house called Plas Helyg is large. Monstrous large. Nothing at all like what he was used to in London.

Why on earth has he been brought here?

It is just as the cart draws up to the grand front doors that they swing open. A tall figure stands on the threshold, supported by a cane. His body is turned to silhouette against the candlelight within, and presently two more shadows join him—the squat form of a woman, a broad-shouldered man—but Henry, unable to concentrate fully now the cart has stopped, feels his head spin and presses his fingers to his temples. What a relief it is to be still!

"Dr. Henry Talbot?"

The voice that calls his name is deep and eloquent. English. *Perfect* English, no trace of a Welsh accent at all, and the shock of it makes Henry look sharply at the man who spoke. There is a dull crunch of gravel against heel as he steps closer.

"My dear boy," the man says. He takes another step forward, right hand clasped tightly on the silver head of his stick. "I've been waiting for you."

CHAPTER TWO

Henry is ushered inside where he finds himself standing within a large and brightly lit vestibule. Blinking into candlelight he sets his portmanteau down on the flagstone floor and looks about him, wide-eyed.

In front of him a broad oak staircase almost fills the entire space, its newels capped with formidable-looking points. The ceiling is high with richly moulded cross-beams, and set into every wainscoted wall are large paneled doors leading off to other parts of the house. But what draws the gaze—indeed, it can scarce be missed—is a magnificent fireplace boxed in by an elegant sopha and armchair. Made of intricately carved stone it spans the height of floor to ceiling, and at the very central point of the mantle there is engraved a symbol. Though fatigued to the point of faintness Henry recognises it instantly: it is the very same symbol that was imprinted onto the wax seal of his letter.

"You are very welcome here. Very welcome indeed!"

He turns. The older man is reaching out his left hand for him to shake. Henry takes it. "Are you Lord Tresilian?"

"I am indeed," comes the reply.

Henry studies the tall man in front of him. In his profession he has become accustomed to marking the tenor of a person by sight alone (dead or otherwise), a skill which made him such a favorite of Bow

18

Street's finest. Lord Tresilian, Henry deduces by the lined contours of his face and shock of thick black hair with only a light peppering of gray, appears to be in his fifties. Not an old man by any means, but the silver-topped cane he holds is telling; he grips it tightly (too tightly) and there is an odd pallor to the man's skin, his lips are pale, his cravat a margin loose at the neck. How long, Henry thinks, has the man been ill?

"Have you eaten?" he asks, releasing Henry's hand. "Do say you haven't! I instructed you to be brought up to the house for the sole purpose of welcoming you to Penhelyg. Such a long journey you must have had, all that way by road!"

Gratified by the gesture, Henry shakes his head. "I've had nothing since the coaching inn at Welshpool this morning."

At that Lord Tresilian clicks the fingers of his free hand, and as he does so a gold signet ring on the fifth digit glints in the candlelight.

"Splendid," he says as the man and woman who appeared behind him in the doorway step forward. "Mrs. Evans, please bring a tray for Dr. Talbot to my study."

There is the briefest of pauses before the woman named Mrs. Evans dips her knees. She is an elderly creature with skin that reminds Henry of damp wrinkled silk, age-spots smattering her face like over-sized freckles. Snow-white hair peeks from beneath a mobcap patched with yellowed darning.

"Thank you," Henry says, managing his first genuine smile in days. "I cannot tell you how welcome that would be."

He addresses both his host and Mrs. Evans, but the housekeeper (Henry presumes she is the housekeeper) appears disinclined to look at him as she shuffles past. His new employer leans forward conspiratorially.

"Forgive her peevishness, Henry. Might I call you Henry? She is not particularly welcoming of strangers at present."

19

"Oh?"

"A family bereavement, I'm afraid."

His dark eyes rove over Henry's features, gaze unnervingly intent, but then he coughs into his fist and turns away. He wipes his hand with a handkerchief, tucks it away into his finely tailored sleeve.

"Come. Powell, our butler, will bring you a glass of port while you wait."

Henry looks at the other man. Broad-shouldered as already observed, he is nonetheless squat in stature with a sour face made all the more unpleasant by the old-fashioned periwig he wears; a dull flax color too long in the front, its curls untamed, which he dips in the direction of his master.

"Very good, my lord."

Strong Welsh lilt, deeply graveled. Polite enough, but Henry is sure he detects a mark of recalcitrance in his tone, and he watches the man walk off toward a plain door tucked behind the cavernous staircase.

"Come," Lord Tresilian says again, just as Henry's driver walks through into the vestibule, depositing his trunk in the middle of the floor.

"Thank you," Henry attempts in Welsh, and for a brief moment the bearded man stares at him before shrugging and retreating back the way he came, the crunch of gravel loud and hurried. Trying not to feel offended Henry lets his host guide him into a dimly lit hallway and thence into a room tucked neatly off to the left.

It is a large room, grandly furnished, but though its decor is bejeweled and rich, there is something about it that seems to swallow light; the armchairs are upholstered in maroon, the ornate furniture is oiled mahogany, the vermilion-colored walls filled with pictures, none of which serve to brighten it. Henry stares up at those paintings, struck by their fantastical scenes. Exotic beasts look out from dark canvases,

20

angels cry through torrid clouds. One painting depicts the fall of Adam and Eve in the Garden of Eden where, halfway up a tree, is entwined a serpent with a human head and arms, offering the damned pair an apple.

Another fireplace here of a more staid and appropriate size is flanked by a mahogany sideboard on top of which sits a baroque globe of the world and a small gun cabinet holding an elegant flint-lock pistol. On the other side stands a cabinet which reaches up to the corniced ceiling, devoted it seems to expensive trinkets. Different-sized compartments hold within them a velvet tray of mounted ancient coins, a group of bronze miniature columns, a model of what looks to be a Roman ship cast in marble, a fine set of plaster intaglios.

"Treasures from my excursions abroad," their owner says with pride, seeing Henry's gaze stray. "Many I collected during the Grand Tour when I was a youth. The places I've seen! Paris and Versailles, Florence and Pisa, the more obscure locales of Baden and Passau. So many treasures to be found there. Never was I happier in my life than I was then, the world so completely at my feet."

Henry has known men like this—men born to privilege for whom the Grand Tour is a rite of passage, a culmination of their expensive education. In Henry's experience, a person cannot ever have the world completely at one's feet without knowing what world it is one treads within. It is clear to Henry—from the trinket cabinet alone to the lushly decorated study and the very house in which they stand—that his lordship lives a rarefied existence, and therefore he cannot match the older man's enthusiasm. Still, it is not his place to voice such thoughts aloud, so Henry forces a smile and politely says, "You're lucky indeed, sir, and it's a fine collection. Most fine."

Lord Tresilian smiles at the compliment. "A modest collection. But nothing at all to these . . ."

He gestures with a wide sweep of his arm, and Henry looks to where the older man indicates.

At the far end of the room stands a deep mahogany desk; behind it, five rows of bookcases spanning from one side of the wall to the other, filled to the brim. In the center of the case—propped up on an ornate stand—is a book far larger than the rest.

"Let me show you," his lordship says, guiding Henry down to the other end of the room, and pinioned in his gentle grip Henry has no choice but to follow.

They come to a stop just past the desk. Lord Tresilian surveys the shelves with a look of unmistakable pleasure.

"Magnificent, are they not? *These* are where my passions lie." He rests his weight on his cane. "The Tour, you know, opened my eyes to many wondrous things besides travel and women. Books, Henry, the source of all knowledge! What do you think of them?"

Diligently, Henry looks. Up close he sees the shelves are encased behind glass doors, the surfaces shining, devoid completely of dust. He cranes his head, takes the books in shelf by shelf, reminded of that obscure Piccadilly bookshop. The seller told him while he was wrapping the dictionary that some of his stock was so old it was best for their preservation to be kept behind glass, and so Henry wonders now just *how* old these volumes are. He steps closer to read the spines. On some, the leather is so cracked with age it makes the words almost unintelligible, but others are clearly wrought in gilt lettering: *Compendium Rarissimum Totius, Petit Albert, Libro de San Cipriano, Epistolae Theosophicae . . .*

Expensive, these. The contents of one bookcase alone would have cost him several years' rent. Henry clears his throat.

"Indeed. They are beautiful volumes."

"Oh, they are far more than that," comes the answer. "Beautiful, yes, but what they contain . . ." Lord Tresilian shakes his head a little. "There is something to be said about esoteric philosophy and the ancient sciences. The old world, you see, has endless wonders just waiting to be discovered. I have," he continues, "at least two hundred books on necronomics and ancient religious practices, on classical invocations, hermetic philosophy, Babylonian mysticism . . . I discovered my first in Italy—" here he points to a volume on a top shelf, though there are so many that it is impossible to make out which precisely he refers to—"and it set about a lifelong fascination. Each place I went I made it a quest of mine to discover a new text. The bookshops in Athens are quite remarkable, as are those in Rome and Montpellier, but it's off the beaten track in Brandenburg that I found some of my most valuable pieces."

He presses the silver ball of his cane.

"Many were difficult to acquire." He pauses, clears his throat, and Henry hears within it a wet, thick-sounding bubble. "Still, I have my sources now, all over Europe."

Henry nods at the larger book, resting high on its plinth. "And this?"

"Ah," Lord Tresilian breathes. "This."

He moves behind the cavernous desk to stand in front of that middle bookcase, reaches out, touches the glass protecting the book with an almost-caress. His fingertips have a clubbed appearance, the nails curving downward, and Henry realises then why his host's face holds such an odd pallor.

Lord Tresilian is a dying man.

"This," he says softly, "is very special to me. Very special indeed."

Henry waits for him to elaborate but when he does not, only stares admiringly at the book behind its glass casing, Henry comes to stand beside his new employer.

Until that moment the light from the room was thrown upon the glass, but now he stands before it Henry can see the thing clearly. It is a great tome of a book bound in thick black leather, a gold clasp holding its gilt-edged pages shut. He bends closer; a raised symbol juts from the cover, set in a circle that spans the width of the front. It is the exact replica of the one above the fireplace in the vestibule, and the wax seal on the letter offering him employment at Penhelyg:

Henry means to ask what the symbol is but Lord Tresilian coughs, pointing at another item which rests at the base of the book, a piece of rock on a small square of black velvet.

"You see this?"

"I do."

The man turns to him with another proud smile. "Gold."

Henry frowns. His host chuckles.

"Of course, it does not *look* like gold, but see at the bottom those tiny flecks of yellow? It was the first we found in the mines. Near thirty years ago now."

"I see."

At that moment a yawn threatens to escape, and Henry must press a hand to his mouth to shield it.

"Forgive me, sir, I—"

"No, no, please forgive me. Here I am wittering away while you're barely able to stand. Come," Lord Tresilian says, steering Henry once more to the other end of the room. "You've had a long journey, I quite understand."

Henry is ushered into a large armchair of red damask in front of the fire. The older man settles down into his own armchair opposite, carefully crosses one long leg over the other so as not to disturb the small table set between the chairs, and Henry does not miss the wince of pain as he does. If Lord Tresilian is indeed ailing as he suspects, then he can be forgiven for finding whatever pleasures he can, eccentric as they are, and so, feeling a little guilty for his less than enthused responses, Henry remarks, "It truly is a vast collection. Surely you did not procure them all on a single tour of the Continent?"

His lordship smiles, dips his head. "I did not. I only purchased three from that first excursion, but the Tour gave me a taste for adventure and for many years I journeyed all over the world. Indeed, I was *very* well-traveled. I should like to be again. Alas, my health does not allow it."

There is a pause then in which the older man places his clubbed fingers together.

"A canker in my lungs, I'm afraid."

Here, at least, is an answer to one of his unasked questions. Henry looks at the man's fingertips. The illness must be approaching its zenith, if the severity of his malformation is anything to judge by.

"What have you been advised?"

A grimace. "That it is deeply rooted, and an operation will be of little use."

"I'm sorry. I can examine you, if you like? Offer a second opinion . . ."

But his new employer is waving Henry off. "I've already been prodded and poked beyond my patience. I know what fate awaits me, unless . . ."

"Unless?"

He says nothing more. Something wavers in his face—a look of sadness, a pitiable desperation—and Henry wishes he could help him.

"Please," the older man says finally. "Let us not speak of it. The notion of it distresses me. What of you? Are you well-traveled?"

Henry blinks. "No, sir. I've never left London before now."

This is not strictly true. He vaguely remembers a farm in the countryside and chasing chickens in the yard, hay bales in summer, a pond where a kindly man had taken him fishing, happy times which, now, are mere whispers of memories that disappear like vapor the moment he tries to catch them . . .

"Indeed!" Lord Tresilian exclaims. "Yet you are a man of languages."

"I am?"

His lordship tilts his chin in the direction of the hallway. "You spoke Welsh before."

"I attempted Welsh," Henry corrects. "When I discovered I was to come here I made it my duty to learn. I shall need to know the language, after all."

The older man looks thoughtful. "A commendable notion, I suppose. I find Welsh to be such an uninteresting language. I much prefer the rigours of Latin and its variations. Welsh is no use to my studies."

"But living here surely the language would be useful?"

A smile. "I'm an Englishman by birth, and rarely spend time here except when circumstances necessitate it. I actually live in London."

"Oh!"

"I didn't say, did I? Forgive me, so much on my mind! The truth of it is that I arranged your employment on behalf of my cousin, Linette. It is she who is mistress here at Plas Helyg but she had no means of orchestrating the task, and so I took it upon myself to assist her."

Henry is surprised. If Lord Tresilian hails from London this explains, then, how he should have come to know about his circumstances, but this cousin, Linette . . . this is new. He is about to press the matter when Powell enters the room carrying a tray with two generous glasses balanced upon it. The butler leans down to proffer them, the deep red liquid glinting in the flame of the fire. Henry claims one and takes a

26

large sip. It is good port, expensive port—rich and smooth with no bitter sediment—and he closes his eyes at the pleasant burn in his throat.

"You needed that, I see! Powell, stay, in case our guest wishes for another."

As the port warms the seat of his belly Henry allows himself to relax. When he opens his eyes, it is to see Lord Tresilian taking a sip from his own glass, watching him over its crystal rim.

"Now then. I invited you here to welcome you, as I said, before you're taken to the gatehouse."

"The gatehouse, sir?"

"Julian, please." A pause. "Yes, the gatehouse." He sits forward a little in his seat. "It's been a long-held tradition that all family physicians live at the gatehouse, to be close at hand, you understand. I regret there is no live-in maid, but Mrs. Evans and the other servants at Plas Helyg will see to it that all your comforts are amply accommodated for."

Henry inclines his head. "Thank you. I'm most indebted, to be sure."

Julian waves off his words of gratitude as if they were gnats.

"Do not thank me quite so soon, for I'm afraid there was another reason I wanted to see you before you settled in. I felt, you see, it could not wait."

His new employer sets down his glass of port on the marquetry table between them.

"Linette is the daughter of Lady Gwenllian, the widow of my cousin, Hugh Tresilian."

He pauses. Henry waits.

"My dearest Gwen," Julian continues, his expression sage, "has a marked countenance of mind. You will examine her in due course, but you'll discover she is much weakened in both body and intelligence. It has been presumed for many reasons that she is a madwoman."

"A madwoman?"

Henry's stomach sinks. He is, if not wholly experienced, familiar with the type. Has he not treated criminals in Bedlam on request of Bow Street often enough? Still, he wants to advise his host that he is no mad-doctor, that he has no wish to take up that mantle, but the older man is speaking again.

"You must forgive me for not mentioning it before when I wrote to you but I confess, I feared you would not accept the role."

Henry suppresses a sigh, for the man suspects correctly. But then, what choice did he have, in the end?

"I do not believe there can be much done except to keep her comfortable," his employer continues. "I care deeply for Gwen, and ask only that you ensure her continued care, to ease any distresses as and when they arise."

Distresses. It is a mild word for what Henry knows is really meant. He thinks of those poor wretches in Bethlam Hospital, confined to their cells. Their tortured screams, their fearsome violence. No amount of leeching or blistering or any other of those more barbaric customs can help them. Indeed, Henry is positive such treatments only make matters worse.

"I shall do my very best," he says now. "Madness cannot be cured, after all, only managed."

At the fireplace Powell shifts on his feet.

Julian inclines his head. "I am comforted you agree. But," he adds, "my telling you of Gwen was merely a prelude."

"Prelude?"

"I wished to warn you of Linette."

Henry waits. Julian reclaims his port and takes another sip, an earnest expression in his dark eyes.

28

"My ward—" he stops, corrects himself—"the woman who used to be my ward, is very dear to me, but a strange creature with little interest in the pursuits many of her position take enjoyment from. Linette has no great talent for music or dancing or embroidery, nor languages either except that of this country and our own. Indeed, no governess could manage her, and I'm afraid that in my fondness I let her follow her inclinations a little too far. She spends all her time immersed in the business of the estate, refusing the help of my agent and our fellow landowners, and her relationship with the villagers is . . . Well, it is all rather unbecoming. Her temper too is questionable. Indeed, she has a sharp tongue when she chooses to use it and is not an easy companion. I confess, it makes me wonder if something more sinister is at play."

Henry represses the urge to quirk a brow.

"Not all females," he says carefully, "are suited to the more genteel of pursuits, or conform to ladylike manners. That does not make her mad."

Powell shifts from one foot to the other once more. Julian, it appears, does not notice.

"But there is something *unusual* about her," he persists, and the expression on his face is full of concern. "She flouts convention at every opportunity. She really is very wild. At six-and-twenty I rather hoped she would grow out of it, but time has only made her worse . . ." A shadow crosses his face. "Gwen was the same age when she first began to exhibit signs. Truly, I worry about Linette a great deal."

Henry contemplates this. "Does insanity run in the family? Beyond Lady Gwenllian, I mean."

Julian hesitates. He looks troubled by the idea.

"On the Tresilian side, no. On the Cadwalladr, I can't be sure. Emyr, her grandfather, was prone to moods of melancholy but . . ." he trails off. "Gwen's condition, however, cannot be denied, nor the fact that Linette acts so strangely." Julian shakes his head. "As I say, I worry most dreadfully. I hope, as her physician, you will keep an eye on her when business takes me back to London tomorrow. It would bring me such comfort."

Thoughtfully Henry takes a sip of his port. He had received very little information about either woman in Julian's letter offering him the position as Penhelyg's physician:

> *You would be required to undertake the treatment of Lady Gwen-llian Tresilian of Plas Helyg, a genteel widow of general ill-health and delicate constitution. Further attention is to be given to her daughter, together with the estate's servants, as and when required. In addition, you would be prevailed upon to undertake the treatment of the residents of Penhelyg, acting in the capacity of village doctor.*

Henry had sneered vehemently at first. While the role of a physician holds far more respect than that of a surgeon and the potential for a much deeper purse, Henry always found it an unexciting enterprise, preferring the ever-changing halls of Guy's Hospital and then, later, the thrill of attending cases under Bow Street's jurisdiction. In London he had been a celebrated surgeon, a lecturer of science. Though the salary offered in Penhelyg was amply generous, for Henry, a village doctor was a great step down indeed. But when it became clear no other offers were forthcoming—each of his queries was met with cold hard silence—Henry realized he had no choice but to accept. As the weeks leading up to his departure passed, he allowed himself to become accustomed to the notion, had conjured in his mind a woman suffering from nothing more than maidenly swoons, or perhaps a weakness attributed to the effects of childbirth on account of the daughter mentioned. He had imagined an entitled pompous woman, or perhaps a mulish one, and as for the daughter . . . well, he had assumed she was a mere child. Now he finds she is mistress of this great estate and—quite possibly—touched by the same affliction as her mother.

What on earth have I agreed to?

"I shall watch her keenly, Lord Tresilian, of that you can rest assured."

Belying his concerns Henry uses a mollifying tone, one he has employed in the past with troublesome elders who presumed to tell him how best to conduct his treatment of their kin. It happened often when they saw his age. His lordship, though, flushes with pleasure.

"Thank you," he says warmly. "I'm most gratified, most gratified indeed."

Henry nods his rejoinder, takes a sip of port; as he places the glass back down upon the marquetry table he marks the butler's gaze lingering on him—unfriendly, hard as hail.

"May I ask?" Henry ventures now, tearing his own gaze away. "You said that Linette was your ward?"

Julian nods. "Until she attained her majority. But as owner of Penhelyg's mines I've maintained a presence here, and I'm still a trustee of the estate. As a consequence I take some responsibility for the needs of both her and Gwen. Linette does not leave the village, after all."

"Not ever?"

"She has no wish to."

"I see." Mentally he marks this. "And why is she not yet married?"

Julian ghosts a smile. "Linette shows no interest in that either."

Henry marks this too. Still, the butler stares.

"Where are they?" Henry asks. "Lady Tresilian and Linette?"

A look of discomfort crosses Julian's features before he shields it with a sigh.

"Gwen is abed. Linette, however . . ." He trails off, shoots a glance at Powell. "I take it she has not yet returned?"

"Not as yet, my lord."

Julian sighs. "You see what I mean, Henry? Past dark and still abroad at so late an hour. Linette truly is a wildling, has not one regard for her own well-being or those that care for her." He sits back in his seat with an expression now of deep concern. "You must understand—I think of Linette as if she were my own daughter. I truly fear her mother's madness might have tainted her."

There is a step at the threshold, and both Henry and Julian look up to find the housekeeper standing at the door, a dinner tray in hand.

"Ah, splendid," Julian says in a much brighter tone. "Please, Mrs. Evans, bring it in. Our guest will be ravenous! You'll forgive me for not joining you—I dined earlier. I couldn't be sure of the time of your arrival."

Mrs. Evans has placed the tray down on the table and the offering, Henry marks, is exceedingly generous—a small chicken, its skin cooked to a perfect golden crisp accompanied by a jug of bread sauce; a tureen of fresh minted greens; a portion of buttered potatoes. Like the port, Henry can see this is expensive fare. Never would he have eaten so richly in London. His purse strings could simply never stretch that far.

"Thank you, Mrs. Evans," he says faintly, and the old woman dips her knees in response. She does not look at him. Instead, she keeps her focus so intently on the ornate rug that Henry feels her gaze would burn a hole in it if the notion were at all possible.

"A most excellent dish, I think," says Julian now. "I never allow mediocre cooking when I am in residence." He clears his throat with another fleshy rumble. "That will be all, Mrs. Evans."

"Yessir."

"You may go too, Powell. Leave the port."

There is a pause. Then the bewigged man fills their glasses once more before placing the decanter next to Henry's tray.

32

"Very good, my lord."

As Powell moves to go Henry tries to catch his eye, but the butler's features are as blank now as a redcoat at orders, and so giving in to his hunger Henry applies himself to his plate.

The bird is tender, its skin beautifully seasoned, and the bread sauce melts deliciously on his tongue. It is (Henry is quite sure of the fact) the best meal he has ever eaten. Julian watches, breaking the silence with observations from his travels—the unmarked beauty of Italy, the dry heat of Jerusalem, the icy climes of Austria in winter— but, at length, Henry begins to tire. All he can think of now is the prospect of finally sleeping in a comfortable bed with a proper mattress, a bowl of warm water with which to wash off the dirt of the day. It is just as Henry is trying to conjure the right words to beg his leave without appearing rude that there comes a loud bang like that of a heavy door swinging open against a wall, and the hurried echo of footsteps on stone.

Julian's dark brows draw together so hard that a deep groove appears between them like a gully.

"And there," he murmurs, "is our errant dove." He loudly clears his throat. "Linette!"

The footsteps stop. Henry can almost hear the reluctance in the pause that follows. Then the footsteps start up again, together with a strange clicking, almost immediately softened by the soft runner in the corridor. As one Henry and Julian look to the doorway where in that very moment a woman appears at the door.

Uncommonly tall, she holds the frame with long-fingered hands. Her cheeks are flushed, and across her shoulders there hangs a mass of long blonde hair that looks as if it has not seen a brush in days. Yet this is not the most surprising thing about Linette Tresilian. No indeed, what takes Henry by surprise is the fact that she wears from head to foot the ill-fitting clothes of a man.

Flouts conventions, her cousin had said. Indeed, there can be no more proof of the claim than *this*!

A gray dog pushes its way in between her thigh and the doorframe, surveys the room before resting its gaze on Henry himself, cocking its head. Henry marks its dark wiry coat, its long snout and flopping ears. A lurcher, he recognises. The governor at Guy's had a sighthound much like it, before he offered the poor beast up to a surgeon's knife.

"My dear Linette." Julian's voice is low now, tired. "Where have you been?"

Linette Tresilian looks slowly between Julian and Henry, eyes bright as if with fever.

"Cousin," she says finally, and her grip on the doorframe is so hard her knuckles are white. "It has been destroyed."

CHAPTER THREE

It is rare that Linette Tresilian finds herself at a loss for words. One of her many failings (so she has been often told), is her inability to keep her mouth shut as a lady should, but at this precise moment she finds herself struggling to force the words from her tongue.

It had been no mean feat to ready Dr. Evans's house for the new doctor's arrival. It took a week alone to clear it of decades of clutter, to sort and remove the old man's personal effects, then another week still to clean it top to bottom, to polish the floorboards, redecorate where needed. Then, of course, there was the ordering of fresh linens and curtains, the restocking of the larder, a whole life erased in order for a new one to replace it. Indeed, such a monumental task had been a painful one, not just for herself but the servants too.

"It has been destroyed," she says again, as the two men sitting before the fireplace simply continue to stare. "The windows. The door! Even from outside I could see the wreck in the hallway. I can only assume the rest, but if the exterior is any indication . . ."

Linette must take a breath, and in that gasped beat her cousin stands. He must clutch the cushioned arm of the chair to support his weakening frame and the new doctor (it must be him, for no one else is expected) half-rises from his own to support him. But Julian, with a grimace, waves him down again. "What do you mean?"

She releases her clutch from the doorframe. She was gripping it so hard the wood has marked narrow gullies on her palms.

"The gatehouse, of course," Linette says, quite unable to keep the waspishness from her voice. "What else would I speak of?"

A look of displeasure crosses Julian's pale features, as it always does when she speaks in so forthright a manner.

"Linette," he scolds, and gestures to the man at his side, standing too now, looking most perplexed. "We have company."

"So I see," she says, casting her gaze to said company, just long enough to mark how young the new physician is. She was expecting someone far older, Dr. Beddoe's age at the very least. "How do you do, Dr. Talbot."

"A pleasure," he returns.

"I regret to say it is not," she answers fast. "Certainly under such circumstances."

"Linette," Julian says, "pray, it is late. What are you saying?"

Has she not just indicated? Dear heaven, her cousin is no more attentive of her when they do converse than when they do not! Swallowing down a sigh, Linette rubs the fading marks on her hands.

"The gatehouse has been destroyed."

Julian is silent a moment, licks port-stained lips. Then, "Ring for Mrs. Evans. She will have to make a room up." He turns to the new doctor, proffers an apologetic smile. "I hope you do not object, but it seems you must stay here at Plas Helyg, at least for tonight. Don't you agree, Cousin?"

It would hardly matter if she did or not; the decision, it seems, has already been made. Dr. Talbot, for his part, still looks perplexed, but he shields this with a polite smile.

"I am sorry indeed to hear this news. But I could not prevail upon your hospitality without her ladyship's express permission." He looks at Linette. "Do I have it?"

She blinks, not expecting this polite recognition; it softens her somewhat.

"I fear there is not much else to be done."

And so Enaid is rung for, the situation explained, instructions given.

The housekeeper ducks her capped head. "Dr. Talbot may have the green room. It is already made up."

Her voice shakes, and no wonder. But Julian does not notice, only turns to the younger man once more.

"I'm sure you have as many questions as we do but I know you're very tired. Perhaps you would like to retire now? Things will be clearer in the morning, I have no doubt."

Another gracious smile has stitched itself upon Julian's lips. The new doctor is shaking the hand Linette's cousin proffers.

"Thank you."

"Of course." Julian dips his dark head. "Linette, stay. Mrs. Evans, if you will?"

The old woman conceals it well, but Linette sees plain the anguish in Enaid's eyes, understands all too well the cause of it. She wants to reach out and squeeze her hand to comfort her but Linette knows that here, now, she cannot.

"This way," Enaid says in a voice so quiet it is bare above a whisper. The new doctor looks between the two women, marking, it seems, their mutual unease, but without a word he makes toward the door and Linette steps aside to allow him room to pass. At the threshold hers and Dr. Talbot's eyes meet; she senses him take her measure, feels the familiar knot of indignation tighten her stomach.

What, exactly, has Julian told him?

Enaid pulls the door shut behind them. The fire cracks, licks the grate with a violent spitting flame. Sensing her discomfort Merlin presses against her leg and she lowers her hand for him to lick.

Julian sinks back down into his armchair, removes a silver case from his inner coat pocket, flips the lid. He selects a thin cigarillo from the top, leans over to light it from the fire, and Linette watches the end glow red at the take. He inhales a steady draw before sitting back again, regards her in that detached way of his which makes her feel as if he were looking through a pane of glass rather than at a fellow human being.

"Honestly, Linette," he says, smoke-wisps escaping his mouth. "What a first impression to make! And to burst in here most unbecomingly . . ." He sweeps a derogatory glance at her masculine clothes. "Where is the green dress I gave you this morning? Well, 'tis done now."

Defensive, Linette folds her arms across her chest. Never has he approved of her clothes, but what harm does it do *him* that she wear her father's old shirts and trousers? The pretty dresses he gives her are simply not fit for purpose, not here, where it rains seven out of the twelve months a year and she spends more of her time outside Plas Helyg than in it. Linette is sure he would feel far more affronted if she ruined all those expensive taffetas and silks on which he has wasted his precious coin! Besides, each and every one of them is damned uncomfortable. Julian certainly would not like it if he felt garroted by whalebones and ribbons.

"Perhaps it makes better sense this way," he is saying now.

Linette frowns. "What does?"

"Indeed, it would be very unfair to leave the poor man to manage at the gatehouse alone, at least to begin with. He is new to Penhelyg, far away from all he knows. It is the mark of politeness to offer him a room here until he is settled."

Politeness, perhaps, but Linette does not like the idea of a stranger under her roof. Still, Julian has a point and so she says, grudgingly, "I suppose you are right."

Julian levels her with a stare. "I'm glad you agree." He twists the cigarillo. "The gatehouse, though. Who might have done such a thing? One of the villagers, I expect," he murmurs. "Hardly surprising, of course."

At this accusation Linette must press her tongue. She wants to defend them, but Julian's comment gives her pause. Is there merit to his words? The thought troubles her, just as much as the other that has been niggling at the back of her mind. Merlin snuffles at her thigh. With effort Linette steps forward. That she must ask him this favor, that she is forced to do it, is humiliating.

"I've not the spare money to make repairs," she says quietly. "What little savings I had left in Plas Helyg's coffers I spent making the gatehouse up in the first place."

There is a beat as the import of her declaration sinks in. When it does Julian sighs, and she hears on it the tenor of his disapproval.

"I did warn you about the risk of spending so much on your tenants."

Linette does not reply. Julian takes one last drag of the cigarillo; he blows out the smoke, and they both watch its snakelike skein take shape.

"Very well," he says, stubbing the cigarillo out into his empty glass. "Go down tomorrow morning, make me a list of what you need. I'll arrange it all when I'm back in London."

"Thank you, Cousin."

He makes her feel like a child, not at all the independent woman she has always striven to be, and her face flushes red with shame. When he says nothing more she turns to leave, Merlin close at her heels.

It is only as she reaches the door that Julian calls her name. One word, two syllables, yet he manages to drag it out. Linette turns. He is watching her with curious eyes.

"How did you come to know of the gatehouse?"

Linette lifts her chin.

"I was on my way home and wanted to offer my greetings to the new doctor. I thought he would be there."

"I see. And what were you doing out so late?"

"I was with Tomas Morgan."

"Who?"

She clenches her jaw.

"A tenant," she replies. "He's been sick. I was merely doing my duty, Cousin."

Linette thinks of the young fisherman, how his body had wracked itself with unrelenting shivers. For near half an hour Tomas coughed up bile the color of pomegranate peel before settling, exhausted, on the bed. Linette gave aid where she could; she helped keep the water warm as his mother bathed him, she read to them both once he had settled. Mair asked for biblical passages since the words were a much-needed comfort, though Linette set no store on the healing power of scripture.

She knows firsthand it does not work.

"Well," Julian says, breaking into her thoughts. "You'd better eat something. Mrs. Phillips has kept a plate back, though it will have spoiled by now, I'm sure."

Linette nods. Hesitates.

"What is he like, the new doctor?"

A pause. "He will do. He will do very well indeed."

Linette's heart sinks. What manner of man has Julian employed? A self-satisfied Englishman, just like him? The villagers, then, will resent Dr. Talbot's presence most keenly. They will resent her too for allowing it, resentment she could well do without. Has Linette not fought hard to gain their trust?

Merlin whines, impatient to be gone.

"Goodnight, Cousin," Linette says, turning away.

He does not answer, nor does she expect him to. She opens the study door and then, feeling spiteful, deliberately leaves it wide behind her.

CHAPTER FOUR

Henry wakes to the infernal chattering of birds. With a groan he tosses in the bed, tries to ignore the steely fingers of a headache which has started to tap like an incessant woodpecker at the crest of his skull.

He feels, quite frankly, like death. No wonder too considering the past few days; last night was the first decent night's rest he has had for some time. Indeed, his head scarce hit the pillow before he succumbed to sleep, but somehow he does not yet feel rested. His body aches, his mouth is dry as sand. He can taste the staleness of port on his tongue. With an effort Henry opens one crusting eye. The light reaching from the gap between the curtains is not so bright that the sun could have risen too high in the sky, and with difficulty he reaches across to the bedside table for his pocketwatch.

Just past eight.

Henry presses the lid shut, rubs his thumb over the engraved H and T. If he could sleep longer, he would, but Henry Talbot has never been one to shirk his duties—it is something he prides himself on most diligently—and with a sigh he rises from the bed, stumbles in his weariness over to the window. Clutching at the heavy silk-lined curtains he parts them, and for a long moment stands there, taking it in.

Though his landlady in London kept his rooms beautifully, the views

from the windows there were decidedly less picturesque. The road outside was always muddy or flush with dust and there was not one single
tree in sight. It is quieter here too—no bustle of carriages, no hawkers
shouting out their wares. Only that birdsong, the distant bleat of sheep.
Something else too, Henry thinks, a noise he cannot place.

He exhales, his breath leaving a lung-shaped fog on the glass.

The difference truly is astounding. Here, Henry is greeted with a
vast valley spotted with grazing sheep and, beyond those, sparsely
settled mountains rising like ramparts that seem to touch the clouds.
The mountains are all green and lush, except for a smaller one that
almost encroaches on Plas Helyg which has no trees at all. Henry
opens the lead-lined window, leans out to get a better view. Skeins of
curling smoke rise from its stony banks, and he identifies now the
sounds of men at work, of pickaxes on stone.

The mine, Henry realizes.

Strange, that it should be so close to the house. He thinks of the
gold-flecked stone in Julian's cabinet downstairs. *It was the first we
found in the mines. Near thirty years ago now.*

At that moment a gentle breeze whips past the window. On its
pass, Henry detects a faint sulfuric smell. He is just about to close
the window when there comes a sharp rap on the door, the creak of it
opening. Henry turns to see the butler, Powell, enter the room carrying a jug of steaming water, a cloth over his arm.

"Good morning, sir."

Henry wipes the rheum from his eyes.

"Good morning."

The older man carries the jug to the washstand, sets it down, the
cloth next to it.

"Thank you," Henry says.

The butler does not respond. Instead he turns, begins a brisk walk
to the door.

"You speak English," Henry calls out as he reaches it. "You and the housekeeper. I had not expected that."

Powell pauses, turns back around to face him. He is still as stony-faced as he was the night before, with a strong jaw that seems disinclined to smile.

"His lordship desires it," the butler replies, clipped. A pause. For a moment Henry does not think he will say anything further, but then—as if realizing more is needed—Powell continues. "It is his wish for all the servants to address him in English." Another pause, this one distinctly disapproving. "Hardly any of the gentry speak the language here, though they are of Welsh stock."

Henry frowns. Julian admitted to his lack of knowledge in the native language last night, but why would the *Welsh* gentry not know the language of their country? He wants to ask, but something in the butler's cold manner makes Henry suspect no more information will be forthcoming.

"Where is your mistress this morning?" he asks instead.

"The Lady Gwen is still abed, sir," comes the reply. Powell says the word "sir," it seems, with a modicum of resentment. "Miss Linette wakes early. She is already down at the gatehouse, assessing the damage."

The gatehouse. In his exhaustion Henry had forgotten.

Destroyed, Linette Tresilian had said. The windows and doors ruined, the inside too, so she seemed to think. But how strange! Is such destruction of property commonplace around these parts? It would appear not, if her reaction was anything to go by; Henry remembers clearly the look of shock on her flushed face as she stood on the threshold of the study, dressed in those ill-fitting garments. He thinks of the way she spoke to both himself and her cousin—so hard and impolite—and the way she looked at him, her gaze altogether too direct and superior, anchored with dislike. He frowns, the memory of Julian Tresilian's words forming in the chamber of his mind:

Linette truly is a wildling.

Well. It is indeed clear that she is a woman of uncommon independence, for no lady of a grand house such as this would wear men's clothes nor venture out alone in the wilderness, day or night. Yet despite all these brief observations, Henry did not mark any peculiar indications of mental weakness.

But then, even the sanest-looking people can be mad.

"His lordship wishes to see you at breakfast before he leaves for London," Powell says now, interrupting Henry's musings. "He awaits your pleasure in the dining room."

"Ah." Henry plucks at the collar of his nightshirt. "Well, then. I'd best be getting on."

The butler inclines his head, and the flaps of his uncouth wig swing forward over his broad shoulders.

"Very good, sir," he says, and promptly he shuts the door behind him with a pronounced and heavy *click*.

In his tired stupor Henry did not pay much attention during the journey up to his room the previous evening and so it is that when he steps out into the hallway, he finds himself blinking in surprise.

He stands in a long gallery filled with portraits. They line the panelled walls, the faces of Plas Helyg ancestors of centuries past looming down at him like stern sentinels. Henry looks up at them with interest, recognizes the changing fashions of Jacobean through to Restoration, through to the earlier years of this century, from the flouncing frills of rococo to the silk and brocades of five decades before. A little further down the hall (and as Henry turns his head he detects the faint scent of vanilla and beeswax) another portrait much larger than the rest catches his eye. It shows three sitters: a beautiful blonde woman seated, with two dark-haired men standing behind her. One of the men rests his hand possessively on her shoulder while the other—Julian, Henry recognises—stands a little further back, as if observing them.

The other man must be Hugh Tresilian. Which means the woman can only be his wife, Gwenllian.

It is a strange portrait, Henry thinks, staring up at it, surely not one likely to be found in a Welsh country seat, for each of the sitters wears what seems to be Middle Eastern costume. Gwen Tresilian has her hair pinned high, a circlet of rubies crowning her forehead, and is dressed in an elaborate style of jewel-colored skirts intricately detailed in the echo of foreign climes. She looks boldly out from the canvas, a small almost seductive smile playing across her lips.

Henry shifts his gaze to Hugh Tresilian. He is a tall man, broad-chested, handsome in his oriental robes. He wears a gold and crimson turban on his head so Henry cannot make out the color of his hair, but from the shade of his eyebrows he suspects Hugh shares the same coloring as his cousin. Julian Tresilian is dressed similarly but wears instead an odd ornate headdress made of what looks to be ivory adorned with dark feathers. He looks very like Hugh—both of them strikingly handsome with hawklike eyebrows and aquiline noses.

He steps further back, cranes his neck. The composition of the painting itself has something distinctly odd about it, something unsavory. It is reminiscent of a Gainsborough Henry saw once, yet it lacks the mellow romance of that artist's style. This portrait is more striking, more severe. In the foreground are the trappings of wealth—gleaming coins, precious gems, swathes of grapes, wine goblets on carved pedestals. A skull nestles between a hoard of sapphires and a gold dagger. Behind the Tresilians a dark curtain sweeps across

45

the canvas, shielding in the corner what looks to be a temple pillar, a stone plinth, torches with glowing flames.

Henry shrugs off a feeling of unease. He has never had much taste for the superfluous frivolities of the gentry. It is a world far removed from the blood and sawdust of surgery, the plain comforting simplicity of lodging in tiny annexes. Henry turns away, only to pause once more.

Below the portrait stands a curio cabinet. Inside are two locks of hair—one brown, one blond—a pair of tiny shoes, a silver thimble, a small finely carved wooden rattle, and a Bible. Not dissimilar from the tome in Julian's bookcase, it is very large, covered with thick boards embossed with ornate patterns of religious persuasion pressed into handsome brown leather, its paper edges gilded. The corners of the cover are encased in brass, attached to which are large filigree clasps that bind the cover shut. Henry's landlady owned one very much like this—she kept it on the dresser in her parlor and read from it every evening before supper. A family Bible, in which were listed the names of all the children she had lost.

A noise makes him look up. The dog from the night before stands looking at him, head inquisitively cocked. Henry reaches out his hand.

"Hullo," he says, and the dog wags its curling tail, pads toward him. Its claws thrum lightly on the worn runner, and Henry realises it must have been those he heard clicking on the flagstone floor in the vestibule when Linette Tresilian crossed it the night before.

The sighthound is so large he need not bend to pet it; the dog presses its snout into his palm, and with a smile Henry scratches under its chin.

"Who are you then, hmm?"

Large brown eyes stare up at him dolefully, and though it is of course impossible, Henry has the notion that the creature understands. It licks Henry's fingers, trots down the gallery toward the staircase.

Henry follows.

There are three flights of stairs; by the time Henry reaches the bottom of them he feels somewhat out of breath. He has done his fair share of walking in London, of course, but the city streets were invariably flat and often Bow Street would provide him with a landau whenever they were in need of him. Henry is just tugging at his cravat to get some air, when there comes the sound of cutlery on porcelain. The lurcher ambles in the direction of a corridor off to the left, and once again Henry follows it.

The dog leads him into a richly furnished dining room, where at the head of a long table sits Julian Tresilian dressed in finely tailored traveling clothes. He half-rises from his chair to greet him, gestures to a seat on his right.

"There you are! Sit, my boy. You must be famished."

In truth, Henry feels too tired for food; the meal from the night before still sits heavy in his stomach but, determined to be polite, he diligently reaches for the platter laid between them on the table and takes a buttered roll. Julian has already cleared his plate; the dog—eager for scraps—snaffles loudly at his elbow.

"Away," he shoos, and the lurcher's ears flatten to its skull before sloping off out of the room. Watching it go, Julian wipes his hands on a napkin before tossing it on the table. "Linette bought it as a runt from one of the farmers up in the valley. It's not a pretty beast at all, unlike Sir John Selwyn's pointer. Pedigree stock, that one. Beautiful russet coat."

"*I* think the dog rather handsome," Henry replies, and in response Julian laughs deep in his throat, twists the gold signet ring on his finger.

"Well," he says, "each to their own. Linette would, I daresay, agree with you."

A beat. Henry takes a bite of his meager breakfast before speaking once more.

"Mr. Powell said she was down at the gatehouse."

"Been, returned, and is now belowstairs with the servants."

He stops twisting the ring, and Henry marks that its bezel has engraved upon it too that strange curling symbol.

"I'm afraid the damage to your new home is rather extensive. It's as well you came here last night and were spared the sight of it."

Henry lays his half-eaten roll down on the plate.

"Is it really so very bad?"

His host nods, grave.

"Linette has provided me with a list of what needs replacing. I begin my return to London today—I'd rather procure what is needed there than rely on local tradesmen."

"I assure you, there is no need for such expense."

"It is not a matter of expense," Julian returns, "but pride. Linette may be satisfied with quaint country fare, but Plas Helyg is a grand estate. It deserves only the best, you see."

Henry does not see. He has never owned anything new himself, has always been happy enough with whatever was provided for him— as long as it was serviceable, it would do. But of course, Lord Tresilian is used to a certain way of living—men such as he are rarely like to give way on such matters—and so Henry says, "I do, sir. Of course. Might I see the gatehouse for myself?"

The question appears to take the older man by surprise. "I advise against it. Surely you would prefer to see it at its best?"

"It will make me appreciate the transformation all the more, I should think?"

Julian stares. Then, unexpectedly, he stands, leaning on his silver-topped cane for purchase. Henry rises in turn.

"Go, if you will. You'll find the gatehouse down the pass; just turn right at the fork. I regret I cannot accompany you for my ship waits in Abermaw, and I must make haste to catch the tide."

"I understand."

"Very good."

He reaches out his hand, clasps it in Henry's own. The hand is cool to the touch, and Henry feels the hard club of Julian's fingernails push into the soft skin of his wrist.

"Farewell for now, then," Julian says warmly. "Remember what I told you about Linette? Do look out for her, won't you? As you saw last night . . ."

Henry inclines his head. "I shall do my best."

"I'm most gratified." The older man releases him. "I shall see you again very soon. Very soon indeed."

CHAPTER FIVE

Henry watches Julian Tresilian drive a fine dapple gray mare down the gravel driveway and thence through the open gates at the bottom, and only when the sound of the phaeton wheels has dimmed to a low rumble does Henry step through the large stone-arched doors of Plas Helyg.

Arriving in the dark as he did Henry had marked little of the house's exterior and so he surveys it now. It really is very large. Far grander than any house he has seen in London, though it must be said that Henry rarely went north of the river except to report to Bow Street or monitor a patient at Bethlem Royal. Indeed, Plas Helyg is like no building he has ever seen: built of dark gray stone it is softened by sweeps of lush variegated ivy that twines itself around the window-panes like gauze; the pediment boasts intricate scrollwork, complemented by high-reaching finials and cupolas on top of four imposing towers. To the far right is a pond, a fountain spouting a stream of water from the middle, and on the other side of the house the gravel drive continues; he glimpses some outbuildings, what appears to be a coach house and stables. And surrounding it all like a vast green cocoon are magnificent ancient-looking willow trees.

Henry pulls up the collar of his coat, walks briskly down the short driveway. As he approaches the iron gates he sees now that the obscure pattern he marked last night is composed of intricately wrought depictions of the same willow trees surrounding the house; he walks through the gates, pulls them shut behind him. Their hinges creak, thick with rust.

On the other side, Henry finds himself on a wide woodland path. He looks both ways, notes a smaller pathway off to his left which disappears up into the trees, takes the larger path downward instead.

The woods are broad and dense. Quiet. Trees thickly bank the sides of the path and ferns grow in clumps about their bases. Wild garlic must grow here too for he can smell a hint of its pungent scent. As he walks, Henry becomes conscious of the pleasant hollow sound produced by his boots against the dry earth beneath his heel. There is a light rustling of a breeze; the humid air tickles the tips of his ears. Above him, the loud trill of birdsong. Henry looks up at the branches to locate its source but sees nothing. Instead—through force of habit, he supposes—he finds himself likening those bands of branches to arteries.

Drawing in the fresh earthen scent of the trees, Henry veers closer to the path's verge. He holds out a hand to touch the dry trunk of what he thinks might be an oak and notes that ivy grows here too, its spindly tendrils reaching up and up as if desperate to escape the woodland floor. There is, Henry thinks, a sense of feeling enveloped within these woods. They have an oppressive quality to them—the trees seem to lean toward him, reaching out with gnarled arms. He turns, peers into the thick vegetation, and realizes he cannot see any trace of Plas Helyg, that he could easily become lost if he were to stray into them. Henry wonders what forest creatures are hidden in the undergrowth, what watches him from its dark depths, and he moves back into the middle of the path, must laugh at himself under his breath.

Do not be a fool.

He replaces his hat. Somewhere, now, the sound of water.

Within minutes Henry reaches the fork; he takes the sharp bend which curves downward for a minute before opening up into a small clearing . . . and frowns deeply at the house that stands before him. It is decidedly less austere than the one he has just come from. Much *much* smaller, it is built with the same gray stone and echoes the pediment and finials of its parent. It is, or could be, Henry thinks, a lovely house, but with the door and windows in such disrepair (the door hangs from its hinges, the windows are splintered or smashed completely), it looks worryingly bleak. Yet it *has* been cared for. As Henry approaches he can see a patch of earth to one side—a small garden, it seems—and peeking from the disturbed soil are remnants of foliage, roots like the bones of fingers.

The sound of water takes Henry to the back of the house. Running behind it is a small stream, and stepping gingerly on the banked earth he bends to take a closer look. The stream is narrow, steeped in shade, coming so close to the house it almost looks as if it disappears underneath. Just then a scent travels upward, and Henry wrinkles his nose. From the dark foam-flecked water there comes the faint but very distinct smell he noted before from his bedroom window: the rotten-egg stench of sulfur.

Pondering, Henry returns to the front of the house. On the ground below one of the lower-story windows there is a crunch beneath his boots. He lifts his foot, marks the numerous shards of glass on the gravel. Strange—this would mean, surely, the windows had been smashed from the *inside*.

Just as he is examining what looks to be a deeply pitted mark in the door there is the rumble of wheels, the hollow-sounding plod of hooves on the path behind him. Henry turns to see a white pony leading a small cart appear round the sharp bend, driven by a young man. In the back sits a dark-headed girl and, jostling next to her, Linette Tresilian.

"Dr. Talbot," she calls, standing when the pony draws to a stop.

Henry makes to assist her out of the cart but by the time he has reached her she has already jumped from it. Like last night she wears breeches and a shirt a little too large for her. Garments, Henry thinks again, completely unfit for a lady.

He studies her carefully. She is striking rather than beautiful, he saw that much last night despite his overwhelming fatigue—blond, boyishly slim with full lips, a pointed nose, arched brows over almond-shaped eyes. But close up he sees there is a hardness to those eyes and her face is weathered; Henry knows the damaging effects of the elements on a complexion when he sees it. He glances at her wild hair, secured only with a tatty ribbon at the base of her neck.

The mistress of Plas Helyg, it must be said, looks every inch a common farm boy.

"Good morning." Henry does not know whether to call her *lady* or *miss* so settles for nothing at all. "I wanted to see the damage for myself."

She helps down the girl who begins to remove three buckets from the floor of the cart. Linette Tresilian looks at him, gray eyes (or are they more a pale shade of green?) sharp, assessing.

"I'm afraid it is rather dreadful." She gestures to her companions unloading the cart—on the patched gravel the buckets have been joined by a rake, a broom, cloths, wire brushes, other items Henry cannot fathom the use of. "This is Angharad, our maid, and Aled, one of the groundsmen. They'll be setting the place to rights."

Henry nods in greeting. They nod back, but neither of them will quite meet his gaze.

"Set to rights," Henry says now, turning back to his hostess. "There *is* much to do, then?"

"As I said."

As last night, her tone is waspish. *She has a sharp tongue when she chooses to use it.*

Aled and Angharad share a look before turning away.

Linette Tresilian smiles tightly. "Come. I'll show you what we are to contend with."

She beckons Henry to follow her into the gatehouse. He does as bidden and inside he stops and stares, open-mouthed.

The hallway is a comfortable size, or would be if not for the debris strewn across the flagstones as if a storm has raged within; there is scarce room to move what with the pictures and ornaments that lie broken on the floor. As Henry raises his head he catches the splintered sight of himself in a mirror, the middle of the glass cobwebbed in its break. A large hole has been made in one of the wainscoting panels, its impact similar to the axe mark in the door.

"My God."

Linette Tresilian folds her arms. Aled and Angharad, who have trailed in behind them, disappear deeper into the house without a word.

"Yes," Henry's hostess replies. "I am not ashamed to say *my* reaction was a little more verbose."

He looks at her. The woman smiles again but it is cold. Unfriendly, almost.

"You will find me very direct, Dr. Talbot. It's a habit I have been scolded for often."

Her temper too is questionable.

"I'd ensured the gatehouse was beautifully prepared," she continues, leaving no room for Henry to comment. "It was cleaned top to bottom, freshly painted. New everything that needed it. Dr. Evans was always happy with the state of his old threadbare pieces—he'd had them for years, after all—but it wasn't right to allow them to be passed on to you. I even procured some English books for you since the old doctor only owned Welsh. So to find it like this . . ."

Henry nudges a torn painting of the sea which lies upturned on an Indian rug with the toe of his boot.

"Who could have done such a thing?"

A beat.

"I wish I could tell you."

Something in her voice.

"That is not an answer," Henry says, directing at her a hard stare which she returns, unflinching. "You will find that I am just as direct as you. 'I wish' is very different from 'I don't know.' Which is it?"

The woman next to him purses her lips.

"It is both, actually. But I cannot deny I have my suspicions."

"And they are?"

For a moment she does not answer. Instead she stares, eyes assessing, as if trying to fathom him.

He wishes she would not.

"You must understand," Linette Tresilian says, "that Dr. Evans meant a great deal to everyone here, and he will not be so easily replaced. Especially by an Englishman."

Henry blinks. "Are you saying someone did this because I'm not wanted here?"

His hostess clears her throat; lightly touches the edge of a curtain half-divided from its rung.

"The gatehouse was Dr. Evans's pride and joy," she murmurs, not looking at him. "He'd be turning in his grave if he saw it now."

The change of both tone and subject is obvious and Henry would have pulled her up on it, if not for those last words.

"He's dead?"

She raises an eyebrow at him.

"Why yes. Didn't my cousin tell you?"

Henry shakes his head. "I knew a position had become vacant, but not the circumstances of how."

Another beat. A look of sadness skitters across her face. "Dr. Evans died in March. He was Penhelyg's physician when I was a child, a man of advancing years even then—needless to say, he was very old. Still, his death was a dreadful shock."

"A shock? He'd not been ill, then?"

Linette Tresilian lifts one shoulder in a half-shrug. "He suffered a little from arthritis, but otherwise, no. I never knew an elderly man to be so robust. Yes, it was a dreadful shock indeed."

Unbidden, Henry feels a familiar pull in his gut. It is the very same feeling he had whenever Francis Fielding, his contact at Bow Street, would profess to some curiosity about the demise of one of his cases. How, for instance, could a man die of a brain haemorrhage when no head wound had occurred? How might a man be poisoned without presenting symptoms of the fact? Such cases were a puzzle to be solved, and Henry always had been extraordinarily good at puzzles. It was what made him so popular with the Runners.

He bites down a feeling of injustice, focuses instead on the matter at hand.

"What was cause of death?"

"A weak heart. He was found on the threshold, there. It was Mrs. Evans who happened upon him. She was most distressed. Dr. Evans was her brother, you see."

This explains why the housekeeper appeared so unwelcoming last night.

"Who attended him?" Henry asks.

"Dr. Beddoe," comes the reply. "He lives in Criccieth, a town across the estuary. He's been seeing the villagers in the absence of a local physician."

"I assume he performed a postmortem?"

"I beg your pardon?"

Her voice comes sharp again. Those gray-green eyes narrow. He is not sure she understands.

"A postmortem," he says. "An examination of a body after death."

56

When a look of distate crosses her features, Henry inclines his head. "I merely wish to ascertain if my predecessor did indeed die from heart failure. Was there no mark on him? Any sign of external injury?"

"No," she says, forceful. But then she repeats the word—softer this time—and licks her lips. "But . . ."

"But?"

Linette Tresilian hesitates. "I just wish Dr. Evans had not died in such a manner."

Again, that tingling in his fingers. Something is missing here. Henry wants to ask more, to exercise that muscle which—until this moment—he thought he had left behind in London, but she is turning away, a pained expression on her face.

"Please, let us not speak of it. He is gone and buried, surely that's the end of it? Come," Linette Tresilian says, brusque, unbending. "Let me show you the house."

She leads him through each room.

The first is the study, where a rattan examination couch lies on its side, its seat ripped. A small bookcase has been emptied of its contents. Sheets of paper litter the floor and pictures have been torn from the walls, a desk and chair upturned; one of its legs has snapped and lies at an angle, splinters pointing upward like little knives.

On the other side of the house is a sitting room, its furniture too upturned, which leads into what Henry must assume was a small but well-stocked library for the shelves are empty, the books they once housed scattered across the rug. At the back of the gatehouse in which Angharad and Aled are already at work are a small kitchen, larder, and washroom. Upstairs houses two bedrooms and an unexpected quantity of feathers, their origins one must assume having come from the mattresses and pillows which have been so brutally shredded. Every single room has been left in disarray with much of the furniture either broken or damaged.

Having returned to the hallway Linette Tresilian excuses herself to speak with the servants and Henry waits, pushes his hands deep into his pockets.

Nothing has been spared; whoever did this ensured that Henry could not stay here, and it baffles him as to why. What possible reason is there? Who would cause such willful damage?

I cannot deny I have my suspicions.

Henry sinks to his haunches, picks at a smashed vase marooned on the rug like flotsam.

Linette Tresilian knows who, though she will not confess to it. Why?

Thoughtful, he runs his hand across the back of his neck. Dr. Evans could easily have died of heart failure. There have been many people who suffered sudden shocks to the heart having otherwise been perfectly healthy. It does happen. Perhaps, he muses, he is deliberately looking for a puzzle to solve. A chance to do what he could not in London . . .

A ray of sunshine glints through the splintered windowpane, sends a shard of light across the floor. Henry's gaze follows the line of it without thinking; the beam ends just at the tapered leg of a satinwood cabinet, and his gaze sharpens.

Something gleams beneath.

He leans over, reaches his hand under the cabinet. Cannot find purchase. With a grunt Henry flattens himself to the floor, reaches once more, and his fingers brush against cool glass. It takes a moment to fish it out, and when he does he narrows his eyes.

A glass vial, no longer than his middle finger, no wider than two.

It is an unusual bottle. Fluted in shape, gray glass, gold Turk's-head stopper. Unmarked. As a man of medicine, Dr. Evans will have housed many apothecary bottles in his stores, but Henry has never seen one quite like this. In fact, it looks more like a perfume bottle of the sort he saw, once, on the dressing table of a Chancery madam he visited a few times fresh out of university. So, then. Why on earth would Dr. Evans own such a thing?

Observation. Contemplation. Interrogation. These are methods that have always served him well when it comes to getting to the bottom of a question requiring an answer, whether that be in the form of a patient in need of a cure or a body concealing the cause of death.

An unexpected fatality. A vandalised gatehouse. Could the two be connected?

He curls his fingers around the vial, weighs the glass within his palm.

I might be wrong, Henry reminds himself. He was wrong before, was he not? But something here does not add up—his gut implicitly tells him so.

"Dr. Talbot?"

Henry rises, hides his hand behind his back.

"I was wondering," Linette Tresilian says when she reaches him, and the imploring look on her face reassures Henry she did not see. "My mother will still be abed, but if you're eager to begin your duties might you accompany me to see Tomas Morgan? I've been seeing him every day this week, but I've done what I can for him now. My services are nothing, I'm sure, to what yours will be."

"Of course," Henry says in a rush, eager to be gone.

He steps aside, allowing his hostess to leave first, and as she leads him from the ruined gatehouse, Henry surreptitiously slips the glass vial into his coat pocket.

CHAPTER SIX

Their walk back up to Plas Helyg is achieved in relative silence, more so because Linette keeps a brisk pace and there is no chance to speak easily at such a speed. Her pace is deliberate—she did not like Henry Talbot's probing questions and what they implied, has no wish to give him the opportunity to ask more. Nor does she like the troubling thoughts now spiraling about her head like a waterwheel because of them.

I assume he performed a postmortem?

Such a distasteful practice. To think of Dr. Evans laid out on a bloody slab, butchered . . . Linette sets her teeth, continues up the dirt path, the new doctor at her heels.

She glances at him briefly. His dark head is down, concentrating it seems on not tripping over the roots of beech trees protruding from the ground, and so Linette turns her gaze back to the path, the ornate gates of the mansion up ahead.

She thinks of the gatehouse, the mess left behind. Linette did not lie when she told the new doctor she had been verbose in her reaction. Indeed, it is just as well she was alone and no one heard her (poor Enaid would have despaired), but seeing it in the cold light of day . . . Such needless destruction! Such waste! Many of the items destroyed had belonged to poor Dr. Evans. Linette remembers how proud he was of the canvas that now lay smashed on the rug in the hallway; a seascape of Harlech Castle he painted himself as a youth. But who could be responsible? Was it the Jones boy? One of the Einions? Linette never would have thought them capable. All the villagers are good people, are they not? Mistrustful, yes, in many ways, but surely they would not stoop to this.

To be sure, Cai or Rhiannon may feel they had cause, and had plenty of time to plot their attack, for gossip travels as swift as the gull in Penhelyg. The linens were brought from Cerys Davies, the ale for the gatehouse's stores from Arthur Lloyd at the tavern and Ivor Morgan knew to collect the doctor from Dinas Mawddwy. It would have been common knowledge Dr. Talbot was coming here. In theory, she thinks, holding open the gate for him, it could have been any one of them.

"I won't be a moment," the new doctor says as they approach the house, and Linette nods in answer, watches him disappear through Plas Helyg's cavernous doors.

As she waits Linette shoves her hands deep into her trouser pockets, worries her bottom lip with her teeth. What to *do* about it is the thing! Not once, not ever has Linette needed to exert authority. She has been a good mistress, and they in turn have been good tenants. Never have they taken her kindness for granted. However they felt about an outsider coming to Penhelyg, Linette finds it hard to believe they could behave so terribly, that they would mistreat her property. And since there is no way of knowing *who* it was . . . can anything be done at all?

Dr. Talbot reappears, a cumbersome satchel in his hand. It looks worn, the leather crusted at the clasp, and Linette thinks she sees a spot of blood on the bottom, as if he placed it down upon a dirty surface. . . . Again, she has a vision of Wynn Evans's lifeless body under the unforgiving blade of a scalpel; swallowing, Linette turns sharply away.

"Come," she says. She walks in the direction of the stables, and her heart lifts a little to see Pryderi poking his head from one of the stalls, flies flitting noisily about the chestnut cob's ears.

There is a shuffle of dirt behind her, footsteps coming to a stop.

"We're to ride?"

The surprise in Dr. Talbot's voice is evident. Linette must suppress a smile.

"You *must* ride," she throws over her shoulder. "Unless you'd prefer to walk the two miles down to the beach?"

"Can we not use the cart—"

"It's cumbersome and would slow us down. Are you afraid, sir?"

There is no answer. She stops, turns to face him. Some distance away now Dr. Talbot looks at her, jaw clenched.

"I cannot ride."

Linette regards him. When Julian informed her Dr. Evans's replacement would be from London she had expected someone very much like this—someone who never had to travel anywhere except by carriage, a spoiled man wholly unsuited to country living. An arrogant man, with the same prejudiced sensibilities as her cousin, and so far he is quite living up to her expectations.

"Then you must learn."

He blinks at her rudeness. And she *is* being rude, Linette knows she is. But she is used to speaking without a mind to others, of managing everything on her own, and it is a hard habit to quench. Besides, riding a horse is not difficult. Surely anyone, including sheltered city men such as he, can master it?

Rhys opens Pryderi's stall, leads out the large chestnut, already saddled. She slips her foot into the stirrup, swings one leg over the cob's broad back, settles herself easily into the leather. Dr. Talbot's eyes widen. Linette knows what he is thinking—no woman should ride astride—for she has been told often enough by both Enaid and

Julian, but she looks down at Dr. Talbot with eyebrows raised, daring him to pass comment.

He does not. Instead he turns his face, stares at the black horse in front of him with a wary expression. Linette shares a look with the young stable hand.

"Rhys, will you assist our guest?"

The stable lad shoots her a look. Linette holds his gaze. Then, reluctantly, he helps Dr. Talbot up into the saddle, begins to explain in stilted English how to instruct the animal. When the new doctor makes it clear he understands, Rhys passes up the medical bag which the man balances across his lap.

"This will take some getting used to," the doctor grimaces.

Linette guides Pryderi into a turn. "You'll have a lot of things to get used to, I suspect. . . ."

She trails off. Dr. Talbot is frowning at the reins in his hands. With a sigh Linette raises her own, shows him how they lie looped between her fingers.

"Hold them as I do," she says.

He peers at them, does as instructed. Linette lets herself be impressed.

"You're a fast learner," she remarks.

The physician shifts in the saddle, evidently uncomfortable.

"I have a mind suited to learning."

"You should find Gwydion easy to master then."

He frowns. "Gwydion?"

"A sorcerer from a story Enaid used to read me as a child. All the animals here are named after the folklore of these lands."

The new doctor stares without expression, but she can read the judgement on his face all the same. Linette raises her chin, cannot help the defensive heat that brims in the hollow of her throat.

"I'm riding Pryderi. He's a prince from the same story."

"And what of those?"

A couple of small black chickens loiter near Pryderi's stall, pecking at the hay.

"Those are breeding fowl. We'd not be able to kill them if I named them."

He says nothing to this. She clicks her tongue, guides the chestnut cob into another turn. Gwydion follows automatically, and Linette leads them back down Plas Helyg's drive, through the gate, onto the woodland path beyond.

They ride in silence. Often Linette wants to ask a question, to break what is soon becoming an awkward tension, but she cannot quite bring herself to manage it. She too has been hesitant to welcome an Englishman here. Are they not all the same as each other? Superior, rude, quick to judge? Will you—she wants to ask—also treat those who live here with condescension? Another question, whispered into her ear like a taunt, rises to the fore of her mind: *Will you be kind to my mother?* But Linette does not ask these things for she is afraid of the answers. Instead, she will simply watch and wait.

Dr. Henry Talbot will reveal himself to her soon enough.

Finally, they emerge from the woodland. Linette indicates the narrow cottages a little further along on the other side, their willow-tree canopies.

"Those belong to some of the miners," she tells him. "It's these you'll likely be attending to the most, since mining is dangerous work. Dr. Evans often visited the mine when the digging proved particularly difficult. He set three broken arms last year."

Dr. Talbot is frowning at the end house as they pass. Linette wonders why.

"Your cousin told me a little about the mine last night," he says. "I saw it from my bedroom window this morning. I'd not realized it was so close."

Linette purses her lips, crosses the dirt road, indicates for him to follow, and they descend a sloping pathway between houses three and four.

"It never used to be," she answers when they are clear. "The Cadwalladr mines began further down the valley, but when Julian took over he expanded their reach."

He nods. "I suppose he was eager to capitalize on the gold deposits."

"Ah. You've seen his little treasure then?" Linette tightens her grip on Pryderi's reins, tries not to let her disapproval rule her. "It is a fool's errand. My cousin has found a few odd nuggets over the years but nothing substantial. He kept digging closer to Plas Helyg because he's convinced a vein runs through the fields."

The young doctor looks confused. "It's not a gold mine?"

"No. It used to be slate, but as they expanded the terrain shifted and began producing copper ore. It does not matter, either way. Julian has ruined this valley in the pursuit of his enthusiasms, torn it up piece by piece."

Her voice wobbles, and from the corner of her eye she sees the young doctor turn his face to look at her.

"I'm not sure I understand. Doesn't the land belong to you?"

Linette shakes her head. "Not the land on the southeastern side of the mansion. My grandfather claimed there were caverns hidden there, and it was passed to Julian as part of the original mine settlement. Even so, if my father had been alive I'm sure he would not have allowed such a thing. It's quite ruined Plas Helyg's beauty."

They have emerged now into the little clearing that acts as Penhelyg's village square. A stone well stands in the middle, surrounded by houses and shops belonging to Linette's merchant tenants, and on the far side a tavern and stable stand at an awkward angle on the edge of a copse of willow trees. It is here Linette brings Pryderi to a stop.

Dr. Talbot, after a moment's struggle with Gwydion, manages to do the same. A few of the village girls loiter outside one of the barns, whispering to each other behind their hands.

"How did your father die?"

Though the doctor's question is asked gently, Linette feels her hackles rise.

"Why? Do you mean to suggest foul play there too?"

Dr. Talbot simply watches her. There is no judgement in his eyes but they make Linette feel, somehow, exposed. Still, she experiences a measure of guilt for her churlishness and turns her face, focuses her gaze on the stone well instead.

"He died when I was a baby," she replies. "Fell from his horse on his return from a trip to London. My mother, unable to cope with the grief, could not care for me. A trust was set in place that made Julian my guardian."

Bitterness digs like a thorn in her chest. It is not on account of her father (how could she feel anything for a man she never knew?) but of her mother, a mother who has never shown affection, who barely seems to recognize her own daughter, a mother who has lived in the shelter of her own troubled mind for as long as Linette can remember.

Henry Talbot is watching her. When she looks at him she fancies she sees a measure of understanding in his eyes.

"I'm sorry."

Linette shrugs. "Don't be. Julian has been good to me, in his own way. I've wanted for nothing."

She does not tell him that despite his care of her in a monetary sense, Julian has never really understood her. How could he when he was so often away, his attentions caught completely by his social circle in London? The majority of Linette's Christmases and birthdays have been spent alone with the servants, and when Julian does come to Penhelyg he keeps to the company of the Pennants and Selwyns, or locked away in his study.

He spends more time with his damned books than he does with her.

One of the girls—Rhiannon, the Einions' eldest—is nibbling at her fingernail, staring at the new doctor insolently over her thumb. Dr. Talbot appears to notice but makes no remark. Instead he says, "Tell me of your mother," and Linette shifts uncomfortably in her saddle.

What to say about her? The truth, she supposes. What else?

"My mother speaks but little and what little she speaks is not worth hearing. Fanciful things. Queer untruths. Sometimes Mamma can hold an eloquent conversation but those moments are short-lived." Linette hesitates. "She is prone to screaming fits, Dr. Talbot, fits that can go on for hours if left unchecked. Mamma says she can hear wings beating in the dark, that there are people in the room. Sometimes she speaks words in a language I do not understand. Often she mentions blades of gold." Linette picks at a fly caught in Pryderi's mane. "It is Enaid—Mrs. Evans, that is—who cares for her, never leaves her side. She sleeps in Mamma's rooms."

A movement to her left catches her eye. A curtain has twitched in one of the holdings that surround the clearing. Rhiannon—joined now by a few more girls—watches them still, and Linette realizes they are too exposed here, that her companion is under deepest scrutiny. Many eyes, she suspects, watch them now although she cannot see them, and Linette thinks again of the gatehouse, her stomach twisting with unease.

"We'd best continue on," she murmurs, gesturing to a pathway that wends itself by the side of the tavern. "The Morgans live farther down, near the dunes."

Dr. Talbot digs his heels into Gwydion's flanks. The horse whickers sharply. Linette holds out a hand to steady him.

"Be gentle. The lightest pressure will do."

This time she keeps a hand on Gwydion's bit, guides them down into the privacy of the path. When she is sure they are out of sight again Linette releases the horse.

They emerge onto the green swards of the salt marshes, the sea a thick band of blue on the horizon. Free of the confines of the lane she urges Pryderi into a trot, turns her head to find that Dr. Talbot has managed to persuade Gwydion to do the same. Above them seagulls dance between the clouds, shrieking loudly into the wind, and Dr. Talbot raises his face into it, holds down his hat, slows his horse. She does the same.

"It must be a lonely life," he says suddenly, and the comment pulls her off guard.

"Lonely?"

"Yes, lonely. Your father is dead, your mother indisposed, Lord Tresilian rarely in residence."

Linette turns her face sharply to look at him. Truth though it may be, she does not like the way he lays her vulnerability out so plainly and so she counters, "I have Enaid and Cadoc, and my friends in the village. Merlin and Pryderi. Besides, I've plenty to keep me occupied."

"Oh?"

A sharp breeze cuts her cheek; she tastes salt on her tongue. In the distance the coastal cottages have appeared, spotted between trees bent with the long push of sea wind. Beneath her Pryderi huffs, and gently Linette reaches out to run her fingers through his tangled mane.

"As a young girl I spent my days exploring Plas Helyg's lands. I loved the call of the sea, the hills, the woods, and would spend hours in its wilderness. Wales is a place of uncommon beauty, Dr. Talbot, as I'm sure you can see." Linette smiles now, wistful. "Over the years I saw how the people of Penhelyg lived. I've come to know them, respect them. They in turn have given me their trust." She gestures at the houses ahead. "The winter after I turned eighteen these lands suffered from severe flooding—homes were damaged, crops destroyed. When I offered to help, the people told me what they needed, what Mr. Lambeth, Julian's agent, had failed to provide. Supplies of food, temporary shelter, men to clear and renew the land. I went to him but he did nothing. I wrote to Julian, and still nothing was done. They were left to manage, alone. So, as soon as the estate passed to me, I dismissed Mr. Lambeth. I trust no one to look after Penhelyg. Only myself."

She meets his eyes. Dark brown, she realizes.

"I care for my people, Dr. Talbot. They're the only true family I have."

The Morgans' cottage is a small holding set within a patch of sandy land bordered by a fence made of driftwood. Shells of all shapes and sizes hang by string from the sea-worn beams and tinkle merrily in the breeze; nature's very own wind chimes. Henry Talbot pauses to look at them, reaches a hand out to cup a grey scallop shell as he passes, a little chip at its fan.

His mouth lifts slightly at the corner, but Linette cannot decide if it is a smile or a sneer.

She knocks on the door. As they wait for an answer Linette glances across at the sand dunes dotted with yellowwort and sedge, at Tomas's small fishing boat moored on the makeshift quay beyond. Its mast rises tall like a javelin, its tattered sail quipping in the breeze. Dr. Talbot follows her gaze.

"He's a fisherman, then?"

Before she can answer, the door opens a crack. When Mair sees it

69

is Linette she begins to open the door wider, but pauses when she notices the man standing beside her.

"It's all right," Linette says, mollifying. "This is the new doctor—I've brought him to help."

The woman hesitates a moment before widening the door. "The Englishman," she says, and though Mair speaks in Welsh there can be no mistaking her accusing tone. No indeed, her companion has marked it well, for Dr. Talbot stands taller, tips his hat.

"Good morning, ma'am."

Mair's lips purse, prune-like. She shoots Linette a look that says without any doubt that she fiercely disapproves.

"It's all right," Linette says again. "Please, let him try. I've done for Tomas all I can."

Mair hesitates. It seems she might refuse, but then there is a cough from within and something sharpens in Dr. Talbot's face. He pushes past both of them into the low-ceilinged house, follows the sound to Tomas's small, cramped bedroom at the back of the cottage.

"Miss," Mair begins, looking put out. "I do not like it. Ivor says he's not fit for a country doctor. How can he know our ways?"

"Maybe that's the point," Linette replies, closing the door behind her. "We've tried a country doctor as well as the old remedies, and they have not worked. Perhaps it's time we try something else?"

Mair's watery eyes watch her a moment. Then the woman sighs, gestures for Linette to follow.

Dr. Talbot already has Tomas sitting up in the narrow bed, the palm of his hand on his forehead, his other hand flat between the young man's shoulder blades. Tomas, Linette notes with concern, is more florid than the previous evening, a sheen of perspiration spotting his skin like dew. The young doctor looks up as Linette enters, indicates to Tomas with a nod.

"How long has he been like this?"

Tomas is looking at Linette above the crown of Dr. Talbot's head, apprehension clear in his wide eyes. Many years ago they used to play together. Once, in the throes of adolescent fancy, she thought herself in love with him. But then age and duty interfered, adoration shifted to friendship and, finally, to polite affection. Linette feels the dull ache of sadness pull at her chest. The villagers are like family to her, she told the new doctor. Not quite then, not really. She is no closer to them than her own mother, but at least she might speak to them and be heard, understood. Liked.

At least she has that.

"Three weeks," Linette replies now, "though it's only this week he's got worse. Fever, sweats. He's been vomiting . . ."

"Vomiting?"

Linette points at the small basin next to the bed and the physician stares down at the bilious material swimming in it. He puts two fingers to Tomas's wrist, extracts a silver-chained watch from his pocket, silently counts. Then, after a moment, he reaches into his medical bag open at the side of the bed. From within the doctor removes a sheet of paper. Linette expects him to take a pencil from the bag too but instead he does something she has never seen a doctor do before— not Dr. Evans, nor Dr. Beddoe, not any of the others she has been acquainted with over the years: Henry Talbot rolls the paper into a tube and puts it between his ear and Tomas's chest.

Beside her Mair unfolds her bony arms.

"What is he doing?" she murmurs, and all Linette can do is open her mouth and close it again. The doctor keeps his position for a full minute before raising his head.

"Will you come here?" he says, beckoning Linette to sit on the other side of the bed. When she does he turns to Tomas, a kind smile on his face. Tomas—who has not yet said one word and looks for all the world like a terrified hare—snaps his eyes to Linette in alarm.

71

"Do you feel any pain?"

Dr. Talbot says the words slowly, with a gentle intonation meant only for Tomas, but Linette deduces she is to act as interpreter. When she asks him the same, he gives a hesitant nod of the head.

"Where?" The doctor begins to pat his hand on his own head, his arm, his ribs. "Show me," he says, and Tomas—evidently understanding—presses his own hand to his left side.

"And does it hurt to breathe?"

Linette translates.

"*Ydy.*"

"Yes," she returns.

"When you lie down? When you sit up?"

Tomas thinks a moment.

"I can breathe better upright. It's painful when I lie on my good side, easier when I lie on the side that hurts."

"When you breathe in, does it feel sharp?" Dr. Talbot himself breathes deep, makes a stabbing motion in the air with his finger. Immediately, Tomas nods.

The physician looks up. "Did this Dr. Beddoe come to him?"

Linette purses her lips. "Yes."

"And?"

"He advised bed rest."

The doctor blinks. "Was anything else done?"

Linette turns to Mair. "Will you fetch the herbs?"

Tomas's mother disappears from the room, returns moments later with a basket, holds it out to Dr. Talbot who looks inside. Linette sees him mark the dried leaves of nettle, coltsfoot, and elderflower with something bordering on distaste.

"You disapprove?" Linette asks, defensive without quite knowing why. Their ways must feel so primitive to him, and heaven knows

72

Tomas's lack of recovery is proof enough the herbs have not worked. But still . . .

"It is not that, precisely," he replies, rifling through his bag without looking at her. "There has been evidence that certain herbs do have some measure of success. But in my experience I find they do not work as well or with such fast results as more proven scientific methods." He stops, frowns. "Suffice to say they do not harm but nor do they do much good; recovery for patients who rely on herbs is slow and unpredictable. I prefer more immediate methods."

"Such as?"

Dr. Talbot sits back, finally looks at her. "There's a fishing boat outside. He *is* a fisherman?"

"Yes."

Linette glances at Mair. Her withered hands are clasped tight to her mouth in prayer.

"And the symptoms began three weeks ago, you say?"

"Yes, he . . ."

Next to her, Mair swallows a sob.

"I made the mark too late," she cries. "I should have done it sooner. My boy would not be suffering so if I had!"

Linette licks her lips. She will not repeat this to Dr. Talbot.

"Yes," she confirms. "Three weeks ago, give or take a day or two."

Dr. Talbot is looking through his bag again. "And I assume this started after Tomas came in after a fishing trip." When no one says anything he looks at Linette. "Am I right?"

Linette poses the question to Tomas, and to her not-quite surprise, the young man nods.

"It were a horrible squall. Freezing cold. But the fish come closer to shore when the weather's bad, so I took the boat out." Tomas coughs. Linette passes him the bowl and he spits into it. "I got such a good haul. We ate well that week. Earned plenty from it too . . ." Weakly he sinks back against the wooden headboard, and it is only then Linette notices what the physician is holding in his hand: a small knife, a thin metal barrel.

She stares.

"What do you mean to do?"

Dr. Talbot looks between mother and son. "A more immediate method," he replies. "Of course, it is entirely up to the patient. But my recommendation is to reduce the swelling in his lungs."

"How?"

"My belief is that Tomas has an inflammation caused by a severe chill that has been left untreated. Pleurisy. The inflammation is made up of fluid that rubs on the lining of the lung which is causing the stabbing pains, making it difficult for him to breathe. I would prefer to drain the fluid by making an incision in the back of the chest and drawing it out."

Linette looks at the knife and the other implement Dr. Talbot holds in his hand, and a cold chill spreads fast across her chest.

"No."

He blinks. "But you've not asked them."

"I don't have to."

"Still," Dr. Talbot says, pointed. "I would rather the answer came from them."

Reluctantly Linette explains in their own tongue, but she can tell by the way both mother and son pale at the mention of an incision that their preference is for the "safer" route, and she tells him so.

Dr. Talbot looks at each of them in turn—Tomas, Mair, Linette. Then, with obvious reluctance, he replaces the implements in his satchel, closes it with a *snap*.

"Other methods are vigorous coughing to release the mucus, bloodletting, cold bathing—" here he picks at the pile of heavy blankets covering Tomas's legs—"all to reduce the inflammation. Drinking milk and consuming fruit would also be of help. This is something that *can* go away on its own, but my concern is Tomas will develop pneumonia, and since he is already so weak . . ."

He trails off. Linette stares, feels the claw of guilt at her chest. All this time she has been helping them, sending those woolen blankets down to keep Tomas warm . . . it is quite possible she has made the situation worse. But how could she have known, when Dr. Beddoe dismissed Tomas's case so readily? Linette clamps the guilt down, repeats everything the doctor dictates, and on the promise she will have milk and fruit sent down to the cottage by evening she and Dr. Talbot rise from the bed. The physician shakes Tomas's hand.

"I'll see you again," he says.

Though Tomas clearly does not understand the words he recognises the sentiment behind them, and for the first time in a long time, he smiles. It is a pained and tired smile, but for Linette the sight of it is almost as good as any cure.

CHAPTER SEVEN

Linette leaves the cottage first, folds her arms tight across her chest as the sea breeze pushes firm like a salt wall. On the air she smells sand, the brine-scent of fish. The shells jangle on their strings. Behind her she hears the doctor close the cottage door, the dull thud of the latch falling into place, and she turns to him with a "thank you" on her lips, but a deep frown is furrowing his forehead, the flat of his hand spread out against the deep grain of pitted wood.

"Dr. Talbot?"

"Why do the doors have white marks on them? I noticed the miners' houses up the way had similar marks."

She looks at the wood, the light washing of white daubed onto it in a haphazard line.

"It's a local superstition," says Linette. "People here think that by whitening their houses they shut the door against the Devil. It is what Mrs. Morgan meant when she said she'd made the mark too late." Dr. Talbot stares as if he does not comprehend. "When she said, '*Fe wnes i'r marc yn rhy hwyr,*'" Linette adds by way of explanation. "She thinks if she had done it sooner Tomas would not have got sick."

There is a beat of silence. Within it Linette watches him twist the fancy of it around in his head, marks the very moment he discards her words for lunacy.

"The Devil doesn't exist," Dr. Talbot says finally, hand slipping from the door. "To believe in such things is the mark of fools."

"Well, while *you* mightn't believe in the Devil the people of Penhelyg do. You will gain no esteem here if you taunt the beliefs of your patients."

"I do not taunt," Dr. Talbot counters, as if lecturing a child, "but there can be no denying the ridiculousness of such a notion. How can marking doors white possibly ward off the Devil?"

Linette shrugs. "White for purity, I suppose?"

"But how is that rational?" he persists, his face bright with the passion of a man determined to push his point. "Even if the Devil existed no amount of white paint could possibly make a difference."

"Perhaps," Linette counters, feeling herself grow defensive again, "it is not the paint that makes a difference, but the *belief* that it will."

Dr. Talbot stares at her from beneath the rim of his hat, dark eyes thoughtful.

There is something familiar about the way he looks at her. It is a calculating regard, one that succeeds in making her feel exposed, somehow, but then he shrugs, returns to Gwydion, and Linette lets out the breath she had not realised she was holding.

When Linette was a child, Enaid used to recite tales of magic and myth to her at bedtime. They were filled with the adventures of young farmhands and gallant knights, of mighty giants and enchanted lakes. Many tales featured wily fairy folk and their wicked deeds; how they would swap innocent children for their own, how they would fool weary travelers into a castle that disappeared once they awoke to find themselves cold and wet on the moors, or how if one were to step inside their stone circles, one would be trapped in dance for ever.

Other tales told of darker beings, much more sinister and chilling—monstrous hounds, tormented banshees, water creatures that would drag unsuspecting victims into the depths of their lairs to feast upon their drowned corpses.

To Linette's mind, they are stories and nothing more. But there can be no denying that sometimes—just sometimes—when she has been out in the fields or woods or mountains, she has fancied to have seen a tantalizing glimpse of an *ellyll* from the corner of her eye, or heard the mournful singing of *Gwrach y Rhibyn* high on the wind. Often she has seen clusters of the moss-bound rocks so favored by the *tylwyth teg* and found a way around them. Just in case.

But it is clear to her there is little point in telling this plain-speaking doctor any of that.

They maneuver the horses across the salt marshes, back up to the narrow path. Linette points at some cottages hidden by a tall hedge, tells him of their inhabitants. (Bryn Parry is not expected to see out the summer, Bronwen Lewis has a baby just weaned, Gareth Griffiths suffers from headaches and his wife, Catrin, is prone to gout.) Henry Talbot responds to these facts in curt polite tones and, beginning to feel as though she is wasting breath, Linette presses her tongue between her teeth.

At length they reach Penhelyg's square. Even at its busiest, the village is quiet during the daytime hours. With the majority of men working up at the mines it is the women who hold sway here; some are weavers of nets which they sell down at the docks of Abermaw, some launder, others bake, and farmers' wives can often be found trading milk or livestock in exchange for these small commodities. Linette nods to them all in greeting, but to her dismay some of the women— women she has known all her life—fail to acknowledge her. Indeed, they appear to take great pains to ignore Linette completely and for a brief moment she cannot fathom it . . . until the butcher's wife narrows her eyes at a point over Linette's shoulder and turns heel.

Oh. She has marked who I'm with.

Linette twists in her saddle to see if he too understands, and it troubles her to find he does; Henry Talbot is watching Delyth Hughes's cold retreat. Is she imagining it, this animosity? She looks about the square, spots Rhiannon and one of the Parry girls sitting now by one of the water troughs near the tavern. Keen to be sure, Linette steers Pryderi toward them, beckons Dr. Talbot to follow. On their approach the girls look up, and like the others their usual friendly smiles do not come. Linette's own smile slips from her face as she reins the horse in.

"Good afternoon, Rhiannon. Good afternoon, Erin. How are you both?"

Erin—the younger of the two—nervously flicks a glance at Rhiannon, then stares hard at the ground. She mumbles a greeting, the words muffled into the rough of her woolen collar. Rhiannon, however, simply watches Linette with steely eyes.

"Well enough, mistress."

Her gaze slides to the doctor then back again. She says nothing else.

"This is Dr. Talbot, our new physician."

Linette gestures to him. The doctor doffs his hat. Rhiannon's pointed jaw clenches.

"I know."

A statement, harmless enough. Why then does it feel like an attack?

"We've just come from Tomas Morgan's bedside," Linette tries in a lighter tone. "Will your father be able to spare some milk for him? Dr. Talbot says it will be curative."

Erin looks taught as harp strings. Rhiannon's eyes darken.

"I'm sure we can spare some. But for Tomas's sake. Not his."

The last words are said with derision, and Linette swallows as her suspicions are confirmed.

Rhiannon Einion is only a few years younger than Linette. Not old enough, not really, to take the rumours to heart. Yet her grandmother had been well-loved in Penhelyg and though—like Linette—the girl never knew the woman, the memory of her has been passed down, the tragic tale with it. Still, it has no bearing on Henry Talbot and Rhiannon should know that.

They all should.

"For Tomas's sake," Linette says now, forcing a smile. "It is all I ask."

For a moment Rhiannon stares. Then she turns up her nose, rises from the bench; Erin stumbles up with her.

"Very well," she replies, and looks at Dr. Talbot once more, a vicious gleam in her dark eyes. Then, with not one word further, Rhiannon brushes past Pryderi's legs. The horse huffs; Linette presses her heels to steady him. Erin—with a shy, apologetic glance—hurries after her, skirts spilling dust, and Linette watches them go with a deep sense of unease. Next to her, Dr. Talbot clears his throat.

"I do not need to understand Welsh to know that we were not well met."

Linette sighs, turns now to look at him. His expression reveals no upset, no derogatory manner, but she hears the reserve in his voice just the same.

"I'm sorry. I do not know . . ." She trails off. Cannot lie. "Your presence here will take some getting used to. That's all."

Something flickers in his face.

"Will it?"

Linette opens her mouth, shuts it again.

No, she cannot bring herself to lie. Instead, it is better to say nothing at all.

They are nearing the fork at the gatehouse when the shot comes. It splits the air with a deafening *crack*, causing an explosion of birds to scatter high into the trees. Linette hears the splinter-break of impacted wood, but she has no chance to see which tree has fallen victim to it, for beneath her Pryderi rears up with a loud whicker, and Linette clings on to his reins, digs her heels into the cob's flanks to keep him steady. Gwydion's cry is louder—the horse's scream pierces her ears, and Linette is vaguely aware of the new doctor clinging desperately on as the cob throws his head.

"*Pwyll*," she says now, leaning forward into Pryderi's ear, "steady now."

The horse snorts deeply, paws the ground, and Linette takes that opportunity to reach out for Gwydion's reins swinging wildly at his neck. Her companion has his fingers buried in the horse's coarse black mane, white-knuckled—it is only when Linette calms his mount that he releases his grip.

"Are you all right?" she asks, breathless.

The doctor is ghost pale. Visibly he swallows.

"I think so, yes. Yes," he says again, more firmly, as if to assure himself of the fact.

There is a snap of twig. Over his shoulder a movement catches her eye. Seeing the direction of her gaze Dr. Talbot twists in his saddle, dark eyes scanning the trees.

"Hello?" he calls.

There is no answer.

"Perhaps," Linette ventures, "it was one of the farmhands. Pheasants are plentiful in these woods. My tenants have free rein to hunt wherever they please."

"Then why did they not call out?"

"Mayhap they did not realize."

It sounds feeble, even to her lips. He called into the woods, loud enough that whoever it was should hear him. They should have heard the horses scream, at least. Why, then, would they not come forward and apologize?

Linette squints into the dense woodland, tries to make out

whatever it was she saw a moment before, but there is nothing. Nothing but the natural sounds of the forest, its creaking branches, its rustle of leaves.

Henry Talbot is looking now in the direction of where the bullet landed. The trunk of a sycamore possesses an ugly splintered wound, and seeing it Linette feels her blood run cold. It is exactly at eye level. This was the tree she had passed a moment before, her companion following close behind. . . .

Furtively Henry dismounts. Handing Gwydion's reins to Linette, he approaches it.

He stares at the tree for a long moment before looking about him on the forest floor where—Linette sees now—his medical bag has fallen among the feathered fronds of a fern. He opens the bag, sifts through it, takes out the small knife he proposed to use on Tomas Morgan.

Linette watches, fascinated, as he angles the blade into the trunk, plucks something from it, places it in his palm. He prods at it with the tip of the knife, his lips a grim line.

"What is it?"

A bullet, of course, but that is not what Linette means. The doctor seems to recognize this, however, for he raises his gaze to meet hers, hard as stones.

"Someone just took a shot at me."

Linette blinks. "I beg your pardon?"

She realizes he is breathing deeply, is striving for a calm he clearly does not feel.

"From the behavior of the villagers just now it's abundantly clear I'm not wanted here." A hint of bitterness. "And when we were speaking of Dr. Evans earlier you said he would not be easily replaced, *especially* by an Englishman. What did you mean by that?"

"I . . ."

He levels her with a stern look.

Linette sighs. "'Tis difficult to explain . . ."

"I'm listening."

She does not respond, for how can she possibly make him understand? But her silence only seems to provoke him.

"Someone *shot* at me!" he cries, and Linette sighs again in answer.

"I'm sorry, but I simply can't believe it was deliberate. A stray bullet, a bad aim, that is all."

The young doctor's face is flushed with emotion.

"First the gatehouse," he says, "now this. I've not been in Penhelyg even a day, yet it seems your tenants are determined to be rid of me."

Linette stares. A sliver of cold runs down her back, making her flinch.

"Are you suggesting someone tried to kill you?"

He slips the bullet into his pocket. "Or warn me off."

"No. No," she says again, shaking her head. "They would not do such a thing." But doubt now is clawing at her insides, burying itself like a worm.

Above them a goshawk lets out a sharp screech. Together they look up, watch it glide through the air before disappearing into the treetops. Pryderi shifts beneath her; Gwydion in turn pulls at the reins she still holds, and suddenly Linette is overwhelmingly tired.

Henry Talbot narrows his eyes. "I deserve to know why they should dislike me so."

"Yes. You do. But now is not the time to tell you."

"Someone shot at me!" he says again, voice raised and pinched. "These villagers, they—"

"Dr. Talbot," she snaps, "I shall not have you slandering my people in such a manner." The physician opens his mouth to counter her with a reply, but Linette holds up her palm to stop him. "I'll discuss this only when we are both calm, and not before. Is that perfectly clear?"

And with that she instructs Pryderi forward, into the now silent trees.

CHAPTER EIGHT

It is a relief to return to his room, finally to be alone.

He can still hear the gunshot in the cavern of his memory, the sound it made when it whizzed past his ear. If he had been only one inch to the left . . .

Henry sits on the bed, removes the bullet from his pocket, balances it again in the center of his palm.

At Guy's Hospital he removed his fair share of slugs. Henry can recognise the lead shot of a Brown Bess musket down to the small balls fired by a standard pistol. This one—despite its flattened tip resulting from the impact of the tree trunk—looks to be of middling size, typical of a pistol or hunting rifle.

The type of gun it belongs to tells him two things. First, that it was a weapon meant for shooting large game. But second and more damning . . . such a gun could only have been fired at close range. Which means that despite Linette Tresilian's protestations, whoever took a shot at Henry could see him, and knew *exactly* what they were doing.

But why? Why would someone shoot at him?

He thinks of the villagers he met down in the square. The pretty dark-haired girl. Rhiannon, was it? Henry felt her resentment, her narrow-eyed glare sharp as knives. He thinks too of the young men with whom he shared the cart from Abermaw, the distrustful looks of Plas Helyg's servants. And the reserve of Mrs. Morgan had been as palpable as ice.

Henry does not understand it.

According to his hostess the villagers had been attended by one Dr. Beddoe from a town across the estuary. If that were the case then that gentleman would have been no worldly use to them at all if they required immediate attention. Surely they would be pleased to have a new doctor, one that was so readily available? The gatehouse is a mere fifteen minutes away from the village square on foot. . . .

The gatehouse. This too he does not understand. To go to such violent lengths of destruction—why? And, of course, there is still the matter of Dr. Evans.

Henry places the bullet onto the coverlet, reaches into his other pocket for the vial he retrieved from the debris of the gatehouse.

Now he is alone, he can look at it with keener attention, and Henry holds the bottle up to the light shining through the window. It is the work of a master craftsman, the shape of it delicate and flimsy, not like his own bottles at all. In contemplation Henry tilts it. Stops. Squints. What he had previously mistaken for dirt is, in fact, the smallest bit of brown liquid, half-congealed at the bottom. Intrigued, Henry pops the gold Turk's-head stopper, lifts the vial to his nose. Frowns.

The faintest hint of sour fruit.

Still looking at it he opens his medical bag with one hand, means to bring out one of his own vials of tincture to compare . . . and pulls back with a hiss. A small bloom of blood pools on the tip of his finger, red as berries. Henry peers inside the bag.

"Damn."

Some of the bottles are broken; it must have happened when the satchel fell in the forest. He had not been able to bring many supplies with him from London—the governor expressly forbade it—and so these items were the last of his personal supply. Henry sifts through the ones still intact, finally brings out a small bottle of laudanum.

Reddish-brown, this. Similar in colour, yet . . .

Henry sniffs this one too. Not sour like the other—laudanum is sweeter. Again, he tilts the strange vial this way and that in the light, watches the congealing liquid slide right to left.

"What are you?" he murmurs, but no answer comes.

Henry shakes his head. It is too much for his tired mind to fathom. And though it is not much past midday he *is* tired, overwhelmingly so. His body aches like—and here he almost laughs—the Devil. All of a sudden it seems as if the past few days of travel, along with today's early start and the ride down to the coast, have caught up with him and taken their toll. Henry grimaces, shifts on the bed. His buttocks are sore, his spine stiff. And his head! He lies down, succumbing at last to the headache that threatened earlier, its insistent tug . . .

A knock on the door wakes him. It takes a moment to rouse himself, a moment more to realize the room is filled with long shadows, that the light outside the window has dimmed. The knock comes again—more impatient this time—and when Henry opens the door it is to find the housekeeper, Mrs. Evans, standing on the other side.

"Miss Linette requests your presence at supper, sir."

Her voice is stiff, measured. As before, she will not meet his eyes. Striving for politeness, Henry inclines his head.

"Please tell her I shall be down directly."

The housekeeper bobs, the scallops of her mobcap trembling, but as she begins to turn away Henry holds out his hand.

"Mrs. Evans?"

The woman stops, focuses her gaze on the doorjamb.

"Yessir?"

Henry searches for the appropriate words.

"I do hope, madam, we can learn to get along together. I appreciate it will take all of us some time to adjust."

At last, the old woman raises her eyes to his. For a long moment she watches him, seems to take him in piece by piece.

"You're very young for a doctor," she says quietly.

"I'm more than qualified, I assure you."

"I've no doubt you are," Mrs. Evans responds, her voice a little stronger than it had been moments before. "You wouldn't be here otherwise. But you might find your age—among other things—will go against you."

It is a loaded comment, delivered with a sharp eye that does not pretend to hide her disapproval.

Henry's hackles rise.

"I hope I will be given a chance to prove myself before I'm dismissed so readily."

The housekeeper says nothing to this. Instead she says, voice clipped, "Miss Linette is expecting you. You'd best make haste."

Mrs. Evans pauses then, glances at his creased shirt, his sleep-mussed hair, and self-consciously Henry raises his hand to tidy it.

"Forgive me, let me change. I'll not be a moment."

"There's no need," comes the reply. "We don't stand on ceremony here, not while his lordship's away." A pause. "Follow me."

The old woman turns, begins a brisk amble toward the stairs in a manner which belies her age. When Henry catches up with her he glances at her face, notes the way the woman's lips pinch shut, as if determined to keep silent.

But he is not. He considers the vial and bullet left marooned on the coverlet in his room.

Henry appreciates that as the sister of the deceased, the housekeeper, at least, has sufficient cause to resent his presence here. Still, he thinks as they turn a corner and walk past a towering grandfather clock, she might be able to shed some more light on today's discoveries, and when else will he have an opportunity to ask?

"I understand," he begins, meaning to soften her before delivering the blow, "that my predecessor was your brother." The old woman pauses in her step, gives a short nod in assent. "Yet you go by *Mrs.* Evans, not Miss? Forgive the impertinence, but I wondered why?"

They have reached the last flight of stairs. The housekeeper rests her age-spotted hand on the carved banister and Henry senses her bristle at the question.

"It is customary for a housekeeper to be called 'Mrs.' A formality, only. And if you forgive *me* the impertinence, Dr. Talbot, you are clearly not familiar with country ways or the workings of a grand house. It makes me wonder if you're quite suited to a position here."

Mrs. Evans has pinned him with such a hard look Henry feels compelled to defend himself.

"I trained as an apprentice at Guy's Hospital in London. I then attended university to train as a physician but found I preferred the study of anatomy and returned to Guy's, where I later taught." Henry hesitates at the memory, feels again that now-all-too-familiar twist of injustice. "I may have no knowledge of country ways or grand houses, madam, but I'm more than qualified in all aspects of medical practice. I'm no inexperienced boy fresh out of the schoolhouse."

The housekeeper watches him. Henry chews his inner cheek. No matter what has happened since, he is proud of his background, of how far he has risen, and Mrs. Evans seems to recognize it for her hard expression softens.

"Very well."

She begins to descend. Henry takes a breath and she stops again, gives him a questioning look.

"I do not wish to cause you pain," he says, keeping his voice as gentle as he can, "but I was told you found Dr. Evans's body."

A small intake of breath. A sudden sheen to her pale blue eyes. "*Ie.*"

"He was discovered on the threshold of the gatehouse, I understand?"

Mrs. Evans looks away, swallowing hard. He thought she would be angry at his prying, but the question appears instead to have weakened her. She stares down into the vestibule, into the fire that burns brightly in its cavernous grate.

"It was like he had seen the Devil himself."

Henry frowns.

"The Devil, madam?"

"*Ie*, as if he worked his way in. Wynn's face . . ."

Henry's fingers tingle with a strange premonition.

"His face, Mrs. Evans?"

The old woman bites the cushion of her lower lip, and it takes a moment for her to compose herself.

"I never knew my brother to be scared of anything in his life, Dr. Talbot, but there was no mistaking the expression on his face." She looks at him, eyes fraught with an urgent light. "Wynn looked terrified. As if he had been frightened to death!"

"Are you coming or not?"

Together both he and Mrs. Evans jump. Guiltily, Henry turns his head.

Linette Tresilian stands at the bottom of the stairs, the gray lurcher at her side. She stares up at them, features haughty and impatient, arms folded across her chest.

"I'll take my leave," the housekeeper says. Her voice is stronger now, the look of pain and panic on her face gone as if they were never there, and before Henry can respond the elderly woman is climbing the stairs. Reluctant, he takes her cue and walks in the opposite direction to meet his frowning hostess.

"What were you saying to Enaid?"

Henry toys with a lie but Linette Tresilian raises one of her finely arched eyebrows.

"I will ask her later, if you do not tell me now."

"I have nothing to conceal. I was asking about Dr. Evans."

Her expression shifts into one of annoyance.

"You had no right."

"I did not realize the subject was forbidden."

She purses her lips, breathes out hard through her nose. The dog—who has been staring up at him, wiry tail wagging—makes a grumbling noise, a little throaty *brrr*.

"Who is this?" Henry asks, and the woman in front of him sighs.

"Your attempt to divert my attention is noted," she retorts, one side of her mouth lifting in what Henry thinks might be a smile. "But I am famished and have no mind to argue. *This* is Merlin."

"Merlin," Henry echoes.

"I told you. All the animals here are named after Welsh folklore."

"So you did."

This time she does smile.

"Come, Dr. Talbot," Linette Tresilian says. "My mother is waiting."

Henry regards the childlike woman sitting quietly at the table, tries to discern similarities to that strange portrait outside his room, but this woman is a mere shadow of her oil-stroked counterpart. *This* woman is painfully thin, pale skin stretched across gaunt cheekbones framed by long thin hair as white as a dove. A statue carved from marble.

"This is Henry Talbot, Mamma, your new physician." Linette Tresilian gently takes the older woman's hand, clasps it in both her own.

"My mother does not usually dine downstairs," she adds to Henry, "but I thought a change might do her good."

Henry bows. "A pleasure to meet you, my lady."

Gwenllian Tresilian merely looks up at him from gray-green eyes the mirror of her daughter's. Dark circles cup them like purple crescent moons.

"Do not mind her," Linette Tresilian says, moving to take a seat a little further down the table. She removes her napkin from its pewter ring. Merlin trots over, settles down at his mistress's feet beneath the table. "As I told you before, sometimes she will carry a conversation as if there were nothing wrong at all. Most days, however, she is as you see her now. Please, doctor, take a seat."

Henry does not move, for Lady Gwen appears to be reading his features like a map—her gaze roves over him, pupils wide, as if looking for something she cannot find.

"How are you, my lady?"

Her eyes move downward then, into the cushion of her lap. Linette Tresilian twirls the napkin ring between her forefingers.

"If Mamma wishes to speak, she will. Sit, Dr. Talbot."

She indicates a seat opposite her, and as Henry takes it she jingles a small bell next to a bowl of apples set in the middle of the table. Lady Gwen does not react to the sound; indeed, it is as if, now, she is in some sort of trance, and Henry watches her thoughtfully. According to her daughter, the tenor of her mind changed after the death of her husband, but can grief really cause such drastic change in behavior? And so long after the first terrible blow?

A small door behind Linette opens and through it comes Plas Helyg's sour-faced butler.

"Are you ready to be served, Miss Linette?"

"Thank you, Cadoc."

Powell bows his head, turns to an ornate sideboard and picks up a glass decanter filled with deep red liquid, pours Henry a glass before serving the women.

No one speaks. The fire crackles gently behind him, the carriage clock on the mantel ticks softly over the turn of its cogs. Linette Tresilian takes a small sip from her glass, eyes meeting Henry's over the rim.

"I wish to apologize for my behavior today."

Powell dips in a bow, closes the dining-room door behind him.

"You'd be forgiven in thinking me an unfriendly, harsh-spoken woman," she continues. "But the truth is I've become rather too used to solitude. I'm not much used to seeing people outside of Penhelyg, and, well, I cannot bear for them to be maligned."

As she trails off Henry reaches for his glass, is surprised to find only a mediocre claret. Perhaps Julian keeps the more expensive goods back for when he is in residence. Thinking of him now, Henry twists the crystal stem between his fingers.

Julian had asked him to be mindful of his once-ward, to judge if she shared her mother's weakness of mind, but so far Henry has seen no evidence of it. An unusual woman, yes, indeed, precisely what Linette Tresilian has confessed to herself: harsh-spoken and solitary. He remembers her defensiveness when he suggested she was lonely. What sort of childhood must she have had, with no parents and a frequently absent guardian? It is clear to him, Henry thinks, that Julian Tresilian simply does not understand his cousin's nature. Still, he must reserve judgment. One day is not enough for him to determine a person's character. And did not Julian say Lady Gwen had been Linette's age when her symptoms first began?

Henry places his glass back down on the table, offers a polite smile.

"I do understand. But that does not change the fact that the gatehouse was vandalized and someone shot at me this afternoon."

92

A flush appears on her cheek—with embarrassment or shame Henry cannot tell—but Linette Tresilian seems not to be led and changes the subject entirely.

"I suppose after the delights of London, Penhelyg is quite a shock. What was it like? Did you enjoy your work?"

It is a question Henry should have expected at some point or another, yet he is not prepared for it, is struck silent a moment, the harsh words of the hospital's governor turning over themselves in his head again and again like the cog of the carriage clock on the mantle:

You are a disgrace to this hospital, a disgrace to your good name as well as mine, a disgrace to all those who put their trust in you. . . .

Henry means to reply with an answer that would serve not to reveal too much, but before he can Powell returns with a plate in each hand, the maid, Angharad, following behind holding another. Immediately Merlin scuttles up, nose raised, ears twitching, and the butler must sidestep the animal before he can set the plate he carries in front of Lady Gwen, her daughter in turn, leaving Angharad to set the final plate down in front of Henry.

"Liver in gravy and onions, with potatoes and greens," she tells him quietly, her Welsh accent pronounced and lilting. Henry looks down at the dish—a less substantial portion than the night before— and he watches the steam rise from the brown sauce, the smell of onions sweet and rich. But, with unease, he notes how the flesh of the liver gleams in the candlelight, reminding him of the kidney he held in his hands all those weeks ago, slick and fat and pulsing.

No tumor. No tumor at all.

Linette Tresilian's voice brings him back.

"When Julian is away we serve only one course," she tells him as the servants leave the room once more. "I don't see the need for three or four as I've heard city folk take. Far too much ceremony and a complete waste of food. I trust you don't object?"

"Not at all," Henry says faintly, disturbed at his unwanted memory. "I'd be at a loss if you were to offer such a spread."

Indeed, his own meals used to consist of cold food parcels delivered to Guy's by his landlady, quick tavern fare, or a late-night penny pie from a street seller en route to his lodgings after his shift at the hospital was done.

"And while we are at it," she continues, brusque again, "please call me Linette. We're to be together far too much to keep up the pretense of formality."

Gratefully, he raises his eyes from his plate.

"Thank you. I confess, I'm wholly sick of not knowing how to address you."

"I may call you Henry, then?"

"I prefer you do."

"Good." She takes a sip of claret. "Henry, you did not answer my question."

That brief flicker of gratitude is replaced immediately by a familiar feeling of dread.

"Why did you ask it?"

Linette lifts one shoulder, begins to slice into her potatoes.

"Well, no doctor I've encountered has been as methodical as you clearly are. Not even Dr. Evans seemed quite so in tune, shall we say, with his patients the way you were with Tomas. He evidently did not possess the same level of learning as you."

While she was speaking, Merlin rested his long chin on the table. Linette cuts a small chunk from the liver on her plate, offers it to the dog who chomps it loudly between his teeth.

"That is not uncommon, considering I imagine he trained as only a country doctor."

"Oh?"

94

He repeats what he told Mrs. Evans.

"I ended up taking a leading position at the hospital which I held for five years," he adds. "I gave lectures on the nervous system, bone structure, anatomy, and dissection. I had apprentices of my own. Patients were often referred to me on recommendation." He hesitates. "Sometimes I consulted on Bow Street cases."

Linette's brow furrows. "Bow Street?"

"Home of the Runners. They are London's law enforcement. My contact there would often ask me to examine a body or a prisoner, advise on either cause of death or best treatment."

"Indeed? You must have been very busy, then. I've heard crime is as common as rats in the city."

"Francis only called on me for the more obscure cases. Cases that required more investigation."

Linette blinks.

"Murder?"

"Occasionally."

"Ah." She sits back in her seat, raises an eyebrow. "Is that why you're so suspicious?"

Observation. Contemplation. Interrogation. But this is a new and unfamiliar playing field, one that Henry must consider carefully before making any further move, and so he simply answers, "That has something to do with it, yes."

At the end of the table Lady Gwen—who has until now simply sat with her hands in her lap—picks up her knife and fork. Her daughter slowly scratches Merlin's chin, watches Henry carefully.

"I see," she says softly. "Tell me, then—if you held such a prestigious position, why stoop to one here? Surely a village doctor cannot begin to compare to that of a city surgeon and all the opportunities it afforded?"

Lady Gwen makes a noise in the back of her throat. It is a strange noise, an odd strangled gurgle. Methodically, she begins to cut the liver into tiny pieces. "*Hoath, Redar, Ganabel, Berith . . .*"

Henry frowns at the whispered words.

"What is she saying?"

Linette sighs. "I don't know."

"It's not Welsh?"

She shakes her head. "Remember I said that sometimes she speaks words in a language I do not understand? Well, this is it."

Her mother repeats the four words over and over as she continues to cut the liver, proceeds to do the same with the beans. Then, once she is done she falls silent and—so very delicately—pierces one of the morsels with her fork and takes a bite.

"I've tried," Linette adds, "to find out their meaning but no dictionary I possess refers to them."

Henry watches her chew with keen interest. Lady Gwen has been served the same size portion as himself and Linette but the pale blue dress she wears hangs from her small frame, her collarbone protrudes from the snow-white skin, and in the candlelight her cheeks look gaunt. He would be very surprised if she clears her plate. Still, she *is* eating, and the fact that she can feed herself without prompt or mess is an encouraging sign. His gaze shifts back to his own plate, and he cuts into the liver. The knife sinks in effortlessly. Henry tries not to make comparisons to the image that imprinted itself upon his mind moments before, raises the fork to his lips.

They eat in silence for some time, the only noises silver against porcelain, the whimper of Merlin begging for scraps. At length Lady Gwen raises thin fingers to her mouth, gingerly removes a piece of fleshy grit from her tongue. She places it on the side of her plate, looks down at it wide-eyed.

"Why *did* you leave London?"

Linette's voice is like a whip-crack in the quiet. Henry lowers his fork.

Hell's teeth, she is persistent! He hoped that her mother had distracted Linette enough for her to forget their earlier subject.

"I shall tell you," he hedges, "if you tell me why I am not welcome here."

For a long moment Linette stares at him across the table, sunbrowned skin pale in the candlelight. She opens her mouth, shuts it again.

Henry leans forward.

"They dislike you because you are an Englishman," Linette says.

He blinks.

"I don't understand."

Very slowly she places her cutlery down on her plate, takes a sip of wine, lingers over it before setting it down.

"To understand it," Linette begins, "you must know our history. Many of the Welsh estates have dwindled dreadfully in recent years, to the detriment of those who relied on the landowners for their care. I'm sure you've noticed there's little to entertain here—many of the gentry took to the cities. As a consequence they left their estates under the care of agents who leeched money from tenants and the land into the purses of their employers, who then squandered it. Some could curtail their spending, like our neighbors Lord Pennant and Sir John Selwyn, but many others were plunged into debt and passed their estates on to English gentry. My grandfather was one of these men. He preferred the delights of London and spent so freely there it put Plas Helyg on the edge of ruin."

Her face darkens.

"Fearing bankruptcy, Emyr Cadwalladr evicted tenants to sell land, and let the mansion fall into disrepair. All he cared about was his pleasure. He was a prolific gambler, lost the mines in a game of cards to Julian. It ruined him."

Linette's gaze shifts briefly to her mother still looking at the gristle on her plate.

"Luckily he had a beautiful daughter to bargain with. My father—being the elder and richer of the two cousins—married Gwenllian Cadwalladr, became sole owner of Plas Helyg, and took on all its debts. Just as well since my grandfather died a few months later, but it was an arrangement that robbed Penhelyg of a Welsh landowner. It was English money that secured the estate."

Henry shakes his head. "But surely that was a good thing? The estate was kept intact."

Out the corner of his eye he sees Lady Gwen has begun to sway, but Linette seems not to notice. She taps a fingernail against the long stem of her glass, its *tink tink tink* a dull chime in the enclosed room, before letting her finger fall still.

"According to Cadoc, my father made moves to treat his tenants more fairly, repair the damage my grandfather wrought. But then he died too, Julian took over, and, well . . ." She sighs. "He wasn't interested in running a rural estate hundreds of miles from London society. Everything was managed in his absence by Mr. Lambeth, another Englishman, hired by my cousin to replace the Welsh agent already in place. My grandfather had been reckless, 'tis true, but Mr. Lambeth charged impossibly high rent, neglected the villagers' homes and ignored their needs when the floods came. As for the mines, they're a profitable enterprise to be sure, but dangerous. Julian's obsession with gold . . ." Linette shakes her head. "He had the workers dig deeper and deeper into the valley, pushed the mines too hard. There have been three collapses in recent years, tragic deaths. All this has made them resent English intrusion. Though I'm half-English myself, they recognize my Welsh heritage and have benefited firsthand from my efforts to make their lives easier since I inherited. But you? You are yet another Englishman."

At the top of the table, her mother's breath hitches.

Henry frowns at the explanation. It seems so . . . flimsy. Yes, he can understand why the villagers might dislike Julian Tresilian's less than mindful treatment of them, but *him*? What of the gatehouse? What of the gunshot? Could his heritage really be so offensive that someone might contrive of a way to be rid of him?

"No."

Linette blinks. "No?"

"No," Henry repeats. "That is not everything. There's something more to this, something you aren't telling me. What is it?"

Though her expression does not change Henry knows instinctively he is right. But there is no time to push her, less time for her to answer, because there comes then a long and mournful moan.

Together their attention snaps to Gwen Tresilian. The older woman is gripping the sides of the table, knuckles jutting against her thin skin, staring at the tiny bit of gristle on her plate with a look of unmistakable horror.

"*O na,*" Linette whispers, and the words are barely out of her mouth before Lady Gwen begins to scream.

CHAPTER NINE

It was bound to happen, of course. Linette had expected it the moment she brought her downstairs, that some small obscure occurrence (for it was never entirely clear what would prompt it) was like to send her mother into a dreadful fit.

Yet.

She had been so desperate to attempt normalcy—to see her mother dressed in something other than a nightgown, her hair clean and combed, smelling sweetly of orange blossom and fir; so desperate that mother and daughter should dine together, as if there were nothing wrong at all. But there was nothing normal about Gwenllian Tresilian when she started to tear at her throat, her nails—cut short, always—scoring ugly red lines down her neck. There was nothing normal about her when she fought off Henry's attempt to help and, in her terror, collapsed upon the floor. No indeed, there was nothing normal about seeing her thin body twist under the physician's grasp, those terrific screams shifting into a mournful wail, eyes dark and wide with fear, long hair spread out beneath her like a white avenging flame.

Linette plays it back in her mind: Merlin crawling beneath the table with his tail between his legs; apples escaping their bowl in the commotion, rolling onto the floor, rosy skins bruising. The bell toppled, the wine glasses fell, their unfinished meals spilled gravy from their plates. And all the while her mother screaming, screaming, screaming. . . .

She clenches her jaw. Never will she get used to it. *Never* will she grow accustomed to such a horrific sight. To see her mother so paralyzed with frenzy week after week, to see her suffer so cruelly year on year, it is more than Linette can bear. Foolish, she scolds herself now as she accompanies Henry to her mother's room the next morning. Foolish to think it could have been any different from all the other times before.

He had been kind, all things considered. He did not treat her mother like an inconvenience, did not pretend she was a body with no soul attached to it. Yes, his grip on her mother's thin wrists was forceful but when the laudanum he administered took effect and her eyes fluttered closed, Henry pulled her long sleeves down to cover them, cradled her head gently on his knees. Yes, Linette thinks, opening the door to her mother's chambers, the new physician treated her with respect, compassion. He carried her upstairs, laid her down gently on the bed without one word of censure or scorn. Not like all those doctors Julian brought from London who denounced her mother a hopeless case, not like Dr. Beddoe with his sneering looks and false pity. . . .

As it did the night before, the smell of vanilla hits them like a wave as soon as Linette opens the heavy paneled door. Unlike last night, however, Henry does not reel back from the sight of it, but she can still see in his dark eyes that he does not quite know what to think. She understands why. Draped over pictures and poking from vases and pots are the spindly branches of Penhelyg's local fauna and flora: the dark mottled limbs of rowan, the lobe leaves of oak, the variegated pattern trails of ivy and, of course, the vanilla-scented flowers of gorse.

Yes, it must look very strange indeed.

They pass through the small sitting room, past Enaid's trundle bed—already made, despite the early hour—and into Lady Gwen's bedroom, with more foliage of the same suspended from the ceiling. Linette marks that the yellow blossom of the gorse is beginning to wilt. Soon, she must send Geraint out for more.

Enaid rises from the chair at her mother's bedside, closes the small Bible she had been reading, presses it hard to her chest.

"'Tis bare past eight, sir." She shifts her gaze to Linette. "Your mother's not long woken—surely the doctor does not mean to examine her now? I've not even rung the bell for breakfast."

Linette frowns at the defensive tone in Enaid's voice, but before she can reprimand her Henry cuts in.

"As I could not conduct an examination last night, madam, now seems the perfect opportunity. The laudanum should have worn off some hours ago."

"But, sir—"

Linette presses Enaid's arm.

"Enaid, come now. Henry will not keep Mamma long."

The housekeeper blinks at the new doctor's Christian name on her lips. She seems to want to challenge this informality (Linette is sure she will, later), but Enaid keeps her mouth clamped shut. She keeps her position by the bed, stubbornness imprinted on her wrinkled features like ink.

Henry levels an annoyed look at her, pointedly clears his throat.

"This *is* what I've been employed for, Mrs. Evans. Would you have me neglect my charge?"

Enaid presses the Bible closer to her heart, as if she might find comfort there. She swallows so hard the lace at her collar jumps.

"Very well," she says quietly, not looking at either of them. "But I'll not have my mistress upset again."

"Believe me, nor would I."

They look to the woman in question. Linette's mother lies pale and dazed in the bed, a mound of pillows propped up behind her bony shoulders, and a knot tightens in Linette's chest like a snakestone. If it was not for her steady breathing and slow-blinking eyes—focused now at the window from where only a slit of light escapes the half-drawn curtains—Linette would think her an effigy or a porcelain doll, no life in her at all. She exists, rather than lives. Sometimes, when Linette feels particularly melancholy, she wonders if perhaps it would be better if her mother *were* dead. Would it not be a release? For both of them? All Linette's life she has wished for a mother who knew her, who recognized her face and voice, the touch of a hand, a kiss on her cheek. A mother who did not scream like a *cyhyraeth* and keep to her bed like the invalid she so clearly is.

"Good morning, my lady. May I sit down?"

Henry has moved to the other side of the bed, and in answer to his question her mother's gaze shifts from the window. She looks at him with childlike interest, eyes wide, pupils deep black pools.

No answer, of course. Henry sits, places his medical bag on the bed between them.

"Please open the curtains."

He could have been speaking to either one of them, but it is Enaid who answers.

"No."

Henry blinks at the curt reply.

Linette stares in astonishment.

"Enaid!"

But the old woman stands firm, Bible still clasped to her bosom.

"No," she says again. "The light hurts her eyes."

Henry regards her with barely laced patience.

"Even so. I should like you to open them all the same."

Still, Enaid does not move.

"Enaid," Linette says, still staring. "Do as he says."

The housekeeper bites her lip. Then, with as much reluctance as a cat pushed to water Enaid crosses to the window, slips behind the harp that stands there gathering dust and violently pulls the curtains open, flooding the room with bright sunlight.

The change is instant. With a loud cry Lady Gwen flings an arm over her eyes, twists her body away from the light, thin legs thrashing beneath the sheets.

"*Na!*" she moans. "*Na!*" and Linette rushes to the bed, helps Henry keep her still.

Shadows return almost instantly; Enaid has shut the curtains again, leaving only a small fraction open in the middle with which to see by. The white strip of light cuts the room in two like a blade, and within it dust motes spot the air brightly like tiny fireflies before gliding out of sight into the gloom of the chamber.

"See," the housekeeper says quietly. Triumphant, almost. "It hurts her eyes. She prefers the darkness. Always has."

Beneath her hands, Linette feels her mother relax. Slowly she lowers her arm from her face and Linette looks into it, marks her paleness, her trembling lip.

"Forgive me, my lady," Henry murmurs. "Forgive me." Then, to Linette, "Has she always suffered from an affliction to light?"

Linette takes a moment to catch her breath.

"It comes and goes. Dr. Evans could never discover why."

"So it's easier," Enaid cuts in, "to keep the curtains closed."

The old woman is standing now at the bottom of the bed, silhouetted against the blade of daylight. Henry straightens to address her.

"Sunlight would do her good," he returns. "Your mistress is far too pale, and keeping to the dark will not help her in the long run."

Enaid ducks her chin in assent. "I quite agree, but since it pains her I can hardly force the issue."

104

Linette heaves an inward sigh. It is not like Enaid to be so difficult.

"Mamma does take a turn about the garden every so often," Linette tells him, "though she wears a veil."

"Hmm."

Gently he lifts her mother's chin, looks at her eyes more closely. They are still wide, pupils expanded so only a thin ring of grey circles the black. For a long moment Henry keeps her chin in his grasp before, finally, releasing it. He turns to his medical bag, pulls open the clasps.

"The dimness of the room is an inconvenience. Still, I shall do my best under the circumstances."

Enaid sighs heavily and retreats to her chair where she begins to slowly leaf through the Bible's pages with fingers that seem to tremble. Linette shakes her head in dismay.

What is the matter with her?

Henry begins. As with Tomas he is gentle, and her mother submits to him with delicate sweetness and childlike trust that belies last night's outburst. At his command she lifts her arms, clasps his hands, sits forward in the bed, does everything he asks of her. It is the blood-taking that makes Linette's stomach turn. To ascertain its consistency, Henry tells her, and Linette must look away when he draws it from her mother's arm into a small glass cylinder. Enaid too cannot bear it, for the pages of her Bible rest still. It is a relief when Henry finally removes a pocketwatch to take her mother's pulse and silently counts the beating blood within her thin wrist. With interest Linette looks at its intricate filigree swirls.

"That's a fine watch," she remarks.

Henry finishes counting before gathering the watch back into his palm, lets the round weight of the dial sit in his hand briefly before slipping it back into his waistcoat pocket.

"It was given to me when I graduated from university," he answers, brusque. "A present from the Foundling. My token."

"Token?" Linette echoes.

He replaces the coverlet. Lady Gwen—looking vacantly now toward the covered window once more—kneads its hem between slender fingers.

"Yes," he says. "Kept back from me until I came of an age to appreciate it."

"Oh."

Before Linette can ask more, her mother begins to hum. Henry touches his finger to the back of her hand, still plucking at the coverlet. Her eyes snap back into focus and she looks up at him as if she has forgotten he was even there.

"I will see you tomorrow, unless you have need of me before then."

She only stares. Henry frowns.

"Does she speak English?"

It is Enaid who answers.

"My mistress always spoke it when Lord Hugh was alive. She comprehends you perfectly."

"I see."

He rises to his feet. Linette's mother watches him, fascinated, until—as Henry turns to leave—she reaches out.

"What is it, my lady?"

"*Berith*," she whispers.

It is one of the words she spoke last night.

"*Berith*?"

Her mother simply stares up at him, wretched, sad. Then she drops Henry's sleeve, starts once more to hum. He shoots a questioning look at Linette, and all she can do is shake her head.

106

They leave Enaid to her Bible, her mother to that strange infernal humming, but on the other side of the door Linette marks the downward lilt of the young physician's mouth, the troubled look in his dark brown eyes.

"What is it?"

Henry hesitates. Linette's chest clamps, though she cannot rightly say why.

"In terms of her general health," he says, very carefully it seems, "your mother appears as well in her person as you or I. A little too thin and pale, but her blood is strong and I see no other cause for concern."

"But?"

He hesitates again. "She is sensitive to light, yet I cannot fathom a reason for it. Can you?"

She shakes her head. "Mamma has always been that way, I'm afraid. Why?"

"Sensitivity to light is not a common complaint, and I cannot recall an illness that would not present itself in an obvious way."

"What do you mean?"

"Only that such a condition would show in the eyes as inflammation, dryness, lack of pigment, none of which your mother possesses."

Linette lifts a shoulder. "I do not find that so surprising. We've already established that my mother's ailments stem from a malady of the mind. Perhaps she merely imagines it."

Still, Henry looks thoughtful. Chews his bottom lip. Then, "You said your mother sometimes leaves her room to walk the grounds?"

"Yes."

"Do you ever mark an improvement in her then? Does she appear calmer?"

Linette frowns. "I'm not sure."

"You see," he says, switching his satchel from one hand to the other, "I wonder if by escaping her room for a spell the fresh air tires her. When someone with a mentality such as your mother is subjected to confinement for long periods, the body becomes weak. You," he adds, gaze flicking up then down (Linette knows he is once again marking her masculine attire), "are robust, healthy. Your mother, on the other hand, has decreased muscular integrity, evidently eats like a bird—"

"So you think that affects her outbursts?"

"Possibly, yes."

"You believe, then, more fresh air would be beneficial?"

"It can certainly do no harm."

Linette frowns. Nothing can exercise the mind like the outdoors; has *she* not found comfort in nature and its gifts, the rolling fields, the snowcapped hills? For years Linette has been taunted with the idea that if her mother is mad then it must surely run in the family and she has—as Henry observed—kept her mind and body active to prevent it. *Just in case.* But now, the more she thinks of it, the more Linette cannot understand why this was not suggested by Dr. Evans himself. Neither did any of those other doctors, Dr. Beddoe included, have the inclination to propose such a remedy. No, each one suggested only restraints, leeches, bodily purges. Failing that, an institution. A place where Linette might pretend her mother does not exist.

Thanks to Julian's refusal, she was spared that, at least.

Henry touches her arm, pulling her from her morbid train of thought.

"I think I shall go into Penhelyg today, visit as many of the villagers as I can."

Linette blinks. "Oh?"

"Considering how they may well be disinclined at present to ask for my help I feel it would be better I go to them instead. It's the best way, under the circumstances."

She hesitates. Linette knows more than anyone the grievances of her tenants. She should tell him, of course, meant to last night before her mother submitted to her inner demons. And yet, now, here in the shadowed corridor . . . well, what use would it be? It is, after all, unsubstantiated village gossip, and would only serve to prejudice Henry against them even further.

"I would not," she says carefully now, "presume to tell you what to do. But remember what I told you last night—they will not take kindly to the intrusion of an Englishman. Are you *sure* you won't allow me to accompany you?"

"I am absolutely sure."

"But how will you manage the language?"

"I have my dictionary."

He really is trying stubborn, and Linette must repress a frustrated sigh.

"You have to understand," Henry says, clearly marking her irritation. "I must command respect. If I cannot do that then I shall be of no use here at all."

There is no arguing, it seems. Still, she attempts one final plea.

"What of the shot? Are you not afraid someone will try again?"

Henry's gaze darkens, and again Linette is struck with an odd sense of familiarity.

"Somehow," he murmurs, before the idea of it can take hold, "I don't think they will. Besides, what use am I if I hide here day by day? No," Henry says, firm. "I will not be frightened off."

CHAPTER TEN

It takes the stable boy some minutes to saddle the cob from yesterday. It snorts impatiently, keen to be moving, and the sound makes the black hens milling around the horse's feet disperse in a flurry of feathers. The boy—Rhys, was it?—passes Henry the reins.

"He'll be glad for the exercise," he says in broken English. "Gwydion's an old soul, used to belong to Lord Hugh as a colt. You need help getting on again?"

There is a hint of mocking amusement in the lad's voice, and Henry eyes the black beast now pawing the ground in front of him. Horses can be lethal creatures, even when handled correctly—he has treated his fair share of accidents. Fractured shoulders, broken legs, once a hand, crushed by the weight of a hoofs, that later had to be amputated. . . . The thought makes him shudder and so, begrudging, he accepts Rhys's assistance. Curtly Henry nods his thanks, guides the horse slowly down Plas Helyg's gravel drive, out through the twisting iron gates.

The cob (Gwydion, he remembers to call him) seems to understand where Henry wishes to go; down the woodland path again, past the fork to the gatehouse, out onto the road at the bottom where he takes the narrow path between the miners' holdings, follows the track that Linette had taken him on yesterday: past the cluster of buildings in the square, the small rickety tavern, thence down the lane leading to the sea.

His journey is not ignored. Hawk-eyed, the villagers watch him as he guides Gwydion through, their scornful gaze stripping him bare, all the while whispering fiercely to one another thick as thieves, and Henry feels exactly as he did yesterday—resented and exposed.

What has Linette not told him?

Above, a gull trills sharply; Henry watches the bird soar across the sky and disappear behind the canopy of trees above. Gwydion snorts. Henry pats the beast's solid neck. When he emerges onto the salt marshes the strong sea air—no longer held back by the trees of the lane—buffets the collar of his coat. Keeping one hand on the horse's reins Henry leans his arm against the cumbersome satchel, raises his other hand to his hat to stop it from flying from his head; and as he concentrates on keeping his balance he realizes this will simply not do. He must find an easier way of carrying his implements, must visit Dr. Beddoe for supplies, ask advice on how best to manage the logistics of a traveling physician as soon as possible.

And he must ask about Dr. Evans.

Again, he could be wrong—Linette did say the doctor was very old. But heart failure tends to be sudden, and typically there is no reason for the face to be contorted in death. Such a thing might happen if the person were to die in anger, in the midst of an argument . . . or if they were afraid. Henry thinks of the glass vial.

Perhaps Dr. Beddoe might know what it contains.

And then, he thinks, steering Gwydion wide to avoid a waterlogged dint, there is the matter of Gwen Tresilian. What, pray, does Dr. Beddoe think of *her*?

The breeze dies down. Henry lowers his hand.

Her case is an interesting one. In his role at Guy's Hospital maladies of the mind were not something he typically dealt with, but there were times Henry had been called to Bedlam to treat the poor wretches who inflicted injuries upon themselves and others. He has seen ear-lobes ripped from the hairline, torn fingernails pulled from their fleshy beds. He has seen deep bite marks in arms, broken jaws, words carved into bare chests with implements either stolen or fashioned in secret. One patient—one of his Bow Street charges—bit off her tongue just so she could not be taken to account. Henry only saw the quieter patients as he passed their cells, but even they could be marked as mad by the way they spoke to their manacles, the way they pushed their foreheads against the walls of their cells. There can be no denying Lady Gwen's unprovoked screams last night, the way she clawed at her neck . . .

Henry thinks of the strange words she uttered before those screams took her in their thrall: *Hoath, Redar, Ganabel, Berith*. Linette said they were not Welsh, but before he went to bed that night he took up the Welsh dictionary anyway, flipped through its thin pages. They were not listed, but there was another word, a word Lady Gwen repeated enough times for Henry to remember it clearly, and he looked through the c's until he found something that might match it, frowned deeply into the dictionary's worn page.

Cythraul. The Welsh word for demon.

The coastal cottages—six in total—are visible now, framed by golden sand dunes, the blue-green bank of water. In the distance, Henry sees the fence of shells outside the Morgans' cottage swinging wildly from their strings in the wind. Gwydion picks up pace. He will check in on Tomas first, Henry decides, then try his luck with the neighboring houses.

The door to the Morgans' is partially open. Henry raps on the whitewashed door, peers through the gap.

The tiny sitting room is empty. The fire is unlit, a spinning wheel stands beside it, its spindles laden with strung wool. On the stone hearth stands a dish containing what looks to be milk. Hesitant, Henry steps inside. There is a wooden bowl by the door filled with seashells of all different shapes and sizes and colors—brown limpets, pale cowries, cream fans that could be scallops or cockles, tiny whelks the shade of sand. On the trail of woodsmoke there is the salt scent of seaweed, and Henry glances up to find bunches of bladderwrack hanging like dark ribbons of dried-out blisters from the low eaves.

"Good morning," he calls. Then, hesitating over the pronunciation, "*Bore da?*"

There is a cough, the sound of movement. Mrs. Morgan appears from one of the bedrooms, wiping her hands on a worn-out apron.

"*O, helo. Mi ddaethoch chi unwaith eto . . .*"

He does not know what that means, but the words are said with some surprise and none of the reserve he sensed the day before, and with a shy smile she beckons him inside.

Between mother, patient, and dictionary, Henry manages to ascertain that the fruit and milk were well received, the removal of blankets and the open window have improved Tomas's temperature, he has bathed with cold water (from the sea, if his translation of *o'r môr* is correct) twice yesterday, once already this morning, and from these small changes Henry feels there is already an improvement.

At the front door Henry thumbs the dictionary once more.

"I'll come again next week." He squints at the word, tests the sound of it on his tongue. "*Wythnos?*" Again, Mrs. Morgan nods her head. She stares at him, a look of consideration in her sharp eyes. Then she turns to the bowl of shells, selects one of the sandy-coloured whelks and presses it into Henry's hand. He runs a thumb over it, likes its spirals pitted with grooves, its grounding rough contours.

"Thank you," he says. Remembers to say it in Welsh.

"*Diolch.*"

A pause.

"*Diolch*," she returns.

The emphasis is different. He raises his head, sees the way she looks at him, her expression kindly, open, and Henry realizes she is correcting him. He repeats the word, makes the *i* sound like an *e*.

This time, Mrs. Morgan smiles.

The other villagers are not so accommodating; only two of the coastal cottages opened their doors. Dictionary once more employed he was able to communicate that he was a doctor, to ask if anyone needed assistance, but their response was a vigorous shake of the head and a hard slam of the door.

Henry knows he must persevere with them. If there is no life for him here, no career for him, where else can he go? What else can he do? Time, he thinks, is the only thing on his side. In time, they will accept him.

They must.

Dejected, Henry leads the cob back across the salt marsh, up through the lane. Halfway he stops, contemplates the hedgerow at his right, the glimpse of cottages beyond. What was it Linette told him? He remembers the names she gave—Bryn Parry, Bronwen Lewis. Gareth Griffiths, his wife, Catrin—all, it seems, in need of assistance.

Henry dismounts, guides Gwydion through the arched gap in the hedge, and in that moment a door from one of the other cottages opens. Out through the low-linteled door steps a man carrying a thick walking stick crudely made from a tree branch. He is dressed all in black, from his buckle shoes to his tricorn hat. The only shot of color is the simple white neckcloth at his collar.

"Ah!" the man exclaims when he sees Henry, face splitting into a wide smile. "You're the new doctor, then?" He ambles across the grass, trampling daisies in his wake. "Dr. Talbot, yes?"

"That I am," Henry replies, cautious, but he holds out his hand in greeting all the same. The man shakes it hard as though he is pulling on a bell rope. Henry tries not to flinch.

"I'm very pleased to meet you," he beams. "I am the Reverend Mr. Owain Dee, Penhelyg's vicar. Well met, Dr. Talbot. Very well met indeed!"

The vicar is lantern-jawed and steel-wigged, severe in his looks, but his hazel eyes are warm, the smile genuine, and Henry finds himself daring to relax.

"I must say," he ventures, "it is a relief to find someone who speaks English—indeed, who is happy to speak to me at all."

The reverend's eyes glint with amusement. "Having trouble, I take it?"

Henry says nothing but he does not have to; the answer must clearly be writ upon his face for the vicar sighs, shakes his head.

"They're an obstinate lot, I'm afraid. Mrs. Lewis there—" and here Mr. Dee nods to the cottage he has just vacated—"might be a little more forthcoming, but I would not disturb her today. I've just blessed her baby and now that the little mite has finally stopped crying his mother has taken the opportunity to sleep. She'll not appreciate the interruption." Next he nods to the furthest cottage where a goat grazes in a pen. "You'll get nothing out of Bryn Parry, either, but he's always been a difficult one, stubborn as a mule. Even Dr. Evans struggled to find him agreeable."

The vicar pauses here, shakes his head.

"Poor Wynn," he says. "Sorely missed. Sorely missed indeed."

Henry's senses sharpen. "You knew the old doctor well?"

Mr. Dee brightens. "Very well! He was a good friend of mine. We

115

often went walking together, climbed Cadair Idris a few days before he died. If I'd known that was the last time we were to see each other. . . . Well, God saw fit to take him, and who am I to argue with the will of the Lord?"

The latter Henry ignores; God or the Devil, he scarce has time for either. But the former . . .

"Forgive me, what is Cadair Idris?"

"A mountain, dear boy! Over the estuary from Abermaw. A beauty of a thing it is, lots of rugged peaks. Good for the legs."

He slaps his thighs at the last with a grin, and vaguely Henry recalls a larger mountain nestled between some others along the coastal road from Dolgellau to Abermaw the day he arrived, a cluster of oddly shaped points that reminded him, strangely, of a giant's sleeping face.

"Tell me," he says now. "Did you find him in good health?"

Mr. Dee leans back on his heels. "I should say so. A little doddery at times, but he made no complaint."

Henry frowns, contemplates his next words, means to glean more information from this barrel-bodied vicar, but then that man's eyes catch at a point behind him.

"Oh, Miss Carew! Come, come and meet our new doctor."

There is a pause, a rustle of leaves. Henry turns. A young woman steps through the arch of the hedgerow, a wicker basket in her hand, and any thought of pressing the vicar flies clean from Henry's head, for approaching them is the most beautiful creature he has ever seen in his entire life.

Miss Carew, as Mr. Dee called her, has the most striking combination of flame-red hair and amber-brown eyes set within a heart-shaped face; her skin is cream-pale, a smatter of faint freckles spans her straight nose like little stars and her mouth is bud-like, coral-hued. He tries not to stare.

116

"Your servant, miss."

A charming dimple appears in the cushion of the young woman's round cheek.

"Dr. Talbot. A pleasure to meet you at last."

A pleasure indeed. Her voice is clear and lilting, with a soft yet very distinct Welsh accent, smooth and fresh like spring water. Henry's pulse thrums in his throat.

"Miss Carew is our resident herbalist," Mr. Dee says. "You will be working quite closely together, I should think?"

Henry thinks of the herbs Mrs. Morgan showed him yesterday. So, that explains it. They did not belong to Dr. Beddoe after all.

"Perhaps we shall," Miss Carew murmurs. "But some doctors do not approve of the old remedies. Are you one of them?"

Not wanting her to think less of him, he chooses his words with care.

"They have their merits," he says.

But Miss Carew clearly sees through the bluff and with a small smile says, "A clever gentleman's answer. Unwilling to commit either way."

Beside him, Mr. Dee rocks again on his heels. "Methinks, Dr. Talbot, you've already made a bit of a faux pas! Rowena is a discerning little thing, are you not, my dear?"

Rowena. What a pretty name.

"I'm sorry," Henry tries, "it is not—"

But Miss Rowena Carew is shaking her head. "Do not trouble yourself. I'm not offended, truly."

"No need to be, either," the reverend remarks. "Your science and Miss Carew's methods can find a way to work in harmony, I am sure."

Henry finds himself at a loss for words. He feels embarrassed now, unsure of himself, green like a novice schoolboy. Seeing his discomfort, Mr. Dee spreads out his arm.

"Shall we walk on?"

He gestures in the general direction of the path, and taking Gwydion by the bit Henry gratefully obliges. The four pass through the gap in the hedgerow, back out into the lane, up in the direction of Penhelyg's square. They walk in silence for a moment until, most delicately, Rowena Carew clears her throat.

"You arrived late on Monday, I understand?"

Her step is light and feminine—not at all like Linette's heavy determined stride. A breeze tickles Henry's nose, and he detects on her the sweet perfume of lavender.

"I did, yes."

"And how do you like Wales?"

Henry hesitates. "It's not at all what I'm used to, I must confess."

"You're from London, are you not?"

"I am."

"A great change, then," Miss Carew remarks, ducking her red head to avoid the branch of a reaching willow. "I've heard medical men from the city are most enterprising in their methods. The people of Penhelyg are lucky to have you."

The reverend, who has been walking up ahead of them, gives a low sigh.

"'Tis a great pity," he says over his shoulder, "they are not more welcoming. It will take a while, I fear, for my flock to make their peace with your presence."

"So I've already been advised," Henry returns. "I cannot fathom why. Linette Tresilian says it is because I am English, but I find it hard to believe they hate me just because of that."

Mr. Dee stops, turns. He and Miss Carew share a look.

"I'm afraid there's a little more to it." He cups the wooden head of his staff with both palms. "Ancient history, you see."

"No," Henry says. "I don't see."

"Hmm." The reverend's open face closes briefly. "The villagers have had some troubling interactions with Plas Helyg over the years. For the household to employ an Englishman, well . . . it is unlikely they should warm to you easily."

"I still don't understand."

They have reached the square. Three young women pass behind the vicar, tilting their yokes. They stare at Henry, eyes narrowed, speak between them without even attempting to lower their voices. Miss Carew says something to them in Welsh, and visibly reluctant the girls move on.

The vicar turns then, raises his whorled stick to point.

"You see the church?"

Henry looks to where the Reverend Dee is signaling. Through the copse of willow trees—across the fields—he spies a distant stone roof, a Celtic cross on its top set in relief against fat clouds.

"I see it."

"My cottage is across the way," the vicar says. "I am ministering to the poor today so cannot invite you now, but do come to tea some time soon for I shall be glad to speak with you further. I'm sure you will appreciate a friendly ear."

Henry would.

"Thank you. I shall come as soon as I can."

Mr. Dee's lantern jaw splits into a toothy smile. "Splendid. Splendid! In the meantime I shall do my best to alleviate the villagers' fears. Take heart, Dr. Talbot. God is on your side."

Henry bows his head in farewell, watches the reverend make his way across the square and knock on the door of one of the houses on the other side. A breeze picks up, on its tail the sharp scent of cut grass, Miss Carew's lavender perfume.

"Had you come from the Morgans'?" she asks him now, and Henry turns to her.

"I did."

"And how is Tomas?"

Henry hesitates. The herbs she gave him clearly did not work—it is only by his own direction that Tomas Morgan begins to improve. Still, he cannot bring himself to say so.

"He does better," he says instead.

She smiles. Her teeth are straight except for one crooked incisor in her upper jaw that overlaps the front left tooth, but instead of marring her beauty, to Henry, it adds to it.

"I am glad."

"Good." Henry pauses. "Forgive me, I had not meant to belittle your ways. To offend you."

"You did not offend me," she replies. Soft, like feathers. It sends his pulse racing.

A line of ducks crosses the square. Distractedly Henry tracks their meandering progress, watches them disappear behind a stone lean-to before speaking again.

"I do wonder why Dr. Beddoe did not do more for him. If he had . . ."

Henry trails off deliberately and, as he hoped, she nods her head.

"Dr. Beddoe lacks patience, 'tis true. Have you met him yet?"

He thinks of what he has just learned about Dr. Evans's good health, and a steely determination settles in his gut.

"No," Henry says, "but I mean to, and soon."

Again, Miss Carew nods.

"I'd go tomorrow. The weather is meant to be fine, and such a journey is best undertaken under good conditions."

"Thank you. I shall."

In that moment Gwydion tosses his black head, snorts loudly through his nostrils. With her free hand Miss Carew reaches out to stroke the bridge of the cob's silky nose.

"Well, then," she says. "Your horse wishes to be away, and I'd best be away myself. *Prynhawn da*, Dr. Talbot."

Henry bows.

"Miss Carew."

She turns, hesitates, turns back again.

"I am glad you're come."

He looks into those brilliant amber eyes, feels his cheeks grow hot. Then Miss Carew turns again and Henry watches her retreat across the square, is unaccountably disappointed when she does not look back. Shaking himself, he turns in the opposite direction. The three milk women are watching him still with narrowed eyes and Henry sighs, clasps Gwydion's reins, steers the horse away.

He tried to call on the houses in the square, with no success. Thoroughly disheartened he set off for Plas Helyg, and it is as Henry is maneuvering Gwydion up the bank toward the main path that he hears sounds of laughter ahead. When he emerges onto the road he sees five boys—the youngest can only be six years of age, the oldest sixteen at most—kicking a wooden ball between them. Henry hesitates, unsure. The lads are blocking his route to the woodland pass; there is no way around them. He considers retreating back into the lane, but then Gwydion whickers and the decision is taken from him for they look up at the sound. When they see Henry they stop, the laughter leaving their faces as if wiped clean with one stroke.

They are only boys, he tells himself as he pushes Gwydion forward. *They can do you no injury.* Still, instinctively, his grip on the reins tightens. The cob seems to sense Henry's disquiet for he begins to weave out of line, tossing his large head. The boys too appear to mark the change in Henry for they close ranks, and a sneer starts to form on the oldest boy's face. He walks, Henry sees, with a limp.

Henry pulls at Gwydion's reins but the horse does not stop. On he plods, shortening the distance between Henry and his would-be aggressors who have straightened their shoulders, begun to come forward, a look of ugly intent in their eyes. Henry pulls the reins again. Reluctant, almost, the cob comes to a stop, and just as he does the oldest boy spits on the ground, narrowly missing Gwydion's fetlock.

"Mynd i rywle, doctor?"

Doctor. That is clear. As for the rest, well, he may not understand them but he does know the words were said with scorn; the look on the lad's sunburnt face is conceited, overconfident, and Henry recognizes that in a battle of words this boy has the upper hand. He should ignore them, ride by without saying a thing . . . but Henry cannot let himself be silent.

"I mean no harm here, lad. Let me by."

He tries to steer Gwydion away but the boys form a semicircle, preventing any movement.

"Rydych chi'n mynd y ffordd anghywir." The boy shucks his chin in the direction of the open country road, the road leading back to Abermaw. Next to him, one of the others tosses the wooden ball from hand to hand. Henry eyes it warily. *"Ewch yn ôl i ble daethoch chi,"* the boy continues. *"Does yna ddim croeso i chi yma."*

Henry takes a breath. They know he does not understand them, well aware they can taunt him without adequate reproach. He looks to the line of cottages, wills someone to come out, but no one does.

"Just let me pass," Henry says. "Your words are wasted on me."

Perhaps it was his lack of deference, or perhaps his stern tone of voice, but the nasty smiles vanish from their faces. The boy holding the ball keeps tossing it between his hands, slow and steady—back and forth, back and forth—and Henry wonders if he means to throw

122

it. But then, suddenly, the older boy lunges for him, too fast for Henry to react. His medical bag drops to the ground with a grating thud, its contents spilling and rolling in the dirt.

Gwydion rears up. Henry swears, desperately hangs on to the reins, but in doing so he pulls at the bit and the horse tosses his head, kicking out his front legs with a high-pitched whinny that cracks the air like a scream.

The boys jump away. For a fearful moment Henry wonders if the horse has struck any of them but his concentration is solely on keeping himself seated on the saddle, on calming the horse down. He clenches his thighs, leans forward, puts his full weight over Gwydion's shining neck. He can hear the cob's heavy breathing through his flared nostrils, and Henry does his best to console the animal with nonsensical words. It is only when he has steadied him that he sees— to both his relief and consternation—the lads are unharmed. Indeed, they are laughing loudly, pointing, without a care for Henry's safety or their own.

"What the hell are you playing at?" he shouts, temper lost. "You could have hurt yourselves!"

He looks again to the cottages. Why does no one come?

The boys are whooping now; two run away into the bank of willow trees. Three remain, staring insolently up at him with hard faces, resentment in their eyes.

"Let me pass. Go home, else your parents will hear of this."

The three remaining boys continue to stare. Then, after a moment, the oldest shucks his head at the other two. The lads exchange a glance but do as they are told—they walk backward at first before spinning on their toes, disappearing round the back of the narrow cottages, out of sight.

The lad that is left stares up at him for one long drawn-out moment. Though Gwydion stands high, the boy's head comes easily to the cob's withers and Henry senses he is trying to use this height to his advantage. But Henry will not under any circumstances be threatened by a bully such as he.

"I said, go home."

The boy smiles unpleasantly. One of his front teeth is cracked. "*Sais*," he hisses. Then, despite his limp, he flees like a rabbit into the willows after his friends.

CHAPTER ELEVEN

Linette's study is a small but airy room situated near the back of the house affording a view of the stables. The view is not necessarily a scenic one, but she loves it all the same; she enjoys watching Rhys groom the horses, enjoys being able to see Pryderi safe in his stall. To Linette, there is gratification in knowing that Plas Helyg functions smoothly, that the old cogs of the estate are well-oiled, a sure mark of all her hard work these past five years. Sometimes she will sit on the window seat and simply watch life carry along on its course, content in her own quiet company. But in this moment Linette sits at her desk, Plas Helyg's ledgers spread open before her like a map.

It is no easy task, managing an estate. Such a heavy workload— the collection of rent, the organization of repairs and improvements for both the village and the farms, the bookkeeping all this requires— is an exhausting enterprise.

Linette adds a tally to the bottom of a column. Bites her lip.

Overall, the estate is performing well enough. Crops are plentiful, the livestock is healthy and producing on time. She was concerned a few months before that they would not be so lucky, for this past winter was especially harsh; hoarfrost had frozen the fields solid and spring, it seemed, was slow to show her face. But then at last the weather turned, made up for its lethargy by becoming unseasonably warm, and so Plas Helyg's lands had flourished and blossomed. The coffers will begin to fill once more.

Still, Linette is aware that the estate is not as prosperous as it could be, and it has made its mark on her books. She offers low rent (too low, according to Julian), and does not make her tenants responsible for the upkeep of their homes as other landowners do. But, as she insisted to Henry, Linette finds this generosity is well-rewarded; her tenants work harder, make no complaints. How many of her fellow gentry can say the same?

There are other ways to make money, Linette knows. She could open Plas Helyg to the public, lease the land and bring in more industry, as Lord Pennant has done this past year and Sir John Selwyn plans to do next. It would help, of that there is no doubt, but Linette cannot bring herself to do it. This land belongs to Penhelyg's people. Their livelihood depends upon it entirely, and she will do everything in her power to ensure its beauty remains untouched by foreign and exploitative hands.

Even if it means less for herself.

The money she inherited on her majority was a princely sum, but she has spent nearly all of it on rejuvenating the land. Flooding down at the salt marshes is scarce now the appropriate barriers have been put in place, and at least—when the weather does prove itself tempest-strong—the cottages are now protected. In addition, each tenant—Linette made sure—had been allocated a small plot of land on which to grow their own produce, keep a goat, a cow as well if they wish it. The farmhands up in the valley too benefited from her generosity: drainage has been improved, new ridge and furrow techniques employed. She has given everything she can to Penhelyg, her own small way of making up for Emyr Cadwalladr's misdeeds, her cousin's neglect. It is why, now, Plas Helyg itself is not all it should be. If one were to look closely, the wainscoting is woodwormed and the tapestries moth-eaten, the roof leaks when it rains, the external stonework is loose. Indeed, every time Linette hears that damned gate creak in its worn hinges it sends a shudder down her spine.

Linette sighs, places the quill into its glass well. She regrets nothing. Not one thing would she do differently. Except, she thinks grudgingly, ask for help. Yet who can she ask? When it comes to running the estate the only people she can rely on are Enaid and Cadoc and the servants who deal with the more menial management of the household, the upkeep of Plas Helyg's grounds. But beyond that, Linette has no support.

She thinks of Julian, feels the familiar reel of frustration churn within her gut. She made light of it to Henry but in truth, Julian had not been entirely willing to relinquish his hold on Plas Helyg's purse. He had, after all, spent two decades in control of it; to step aside must have vexed him greatly. She remembers perfectly her twenty-first birthday when she received a letter from a Dolgellau attorney requesting she and Julian grant him an audience. Linette remembers them sitting side by side in front of a man who reminded her of a trussed ham, round cheeks pink and shining (a predilection for wine, she later found), as he explained in a manner most clear how, in accordance with her father's will, all estate accounts would be transferred into Linette's name. She remembers how Julian—quietly and somewhat in shock—provided the information required, but when they were left to discuss the matter between them, he asked her, very gently, if she was *quite* sure it was what she wanted.

It can be overturned, you know. It's a lot of responsibility for one so young. For a woman.

He offered to run Plas Helyg on her behalf, to run it just as he always had, but it was that very offer which had prompted Linette to sign those papers without a second thought. No more would he neglect the people who had come to mean so much to her, no more would he treat her friends as if they were nothing more than commodities. *She* meant to treat them fairly. Linette had a purpose, at last.

Julian simply did not understand.

There was no denying the transition had been hard. The attorney— Mr. Ellis—had been unfailingly kind. It was he who opened up a new account with the bank, he who arranged the dismissal of Mr. Lambeth (to Julian's disbelief), he who put in place everything she asked for with regards to Penhelyg's well-being. It was Mr. Ellis who instructed her on the more complex particulars of managing an estate until Linette could get by on her own. She had been grieved indeed to hear of his death some months later, his bloated body found on the banks of Dolgellau's river, having drunk himself blind in the tavern and fallen into its harsh winter currents.

After this Linette begged Julian to send her the latest treatises on land management from London, for how else could she keep abreast of new developments? And while he procured the literature she required and arranged subscriptions to periodicals on agriculture and farming it was all done with a look of long-suffering skepticism, as if he could not quite believe a woman should take such a thing into her head. Thankfully those subscriptions have since enabled her to send for books on other topics such as religion and philosophy, science and industry, the more distasteful but enlightening subject of slavery, books she is sure Julian would prefer she did not read. Unbecoming, he said. Unladylike.

Linette has devoured them, every single one.

Somewhere outside, Merlin barks. It is followed by the squawk of a bird, the harsh admonishment of the gardener, and pinching the corners of her eyes Linette sits back heavily in her seat. The ledgers in front of her have become a blur, her black cursive trailing across the pages like ants. Perhaps, Linette thinks grudgingly, she is done for today. She looks at the small carriage clock on the mantel. A quarter to four.

She has been working solidly since Henry left that morning.

With a groan Linette gets up. She winces at the rise—her back is stiff from sitting so long—but she presses her hands into the base of her spine, bends into a stretch and moves over to the window, half-open in its casement.

It is a lovely day. Too lovely to waste it hunched over a desk: the sun is shining, the clouds cotton-like in the azure sky. Linette can smell how fresh the air is, its floral tones undercut by the smell of hay and manure from the stables. She looks across to them, at Pryderi drinking from a water trough, tail swishing against his hocks. One of the hens loiters around the stalls. Merlin bounds out of the hydrangea borders with an excitable bark and gives leggy pursuit. Linette shakes her head.

That dog must chase everything he sees.

She watches the poor hen flee toward a small pen on the other side of the stables where the rest of the chickens are busy pecking the ground. Merlin lurches after it, narrowly missing Geraint and his wheelbarrow; wood chippings spill from its sides as the gardener pulls himself up short, and he swears at the dog who, again, ignores him completely.

It is never a good day when Geraint finds the remains of one of the hens in the gardens. Merlin is scolded something rotten by Enaid and Mrs. Phillips (who is most put out by the waste of a potential dinner), but even though she knows he deserves it Linette cannot bring herself to be angry with him.

Just as one of the hens loses a black feather in its desperate bid to escape, there comes a soft knock on the door.

"Yes?" she calls tiredly.

With a creak the heavy door opens, and Henry peeks his head through.

"Am I disturbing you?"

"Not at all," Linette sighs, turning from the window. "I'd be glad of the distraction."

He comes in, moving as tiredly as she feels, and in that moment she realizes how frightfully pale he is. His dark hair is disheveled, his clothes rumpled; the satchel he carries is scuffed even more than it was yesterday, its handle askew. Linette looks more keenly. Pale, as she already marked, but there is also a tightness to his face and it takes her a moment to realize what it is.

Anger. Unmistakable anger.

"What on earth is the matter?" she asks, and the look he levels at her is hard as stone.

"I had some trouble in the village."

Linette sucks in her breath. "Not another shot?"

"No, not that," and as the physician explains Linette listens with a rising sense of displeasure.

"I'm sorry," she says when he is done. "But they *were* only boys."

"Only boys?" Henry counters, voice pinched. "They were old enough to know right from wrong. They wished me harm, even if they hadn't the compunction to act on it. And," he adds, "no one came to help. We must have been watched and yet no one came. Is there no discipline here, no compassion? What of conscience? Should their actions not be dictated by that?"

Though he is perfectly justified in his anger, Linette feels the beginnings of hers set to boil.

"You accuse them of being quick to judge," she shoots back, "but are you not the same?"

He stares, clamps his mouth, and Linette narrows her eyes.

"You are a proud man," she continues, "I see that, but your city ways are imprinted on you like ink for all to see. You're as unlike them as the sun from the moon. You cannot come here and expect them to welcome you with open arms after only one day!"

130

At this, Henry's nostrils flare.

"While your loyalty to them is commendable, you are also blind to their faults. I've never known a people like it. So unwelcoming, so coarse!" He takes a step closer. "My new home is ransacked, someone takes a shot at me, youths harass me in full view, the villagers turn me away from their doors. You claim your tenants are like family, but if these are the type of people you consider your kin then—"

"Then what?"

"Only that it makes me wonder what manner of woman you are, if you can so easily mix with heathens."

Linette stares. "*Er mwyn y mawredd!* You sound just like Julian." She stops short as a thought occurs. "You've been *speaking* to Julian, haven't you?"

He does not look ashamed at this. Indeed, Henry looks her square in the eye.

"Your cousin asked me to take my professional measure of you, yes."

She would laugh if it were not so galling.

"Well, then, doctor." She spreads her hands. "How do you find me?"

Henry hesitates. "I don't know yet."

"You don't know yet? Considering you've judged my tenants so quickly I find that surprising."

He says nothing.

"Are you Julian's spy then? Come here to keep an eye on me at his instruction?"

Something flickers in his dark eyes. "No. I come here as a physician. That is all."

Outside, Merlin barks again. Linette hears Geraint spout a long and vitriolic curse and—more to hide her frustration than anything else—she turns back to the window, raises the peeling sash.

"Merlin, *gad o!*" she shouts. "*Tyrd yma!*"

The lurcher pauses in his relentless chasing, looks toward the

131

window, tongue lolling. His ears twitch, gaze sidling to the chicken pen, but then Henry is at her side and when he whistles the dog cocks his head, finally takes heed. Merlin trots away around the side of the mansion, and if Linette did not know any better she would think the animal was grinning.

"He's taken to you," she remarks grudgingly, pushing the window back down into its frame. "He does not take to everyone. Heeds them even less."

Henry shrugs. "I like dogs," he says. "They are more truthful than humans—what you see is what you get with them."

Linette says nothing to that. Instead she moves toward the small round table near her bookcases, sinks into one of the spindly wooden chairs, buries her head in her hands.

The room is silent but for the ticking of her carriage clock, the buzz of blood in her temples.

"I did not mean to upset you," Henry says. "I'm sorry."

His voice is quiet. Kind, almost. Linette raises her head.

"Are you?"

"I am."

She is not quite sure she believes him. He steps forward.

"What does 'sais' mean?"

A beat.

"Where did you hear that word?"

"It's what one of the boys said to me before he fled."

"What did he look like?" she asks.

Henry describes him.

"Cai Jones," Linette answers with a sigh. "Lives in one of the narrow houses down on the road. He is troublesome, I must admit. Cai's father works in the mines; he worked there too, once, but then he broke his leg two years ago in an accident which made continuing impossible. His brother died in that same accident. Cai plays up

132

sometimes, pilfers from the tavern mostly. Boredom, I suspect, but he's harmless enough."

"Are you sure?" Henry asks. "Perhaps he was responsible for the gatehouse. Perhaps it was him who shot at me."

Linette considers this. Though unlikely, it is not impossible. Out of all the villagers aside from the Einions, Cai Jones would be the most likely to rebel, to resent another Englishman in Penhelyg's midst. The gatehouse she might just be able to accept as his doing, and it is true a gun could easily be procured. All the farmers had one, after all. Even Arthur Lloyd kept a shotgun in the tavern. But would Cai actually take the risk to do it? She told Henry before that mining was dangerous work, and it was the truth. Cai never forgave Julian for not securing the cave shafts; the lad holds him personally responsible for the collapse of that tunnel, for the death of his brother, for making him a cripple, and Linette cannot blame him for thinking it either. He has not been the same since, either in body or mind.

"Linette?"

She looks up, catches her nail against a whorl in the tabletop.

"I cannot deny," she says slowly, "that Cai might be a likely culprit. But without proof I can do nothing. And neither can you."

Henry gives a short sharp nod. "I'm not unreasonable. Of course I'll do nothing. Not unless I have cause."

"Such as?"

"Let's put it this way. If Cai lays one hand on me or my property I shall have the magistrate called and he will be punished then, mark my words."

Linette smiles without humor.

"As the magistrate is Lord Pennant I fear you'll be disappointed."

"Why?"

"Because it is a matter of status for him, nothing more. As long as his own property is secure then Pennant has no interest in dirtying his hands with those of lower social standing. Besides, like Julian, he's rarely in residence. You would have better luck consulting Mr. Dee—he holds more sway with the villagers. But the reverend is very protective of his flock; he prefers a Christian solution, a charitable one. Not that he has ever had to employ such a measure," Linette adds. "We have no crimes committed here."

"Except for shooting at people, ransacking a gatehouse, and thieving from taverns."

Linette presses her lips. Henry gives her a pointed look but, thankfully, falls silent, turns away.

Their argument, it seems, is at an end, though neither of them has won it. She considers the young doctor's broad back. Never has she met anyone who could hedge around a subject as well as she, never has she met anyone whose temper blows similarly hot and cold, and Linette cannot decide if she likes the fact.

At present Henry is looking at her wall of bookshelves. One is set aside for Plas Helyg's ledgers, the other for her books on farming and agriculture. Linette watches him take in the treatises and annuals, subscriptions and journals. He stops at a middle shelf, reads the spine of Anderson's *Essays Relating to Agriculture and Rural Affairs*, his mouth moving noiselessly over the title.

"Impressive," he murmurs.

Linette feels a twinge of pride.

"I order them in from London. Nowhere here stocks texts on modern methods of land management."

"You read them all?"

"I do."

"*All* of them?"

"Of course."

"And these ledgers . . ." He counts them. "One for each season?"

"*Ie.* I keep meticulous records."

Henry turns around. His look of admiration is unmistakable.

"When you told me you managed Plas Helyg's estate I never fully appreciated the enormity of the task. Seeing your library—" and here he gestures at the shelf housing the ledgers—"the administration such a task requires . . . well, it puts things into a different light."

She touches her tongue to the roof of her mouth, dares to test him.

"You must agree that a madwoman could hardly be so well-read."

He stares a moment. Then he barks a short laugh, turns back to the shelves, continues perusing them. At length he reaches out to stroke the spine of a green book lower down.

"You have some Welsh texts here too."

Linette rises from the chair, goes to stand next to him, plucks the volume of Welsh folklore from the shelf.

"A book from my childhood," she murmurs. "It tells of the namesakes of Gwydion and Pryderi. Of Merlin."

She flicks through the pages, the old myths and legends she could recite off by heart. Linette remembers how Enaid would read them to her as a little girl tucked up tightly in bed, and even then—at so young an age—she would wish it were her mother telling the tales of Branwen and Blodeuwedd and Bedwyr instead.

The memory pains her. Linette places the book back on the shelf.

"How went your visits today?" she asks. "Aside from your encounter with Cai."

Henry grimaces. "I looked in on Tomas—he does a little better, by the way—then the coastal cottages, then tried my luck with the ones in the square. All refused to see me."

"I am sorry for it. Truly, I am."

Henry says nothing. Linette licks her lips.

"You asked what '*sais*' meant."

"Yes."

She hesitates. "There is no literal translation for the Welsh language does not always work that way, but . . ."

"But?"

"It is an insult. Cai was essentially calling you an Englishman, but the word—and the intonation of it—is generally derogatory. Like a curse."

"I see." A pause. "No, actually, I do not see. Don't you think it time you tell me the real reason why the people of Penhelyg should resent me so?"

He is looking at her with such a hard unflinching gaze that Linette knows she cannot avoid the subject again, and with a sigh she rubs her nose, lays her palm flat against the spines of her books as if she might find strength there.

"There have been rumors—"

"So the vicar advised when I saw him in the village. Ancient history, he said, troubling interactions."

Linette purses her lips. "Will you let me speak or not?"

Henry falls silent. Linette tries again.

"There have been rumors," she repeats quietly. "Tomas told me of them, many years ago." Linette takes a steadying breath. "I said last night that all my grandfather cared about was his pleasure. Well, his pleasure, apparently, went beyond gambling. Before the Tresilians took over the estate, he used to invite his English friends up to Plas Helyg. It was said . . ." Linette stops, feels shame at even saying the words. "It was said there had been distasteful gatherings, that village girls were used in illicit ways for their own entertainment."

"Like whores."

Linette flinches at the term. "If you must be so blunt. One of the girls died."

"Died?"

136

"Her body was found down by the road, under the willows. Do you remember the dark-haired girl I spoke to in the square?" Henry nods. "Her name is Rhiannon, Heledd Einion's granddaughter. Of course, all this was long before I was born so I cannot vouch for the truth of it. Enaid tells me I must not listen to village gossip, and it does all seem incredibly unlikely—it's perfectly possible Heledd simply slipped on the tree roots and broke her neck. But whatever the truth of it the people of Penhelyg believe wholeheartedly that my grandfather was responsible, and that if it were not for his English friends none of this would have happened. As a consequence they do not trust Englishmen, and so they do not trust you."

Henry is watching her.

"I see," he says, and this time, it seems, he does. Instead of looking angry as Linette thought he might, Henry instead looks contemplative.

"You kindly offered your assistance earlier," he says, "to come with me when I visited your tenants." Linette waits. He clears his throat. "I still want to make a try of it on my own. I think that's important. But you accused me of being quick to judge just now and it did not sit well with me. Perhaps you might agree to help in other ways."

"Oh?"

"I need to learn your language. For my sake, as well as theirs. How can they learn to trust me if I do not speak their tongue? I have the dictionary, of course, but it's clear I need more specialist knowledge, of the kind only a native speaker can provide. The pronunciation, the nuances, all of that." His dark eyes are bright, suddenly keen. "Will you teach me?"

Linette feels a rush of unexpected pleasure, of gratitude, and she says, more brightly than she is prone, "I would gladly teach you, if you really wish it. Shall we start tomorrow?"

But Henry has hesitated, is shaking his head.

"I planned to visit Dr. Beddoe tomorrow."

137

He indicates his medical bag which he left by the study door, and Linette once again marks its scuffed hide, its lopsided handle.

"I need more supplies, something suitable in which to carry them if I am to visit my patients on horseback." He hesitates again for the briefest moment before continuing. "I was hoping he might advise me."

Linette marks his hesitation with guarded interest.

"There's a boatman who can take you across to Criccieth."

"A boatman?"

"It's the only way over the estuary. You must catch it from the port six miles from here. I'll have Cadoc send word down to Mr. Morgan who can take you. But why the rush? I can advise you just as well as he can on such a trifling matter."

Something shadows his face. "There are some things only a doctor can answer."

CHAPTER TWELVE

The same driver who conveyed Henry to the village met him outside Plas Helyg's iron gates, but rather than greeting Henry with his previously evasive demeanor the older man spared upon him a broad smile.

"I feared," said he in his slow and stilted English as he directed the pony down the woodland pass, "that we'd lose Tomas not three days ago. Mair said you came to see him again yesterday. That was kind. Unexpected." The older man sidled a glance at Henry then away again, flushing into his whiskers. "You've my sincerest gratitude."

"You're very welcome."

He offered Henry his hand.

"Name's Ivor."

"Henry."

"*Ie.*"

Ivor's gratitude loosened his tongue. Henry soon found that aside from acting as Penhelyg's messenger and errand man, he also made his living as the village coachman, though his mode of transport does not suit the term; the open cart would do just as well for the transport of hay and livestock but Henry was grateful for the ride, tried to enjoy the journey down pebble-laden tracks and the boggy marshlands of Harlech (a small market town where an abandoned castle nestled on a rocky outcrop overlooking the Irish sea), the dirt roads which led to a small riverbank port named Twgwyn. Despite the best efforts of the ferryman it was a rocky, tumultuous ride across the estuary; as the barnacled oars sliced into the choppy sea Henry gripped the sides of the vessel so hard his palms became host to some nasty splinters. Now on terra firma again Henry swallows, runs a handkerchief across his forehead. As with horse riding, sea travel is a pastime to which he must adapt, and quickly.

Henry shields his eyes, looks upward to the town waiting for him on the hill. On a cliff to his right stands another castle (this one decidedly less put together than the one at Harlech) and he watches as a gull lazily circles one of its fractured turrets. There is a commotion behind him, a loud offloading of wares, the boarding of a passenger for the return journey. Henry walks up the beach out of the way, pebbles crunching underfoot.

He must ask for directions, thumbs the Welsh dictionary until the pages tear. Having finally made himself understood he is pointed in the right direction and soon finds himself standing in front of a tall townhouse situated down a narrow road just off the main, the stone partition walls spilling fat roses the color of lemons. He licks perspiration from his top lip. Secluded here there is no breath of sea air, no clouds provide cover. The air has within it a prickly heat and the sun beats down, unrelenting. Puffing into his collar Henry climbs the narrow stone steps, tugs on the bell-pull, and within moments a young maid opens the door.

"*Oes gennych chi apwyntiad?*"

Henry repeats his rehearsed question.

"*Gweld Dr. Beddoe? Dr. Henry Talbot ydw i.*"

The maid nods, opens the door wider, and Henry steps past her into a cool hallway. She indicates he take a seat before disappearing into a room off to the left, and as he sits down on a chair with eagle heads carved into the arms, he looks about him with interest.

Money has been spent in this house, more money than Henry expected a country doctor to have. An expensive and intricately patterned rug runs down the length of the hall, its seam meeting the solid base of an ornate grandfather clock. The wooden floor is polished to a high shine, the whitewashed walls crisp as if newly painted and lined with a still-life gallery of overly bright fruit and gaudy flowers. He looks across from him to where a large mirror sits above a mahogany side table; on its waxed surface stands a bowl of those same lemon-yellow roses, spilling like taffeta from its glass brim.

Henry loosens his cravat, rests his battered medical bag on his lap, looks at the grandfather clock. Nearly midday. He left Plas Helyg promptly at half past seven. So, then, it took near four and a half hours to reach his destination. No earthly use at all if a patient needed him urgently. True, he has only been employed as physician to the residents of Penhelyg, the private aid of the Tresilian household. But what of the neighboring towns and villages? Dr. Beddoe surely cannot accommodate them all.

He scratches at his hand, tries to squeeze one of the splinters free. In winter, especially, travel will be near impossible. He has heard winters are harsh in the country but *here* this means a churning sea, perishing cold, muddy roads too dangerous to traverse. The nights would be long as well, the dark impenetrable.

The door opens. The maid beckons. Henry rises, follows the girl into a large and comfortably appointed room.

There is a similarity to the gatehouse study in its layout—a sizeable desk, a chair and recliner meant for a patient, what appears to be a well-stocked library, a large cupboard in the corner. Dr. Beddoe is lucky. In London Henry's "study" had been one of the many surgeons' slabs to be found at Guy's, the confines of that hospital's tightly packed operating theater. Dr. Beddoe himself sits in a large, richly upholstered armchair behind the desk. A thin, sallow-looking man wearing a full-bottomed white wig, he does not rise at Henry's entrance, merely watches his approach over long steepled fingers. The maid shuts the door, leaving them alone.

"Take a seat."

He speaks English, Henry notes, but with no Welsh accent. It is a measured voice, one that denotes a watchful and critical mind, and Henry is reminded of his tyrannical schoolmaster at the Foundling who caned him once until his fingers bled.

The seat proffered is simple wooden fare, hard and uncomfortable as Henry discovers when he has taken it. No comfort, then, he thinks, for a patient.

"So," the doctor says before offering a thin-lipped smile. "You are Henry Talbot. Your arrival has been long anticipated."

Henry blinks.

"Has it?" he says, careful. "My understanding is that my presence in Penhelyg has not been taken with much enthusiasm."

"For the villagers, perhaps. But it saves me a great deal of time."

"I can imagine. I've been most intrigued at how you managed considering how busy you must be. Indeed, it took me quite a time to travel here myself."

"It was not so much trouble as you might expect," the older doctor replies. "My services were not required overmuch. Superficial ailments, hardly worth my time at all. Mere headaches, a shallow cut, an innocent cough which turned out to be the oncomings of a common cold. It helps, of course," he says with something of a scoff, "that the good Linette Tresilian paid me for the trouble of a weekly visit, else I'd have been inclined to leave them to their own devices."

"One of my new patients is not the subject of a superficial

ailment," Henry counters. "If his condition had been left any longer I fear nothing could have recovered him."

"Oh?" Beddoe sends him a lopsided smile. "And who was this person, so near to death's door?"

He tells him of Tomas Morgan. The older doctor sits back in his seat, leather creaking.

"While the early symptoms of pleurisy would have indeed demonstrated themselves as a cold," Henry adds, "I feel that perhaps a little more discernment on your part might have made all the difference."

Beddoe pierces Henry with a look.

"Do you presume to tell me how to conduct my work? To question my methods?"

"I simply confess myself surprised his symptoms were not accurately interpreted."

The older man stares.

"At the point I saw the boy his symptoms had not presented themselves beyond, as I said, a common cold, and the mother was more than happy to treat him using traditional methods, under the advice of Miss Carew."

Rowena Carew. Those beautiful amber eyes. . . .

"I met her," Henry says, embarrassed to hear his voice falter. "I happened upon her yesterday in the village."

"Indeed." Beddoe licks his lower lip. "She is a member of the old school of healing, shall we say. She knows her herbs, their medicinal qualities. She has assisted me occasionally in my consultations, provided alternative means of treatment when it was preferred. Mrs. Morgan chose to listen to her in this instance. I have made no error in my administrations, Dr. Talbot. But tell me, why have you come here today? I presume it was not to belittle me for any wrongdoing on my part. If it is, a letter would have sufficed."

The scold is justified. It has always been the way with Henry; at

Guy's he never hesitated to rebuke a colleague or student when they made a mistake. Human lives are at risk in this profession, he used to tell them—there is no room for error, as he well knows. But courtesy should not have allowed such rudeness. Henry is sitting in the study of another medical professional. *He* is the outsider here, and politeness should have dictated his conduct better.

"Forgive me. It was not my place."

There is a pause. The older man gives an imperceptible nod of the head. Henry takes a breath. He must be very careful, he realizes, in what he says next.

"I came because I need supplies. I hoped you might be able to advise on where best to procure them."

Beddoe clears his throat, his fingers still steepled into a pyramid, and Henry's gaze involuntarily drifts to them. On the little finger the doctor wears a gold signet ring.

"Criccieth houses an apothecary," the older man says, oblivious to Henry's frown. "Anything you need can be purchased there." He looks down at Henry's satchel on his lap. "Is that all you have? Yes, a knapsack would better suit your needs. I'm sure by now you've ascertained that carriages are not quite so obtainable here. A bag such as that will be cumbersome." Beddoe's lip twists into a smile that looks to Henry more like a sneer. "I should advise that you'll struggle here, Dr. Talbot. While your more particular medical knowledge is, I'm sure, perfectly sound, it will be of little use to you in these parts. The people of Meirionydd, especially the inhabitants of Penhelyg, have a rather archaic view of modern medical practices."

Beddoe taps his fingers together, the gold ring glinting in the light shining from the window. Is that a pattern etched into the circular disc?

"Oral tradition, you see. Medical knowledge has been passed through word of mouth here for centuries. They still consider illness to be a God-given punishment, and prefer natural remedies. Rosemary sprigs mixed with honey to prevent nausea, ground fennel for diseases of the eye, a clove of garlic in the ear for earache, that sort of thing. For the more superstitious, a cure for jaundice might involve placing a coin into a mug of clear mead. Most, then, would rather implement these methods than call on a doctor. I know Dr. Evans had more sympathy for such practices, often purchased plants from Miss Carew as a mark of goodwill. Grew his own, in fact."

Henry thinks of the abandoned patch of earth at the gatehouse, those dried-out spindles of foliage that reminded him so keenly of finger bones.

"You will find that, like me, you are best employed as a personal physician, as I understand you already are. My employer is Sir John Selwyn—he owns the lands around these parts, is Plas Helyg's closest neighbor other than Lord Pennant on the edge of the Mawddach estuary." The doctor lowers his hands, spreads them flat across the red leather-topped desk. "This practice is my home first and foremost, and only those who can afford my services are like to come here for more progressive treatment. The rest, as I say, prefer the old cures."

Henry dislikes the man's derogatory tone. He sits straighter in the hard chair, tries for a polite smile that does not quite come.

"Thank you for explaining so clearly, doctor."

Beddoe inclines his head. "I shall write you a list of supplies to get you started. The apothecary can furnish you accordingly."

He removes a crisp sheet of expensive-looking paper from a drawer, reaches for a quill resting in a marble inkwell next to him on the desk. Henry watches him write, the only sound being the scratch of nib.

"Have you ever treated Gwenllian Tresilian?"

Beddoe continues to write, does not look up.

"I've given the family a second opinion, yes."

"And what did you find?"

"That Plas Helyg is unfit for a woman such as she." He dips his nib, and without looking up he says, "She belongs in an asylum."

Henry feels his growing dislike for the man coil in his gut.

"You approve of the barbaric methods such places employ?"

Beddoe makes an amused noise in the back of his throat. "I do not consider such treatments barbaric. Not if they work."

"Do they, though?" Henry shoots back. "Asylums will provide drug upon drug to a patient without knowing anything concerning the root of the disorder. Such places . . . they are enough to turn even the sane mad. Indeed, I cannot be induced to think their so-called cures to be of any benefit at all."

"That, Dr. Talbot, is a matter of opinion. But it does not signify—it is where I believe Gwen Tresilian should be. Alas, his lordship would not allow it, ignored my recommendation. He felt she was better kept at Plas Helyg."

The coil tightens. The quill scratches on. Henry tries another avenue.

"You attended Dr. Evans at his death, I understand."

The quill pauses on the curve of a P.

"I did."

"Heart failure, apparently."

"Correct."

"Odd, though. I am told he was generally in very good health. Climbed a mountain the week before." Henry licks his lower lip. "Was a postmortem done?"

The doctor pauses from his task, raises his head, a wiry eyebrow raised.

"Such practices are not condoned in these parts."

"Why not?"

Beddoe frowns, lays the quill flat beside the unfinished list.

"Because," he says, "it is wholly unnecessary. People here tend to die from natural causes, as was the case with Dr. Evans. Heart failure, that much was clear. If he'd recently climbed a mountain that can come as no surprise, not at his age." The older doctor pauses. "But you evidently think otherwise."

Henry hesitates. "Not necessarily. The man *was* elderly. Even so . . ."

He thinks of what Evans's sister had said—*Wynn looked terrified. As if he had been frightened to death!*—the strange vial he found in the gatehouse. Henry touches the inner pocket of his coat where it sits nestled against his chest.

"What did you think of the contortion to his face?"

"What contortion?"

A beat. "Mrs. Evans intimated—"

But Beddoe is brushing him off. "The fancy of females, to be sure. I noticed no such thing."

"I do not see why she should lie."

The older man levels a hard look at Henry across the desk.

"I hope you might, as a fellow man of science, take my professional opinion over those of a mere woman?"

Henry stares. "Might I see the coroner's report?"

"There wasn't one."

A beat. "There wasn't one?"

"No."

"Why?"

Beddoe sighs impatiently, sits back in his chair, steeples his fingers again. They are thin and grey, like riverweed.

"Because there were no suspicious circumstances."

"Are you quite sure?"

Henry says it to see what the reaction might be, and he is not disappointed. Something shifts across the older doctor's face, his eyes

147

darken, his fingertips press against each other ever so gently, and Henry knows now—*knows*—his suspicions have merit.

"I am surprised at you, sir," that man says now, "for asking such a thing. Even if there had been one *you* would not show the records of your London patients to a stranger, surely?"

And now, Henry quirks a brow. He did not mention that he hailed from London. News, then, travels fast in these parts.

"It is only," Henry says now, pretending a more reasonable tone, "that Dr. Evans was a resident of Penhelyg. It's right I should know the facts."

"You have the facts. I have given them to you. Heart failure. It really is that simple."

They look at each other across the table. Beddoe meets Henry's gaze without batting an eye, and Henry understands then that he will glean nothing further from him.

"Very well. Perhaps, though, you would be willing to relinquish the case notes of the patients from Penhelyg you have seen these past weeks?"

The older man's eyes narrow. He picks up the quill, resumes the list. Then, without looking up he says, "I only make notes for my own patients. Besides, as I told you, their ailments were superficial. Not worth the paper and ink to write them down. Now then, Dr. Talbot," he adds, offering the sheet between bony fingers. "Is there anything else?"

It is in that moment Henry sees clearly the signet of the gold ring he wears, and it is all he can do not to clutch at the doctor's hand, draw it toward him, take a closer look. Is that not a familiar symbol etched within its shining disc?

"Dr. Talbot," he says, still holding the paper across the desk. "Is there anything else?"

Henry tears his eyes away. There is, of course. There is the matter of the strange vial in his pocket, the residue inside which he suspects to be something far more sinister than laudanum. But clearly there is no use in voicing any of it to this man.

Observation. Contemplation. Interrogation.

"No," Henry says, taking the list. "That is all."

Beddoe splits a smile.

"Splendid. My next patient is due, so you'll forgive that I cannot accommodate you for longer. The list I've made here should suffice. I trust," he adds, "you're not yet acquainted with where the apothecary is located?"

"No, sir, I am not."

Beddoe sounds a small brass bell on his desk. "My maid shall direct you."

He smiles again, fake and tight.

"Good day, Dr. Talbot."

CHAPTER THIRTEEN

Linette's mother was once proficient at the harp, so Enaid told her
many years ago. It had been one of her greatest pleasures to listen to
her mistress play, to have fluting folk tunes fill the mansion's cavernous walls. Servants would stop in their work and listen, such was the
quality of her playing.

It is hard to imagine such a thing now; Linette's mother sits at the
little stool beside the harp absently strumming the strings with a
look of bewilderment on her face, as if desperately trying and failing to conjure in her memory sounds that had once been pretty, but
are now merely tuneless noises that send Linette's ears into a painful ache.

Linette shifts on the armchair beside the bed, squints down at the
recent treatise on farming resting on her lap. It is late. The sun's dying
rays are barely visible through the chink in the curtains, the room lit
only with candles tiered in lofty corners about the room so as not to
hurt her mother's eyes. Some might think such a display beautiful and
peaceful, the way the tapers flicker and bend, how the sprigs of gorse
appear to glow in the wake of their flames, but to Linette it is distasteful. To Linette it echoes the somber confines of the Cadwalladr crypt
in the forest, a living shrine keeping out all the beauty of outside.
What a wonderful sunset there must be across the horizon, she thinks,

glancing up at that golden gap in the curtains. What a view it must afford from those great windows, a view her mother can never see!

On the opposite side of the bed, in a chair of her own, Enaid coughs. She is sewing up the tear in her mistress's blue dress, a tear made when she writhed so violently on the dining-room floor the other night. Linette stares at the methodical rise and fall of the needle and thread, bites her bottom lip.

"Why were you so difficult with Henry yesterday? You know he is here to help. He'll not harm Mamma, I'm sure of it."

Linette is not sure what she expected Enaid to say. A dismissive shrug, an apology, or, even, a denial. But whatever she expected, it was not this—the old woman rests the needle, and her pale eyes fill with tears.

"Oh, Enaid. Please don't upset yourself."

"I cannot help it," she whispers. "I love her as my own, as I do you. It hurts to see her like this. And to not have Wynn here . . ."

Feeling her own tears threaten to rise, Linette looks back down into her lap, grips the treatise hard, determined to keep her eyes dry.

"I know," she says, with effort. "But it is Henry that must care for Mamma now. Be thankful, at least, she is not in the care of Dr. Beddoe."

Enaid sucks in her breath. "No," she whispers, "no," and a spark of resentment rises in Linette's throat.

Dr. Beddoe, who harshly told Linette that her mother should be kept chained to her bed, then left her weak as wet paper after bleeding her nearly dry with a vigorous course of leeches. Such a horrible, disagreeable man. Linette thinks of how kindly Henry treated her mother in comparison, his gentle touch when he held her wrist, counting her pulse.

The silence that settles between Linette and Enaid is broken by a plucked minor of the harp, two majors in quick succession. Linette

151

returns to the treatise, Enaid tackles the particularly tricky tear. But, after a while, the housekeeper looks up.

"Dr. Talbot *was* kind to her. You've taken to him, I think."

Linette raises her gaze to Enaid's, but her eyes instead hold within them an odd expression of reserve.

"I would not say I have *taken* to him, Enaid."

"You called him Henry."

Ah, here it comes. That anticipated lecture on propriety, on social boundaries that she has never—not once—listened to. Linette lifts her shoulder in a shrug.

"Only because it is easier. That is all. I barely know him." She pauses, rests the treatise on her thigh. "But yes, he was kind. Far kinder than I expected."

"Yes." A beat. "You must be careful."

"Careful? Of what?"

The old woman licks her lips. "You know so little of the world, of men. I could not bear . . ."

She glances at Lady Gwen who plucks another major note, then a few more together in the semblance of a melody that is not altogether tuneless.

"Oh, Enaid," Linette teases, "you can hardly think me like to be in danger? You know I have no interest in matters of the heart."

The housekeeper shakes her head, but at what she is not quite sure. Very carefully Enaid places the dress on the bed, reaches up to snap off a sprig of gorse from the floral canopy above them.

"Take it," she says, reaching over the coverlet to hand it to her.

Linette sighs. "Enaid, I—"

"Please," the old woman says, an urgent light in her pale blue eyes. "I know you do not believe in its powers, but I would feel happier if you kept it with you. Take it. For me."

Often Enaid does this, presses a piece of gorse or rowan into her

152

hand as if it were a talisman, and Linette sighs, takes the spiky sprig of yellow flowers, slips it into the pocket of her dressing gown. If it gives Enaid comfort, then she supposes there can be no harm.

There is a soft knock. All three women look in the direction of the sound. Placing the treatise on the bed, Linette goes to open the door.

"Henry!" she exclaims. "You're back later than I thought. Is everything all right? Have you eaten? I asked Cadoc—"

"Might I speak with you?"

Linette blinks. "Of course." She shuts the door behind her. The hallway is narrow, and at such close proximity she smells on him the briny essence of the sea.

"What is it?" she asks.

The young physician looks tired, travel-worn.

"Beddoe. How long has he been in Criccieth?"

His tone is one of displeasure. So then, he does agree with her measure of him!

"As long as I can remember," she says. "Why?"

"It's a Welsh name, is it not?"

"It is."

"But he does not sound Welsh."

"No. He comes from a local wealthy family so does speak the language when it pleases him, but he was educated—like you—in London. There are many Welshmen like him in these parts; some hold a profession, others do not. Sir John Selwyn and Lord Pennant are two. I mentioned them before, remember? They own the estates neighboring Plas Helyg."

"Did Beddoe and Evans ever work together?"

The question surprises. "No, not really. Julian asked him to offer a second opinion on Mamma's condition, and Dr. Evans was present for that. But otherwise . . ."

"How did they get along?"

Linette hesitates. "They had different opinions, different methods."

"They argued?"

Again, Linette thinks of the leeches. Dr. Evans was appalled, but under Julian's orders he could do nothing.

"Sometimes," she says.

Henry looks thoughtful. Linette frowns.

"Why all these questions?"

He pauses, seems to contemplate his next words.

"I believe there is more to Dr. Evans's death than you originally thought."

Linette sighs. "Oh, for pity's sake, not this again."

"Yes, this again!" he hisses, and his hard tone makes her stare. Henry marks it, pulls back. "Forgive me, but can you honestly expect me to believe he should die so suddenly, with no previous intimations of ill health? You yourself said he did not appear sick, and Mr. Dee told me that he and Dr. Evans climbed a mountain a few days before he died. A man who would endeavor such a thing does not strike me as a man of poor constitution."

"Who's to say that signifies? Climbing mountains is hardly preservation against premature death. He died because he was *old*!"

"Did he?"

She is about to scold him, to tell him his imagination is running wild, when Henry produces from his pocket a small and strangely wrought glass vial. Linette stares at it in the semidark.

"What is that?"

Henry hands it to her.

"I found it in the gatehouse," he replies, and Linette vaguely remembers how—after giving Angharad and Aled their instructions— she found the doctor sifting through the wreckage on the gatehouse floor.

"Did Dr. Evans ever use a vial like this?"

Linette turns it in her hand, presses her thumbnail against the unusual gold stopper.

"Not that I ever saw."

"What of Beddoe?"

"I don't know."

Henry sighs, runs his fingers through his hair.

"Listen. I know something isn't right here. If Dr. Evans did not use such vials, then someone else certainly did, and my bet is on Dr. Beddoe."

"But why?"

Henry looks at her meaningfully. "If my time working with Bow Street taught me anything, it is to trust your instincts. And my instincts tell me this vial has something to do with Dr. Evans's death. Think about it," he continues, when Linette stays silent. "An old but otherwise healthy man dies suddenly—Mrs. Evans said it looked as though he had been frightened to death. But when I mentioned this to Beddoe he insisted this was not the case."

Linette's mouth goes dry. She had not mentioned Dr. Evans's face to Henry that day at the gatehouse, had found the memory of it too horrifying. Linette shuts her eyes, pictures the old man's wide eyes, his twisted mouth held open as rigor mortis took hold. She assumed that was simply what happened, when one died in such a way, and it has haunted her, that expression; no one—not she nor Enaid and certainly not Dr. Beddoe—could deny having seen it.

"Impossible," she whispers. "It was obvious."

"So why did he deny all knowledge? Beddoe was hiding something, of that there can be no doubt. And, I was sure I saw . . ."

He trails off, looks confused, but Linette is no longer listening. Feeling ill she raises the vial up in the meagre light of the hallway. Something brown sits at the bottom.

"What was in it?" she asks, and slowly he takes the vial back, holds it at eye level between them.

"I don't know," he says. "But I do know this. Whatever it was, it wasn't laudanum. I think, Linette—" and here Henry's expression grows grim—"it was some kind of poison."

BRANCH II.

How hard it is to keep the middle way ;
Not to believe too little or too much!

REV. JOHN WESLEY
Journal, Vol. III. No. 26.
Mon. 10, December (1764)

CHAPTER FOURTEEN

The next morning Linette leads Henry up the small winding path he marked that first morning into the dense trees abutting Plas Helyg's boundary walls. It is a steep uneven path; Henry must watch his footing as he follows Linette's more confident journey upward and Merlin bounds happily ahead, wiry legs navigating the exposed roots and overgrown bracken with careless ease. How unfit I am, Henry thinks as he puffs behind them—at least in London he did not have to contend with sheer hills—and it is a relief to emerge onto open fields, a relief when Linette allows him to stop for breath.

She puts her hands on her hips, looks out on the vista, the breeze whipping strands of tangled blonde hair about her shoulders.

"I will never tire of this place."

Perspiring, Henry removes a handkerchief from his pocket, presses it to the back of his neck. He loosens his cravat, and as he turns his head to let the warm air dry his skin Henry catches sight of Linette's face. She took the news of Henry's suspicions with obvious distress, and had a haunted look for the rest of the night. Now Henry is relieved to see an expression of calm.

"Don't you think it beautiful?"

It *is* beautiful. Like a grassy sea the fields spread wide below them toward the distant rise and fall of craggy mountains, and the warm morning has been blessed with such blue sky and stark sunshine that their colors are prominent—lush green and rich brown, the pretty purple of summer heather.

"Very."

"Nothing to match it in London, I dare say."

"Not at all."

The wind catches another strand of unruly hair. Linette pushes it behind her ear.

"We stand now in Cwm Nantcol."

"Cwm Nantcol?"

"It's a valley, part of Plas Helyg's lands." She points to the right. "Over there are the remains of some ancient settlements. See that stone structure in the distance?"

Henry nods.

"It's called a cromlech, a relic of the druids. There are many dotted across these fields. And, to the left, you can see the mountain range of Eryri. See," she says, raising her finger in a point. "That little misshapen triangle between those two knolls? That's the summit of Yr Wyddfa."

"Yr Wyddfa," he echoes, trying his tongue across the sounds.

Linette nods. "The English call it Snow Hill, but the translation is wrong. It actually means 'the grave.'"

"The grave?"

"Legend says it's the resting place of Rhita, the giant that King Arthur slew."

Another local superstition. Henry says nothing; despite Linette's apparently calm demeanor he is unsure of her true mood today. No indeed, better to hold his tongue than be on the receiving end of hers. She does not seem to notice his lack of response; she is pointing at the stony outcrop rising to their far left.

"The mines," she says. "I go once every fortnight to take up food parcels Mrs. Phillips prepares. I'm due to go tomorrow, in fact, if you'd like to accompany me? Julian prefers I do not interfere, but mining is unforgiving work and they deserve some respite every now and then." A shadow crosses her face. "Come, let's take the path up toward Moelfre. Miss Carew's cottage isn't too far."

It had been her idea to visit Rowena Carew. As a herbalist if there was anyone (so Linette said last night) who could know what the strange liquid in the vial might be, it was her.

"Do you know Miss Carew well?" Henry had asked, and even then he felt his pulse pound at the thought of her.

"Not well," Linette replied, "for she keeps much to herself. She came to Penhelyg a few years ago, and has never sought my assistance."

"Why not?"

"Because she does not need it. Miss Carew has a serviceable cottage and is not in want of work. She has a good relationship with my tenants since many of them—" and here Linette had looked at Henry apologetically—"prefer the old herbal methods."

Henry was not sure whether to be pleased or disappointed. On the one hand, Linette might have been able to tell him a little more about her. On the other, he now has a chance to discover Miss Carew for himself without any other opinion to influence his own.

"Moelfre," Linette says now as they walk briskly across the field, Merlin at their heels, "is another curious mountain." She looks up at it with a smile. "Enaid used to read me a story about three women who were turned into standing stones at its summit when they chose to work on the Sabbath. They went up the hill to winnow their corn but because they were unobservant of the holy fourth commandment they were transformed into three pillars of stone for their wickedness, each the same color as the dresses they wore—Blood Red, Bone White, Vein Blue."

This time, Henry is not quite able to stem his disapproval.

"Really," he says, sour, and Linette glances at him.

"You've no patience for our ways, have you? Can you not at least *pretend* to suffer them?"

"Do you expect me to believe three women turned to stone?"

"No. But I expect you to enjoy the story for what it is—a fable—and not mock it."

He thinks for a moment. "Why disregard the logic of science in favor of archaic philosophy that has no foundation of truth?"

She quirks an eyebrow at him. "How do you know it has no foundation?"

"Because reason dictates there is none. Besides, you just called it a fable."

"So I did. But is that not very stubborn of you, nonetheless? To disbelieve something so assiduously? Legends are legends for a reason. They came from somewhere."

A stone cottage comes into view. At their side Merlin barks, runs ahead, and Henry watches him jump over a stile. Once the lurcher has bounded further down the field, he clears his throat.

"I do not mean to mock. But you must understand my upbringing. I am a man of science, not magic."

"Interesting," Linette murmurs, burrowing her hands deep into her pockets. "I think of them as the same thing."

"Oh?"

"Well, in medieval times science *was* magic. Scholars believed that God created the heavens according to scientific principles, yet they were still considered divine. So to them, magic and science were one and the same."

Henry looks at her in surprise. Linette shrugs.

"I read," she says, and her tone is so matter-of-fact he cannot dispute it. "Besides, our legends are not magic, not neccessarily. They are simply the myths of our homeland, common folklore. They're to be respected."

He has nothing to say to this, nor does Linette seem to expect an answer. Instead she picks up pace as they draw closer to the cottage, and as they reach the lower reaches of Moelfre the land begins to change terrain; half-earth, half-turf, half-water. Bog plants blossom about Henry's feet, marsh insects buzz about their heads. The ground becomes soft underfoot. Just when Henry feels they must wade through water to reach the cottage Merlin leads them across a small makeshift bridge of mountain rock onto drier planes where rabbit pellets litter the ground like tiny round bullets. A few more steps take them past a dilapidated stone wall. A desiccated jackdaw lies against it, the sun having already dried its sinews to crisp ribbons.

The cottage itself is on the other side, and Henry looks at it with interest. A low and rambling one-story building made of the same stone as the bridge, topped with a slate roof, and as Merlin trots up to the door (no whitewash mark here, he is gratified to see) Henry perceives a small garden not unlike the barren one at the gatehouse, but this one is filled to the brim: wildflowers vie for attention among a bed of thyme, rosemary, mint, and numerous other herbs Henry does not recognize.

It is Linette who knocks, fast and firm. A black-stemmed tree sprigged with delicate flowers grows around the doorway, its spicy, almondlike scent heavy in his nostrils, the tiny white flowers shaking on their thorny stems. Footsteps sound within; Miss Carew opens the door. Her cheeks are flushed, red hair loose down to her waist, and as before all Henry can do is stare.

He has known his fair share of women in his time, of course; he has his needs. Still, it has seldom been Henry's habit to indulge in such things—often his role at the hospital meant he scarce had opportunity—but when he did, he chose respectable houses. The women he partnered only ever evoked in him a sense of release and polite consideration. Some of them had been pretty, some plain. But none of them looked like *this* one, and never did they make him nervous and hot-skinned the way this one does now.

"Miss Tresilian!" Miss Carew exclaims. "Dr. Talbot." She hesitates at the threshold, looks between them both. "Am I needed in the village?"

Again it is Linette who answers, and Henry is glad for it allows him to catch his breath.

"Miss Carew," she says, "I apologize for visiting unannounced. We were hoping you might identify something for us."

She frowns. "Identify something?"

Henry clears his throat. "An ingredient. It is not one I recognize, and we . . ."

Miss Carew opens the door wide. Merlin sneaks his way through.

"Of course," she says. "Do come in."

As pretty as the outside of the cottage is, Henry is surprised at the interior. Serviceable, yes, as Linette said, but simple. A little too simple, even for him.

It is an open room—no internal walls divide the space—and upon the earthen floor lies a large reed mat, some worn Indian rugs. At the back of one wall is a single bed with a lumpy mattress, next to it a basket of blankets, a battered chamberstick holding a candle nub resting on top. On another wall stands a large stone hearth, its fire lit and low despite the warmth outside, an iron kettle hanging from a spit. A threadbare armchair is positioned close to the fire. On the far wall a long table is home to flowers and leaves in various stages of preparation, stone bowls, a pestle and mortar, glass bottles and jars. Next to it stands a Welsh dresser, its cavernous doors tied shut with twine. To hold Miss Carew's ingredients, Henry supposes, though the ceiling itself seems to be its own store—dried bunches of lavender hang from the eaves, other clumps of foliage with woody stems that again Henry does not recognize, and it gives him confidence that Miss Carew might be able to answer their question.

"Forgive me," she says, wiping her hands on the apron she wears. "I'm preparing a tincture for Bronwen Lewis's baby to help her sleep, so I'm afraid I cannot offer refreshment. The kettle, you see—"

Linette is shaking her head. "We shall not keep you, Miss Carew."

Miss Carew nods, looks relieved. Henry retrieves the vial from his pocket.

"It is this," he says, handing it to her. Her fingertips graze his. Henry pulls back as if stung.

Confound it man, control yourself!

"There's not a lot left," he adds, flushing, "but if you could give us an idea of what it might be we'd be very grateful."

Miss Carew hesitates. Then she takes the vial, sniffs it. A frown mars her forehead, and she crosses the room to the small window set back behind the armchair, raises the bottle to the light. Linette—a pinch having formed about her mouth—watches the young woman like a hawk.

"Well?"

"Wait a moment."

This time Miss Carew crosses to the table of herbs, begins to sift through the bowls and jars.

Henry is fascinated, cannot take his eyes off her. She moves like water in a gentle stream, her skirts whispering along the reed mat, and he is inordinately glad the dimness of the cottage hides the blush he is sure has appeared on his cheeks.

Linette steps forward.

"Well, Miss Carew?"

Her tone is insistent. If it were not for the seriousness of the situation, Henry might ask Linette to show a little bit of patience, but he too is anxious for the answer. If he is right . . .

Miss Carew has selected a glass pipette from the table. Very carefully she inserts it into the vial, removes a tiny drop of the brown liquid from its depths. Then—before Henry can prevent her—she has placed it on the tip of her tongue.

He watches, heart in mouth. What if it harms her? But a contemplative look has crossed her face, and she takes a handkerchief from her sleeve, spits into it hard.

"Deadly nightshade," Miss Carew announces.

She holds out the vial. Henry takes it.

"Are you sure?"

Miss Carew nods.

"The tincture is old, so the potency is much diminished. But yes, it cannot be anything else."

A sliver of triumph runs up his spine. Deadly nightshade. One of the strongest natural poisons to exist. He knew it. *Knew* it!

It is the first feeling of justification Henry has felt since coming here. His dismissal from Guy's Hospital made him doubt his talents, made him believe he was a failure. But here, here is proof that he is not so hopeless as the governor had him believe! Joyfully Henry turns to Linette, but his triumph turns to guilt as he sees the look of shock on her face.

She had not truly believed him, that was clear. Yet Linette doubted enough to suggest coming to see Miss Carew, doubted enough to ask the question. And now she has her answer.

"I'm sorry, Linette."

Merlin, attuned it seems to his mistress's distress, presses his head against her thigh. Absently Linette lowers her hand, and the dog gently licks her palm.

"His face was contorted when we found him. Did he suffer greatly?"

Her voice is quiet, sad. Henry hesitates. How to tell her? But here, Miss Carew steps forward.

"I don't understand. Someone has taken this?"

Linette's mouth opens and closes. Henry takes a breath.

"I found this bottle in the wreckage of the gatehouse."

Miss Carew's hand rises to her mouth. "You mean . . . Dr. Evans?"

"I'm afraid so."

Her eyes widen. Slowly she lowers her hand, presses it against her chest.

"Poor Wynn," she murmurs. "I had not . . . it did not . . ." Miss Carew trails off. "I was saddened to hear he had died. He was a good man, a kind man. He did not taunt my work as others have."

She pauses, and Henry wonders if she thinks of Dr. Beddoe. In the beat that follows, Miss Carew looks to Linette.

"To answer your question, my lady, deadly nightshade is a potent poison when used in its purest form. To eat the berries or leaves would in itself be deadly, but as a tincture its potency is magnified. Within minutes Dr. Evans would have experienced severe pain, difficulty breathing, loss of sensation. His heart rate would have increased rapidly." Miss Carew nods at the vial in Henry's hand. "If he was given the full amount in that bottle his heart would have given out very quickly. Yes, I'm afraid he would have suffered greatly indeed."

Linette closes her eyes.

"Good God," she whispers. "What do I tell Enaid?"

"Tell her nothing," Henry says. "At least not until we've got to the bottom of this. It wouldn't be fair to distress her when we still know so little."

She takes a shaky breath, a single nod. When she opens her eyes again they are hard, an angry light in them.

167

"What do we do now?"

Henry turns the vial over in his hand, thoughtful.

"At Bow Street," he says, "such matters follow a very simple course. Francis Fielding always considered the facts and took note of all the people who link to them. The facts are these: my predecessor has been poisoned with a tincture of deadly nightshade, administered from *this* bottle." Henry holds it up so both women can see it clearly. "Said bottle is not typical of one purchased from an apothecary, so must have been specially made for the purpose by someone of means. It must be noted that Dr. Beddoe lives very comfortably for a village doctor, but that observation would be nothing if not for this—the tincture's effects account for the expression on Dr. Evans's face when he was discovered, yet Beddoe denied noting any such expression when I asked him about it yesterday."

Henry hesitates. Should he say?

"And there's another curious thing I noticed."

A weary expression passes across Linette's face. "What else can there be?" she asks, and Henry takes a measured breath.

"Your cousin wears a signet ring, does he not? A ring with a strange symbol upon it."

"The family crest, yes."

"Are you sure that's what it is?"

Linette stares. "Why wouldn't I be sure?"

"Because," he says, careful, "while I admit I only saw a fleeting glimpse of it I'm also sure I did not imagine it, either."

"Henry, speak plainly. Imagine *what*?"

"Beddoe," he answers, "wears a ring with that very same symbol."

CHAPTER FIFTEEN

"Tell me everything you know about it."

They are in the vestibule of Plas Helyg, standing in front of the vast fireplace. Until now, Linette has rarely thought about the symbol. It has always been familiar to her, of course; on the Tresilian portrait upstairs, on the book in Julian's study displayed so grandly inside its glass cabinet, on his ring . . . All this she marked years ago. Until now, the only other place Linette knew it existed was on the fireplace:

The symbol was simply *here*, as familiar to her as Plas Helyg's creaking gate and smoking chimneys, the stained-glass window in her bedroom depicting the white and red *dreigiau* of Dinas Emrys. Indeed, she had accepted it without a second thought. So why *should* Dr. Beddoe possess a ring with the Tresilian crest?

Linette tries to consider whether she ever noticed him wearing a ring before, but she is not in the habit of taking particular interest in a person's hands, nor does she encounter Dr. Beddoe enough to mark his. The last she saw of him was the other week on his final visit to Penhelyg when she paid him his extortionate fee. Did he wear a ring then? Linette cannot remember. Whether she marked it or not, Henry has, and yes, there can be no denying it is most unusual. But despite this strange discovery, that is not what concerns Linette at present. No indeed . . . what concerns her is the deadly nightshade found in the vial, and Henry's terrible suspicions.

A surge of sorrow overtakes her then, followed closely by anger. Dr. Evans. Poisoned! He had no enemies—the old doctor was liked by everyone. And though he sometimes did not agree with Dr. Beddoe, the latter would have no reason to kill him. What motive, after all, could there possibly be?

"Linette?"

Henry's hand on her wrist brings her back with a jolt, and she releases a shaky breath.

"All I know is that it's the crest of the Tresilians." She gestures to the stone in which the symbol has been carved. "The original stone was replaced with this one once my father took over the estate. It was a willow tree before."

"A willow tree?"

"*Pen* means head, *helyg* means willow, *plas* means mansion. Essentially then, the village name loosely translates to Head of the Willows, or Village at Willow's Head, and the house itself is Willow Mansion." Linette frowns, angles her face to look at the symbol again. "I often thought it sacrilege that Plas Helyg's Welsh connections should be removed in favor of the Tresilians. But after I inherited it seemed too much effort to change it, not to mention the expense. The needs of my tenants were my priority."

Beside her, Henry looks thoughtful.

"And that's it?" he asks. "That's all you know?"

"I'm sorry, yes."

170

"Then let us look at something else."

He is crossing the vestibule before Linette has a chance to register what his intentions are. She rushes to catch him up.

"Where are you going?"

"Where do you think?"

He is already through into the corridor, striding down it to reach Julian's study at the far end, and as they cross the threshold Linette looks about it with distaste.

It is, she thinks, an unhappy room. While Julian might consider it elegant with its shades of red and mahogany, Linette finds it dark and somber. The religious paintings are foreboding, the baroque globe a muddy ball on its axis, Julian's trinket cabinet a profligate display of his wealth.

But it is the books at the far end she likes even less.

As a booklover herself it seems silly she should be so adverse to this ornate collection, yet as Linette and Henry approach those five rows of shelves filled to the brim with ragged tomes, she finds herself looking upon them with resentment.

All they are, all they have ever been, is a reminder that Julian cares more about them than he ever has about her.

Henry clears his throat.

"Your cousin told me these were his collection of books on hermetic philosophy."

A hazy memory is spooling at the back of her mind. Strange circles, complicated star charts, obscure banks of tightly packed text, and Linette shrugs with uninterest.

"Yes. He showed me them once when I was ten."

Henry reaches out his finger to tap the glass that holds the large tome within its own compartment, Julian's gold-flecked stone glinting dully before it.

"Why would an ancient book of philosophy have on it the Tresilian

171

crest? It makes no sense. Such a crest would more likely appear on a family Bible but you have one of those in the cabinet upstairs, and no such symbol appears on *that*."

Linette stares at the book's black leather bindings, the symbol jutting from the cover like veins in a hand.

"What are you saying?"

"I'm saying, is this symbol a crest at all?"

She frowns. "I don't understand."

"Think about it. The likelihood of Beddoe wearing a ring that matches Julian's—a ring with the Tresilian crest on it—is low, unless someone in your family gave him one, which would hardly be appropriate. What gentleman would wear the crest of a family not their own? As I said, it makes no sense. Besides, it doesn't *look* like a crest. What if, then, this symbol is something else entirely?"

"I still don't understand. Are you accusing Julian now?"

At this Henry frowns, as if it were a new consideration.

"You did say," Linette points out, "that your Mr. Fielding always considered the facts and took note of all the people who link to them. It seems you're suggesting that my cousin plays some part in this because of a connection to Dr. Beddoe?"

He blinks, opens his mouth, shuts it again.

"No, that wasn't—I did not—"

"Because such a thing is ridiculous. My cousin barely gave Dr. Evans any mind. How could he, when he was never here?" Linette presses her bottom lip with her teeth. "The Tresilian crest is unusual, I admit, but it has nothing to do with Dr. Evans's death, and surely that is where our focus should lie?"

A muscle ticks in Henry's jaw.

"I am not accusing your cousin of anything. But you have to admit Beddoe has behaved suspiciously and the significance of his ring is perplexing."

172

"Perhaps you were mistaken in that! A fleeting glimpse, you said."

He falls silent, and Linette can see from his expression that doubt has crept its way in. He looks once more at Julian's book.

"All you're doing is chasing shadows," she reasons. "The only thing we can *both* be sure of is the vial and what it contained, and it is that we should be pursuing."

At this Henry's expression grows pensive, and Linette can imagine his thoughts turning like cogs within his head.

"You said Dr. Evans and Beddoe argued?"

Linette considers. "They exchanged the odd disagreeable word about Mamma's treatment. But Henry, that can hardly be a reason why he would want Wynn Evans dead."

"Even so, Beddoe is the only link we have, so we must contrive a way to find out more. Discover if he had a motive, even if one is not immediately obvious."

"All right," she agrees. "I shall ask Enaid, see if there is anything she might know about the nature of their relationship."

"And I can ask the reverend. Mr. Dee said himself they were good friends."

"There then. We can always ask Julian on his return to enlighten us as to the mystery of the rings, if you did indeed see what you thought you saw."

Henry chews his inner cheek. Linette sighs.

"Come. We gain nothing by staying here."

In the soft grip of her hand he reluctantly allows her to lead him away, and together they cross Julian's sitting room. Near the armchairs, however, he pauses. Narrows his eyes.

"What is it now?"

Without a word Henry squeezes past, and it is only when he stops to stand at Julian's gun cabinet that Linette realizes what he is about.

"No one *here* shot at you."

She comes to stand next to him where he is staring at the pistol behind the glass in consternation.

"How do you know?"

"Because my servants would never do such a thing."

He throws her a frustrated look. "And I ask again, how do you *know*?"

Before she can reply Cadoc Powell appears at the door, carrying an empty decanter between both gloved hands. The butler stops when he sees them, ducks his head in acknowledgment, his stiff wig making him look like a stern judge.

"Miss Linette. Dr. Talbot. Might I be of assistance?"

Linette and Henry share a glance.

"I wanted to look at the flintlock," Henry says, and one of Cadoc's bushy eyebrows quirks.

"To what purpose?"

"I wished to hold it, that's all."

There is a pause. The butler looks to Linette for permission and grudgingly, she nods her assent. Cadoc crosses the room, places the decanter on a silver tray set upon the marquetry table beside Julian's armchair. Then he removes a chain from within his waistcoat, from which in turn dangles a set of keys which unlock the cabinets that hold the Cadwalladr heirlooms.

Cadoc selects a tiny brass key from the chain, inserts it into the cabinet's minuscule lock. Carefully he removes the pistol, places it into Henry's waiting hands. Linette watches him admire the barrel's inlay of tortoiseshell. It is a beautiful thing, more a decorative piece, not suited for hunting at all. Linette cannot understand why he should think this was the gun which had been used.

"How do you load it?"

Cadoc frowns, looks to her. Linette shrugs.

"Show him."

The butler takes the flintlock back from Henry, turns it over. He does not seem to know how to open the barrel, is frowning in concentration, but then he pushes his thumb against a curved node at the top, something clicks, a canister opens, and five bullets roll into the butler's gloved hand.

For a moment Henry does not speak. Is he relieved? Disappointed? From the blank expression on his face, Linette cannot tell.

"Thank you," Henry says faintly. "That's all I wanted to see."

There is a pause in which Cadoc stares at him. Then the butler neatly reloads the pistol, returns it to the cabinet, turns the key.

"If that will be all, Miss Linette?"

"Yes, Cadoc. That will be all."

The butler looks between them. She cannot read the expression on his face, either, but she can feel the force of Cadoc's disapproval coming off him in waves.

"Very good."

He stares at them each in turn one final time before leaving the room. It is only when the heavy door swings shut behind him that Linette turns to Henry.

"Would you mind telling me what that achieved?"

"The shot was fired from a pistol," he says, eyes fierce. "One that would be fired at close range. A flintlock."

"How can you know that?"

"I know bullets. I used to remove them regularly in my line of work. I recognize a flintlock ball when I see one. Still," he says, begrudging. "Flintlocks only carry five bullets."

"Exactly. The one here still has all five."

"Yes." He runs a thumb over his lower lip. "It could have been reloaded."

She says nothing to this. Cannot.

Suspecting Cai Jones is one thing—her servants, quite another.

CHAPTER SIXTEEN

The main entrance to the mines is reached by taking a northeastern track out of Penhelyg, deep into the valley of Cwm Nantcol. The way is orderly and well-maintained, free of stray rocks and errant branches, allowing Ivor Morgan's cart to trundle up without incident— it is the one good thing Linette's cousin has done for the miners, although in truth he had Mr. Lambeth build the path for *his* ease and requirement rather than theirs; Julian never travels in anything but a carriage or his own phaeton if he can possibly help it.

Torn down in the name of industry, no trees grow here on this path, but it is banked by buttercup meadows and affords a pleasant view of the valley; down in the fields can be seen lush copses of vegetation that border the farmlands of Linette's hill tenants, and she can spy the finials of Plas Helyg peeking from the dense woodland that surrounds it.

The mine is in a unique position—built horizontally into the lower reaches of the mountains, the spoil-heaps face out to sea. Nowhere else in North Wales can one emerge from caverns in the heart of the rock to find oneself confronted by a grand expanse of ocean, and as Ivor guides the pony and cart upward, Linette twists in her seat. The mid-morning sun is high in the turquoise sky, casting the water into shades of deep cornflower blue, and the brisk wind causes waves to break the surface in long curling crests.

"White horses," she murmurs, and beside her Henry quirks a brow.

"I'm sorry?"

"White horses. It's a term for how the waves look when they rise and fall on a choppy sea. Look how the white ridges appear like a horse's mane?"

The glance Henry spares her is laced with impatience.

"Another superstition?"

"No," Linette says, drawing the word out. "Just a metaphor."

She keeps her eyes on those foam-ridged waves, yawns deeply into her hand. Sleep had not come easily last night, for all Linette could think of was poor Dr. Evans. Before supper she had asked Enaid, as promised, and was not surprised when the old woman only stated with evident confusion (how cruel to keep such dreadful secrets from her!) what Linette already knew: there was no love lost between Dr. Beddoe and her brother, but certainly nothing to cause concern—the two men simply had differing opinions of professional practice. Yet while Linette had not been surprised by the revelation (or lack of, in this case) Henry had been most disappointed. When she told him Enaid's answer his expression turned grave and contemplative, his conversation grew less and less as the evening drew on, so that in the end dinner had been such a stilted affair Linette had excused herself to bed earlier than was her habit. Today Henry has been vexing irritable, right from breakfast to the very moment they boarded Ivor's cart, so she is relieved when Ivor finally brings them to the cavern entrance.

Perhaps meeting the miners will distract them both.

Linette raises her hand in greeting to where the miners are sifting through the yield. She expected them to smile and wave back as they have always done, but now they simply stare as the cart is brought to a stop. Even beneath their dirty faces Linette sees their hostility, the nasty curls of their lips, the pointed stares. Not just the men, but the boys as well.

She jumps down from the cart. Henry follows, slapping straw from his trousers. The air falls silent with an unspoken threat, tempered only by the muted hammering that echoes up from the caverns below, the waterwheel by the entrance, and Linette marks now what Henry did from the very start: their dislike is unreasonable, unprovoked and dangerous, and it fills her with deep-seated dread.

"Good day," she says in Welsh over the sound of rushing water. "The doctor and I have brought refreshments—won't you rest a little?"

The miners shift on their scuffed boots, look almost as if they might refuse her, but then to Linette's relief they lay down their tools. The overseer—Cai Jones's father Rhodri—rings the bell at the mouth of the cavern, and the echoing sounds from within come to a stop.

Linette steps closer to Henry. The look he gives her is clear—*I told you so*—and she cannot quite meet his eye.

"Let us set up over there." She points to a large block of stone that she has always used as a makeshift table. "We won't stay long."

In silence they unload the cart, spread out Mrs. Phillips's fare—baps and cured meats, cheeses and *bara brith*—on cloths of muslin. Henry and Ivor (who, Linette was gratified to note, greeted Henry warmly this morning) maneuver between them the barrel of *cwrw* brought up from the tavern, and all the while the miners watch him, like red kites on the hunt. It is customary for the men to line up with their tin cups, to take their food from Linette with a smile and a pleasant word, and it was her intention that Henry should serve the miners by her side. She hoped the familiarity of the act would help them thaw to their new doctor, help them see him as a decent man, but the miners continue their frosty-faced silence, and Linette begins to question the merit of her plan. As she and Henry serve them not one of the men says thank you and worse, to her dismay, not one of them will look her in the eye, either. All the while Linette keeps the conversation light, asks after their health, their families, but even though

178

they respond in kind the rapport she has always felt with them seems to slip further and further away. As the line lengthens and more miners emerge from the cavern, the atmosphere turns from uncomfortable silence to something like an unspoken threat, and Linette wants to shout at them for their belligerence.

It is as the line begins to dwindle that there comes the loud rumble of wheels. Peering over the shoulders of the remaining miners, she feels her stomach sink.

"*O na.*"

Henry looks to where Linette stares.

"What is it?"

"An unwelcome visitor."

Indeed, the sight of the small black carriage that has just come to a stop by Ivor's cart is most unwelcome. The fine-legged horse which pulls it tosses its head in the heat, and Rhodri—noting the sweat that dampens its coat like dew—places a tin bowl of water down on the ground. The filly bends its head to drink. As the driver expresses his thanks the carriage door opens and his master, Lord Pennant, steps down, Julian's agent Mr. Lambeth following closely behind.

They lock eyes. Linette has never liked Lord Pennant. Though a Welshman by birth he is just as uninterested in his workers as Julian is, and she scowls at him from beneath the wide brim of her hat. Lord Pennant disguises his surprise at seeing her with a look of amusement. Mr. Lambeth—whom she likes even less—shakes his head in disapproval. Linette turns to Henry.

"Will you be all right a moment?"

She glances at the miners. Only ten or so left.

Henry nods. "I hardly think any of them will try to kill me here, do you?"

There is a sardonic twinkle in his eye. Linette feels a tug at her lip.

"You're incorrigible."

She does not wait for him to answer. Instead, Linette wipes her hands on the front of her trousers, stalks over to the two men with as much dignity as she can muster.

"What are *you* doing here?"

The remaining miners loiter, sullen eyes flicking between Linette and the finely suited men. An element of fear has crept into the air now that was not there with Henry alone, and Linette can well understand it for Mr. Lambeth is a nasty weasel of a man with a tongue as sharp as shale.

"Get back to work," he snaps in clipped mispronounced Welsh. In his gloved hands he holds a leather folder and pencil. A report book, no doubt, and Linette narrows her eyes at him.

"They deserve a rest, surely? One hour's respite will do no harm."

The agent says nothing, merely lifts his mouth into a sneer. Lord Pennant steps forward, fingers tucked around the wide lapels of his dress coat. A gold ring on his fifth catches in the noonday sun, and Linette's breath falters in her throat.

Has he always worn one? But of course, many men of his station do. It means nothing at all.

"Linette, my dear," Lord Pennant says now, cloying as treacle. "Gracious as ever. A beautiful day, is it not?"

"Lord Pennant," Linette says with every ounce of patience she possesses. "You have no business here."

"I do, as a matter of fact." The older man licks a fingertip, teases a stray hair of his brown coiled wig back into place. "But I might ask you the same thing. The mines are your cousin's concern, not yours."

"I bring my *tenants* refreshment," she replies, scathing. "I also thought it an opportunity to show Dr. Talbot the mines."

Linette gestures to where Henry serves the last of the miners. One of them snatches his tin cup back the moment it has been filled, and stalks away into the shaded canopy of a stony outcrop. She can see the hard jut of Henry's jaw, the effort it must be taking him to keep his temper, and Linette is sorry now they ever came at all.

"Ah, the elusive Henry Talbot!"

Henry looks up at the sound of his name.

"What a relief to finally see him here," Lord Pennant adds, preening almost. "Will you not introduce us? I should *very* much like to meet Penhelyg's new physician."

She would very much like to push him over the spoil-heaps, but with a tight smile Linette beckons to Henry, and with an expression bordering on relief he joins them.

"This is Lord Pennant. His lordship owns the shipbuilding business in Abermaw and is Plas Helyg's nearest neighbor." The men shake hands. Pointedly, the other man clears his throat. "And this is Mr. Matthew Lambeth, Julian's agent."

"A pleasure," Henry says, and Linette is gratified to hear he does not sound pleased.

Lord Pennant releases Henry's hand, looks him up and down as if he were a specimen in a bell jar.

"Well, Dr. Talbot," he says, "your new charges are fortunate indeed to have such a young and hearty-looking fellow take on the position. Beddoe was telling me only the other week how frail old Evans had become, near the end."

Beside her, Henry goes very still. "Indeed?"

"Indeed so," comes the answer. "I saw him up at Selwyn's place, treating one of her ladyship's migraines—" here he leans conspiratorially in, and Linette detects the piquant scent of garlic on his breath—"she worries most dreadfully, poor thing, and we spoke of it then. We both agreed Penhelyg needed an able-bodied doctor, not one who seems likely to keel over the moment a gust of wind touches him. And here you are!"

He laughs. Mr. Lambeth joins in. All Linette can do is scowl.

"It is my understanding," replies Henry, "that Dr. Evans was fit as a fiddle."

There is a beat of silence. Lord Pennant raises his eyebrows in a show of surprise.

"Is that so? Well, I never knew him personally, of course. We followed very different social circles, you see. *Very* different!"

They laugh again, and a stone of dislike slams into the cushion of Linette's gut.

"I confess," his lordship resumes, "I think Beddoe should always have had the role as part of his practice. And your cousin does pay uncommonly well—Sir John is far less generous, I'm afraid." His lordship sighs dramatically. "Still, no matter! Everything has turned out beautifully for here you are, and just the ticket too!"

Linette steals a glance at Henry, his narrowed eyes. Is this what he might call motive? Not trusting herself to hold her tongue, she turns her face away toward the sea. Far out she spies the white sails of a coasting brig, a schooner heading into high waters.

"Of course," Lord Pennant continues, falsely commiserating, "I imagine you must be having some difficulty acclimating. The language is *devilishly* hard!"

"I agree, but Miss Tresilian is teaching me."

After their less than fruitful visit to Julian's study, Henry suggested they begin their lessons. Linette had chosen the green book of Welsh folklore for him to translate, to which Henry's response was to look at her sourly.

"Are you trying to vex me?"

"Not at all," she returned. "I'm trying to make you understand."

"I don't need to understand your folklore," he replied stubbornly. "Just your language."

"But they are one and the same. Our language is part of our identity, and with that identity comes an understanding of our past. This," she added, giving the book a tap, "*is* our past. You cannot learn one without the other."

Henry had looked dubious. "Even so—"

"You don't need to believe them," Linette replied with more patience than she felt. "You don't even need to appreciate them. You just need to acknowledge them." She opened the book of folklore to its first story. "You may begin with 'The Lady of the Lake.'"

In truth, Linette finds many of the tales fanciful herself—how, for instance, can a woman live at the bottom of a lake and bring forth from it a whole herd of cows? Yet while she may not accept them as truth, she can never dismiss the stories completely. As she told Henry, legends must come from somewhere, and to be blind to them would be to turn her back on her homeland, something Linette is unable to do.

Now she turns her face back, and Lord Pennant is pinning Linette with a smile that does not reach his beady eyes.

"Is she now? Well, I commend you, doctor, though I hardly think it necessary."

"I can't do my job without the language," Henry responds, sharp. "It seems a necessary requirement to me."

"Are you sure?" Mr. Lambeth, this, his mid-county burr in full force. "The people of Wales must learn English at some point. It is the future."

"Then how do you manage, as agent?"

Mr. Lambeth shrugs. "I know enough Welsh to give orders. That's all that is required, and thankfully mining is not a difficult job. Even dogs know how to follow simple instructions."

Linette's anger begins to boil, a hot ache in her throat that has her fists clenching. Henry moves imperceptibly; she feels the warning touch of his hand in the small of her back.

"What business do you have here, my lord?" Linette manages. "You did not answer."

"I didn't, did I?"

Henry removes the pressure of his fingers. The older man clucks his tongue to the roof of his mouth. He and Mr. Lambeth share a look.

"Well," he says with a shrug, "it's no secret. Your cousin is expanding again, plans to go deeper. He has asked me to inspect the lower caverns for the new pulley systems. I need to know how much wood to provide for the job."

Linette stares. "He plans to expand again?"

It is the last thing the miners need. It is the last thing the *mines* need—have they not been unsafe for years? But before she can voice her concerns, Henry does it for her.

"Surely it would depend on the capacity of the mountain and what is safe for the workers?"

"Very true," Lord Pennant replies, "but we have requirements, a very particular vision to fulfil. Is that not so, Lambeth?"

The agent smiles, gives Henry a long appraising look.

"Just so, my lord. I used to be a stonemason, many years ago—I know how best to make stone yield safely. But perhaps, Dr. Talbot, you would like to see for yourself?"

The caverns are cold.

It is a peculiar feeling, to experience such cloying heat and then—as if by the turn of a wheel—a coolness that seems to strip heat from bone. Linette's shirt (which outside had started sticking between her shoulder blades) is chill now against her skin, and she begins to unravel the full sleeves to cover her forearms, shivering into her necktie.

She has never been down the copper mine before. The cavernous ceiling is high; in the moss-lined eaves pigeons coo in their stone roosts, and as they continue their descent down narrow steps the color of rust Linette is reminded of a holy shrine, a natural cathedral. All around her are the sounds of water droplets tapping rhythmically down from the rock, and she can hear the different cadences of them—a metallic *tick* when they hit a cart or tool, a light *slick* when they land on stone, a dull *thud* when they fall on the lip of her hat.

Ahead, Lord Pennant pats his coiled wig.

Rhodri leads them down into the lower caverns, pebbles skimming beneath their boots. The echoing sounds that could be heard from above grow louder for they are in the thick of it now, and as they reach the bottom of the steps the light becomes denser. Linette looks over her shoulder. Above, the cavern entrance is now a crescent moon; the rock ceiling has reduced by half, and the only light is from the guttering candles on the miners' tin hats. As they pass by them their faces are thrown into devilish relief, making the scowls that line their faces more pronounced. This time, though, those scowls are directed at all of them, not just at Henry. As they squeeze past a windlass, Linette worries her bottom lip.

Colder now. The chambers begin as large and spacious caverns— remnants of earlier dig sites with no more yield—and in some Linette catches a glimpse of strange formations like rough downward spears.

"What are they?" she calls up to Rhodri, and his voice throws echoes behind him.

"Stalactites, milady. Nature's taking the mine back. We've not worked those particular caverns for years."

The deeper they go, however, the more oddly shaped the chambers become, making it necessary to walk in single file and duck their heads to fit through. How many years has it been since they began mining for copper here? Twenty? More? So many empty caverns! No wonder Julian wishes to go deeper into the mountain. As they pass

185

even smaller caverns veering off from the silt track, Linette spies blocked-off doorways barred with timber, others with offerings of food and water for the *bwcaod* and *coblynau*. With a wry smile Linette wonders what Henry will think of *those* when he reads about them in her book.

That is not all she sees. The too-narrow way is cluttered with wooden carts led by hunch-backed donkeys, the ground littered with discarded pickaxes, chisels, and shovels. The walls and lowering ceilings are held up in places with large pillars of wood which, to Linette's mind, cannot safely secure them. Shooting off the tapering path are more active chambers, every one filled with a crowding of dirty-faced miners. Some kneel at the bases of walls, a mutton-fat candle at their side, but others—to reach the higher walls of the caverns—hang suspended from chains around their left leg, balancing their weight on the other as they chip away at the stone. Linette swallows as a younger lad bows over a large crevice in one of the upper corners, chain swinging precariously.

The path inclines briefly before slanting down again. They pass under carved-out vents in the ceiling, the air growing cooler the deeper they go, and a sharp sort of cold settles uncomfortably between Linette's ribs. For a moment she experiences a sense of claustrophobia, and though she can see Rhodri's candle leading the way she runs a hand along the rough-hewn walls to keep her bearings in the semi-dark. Beneath her palm the stone is slick with water and algae, and while the air is sharply fresh, every now and then there comes a faint sulfuric smell.

"Nearly there."

Mr. Lambeth's voice trips itself down the line. Linette swallows in relief. How, she wonders as they continue down, can the miners bear it? Even though she knew generally what mining entailed she has never seen them at work, and the reality of it claws at her heart.

Finally, the group reach a chamber, three barrels propped against its entrance. Rhodri guides them in. It is deathly quiet. Two candles are set on some wooden planking beside a pair of rusting cartwheels. The walls are extremely rough here, barely chiseled out from the rockface, red and ochre-tinged. This final cavern is only high enough to stand in with their heads tilted at an angle, but Lord Pennant—a much smaller man—can remain fully upright with no trouble at all, and he looks about the chamber with interest.

"Hmm. I see." He taps a fingernail to his chin. "I imagined the deeper into the mountain we went, the larger the caverns would become. Getting the wood down here will be monstrous difficult." Lord Pennant spreads his hands in a sweeping gesture. "I pictured a wonderful open cave, a little like the one we entered through, with pulleys and levers that would send the miners up and down, allowing them to work across a much wider area. The mines, as I'm sure you must agree, would benefit greatly from such a system."

The candle Rhodri holds flickers. In the wake of it, Henry clears his throat.

"Do the mines *need* expanding?"

"Oh yes!" Lord Pennant exclaims. "And we shall, I'm sure, find a more lucrative yield by doing so."

"More lucrative than copper?"

He looks inordinately pleased with Henry's question.

"More copper, certainly. But . . ."

Lord Pennant and Mr. Lambeth share a look.

"Gold."

Linette laughs then, cannot help it. The older man narrows his eyes, the pandering smile he has been wearing slipping like water over slate.

"Not this again," Linette says, quite unable to keep the scorn from her voice. "My cousin has been searching years for such a yield without success. You're both fanatical."

187

Mr. Lambeth regards her coldly.

"And you, Miss Tresilian, would do wise to keep a civil tongue in your head."

"A little difficult when his lordship speaks such nonsense."

Beside her, Henry lets out his breath. "Linette . . ."

"Ah!" Lord Pennant exclaims, buoyant again. "Dr. Talbot also dislikes that vicious sting in your tongue. Do *you*, my dear doctor, not see the merit in our plans? Expansion, investment, that's the ticket! These are rich lands, to be sure, and I do not think the scheme so far outside the realms of reality."

"Perhaps not, sir, but matters of safety must be considered. These mines are already overcrowded and I see precious few measures in place to secure the workers' protection. Some of them are mere children. I've already been advised there have been accidents. Deaths. Dr. Evans set some broken arms this past year, so I understand, and two years ago one lad—a Cai Jones—broke his leg and has been unable to work since. If you wish to expand, such considerations *must* be made."

At his son's name Rhodri had looked up and stared at Henry, hard. It is a shame, Linette thinks, that the man does not understand how Henry came to Cai's defense just then. Lord Pennant, however, does understand Henry's words but has no care for them—Linette can tell by the stubborn pout of his lip, the dismissive nodding that makes the tight curls of his mousy wig bob.

"That," he says, "is all by the by. There's no shortage of men available for challenging work—"

"Not here," Linette cuts in. "The only men left in Penhelyg are the farmers, and you cannot employ *them*."

"The shortfall can be employed across the border, if the Welsh will not oblige. Further afield, if necessary."

"But not everyone will agree to work in such conditions. We do not have slaves here, unlike in your Jamaican plantations."

188

Lord Pennant hesitates. He did not, it seems, realize she knew.

"How do they fare, by the way?" Linette adds drily. "I would have thought that with the abolitionists gaining ground your days of easy money are numbered. I wonder, sir, if that is why your ships are such a commodity? You must be rather desperate to fatten your pocketbook nowadays."

Again, Henry touches her back, but she cannot help it—it is one of Linette's few pleasures in life, to watch men like Lord Pennant squirm. Indeed, despite the dimness of the cavern she can see his cheeks have reddened to puce.

"Your tongue will get you in trouble, one day," he says softly. "It is a shame that you have such a narrow-minded attitude. Your cousin is completely the opposite, a truly enterprising man."

Linette presses her lips. Henry drops his hand from her back. Rhodri, still hovering at the cavern entrance, sniffs loudly, clearly impatient at listening to a conversation he does not understand, and Mr. Lambeth notices, tucks the leather folder underneath his arm.

"Time to go, I think."

"Yes," Lord Pennant returns. "I believe I've gleaned all I can here. Shall we?"

With one last pointed look at Linette, Lord Pennant turns on his heel and the men retreat from the cavern, Rhodri leading the way, leaving Linette and Henry alone. She turns to him, fully expecting him to scold her, but strangely he is staring at the far end of the cavern into the deep dark, eyes narrowed into slits.

"Henry, what is it?"

"I . . . I thought . . ." He sounds confused. "I thought I saw some lights."

"Lights?"

"Like candles, but somehow . . ."

Linette steps past him, looks into the murk.

"I can't see anything. Candles, you say?"

"Yes," Henry murmurs, "but they were different colors. Two red, one blue. Of course, that's ridiculous."

Uneasy, Linette stares at him.

"A trick of the light," she murmurs. "The tunnels must go farther back, and you saw some miners crossing one of the paths. That is all."

Henry stares a moment longer, then shakes himself as if coming to his senses.

"You're right, of course. The enclosed space must be playing tricks on my mind."

His words are firm, but Linette can see from his face he does not believe them.

"Come," she says. "Let us go back before we cannot see our way out."

CHAPTER SEVENTEEN

Henry sleeps fitfully, his mind too alive to settle properly, and at a quarter to one o'clock he finds himself wide awake, staring up at the ceiling and its ornamental grooves. Absently he presses the rough points of the whelk shell Mrs. Morgan gave him with his fingers; he finds it soothes him, helps ground his perilous thoughts, nature's own little anxiety relief.

A murdered man. A poisoned vial. A strange symbol. These are facts he is sure of. What he is not sure of are the circumstances of those facts. Why is the vial of such unusual design? Why should it possess the remnants of nature's deadliest poison, a poison obviously administered to Dr. Evans? He had no enemies, according to Linette, but that is blatantly untrue. *Someone* wanted him dead. His sister claims there was no ill-feeling between the rival doctors, but that Beddoe is involved seems at present far too likely—from what Lord Pennant revealed earlier at the mine, it seems Beddoe had his eye on Wynn Evans's position in Penhelyg, and there can be no denying that Criccieth's doctor was altogether too suspect in the answers he provided when Henry questioned him.

And, of course, there is the ring. He has played the final moments of his visit to Beddoe over and over in his mind, and Henry is sure— absolutely positive, despite his glancing view of it—that he saw the symbol on the older man's ring. So, then, what does that signify? What connection does it have to the Tresilians?

Before, Henry prided himself on logic. *Before*, before the mess with Viscount Baverstock, Henry had always felt sure of himself, especially in matters of medicine and science. But this is beyond his capabilities. He feels utterly at sea.

Should he write to Francis, ask for his advice? For a brief moment Henry seriously considers the notion, sits up in bed to fetch paper and quill, until a thought makes him sit back against the pillows again in disappointment. Meirionydd is out of Bow Street's jurisdiction. He would only advise Henry to seek out the magistrate. But considering that magistrate is Lord Pennant, a man who appears to be closely acquainted with Criccieth's doctor . . .

Henry clenches the shell. He knew he would not like Plas Helyg's neighbor when he finally met him. His opinions on Dr. Evans aside, Henry found him a self-centred, condescending man. All the while Lord Pennant was speaking in that last cavern Henry strived to practice patience. He will not ever forget the boy he saw hanging from the ceiling, a chain around his leg. A boy! The lad could not have been more than fifteen years old. With unease Henry thinks of Cai Jones, his ungainly limp. And so while Linette and the two men exchanged their loaded words he stared into the dark . . . until that dark was marred by those strange colored lights.

Two red, one blue.

They truly had looked like candles at first, but what candle flame possesses such strange hues? It is true that sometimes a flame might burn blue at the very center of the wick if one were to look closely, but from where Henry was standing in the cavern he would not have been able to see it. And as for red, well, no candle he has ever seen could burn that fierce a color. So, what were they? He knows he saw them, despite what he told Linette.

He knows he did.

Henry puzzles over it now as the grandfather clock below chimes the hour. His pocketwatch sounds the minutes, and he lies there listening to its regimental *tick-tick-tick* with growing frustration. At one-thirty he gets out of bed, uses the chamber pot. At two Henry gives up completely and lights a candle, fetches the Welsh dictionary, the book of Welsh folklore, his creased and scribbled translations.

It is a distraction, if nothing else.

He has already translated the tale of "The Lady of the Lake," one chapter about an old woman who outwitted the Devil after he built her a bridge, and another about a witch who turned into a hen and ate her son. One chapter spoke about the dastardly deeds of fairies. *Y tylwyth teg* they are called here, and Henry has never heard of anything so ridiculous. Some (so the book says) make violins that bewitch people to dance without stopping, others tempt people with gold, only to then curse them for touching it. Some even steal children.

In London children go missing as often as whores open their legs. Many are runaways, escaping a life of abuse and poverty; many more are sold into slavery or to brothels and molly houses. Others . . . well. Bodies are fished out of the Thames every month. Sometimes the surgeons at Guy's use their cadavers for anatomy lessons, including Henry himself.

These are true stories. These are unfortunate facts. Nothing fanciful about them. But for children to go missing at the expense of a *fairy*?

Complete and utter nonsense.

Henry opens the book on the next chapter, reads the title.
Coblynau.

It takes Henry a while to translate the first paragraph. In the guttering candlelight he squints between page and dictionary, diligently marks the vellum with his pencil until, at length, he is done:

A creature similar to the bwcaod, which haunts the mines, quarries and secret places of our majestic mountains. Such beings are known to knock on the walls so as to lead miners to rich veins of ore, and are therefore considered to be creatures of good luck and fortune. Ensure they are given ample award of food and water, for they have a nasty temperament! It is said that if one were to offend such a being they have been known to throw stones, steal food and tools, extinguish lanterns or, worse, may endeavor to cause a rockslide or cave-in, resulting in a most terrible and dastardly death.

With a huff Henry flings the books on the coverlet, his translations with them, rests back against the headboard. He looks at the pocketwatch:

Three twenty-two.

He snaps the lid shut. Stares at the ceiling.

Tick-tick-tick.

A hoot of an owl outside.

Tick-tick-tick.

Henry presses his temples.

Tick-tick-tick.

A rustle at the door.

Henry shoots up in bed, instantly alert. For a drawn-out second there is nothing, but then the sound comes again.

Shuffling on carpet.

"Linette?"

No reply. Instead the sound moves off, retreats down the corridor like a whisper. Henry swings his legs out of bed, swiftly moves to the bedroom door. Opens it.

Nobody there.

Uncertain, Henry steps out into the corridor. The moon is waxing; he can tell for the corridor is bright, and he shifts to look at the view from its windows.

There is a whiteish light across the willow trees. The silhouettes of mountains stand tall against a royal blue sky, marred only by a thin whisp of silver cloud, and Henry presses his face to the window. Stars blink down at him like milky eyes. He is amazed how bright they are, and it occurs to him then that this is the first time he has ever seen the stars look like this. Did he even see them in London? Did he ever dare look up? Or had he always been too distracted by work, too preoccupied with flesh and bone to notice nature's more palatable gifts?

He turns away, walks the corridor. The family portraits stare down at him, and he comes to a stop beneath the one of Gwen, Hugh, and Julian. Again he regards its unusual detail. His eyes pass over the gleaming coins, the sapphires, the skull, rest then on the gold dagger. Henry sucks in his breath. *Again*, that symbol: it has been painted on the dagger's blade!

Suddenly a muffled cry breaks the silence from the floor above, and there comes then the sound of a door, thundering feet that beat across the upper corridor. They rush down the stairs with all the ferocity of a bull, and then the small door leading to the third floor flies open with a bang.

Enaid Evans stands at the threshold in her nightdress, eyes bright with fear.

"Dr. Talbot!" she cries upon seeing him. "The mistress—she's gone!"

"Gone?"

"I woke up and she was not in her bed!"

Henry takes her soft arm. The old woman trembles in his grasp, the frills of her lace nightcap trembling with her.

"I'm sure she's not gone far," Henry soothes. "I heard a rustling at my door not five minutes ago. It must have been her."

"You don't understand!" the old woman cries. "She's been known to wander outside at night. We must retrieve her before she gets to the front door!"

195

"Enaid?"

Linette—eyes heavy with sleep—appears at the bottom of the stairs. She is pulling an oversized dressing gown around her lean shoulders, trapping her long hair underneath its collar so it looks as though it has been cut short at her neck. Henry can smell that now familiar hint of vanilla on the air.

"What is it? What has happened?"

"Your mother's out of bed," Henry provides, and Linette pulls the strings of the gown tight around her waist.

"Why didn't you lock the door?" she asks Enaid, to which the old woman wrings her hands again.

"I did! She took the key when I wasn't looking!"

Linette sighs, meets Henry's gaze across the old woman's head.

"She does this sometimes. Will you help?"

Henry inclines his head. "You know you need not ask."

They find Gwen Tresilian in the vestibule, though she is not attempting to open Plas Helyg's wide front door as Mrs. Evans had feared. Instead she stands, motionless, in front of the chasm-like fireplace.

The housekeeper sighs with relief.

"My lady! Come, now, come back to bed."

Lady Gwen is swaying. Henry approaches her cautiously on one side, Linette on the other, and he is struck with the notion of them stalking innocent prey, a cruel game of cat and mouse.

"Can you hear them?" she whispers.

"I can't hear anything," Henry says. "What is it you hear?"

"Wings. Beating. Poor, poor thing!"

Henry shares a look with Linette. She shakes her head tiredly.

"Mamma," she says, gentle. "Do as Enaid asks. There's nothing for you down here."

"But there were people in the room," Lady Gwen replies, and takes a breath that sounds more like a sob.

"Which room?" he presses. "What people?"

"They were calling him."

"Calling *who*?"

But she does not answer. Henry reaches out; the older woman allows herself to be turned. She looks up tearfully—eyes like pools of ink—before her gaze falls downward to his throat.

Her eyes widen. Before Henry can stop her she reaches for the collar of his nightshirt where it lies open at the neck.

"No," she moans, pressing her fingertips against his skin. "No," she cries, louder now, and again she looks up into his face. Her eyes shine with unshed tears. "You're marked! Not real. Not real! You cannot—"

But Mrs. Evans is dragging her away, Linette at her other arm, concern and confusion etched across her face, and Lady Gwen says nothing more.

CHAPTER EIGHTEEN

He rises late, the sun already high in the sky, blinding-bright.

In front of the mirror Henry dips his razor into the fresh bowl of warm water that Powell brought up together with his clean clothes. He scrapes the blade across the plane of his jaw, sucks in his breath as a spot of blood blooms on his neck. Henry reaches for the towel, pats his skin to stem the flow.

When it stops bleeding he examines the birthmark that so upset Gwen Tresilian last night. He always made care to keep it hidden by collar and cravat, but the sight never particularly bothered him. In fact he found the mark fascinating as a child, perhaps it was even the initial reason for pursuing a career in medicine. What made the skin produce such discoloration? What differentiated the anomaly from that of normal tissue? The notion was captivating.

Venous malformations was what the anatomist William Hunter called such marks, though Henry did not know the name in those early years. No, indeed, this information was imparted from a lecture he once heard the older man give during his apprenticeship, and Henry credits him for his own pursuit of the task at Guy's. He stretches the skin with his fingers. The mark is livid purple in color, like grape juice on linen. He runs his thumb over it—no raised bumps, no hairs . . . no change.

Satisfied, Henry reaches for his cravat.

He needs to check on his charge. Henry takes the stairs to the third floor and the vanilla scent hits him as soon as he opens the door, making his eyes water. The smell is not unpleasant but it is cloying, and for the first time he finds himself more than passing curious as to why Lady Gwen's rooms are filled with the flowers responsible for that perfume. Is it another superstition? Or mere decoration only?

There is no answer to his knock. He tries the handle; the door opens easily. The rooms are, for once, flooded with light, the windows open wide, and the sound of birdsong trickles through them, taffeta curtains blowing gently in the breeze. Mrs. Evans's trundle bed is neatly made. He crosses beneath the floral overhang to the bedroom, but Henry can already see from the threshold that the bed is empty, its sheets pulled back for airing.

No one is here.

Henry looks about the room. In daylight it appears drab—threadbare carpets, moth-eaten curtains. Even Mrs. Evans's trundle bed seems, somehow, *less*. Henry regards the lumpy mattress with distaste. What way is this to live? He sighs, turns his head. A harp stands near the window and he goes over to it, plucks its strings. The sound is gentle, resonant, the mellow note lingering in the air. Thoughtfully he looks out over the grounds. The bedchamber faces the gardens; box hedges, a large pond filled with lily pads the size of dinner plates. And there, walking the paved footpath surrounding it, is Lady Gwen, a wraith in white.

She is alone. This, then, is an advantage. Henry told Linette that he could not deduce madness from one hysterical episode alone. Here is an opportunity to observe her without the eagle eyes of Enaid Evans to curtail him; always she has hovered like a stern sentinel, making Henry's job damnably difficult. Even though the housekeeper's reserve has begun to thaw these past few days, Henry has not missed the way she still looks at him as if trying to take his measure.

If Henry does not speak to Gwen Tresilian now then his chance at finding her alone again is very slim indeed.

Outside, Plas Helyg is steeped in bright sunshine. The air is sweet, and a warm breeze lifts the curls at his crown. In the far distance he can make out the faint sound of the sea like a rumbling sigh upon the horizon.

Henry follows the gravel path around the side of the house in the direction of the ornamental garden, crosses the lawn in long fast strides. Lady Gwen is lingering now at the top of the pond under the shade of some trees, watching the fountain with a dreamlike expression on her face. She is dressed in a flowing nightgown; from beneath the hem peek bare toes. Her long white hair is loose; it hangs down her back in thin ropelike strands, but the way they capture the glow of sunlight makes them look, almost, like spun silver.

How different she looks from the portrait, he thinks. How changed. Though her beauty is still etched into the thin plane of her face it pales in comparison to the loveliness captured in oil. The boldness Henry saw staring out of the canvas no longer exists, a mere watermark on silk.

"My lady?"

Gwen Tresilian tears her gaze from the fountain. She looks for a long moment as if she does not know him, but then her face splits into one of recognition.

"*Bore da*, Dr. Talbot."

Her voice is soft, quiet, as if that too has been watered down.

"Good morning. How do you feel today?"

When he, Linette and Mrs. Evans guided her back to bed last night she had cried the entire way. Henry wants to ask if she remembers what she said—such odd things—but then Linette warned him that her mother uttered many things which made no sense. Would there be any use trying to remind her of it?

She answers him now with a sigh, reaches up to rub her left eye.

200

Gwen is not wearing the veil Linette mentioned. Perhaps, Henry thinks, she does not need one for the trees here provide plenty of shade. Still, it is bright outside, bright enough that it should cause her eyes discomfort of *some* sort. . . .

"Do they bother you, my lady?"

She nods. "Ache."

"Where is your veil?"

"I do not like it."

"But where is it?"

Lady Gwen looks as if she is trying to recall, but then she plucks a creamy flower from one of the nearby trees, holds it out to Henry in her small and delicate hand.

It tremors slightly. He has not noticed a tremor before.

"*Criafolen*," she murmurs. "Rowan. The tree of enchantment. Its berries will come soon."

Henry hesitates, takes the flower from her. She turns back to the fountain and politely he watches it with her, its merry trickle.

"You play the harp," Henry says after a moment, and Lady Gwen pulls her eyes back, the soft smile that crosses her lips the very twin of Linette's when she chooses to bestow it.

"*Ydw*, I've played since I was a child. The only true pleasure I have."

"What of your daughter? Is she not a pleasure?"

A beat. "My daughter?"

"Linette."

Gwen Tresilian frowns. "I don't have a daughter."

A knot tightens in Henry's stomach. Once, in his most lonely years at the Foundling, Henry thought it was the worst thing in the world to have no mother to love him, but now he realizes he was mistaken. This, *this* is worse—it is better to have no mother at all than one who does not recognize her own child. If she cannot even recall her own daughter, what else does she not recall?

"Do you miss your husband?" Henry asks, testing her, and immediately Lady Gwen's face fills with an acute sadness. She remembers *him*, then.

"Every day."

"Can you tell me about him?"

Lady Gwen nods. "A kind man, of noble birth. Father was so proud to unite us." She ghosts a smile. "The Tresilians are of an old Cornish bloodline, did you know that? 'Tis thought the Welsh and Cornish are the purest of Britons, and it pleased Papa to think our ancestry could be joined together. Hugh and Julian, you see, are the last of them."

"The last?"

Another nod, a wistful sigh.

"My husband and his cousin were the only surviving heirs. Their fathers both died young of a wasting disease."

In the lilting pause that follows Henry thinks of Julian's illness. Hereditary, then. If not for Hugh Tresilian's accident, might he have eventually suffered the same fate?

"I'm sorry," he says now. "It's no wonder your husband wanted to memorialize the Tresilian line by adding his family crest to Plas Helyg's furnishings. The symbol above the fireplace is particularly impressive. One would not forget it."

He has said it to test her, to see if—in her more languid state—she might rise to the bait, and her next words confirm his suspicions.

"That is not a crest."

"It isn't?" Henry asks, feigning surprise. "Then what is it?"

But she does not answer, stares unseeing across the pond. Henry touches her arm; the gesture brings her back.

"The goats," she says softly.

Henry frowns. "Goats?"

"It's said they represent vitality."

It seems he is losing her to more of her strange fancies.

Disappointed, Henry is about to change the subject when Lady Gwen turns her pale face to look at him.

"The Tresilian crest, you see. Three goats within a chevron."

That familiar tingle in his fingers again. Wait, he thinks, just *wait* until I tell Linette! Instinct told him that the symbol could not be a crest. But if the symbol is not associated with the Tresilians, what on earth is it?

Suddenly she takes his hands in hers, making him jump. They are very small; Henry feels the barely-there weight of them, marvels how childlike they are. He squeezes her fingers, wills some warmth back into them for despite the heat of the day her hands are freezing cold. Lady Gwen squeezes back.

"You have been wronged, haven't you? Wronged by people you trusted."

The thrill of just moments before cools as Henry's chest tightens, and he automatically pulls away from her.

"Ah yes," she whispers. "I see it clearly. I see many things, you know."

Wary now, Henry watches her. How can she *possibly* know such a thing?

"What things do you see?"

"Things that would terrify you."

He remembers her ravings the night before: *Wings, beating. People in the room, calling him.*

"What things?"

She gazes up at him, gray-green eyes guarded. There is something else about those eyes too, something odd that Henry cannot place. She releases him. The air between them grows so quiet one might hear a pine needle fall in the woods, and in the wake of it the woman takes a shuddering breath.

"Within each of us there lies a devil."

It is not the answer he expected, and Henry is silent a moment. He thinks of his unsympathetic ward nurse who dismissed his nightmares and ignored his cries, the schoolmaster who struck a little too hard with the birch and took pleasure from it. He thinks of the men and women in Bedlam and the people who keep them there. He thinks of the gentleman who died under his scalpel, of the governor's unkindness.

He thinks of himself.

Within each of us there lies a devil.

Flustered, he pulls at his cravat. The humidity of the day must be getting the better of him, he thinks, and in that instant Gwen Tresilian's gaze drops.

"Oh," she says softly, stepping closer. "You've cut yourself."

She reaches out thin fingers to touch his throat. The action shocks him, holds him still. Henry remembers her desperate grasping of last night, but he sees no fraught emotion in her now. Instead he sees only bewilderment; the moment she touched him her forehead had furrowed, causing a deep gully between her fair eyebrows.

"What is it, my lady?" he asks softly.

"I thought . . ." She shakes her head, sucks in her breath. "Last night I had a dream. But it's nothing. 'Tis nothing."

Lady Gwen drops her hand, turns away to the rowan tree, strokes its bouncy blossoms as if they were a robin's breast.

She does not remember, Henry realizes. Her mind does not acknowledge the truth of her subconscious. The laudanum Mrs. Evans administered, then, must have been very potent indeed. He will not trouble with reminding her—her upset last night was so great he does not wish to risk distressing the gentle woman further. And she *is* gentle, Henry thinks, watching Lady Gwen touch the trunk, how she hums a lilting folk tune under her breath . . .

"Milady?"

Across the grass strides Cadoc Powell. He pauses at a bench on the far side of the pond, retrieves from its wooden seat a piece of white diaphanous material (the veil!), before continuing on. As the butler draws closer Henry can see the deep expression of disapproval on his face.

"Come, madam," he says when he reaches them, veil fluttering in the breeze. "Mrs. Evans has charged me to fetch you. It is time for your nap."

As Henry rounds the mansion back the way he came, two things strike him.

The first, that Gwen Tresilian cannot have been awake more than two hours which means a nap is entirely unnecessary. The second is that madness does not rule her.

It is something else altogether.

But what? What caused Lady Gwen's outburst last night, the one before it, all the rest he has not seen?

When a mind is not engaged it becomes stagnant, repressed. There is nothing to entertain her here, nothing to keep her engaged. It is easy to trap oneself within the confines of one's mind, to torture oneself with unpleasant memories when there is nothing else to do. Henry slows a moment before picking up speed once more. Perhaps that is it. Does a *memory* set off her anguished fits? Linette said it was grief that made her mother the way she is. In Henry's experience, grief manifests itself in a variety of ways, all of which the lady of Plas Helyg exhibits in abundance: confusion, sadness, anxiety, agitation. But Henry saw no madness in that pale face just now. Even the strange things she says do not account for such a condition. No indeed, never has he dealt with a patient such as she. Give him a body with something obviously wrong with it and he can apply himself with skill. But Gwen Tresilian has no superficial ailment. Here, he is working blind.

He strides through Plas Helyg's cavernous front doors. There is something else that troubles him about her too, something his trained eye is missing but cannot place. What was it about her today that bothered him so? That has, he realizes, bothered him right from the start?

It is a niggling and frustrating thought to be sure, but it is another more pressing one that drives him in this moment as Henry crosses the vestibule in the direction of Julian Tresilian's study.

Three goats within a chevron.

By rights he should go straight to Linette, but this time Henry needs to look at Julian's book in the cabinet alone, needs to consider this new piece of information without her challenging him at every point. He thinks of the question he asked Linette the other day. Why *would* an ancient book of philosophy have on it a family crest? It made no sense, he told her, and now Henry thinks with a satisfied smile, he has been proved right.

The symbol is something else.

This assurance buoys him, and Henry steps over the threshold of the study with a rising sense of excitement, only to stop dead on the rug.

"Can I help you, sir?"

Angharad is standing at the cabinet of curios, duster in hand. Impossible to look now.

"I got lost," he says, and Henry finds himself flushing at the weakness of the lie. "I meant to find Miss Tresilian's study."

Angharad looks at him shyly.

"That way, sir." She indicates with the duster. "East wing," the maid adds when Henry hesitates too long.

"Thank you. Of course."

He turns, clenching his fists in disappointment. In the vestibule

206

again he considers his next move, and, restless, finds himself returning outside to consider his thoughts on foot.

Books on philosophy, Julian claimed. What else? What were the precise words he used?

Frowning deeply Henry strides up the driveway, passes through the squeaking gates of Plas Helyg. The two paths—the one that takes him down into the village, the other leading to Moelfre—he ignores. Instead he plows into the woodland, and with each stride into the forest is conscious of a rising sense of frustration.

Religion, mysticism . . . Babylon? Henry remembers those words, but not the others connecting to them, for in truth he was not truly listening. He was tired and travel-worn, considered Julian's enthusiasm as nothing more than the arrogance of the *beau monde*.

No matter what the books are, the symbol must be significant for the original stone above the fireplace to be changed. Significant enough to be included on the Tresilian portrait, and—more tellingly—etched into the rings that both Julian and Dr. Beddoe wear.

Henry comes to a patch of wild garlic, slows his pace. A light breeze rustles the hair at the nape of his neck and he removes a handkerchief from his pocket, presses cotton to skin. He breathes in the pungent smell of allium, counts the beating pulse of his heart, and as he waits for it to slow Henry becomes conscious of the distant sound of running water. Deeper he goes, the forest floor twisted with exposed roots, cosseted with bracken, its green fronds spreading across the route like splayed hands, and it occurs to him suddenly what a foolish notion this was—if he takes a fall, no one knows where he has gone.

Beyond, the sound of water grows louder, a crushing roar. At length the woodland opens up to reveal a river, and Henry takes a moment to appreciate it; the water is clear, its bed a mass of pebbles. A heron stands tense on the bank. His eyes follow the river upward, sees that it drops thrice, waterfall upon waterfall.

For a long moment he stands, staring.

There is nothing like this in London. Nothing at all can compare.

Pulling himself away Henry stays close to the riverside, where fading bluebells line the bank, and walks downward until, eventually, the land levels off into a deep grove of willow trees. There is a dirt track here, a sure footpath, and Henry peers back into the dense woodland, tries to think where it might have led from. He listens to the rushing river behind him and then, with a spark of realization, remembers the small stream running behind the gatehouse. Is that where it eventually leads? He is positive he is right, but Henry does not want to go back the way he came to prove it—he wants instead to go further on—and so he meanders along the winding footpath, the grove of bending willows forming an inimitable shade. Above there comes the gentle cooing of a dove and, suddenly, the willows open out.

He stands within a clearing. Above him tower stone walls carved out of the hillside, stark shards of shale and slate, and Henry must crane his head to see the top of its wooded banks. It is a sheer drop; one could break their neck if they fell. Across the whole length of the stone, ferns explode from the cracks like lush green fireworks and moss blankets the lower reaches of the wall like a curtain.

But it is the stone crypt that holds Henry's attention.

It is a large structure reminiscent of a small-scale abbey, constructed from stone with intricate finials which mirror Plas Helyg's at its top. They are connected by an ornately carved arch, a great moss-mottled skull set high in the middle, a cross of Celtic weave design above that. One word has been carved into the arch—CADWALLADR—age having smoothed the letters until they appear to meld together in the stone. The wide doors are decorated with carved willow trees, two large urns spilling more ferns flanking either side. And, kneeling between them, is none other than the Reverend Mr. Owain Dee.

CHAPTER NINETEEN

If Henry had been asked to imagine a traditional Welsh cottage, Mr. Dee's might be what his mind would conjure up. Not ten minutes' walk from the crypt it is a small, whitewashed house with a low lintel which Henry has to duck under to avoid bumping his head. A tiny entryway divides the cottage in two—a small kitchen to the right, a sitting room to the left, with a set of poky stairs leading upward to the first floor. It is pleasantly furnished for a man living on his own, with rustic wooden furniture happily situated, woven rugs lining the stone floor. The house feels too small for the reverend's bulk, but that man moves through it with ease and directs Henry left, gestures to some high-backed wooden chairs and a circular table set under a window overlooking the lush green valley. The mine is visible through the open window, and Henry can even hear the faint sounds of pickaxes on stone, the shouts of miners hard at work. If he squints, Henry can just make out a wagon filled with timber resting near the spoil-heaps.

Lord Pennant, then, wasted no time.

"I only have nettle, Dr. Talbot," Mr. Dee calls from the kitchen. "Will that suffice?"

"I've never had it," Henry calls back.

There is the clatter of pots and pans, then the reverend appears at the sitting-room door, wiping his big hands on a cloth.

209

"I'm afraid a lowly vicar like myself cannot afford such luxuries as brown tea. I'm sure the Tresilians serve better fare, but I'm happy enough with my simplicities."

"I assure you, nettle tea will suit nicely."

Mr. Dee nods, retreats back into the kitchen.

Henry had been startled to see him at the crypt. The reverend too looked surprised but then his face broke into a welcoming smile, and he lifted himself from the forest floor by his crude walking stick.

"Dr. Talbot!" he exclaimed, ambling over, grass stains on his knees. "What a pleasure to see you."

"How d'you do?" Henry answered, hesitant, for it is not common to meet someone in such a strange otherworldly place. Mr. Dee seemed to understand his reserve, for he gestured across to the crypt with his lantern jaw.

"The Cadwalladr tomb. It's where Hugh Tresilian is buried as well as Lady Tresilian's parents, her ancestors before them. I bless their resting place every week."

"At Linette's request?"

"Oh no." He laughed low in his throat. "I've never even known the Lady Linette to visit here, and she has no fondness for prayers. Indeed, she only attends the Sunday service at church because it is her duty. No," he sighed, raising his eyes up at the sheer bank, "I do it because I feel compelled to. As a man of God."

"Ah."

The vicar regarded him. "Are you a man of God, Dr. Talbot?"

"I am not."

"A pity. Are you a man of tea?"

It had not taken much to persuade Henry to return to Mr. Dee's cottage with him. Henry was, he realized, parched and hungry for he had not yet taken breakfast, and so was gratified to accept the invitation. Together they crossed the clearing, took another willow-lined path on the other side. Within minutes they had emerged onto an open field, and Penhelyg's church came into view.

The large man—tall and blocky rather than fleshy and round—had walked briskly, wooden staff swinging between the long grass, and Henry had to rush to catch up with him. The sun disappeared behind a suspect-looking cloud.

"It will rain soon," the vicar said, eyeing it dubiously. "It's in the air. Too hot by half, and the sun doesn't seem to know what to do with itself."

Henry tripped over a hard clod of earth beneath the grasses. Mr. Dee reached out to steady him.

"You'll need a staff if you plan to stay here, Dr. Talbot. Mighty handy if you like to walk, as I do." He tapped his own. "Good solid oak will do you right. Sturdy, stalwart. The forest provides plenty of broken branches in the storms."

They climbed a stile, reached the church on the other side.

Tucked behind a border wall it was small and pretty, with pointed arched windows and trefoils that reminded Henry of clover leaves. Trees stood tall between the gravestones, and lush green ivy coated the walls, spilling over onto the slate roof of the lychgate. He thought Mr. Dee might take him through for a closer look, but instead the man gestured to a path on the opposite side of the lane, leading to the cottage Henry finds himself seated in now.

Penhelyg Church can be spied through a smaller window on the opposite side of the room. He means to look at it again, but as Henry steps toward it his attention is drawn to the stone wall that has, until he stood up, been concealed by a wooden beam. Henry stares, transfixed—hanging from hooks top to bottom are row upon row of wooden spoons.

Mr. Dee returns with two stoneware mugs. Henry takes his, still staring at the wall.

211

"What are they?"

"Lovespoons," the vicar replies, a note of pride in his voice. "A little hobby of mine."

"Lovespoons?"

"Tokens of love," he explains with a slurp of his tea. "It's a custom here."

Henry moves to the wall to take a closer look.

The spoons are all intricately carved with different shapes and patterns. Some have etched within the handle a bird, a vine, a heart. Others a cross, a horseshoe, a lock. The detail, Henry thinks, is remarkable, and he says so.

"How do you make them?"

The vicar puts his mug on the circular table, reaches to the hearth in the corner, picks up a spoon and knife from the mantel and shows them to Henry in explanation.

"I carve them from the oak trees, those here in the woods. Sturdy and stalwart, as I said."

"Do you sell them?"

Mr. Dee rubs the bowl of the spoon with his thumb. "Ethically I shouldn't, of course, considering my profession, but my income is such that I find the extra coin helpful. I take them to market at Harlech, sometimes Abermaw. I don't get much for them, but I must admit it's not just about the money. I carve for pleasure."

With his free hand Henry unhooks one of the lovespoons from the wall, turns it over in his palm. The ladle is small, no different in style to a spoon found on Plas Helyg's dining table, but it is the handle that bewitches. This one has a series of intricate knots intertwined with a heart. Henry runs a thumbnail over the ridges, marvels at the smooth finish.

"This must have taken days," he murmurs.

"It did," the vicar says, smiling at the compliment. "The romantic thing is to think of a young man whittling away in front of the fire for his *cariad*, but these spoons are made by craftsmen. They take years of practice to make well, and I began my craft very young, long before I took my orders. There's a skill to it. This one here," he says, raising the unfinished spoon in his hand; the handle is made up of six wooden spheres in a cage. "The balls are not placed in—they're carved from a single piece of wood."

"Incredible. What do the balls denote?"

"Whatever you like! Some more soft folk like to think of them as the number of children they want to have."

Henry takes a sip of the nettle tea; when he swallows he immediately coughs. The reverend bares his teeth in a grin.

"Bitter, I know. It's an acquired taste, but you get used to it." Mr. Dee watches him with interest. "I suppose you have a lot of things to get used to here. How *are* you settling in?"

Henry does not answer a moment. Instead he replaces the love-spoon back on its hook, picks up another. This one has tiny wheels and elaborate cogs—so delicate—weighing nothing at all in his hand. To think, it's been carved from a single piece of wood.

A skill to it, indeed.

In London people would pay good coin for these spoons. Far more, Henry suspects, than Mr. Dee sells them for here.

"I wish," he says, setting the spoon back on its hook, "that I could say well."

The vicar nods knowingly. "I did think you would struggle."

He replaces the unfinished lovespoon on the mantel, gestures for Henry to take his seat at the table and joining him there, raises his mug of nettle tea to his lips.

"Linette has told me the rumors," Henry says. "About Emyr Cadwalladr."

"Ah."

The reverend does not say anything further, continues to drink his tea with slow measured sips, and it takes Henry a moment to realize he is waiting for him to break the silence. Thoughtfully, Henry regards him. Though he is not a man of God, Henry is perfectly aware of the sanctity of the Church—can Mr. Dee be trusted? Trustworthy or not, he cannot think of anyone else who might be able to shed light on everything that has occurred here, and with a deep sigh Henry sets his own mug of tea down on the table.

"May I speak to you in confidence?"

"Of course you may."

"Did you know the gatehouse was destroyed before I arrived?"

Mr. Dee blinks. "I did not. Who was the culprit?"

"It can only have been one of the villagers, for everyone I've met treats me with a loathing they do not bother to conceal. Some of the boys intimidated me up on the road and scared my horse. Yesterday Linette took me up to the mines, and their dislike was as palpable as if I had struck them. The other day I was shot at."

Until now the vicar has been nodding his head in slow sympathy over the rim of his mug, but this brings him up short.

"Shot at," he echoes.

"Yes."

"Heavens, I am sorry. That is most troubling news indeed."

Henry pauses. *Can* he trust him? But he must say something—it does no good at all to sit and do nothing.

"Indeed," Henry says carefully now, "most troubling. But not so much as what I have to tell you next."

The vicar raises his eyebrows.

"Some days ago I discovered a vial in the wreckage of the gatehouse. It has within it the remains of deadly nightshade."

"Deadly nightshade?"

"A very toxic poison."

214

Mr. Dee lowers his tea. The man's pallor has paled to milk-water.

"Dr. Talbot. Are you intimating what I think you are?"

"I am. Wynn Evans was poisoned."

The vicar sits heavily back in his seat, the look of astonishment on his face unmistakable. He opens his mouth then closes it again, grasps his mug tight between his hands. Then, finally, he shakes his head.

"Are you quite sure of this?"

"The vial was found in the gatehouse—"

"Which you said had been destroyed."

"Yes."

"Perhaps the vial *belonged* to Wynn?"

Henry hesitates. "It is possible, I admit. But it is not a typical apothecary bottle." He describes it. Mr. Dee frowns. "Besides, why would Dr. Evans possess a tincture of pure deadly nightshade? If we consider that, and the look of contortion on his face—"

"I'm sorry?"

The reverend appears confused. It is clear he does not know. Gently Henry explains what Mrs. Evans told him, Rowena Carew's description of the poison's terrible effects.

Mr. Dee stares hard into his mug until a watery sheen appears in his eyes. With a shaking hand he pinches his fingertips to their corners. It is some moments before he lowers them again, and when he looks at Henry once more his cheeks are flushed.

"Who do you suppose could do such a thing?"

Outside, the sounds of chopping wood wend themselves down across the fields from the mine. The sun peeks briefly from behind the billowing clouds before disappearing again, dipping the cottage into shade.

"I have some concerns about Dr. Beddoe."

The reverend sits back again into his seat.

"Why should Elis Beddoe harm Wynn?"

"I was hoping you might be able to shed some light on the matter. Did they get along? Did Wynn say anything to you?"

Mr. Dee shakes his head. "It is true they disapproved of each other's methods. Wynn felt Dr. Beddoe's bedside manner was distinctly lacking, and did not like his caustic attitude to Lady Tresilian's, ah, ailment. He often scolded Wynn on his sympathy towards the villagers and mocked his tolerance of Rowena's herbs." The vicar spreads his hands. "But it was merely professional disagreements, nothing more than that. If it had been he would have surely told me, and the only person who knew him better than myself was Enaid. Have you asked her?"

"Linette did," Henry replies. "And her answer apparently was much the same as yours."

"Well, then. You must be mistaken."

"Perhaps on that point. But there is another. Lord Pennant intimated that Beddoe had designs on Dr. Evans's position here in Penhelyg, that Sir John Selwyn does not pay him well."

Mr. Dee sniffs. "I've heard that Sir John's fortunes have not been favorable for quite some time. He breeds horses. Racing fillies, fine creatures of Turkish lineage. The dapple gray of Lord Tresilian's—that comes from Selwyn stock. For many years he gained quite a profit from them but his thoroughbreds have since stopped producing, and he's lost the sponsorship of the Crown. It does not surprise me that his coffers cannot stretch to paying a personal physician the appropriate wage. Still," the reverend adds, "it's a stretch to say Dr. Beddoe would resort to such extremes. Murder? He had no particular like of Wynn, that is true, but no liking for Penhelyg, either. Salary aside, why should he want the position? Even Criccieth, he once said, held little appeal. I believe he owned a practice in London some twenty years ago, catering exclusively to the rich. It's a wonder he does not return to it—he'd have no lack of patrons, I'm sure."

"Then why doesn't he?"

"I couldn't possibly say."

Thoughtful, Henry taps his cooling mug. Interesting, that Beddoe once kept a high-end London practice. Why on earth, then, would he have relinquished it for a position in Wales? Henry thinks of the doctor's expensively furnished house. His background explains that, at least. Or, perhaps the house has been furnished using different means. Maybe creditors are the problem, and Beddoe *cannot* leave Wales. If the doctor has since fallen on hard times, that could be his motive for murdering Dr. Evans in order to take his more lucrative position. Still . . .

"My suspicions," Henry says now, "arose before I met Lord Pennant. When I questioned Beddoe some days before about Dr. Evans's death he was particularly evasive. And . . . there's something else that's been bothering me."

"Something else?"

"Yes. He wears a ring identical to that of Julian Tresilian. It has a symbol on the signet."

"A symbol?"

Again Henry's fingers tingle, that familiar instinctive pull of intuition.

"Linette always believed the symbol to be the Tresilian family crest, but today I learnt from Lady Gwen this is not the case. The symbol appears too on an antique book Julian collected on his travels, but it's also present on the fireplace at Plas Helyg, and in a portrait of him with his cousin, Hugh, and Lady Gwen. Each of them wears gaudy robes, jeweled turbans, clothes no English aristocrat would usually wear. The background is the kind you might see in the British Museum—temple ruins, that sort of thing."

Something has shifted on Mr. Dee's square face. Henry leans forward.

217

"What is it?"

The reverend looks grim. He takes a long sip of nettle tea before answering, and Henry tries not to squirm with impatience.

"I do not know the symbol of which you speak," he says, slow and measured. "But I believe I can at least enlighten you as to the connection."

"Yes?"

Mr. Dee places his mug very carefully between them, taps the stoneware rim.

"Julian Tresilian, together with Lord Pennant and his wife, as well as Sir John and his, are all part of their own exclusive gentlemen's club. It is, as I understand it, a club for those belonging to the higher echelons of society to promote one another's professional interests, but they've been known to take others of lower stations into their fold. Dr. Beddoe, for one. The land agent Mr. Lambeth, for another." Here, he hesitates. "I know this, because they invited me to join them some years ago. Lord Tresilian showed me a few of his esoteric books. Quite sacrilegious, in my opinion."

"Sacrilegious?"

"Works that held reverence to philosophical magic. The four elements, astrology, scrying, alchemy . . . that sort of thing. Obviously I declined." The vicar shrugs his shoulders. "In any case, *that* is your connection to Elis Beddoe. And from what you say—if the symbol appears in Plas Helyg as well as on the rings—perhaps Gwen and Hugh Tresilian were part of the club too."

Henry sits back in his seat, a suspicion spooling in his stomach.

This makes sense. He has heard of such clubs from his time in Bow Street; the governor at Guy's belonged to one himself in his youth, and had once (so Francis alleged) used its connections to get himself off from a charge of fraud thanks to an affiliated judge. There were whispers, even, of a Bow Street official keeping similar company (a fact of which Francis was rather more close-mouthed). But for a club to favor works on philosophical magic . . . There was a name for such fellowships, a name that left a bitter taste in Henry's mouth:

"Hellfire."

Mr. Dee blinks.

"I'm sorry?"

"Hellfire clubs," Henry repeats. "Secret societies rumored to dabble in, as you put it, philosophical magic. Mostly, though, they were thought to take part in irreligious and immoral acts."

The vicar looks displeased.

"Immoral acts?"

"Indeed. They are a place where one can indulge freely in more unsavory pastimes—unchaste women, gambling, drinking to excess, that sort of thing."

Suddenly another thought occurs. Unbidden, Linette's words echo inside the chamber of Henry's skull: *Rumors of distasteful gatherings. All he cared about was his pleasure.*

Village girls. Heledd Einion. Was Emyr Cadwalladr a Hellfire member himself?

The reverend is shaking his head.

"I confess, I find that hard to accept. Why would they ask me to join such a club, knowing my profession? In any case I do not understand what any of it has got to do with Wynn's death. What proof do you have?"

In that instant, the sun makes its appearance from behind the clouds. It floods the cottage with golden light, one of its rays shining into the vicar's eyes, making his pupils constrict into tiny pinpoints. Any answer Henry might have made is overturned by another answer, an answer that, now he sees it, he can scarce believe he missed, and another part of the puzzle slips into place.

Mr. Dee's expression shifts from skepticism to concern.

"Dr. Talbot?"

"I'm sorry," Henry breathes, rising from the table so fast his chair wobbles. "I'm so sorry," he says again, "but I need to get back to the house."

It is lucky Gwen Tresilian is sleeping when Henry returns to Plas Helyg. Or, rather, it is lucky that she is not awake. It is also lucky no one is in the room to stop him from opening the curtains, to stop him from lifting her thin blue-veined eyelids, to see him confirm his suspicions.

It does not take long for Henry to find the bottles beneath the bed, to remove one from the box and rearrange them in such a way it is not obvious one is missing. It does not take long to open the stopper and sniff its contents, to form his grim conclusion.

The vial from the gatehouse. The vial in his hand. The bottles are exactly the same.

Not one hour ago he had been convinced Dr. Beddoe was responsible for Wynn Evans's murder. He had, after all, been the only obvious suspect. But now? Henry's mouth splits into a grim line as he remembers Owain Dee's words:

The only person who knew him better than myself was Enaid.

CHAPTER TWENTY

In Wales the weather changes as fast as the snap of a finger. Linette woke to bright sunshine, and in Henry's absence she passed a wholly distracting morning tallying the ledgers with the window wide open to the sound of birdsong. But, as the day edged into afternoon, the clouds gathered and the heavens opened, causing the fountain outside to overflow and the hens to seek shelter in their pen. Plas Helyg's stone walls held little of the morning heat, and the house was thrown into such an oppressive gloom that Angharad was soon tasked to build up the fires.

Now, Linette closes Julian's study door behind them, presses her hand against the casement so it clicks quietly into place.

Just moments ago she had happened upon Henry leaving her mother's room; in the dimness of the corridor he looked somber, as if his mind were preoccupied with some dark thought, and that somber expression was enough for her to feel some semblance of alarm.

"Is Mamma all right?"

A beat. "Yes."

Linette sagged with relief. "Does she still speak in riddles?"

"No," he said, hand straying to his trouser pocket.

"Well, that's something, surely?" He did not reply. "I am so sorry about last night. Did she hurt you at all?"

She had peered at his neck then, tried to get a better look at the birthmark she spied on his collarbone, but it was hidden neatly away beneath shirt and cravat.

"Not at all."

How strange he sounded.

"I missed you at breakfast."

"I apologize," said Henry. "I . . . I went for a walk."

"'Twas a long walk, then. You've been gone some time."

Another odd beat passed between them, and Linette regarded him, unsure.

"I hoped we might go to Criccieth today," she said slowly, "to visit the apothecary and ask if he knew anything about the vial, but now, well." Linette gestured to the paneled ceiling then, the faint patter of rain. "The weather's turned."

"So it has." In the dimness of the hallway his frown was so deep a line had appeared between his brows. "Linette, I . . ."

"Yes?"

It felt, then, as though he was on the cusp of saying something, and troubled by his expression she had moved closer, smelt on him the faint scent of sweat.

"What is it?"

He chewed his inner cheek.

"It was a good idea, to visit the apothecary. But if we cannot go now perhaps we might occupy our time in some other way? Your cousin's study, for instance."

"This again? Henry, we are *not* breaking into the cabinet," Linette said in terms that broached no argument, but he was shaking his head.

"I meant that we could look at the other books. You see . . ."

Henry told her then of how he happened upon her mother in the garden and what she revealed. Linette had stared.

"Mamma told you that?"

"I'm afraid so."

"That the Tresilian crest . . ."

"Is not the symbol at all."

"Are you *sure*?"

But why would Henry lie? It was as Linette was reeling from the shock of it that he then told her of his encounter with Mr. Dee on his walk, and their subsequent conversation. It is why, now, they find themselves once again in Julian's study.

"Hellfire clubs," Henry says as he crosses the room, "have been in existence from the beginning of the century. The Duke of Wharton created the first."

"How do you know this?" Linette asks, still somewhat dazed by what he revealed upstairs.

"I don't know that much, not really," Henry throws behind him, coming to a stop in front of Julian's bookcase. "This has been told to me in passing by Francis Fielding, or overheard in coffee-houses and taverns. It's all common knowledge in London. The term 'Hellfire' has become a bit of a running joke."

"A joke?" Linette asks, coming to stand beside him, and Henry nods.

"They called Wharton the 'Hellfire Duke.' Before the Hellfires came into fashion, clubs were a means for men of high rank to meet and discuss their interests. Poetry, philosophy, politics, that sort of thing. But apparently Wharton's group was known to ridicule Christianity. It was said their president was the Devil, members attended meetings dressed as characters from the Bible, and their activities included sacrilegious ceremonies. Nonsense of course, it was all merely satirical; a way to demonstrate how liberated and forward-thinking they were, an opportunity for the rich to play dress-up and pander to make-believe. Then, of course, there was Dashwood's clan."

"Dashwood's clan?"

"Francis Dashwood, Earl of Sandwich. His club was called many names, but most often the Medmenham Friars. They had a motto: *Fais ce que voudras.* Do what you will. And they meant it too. There were rumors that their meetings were of a more . . . physical nature."

A beat. "I see."

Despite her stalwart sensibilities, Linette is conscious of a sick taste on her tongue, has no trouble in understanding what he means.

"Like Wharton's club it was implied there was a connection to the Devil," Henry continues, and here he reaches up to the bookcase, hovers his fingertip over the glass as he peruses the titles of the ancient volumes housed there. "An account was circulated which accused the Friars of practicing black magic. Again, nonsense. Written no doubt by a member who had fallen out with Dashwood over some petty grievance or other, but it eventually put a stop to the club's meetings sometime in the late sixties, I believe."

"All right," Linette says. "But what does any of this have to do with Julian's books?"

Henry stops. Taps the glass.

"See, here?"

Linette must squint up to a higher shelf. He is indicating the spine of a book bound in faded red leather.

"*De Occulta Philosophia Libri III,*" he reads. "My Latin is rusty, but the word 'Philosophy' is obvious. '*Libri*' means book. And there . . ."

He trails off. Linette tilts her head. "'*Occulta.*' Occult."

"Occult," Henry repeats, "yes. Mr. Dee said that Julian had shown him books on philosophical magic. Books that—he said—were sacrilegious. Of course, a man of the Church would say such a thing, but for a man of your cousin's learning, he'd simply consider books like this to be of academic interest. I mean, look," he adds, turning to the next shelf. "*Clavis Inferni.* 'Inferno'? *Histoire des Diables de Loudun.* History

of Devils, seems straightforward. Loudon . . . somewhere in France?"
Henry shrugs, moves on. "*Lemegeton Clavicula Salomonis.* Solomon, I
think. *Epistolae Theosophicae*, that's an easy one too—Theosophical
Epistles. So you see, Linette? All these are occult texts. Julian and
Beddoe, Lambeth, the Pennants and Selwyns. They're all part of their
own Hellfire club, and these books are their collected philosophy."

"What of this one?"

She gestures to the large black tome.

"Their rubric, perhaps? I'd love to get a good look at it. Don't
suppose . . ."

Henry reaches out his hand to the handle and attempts to pull, but
Linette stays his arm.

"It's locked. Julian would never risk sullying these books. He
values them far too highly."

"Surely you have the key?" Henry returns, and Linette laughs
without humor at the notion.

"Julian would never trust me with one. No one touches that bookcase, not even the servants."

"Well, can't we pick the lock?"

"With what?"

"Do you not have hairpins?"

This too would be amusing if it were not so absurd, and instead of
laughing again she simply levels him with a look. Henry takes in her
unruly hair, the wild curls at her temples, seems then to understand
her unspoken point, and together they turn their gazes back to the
bookcase. Uneasily Linette marks their ancient spines, reads once
more one of the titles Henry translated: History of Devils.

*For a man of your cousin's learning, he'd simply consider books like
this to be of academic interest.*

Julian is a man of sense. All the countless times he has cocooned
himself away, pouring over his collection for hours on end . . .

Certainly he was doing nothing in his study beyond simply reading! It was all satirical, as Henry said; a mere bit of fun, a means to entertain. Frowning, Linette stares at Julian's tome on its stand, the symbol jutting sharply from the black leather. *Not* the Tresilian family crest, but a symbol signifying a Hellfire club. *Julian and Beddoe, Lambeth, the Pennants and Selwyns.* Who else? Suddenly she pictures the portrait upstairs, the symbol etched into a golden knife, sucks in her breath. Not a family portrait at all, but something else.

There were rumors that their meetings were of a more . . . physical nature.

"My parents were a part of it."

Henry looks at her, notes the revulsion he sees in her face.

"You're thinking of the portrait," he murmurs. "Mr. Dee seems to think so too. It makes sense, doesn't it?"

Linette swallows hard, looks away.

"This is getting us nowhere."

"Isn't it?"

"Of course it's not!" she snaps, and Linette hears how shrill she sounds, must clamp her tongue, stamp down her revulsion at everything she has learned. "You've been proven right inasmuch as the symbol on his ring links Dr. Beddoe to this book. To Julian. A . . . a club. But this fact alone has nothing to do with Dr. Evans, does it?"

He does not respond to this, keeps his eyes pinned on the ancient books, the symbol on the tome.

"Henry," she begs, tugging at his sleeve. "We're no closer to discovering anything in connection to Wynn's death than we were last night. Please, come away. We gain nothing by being here. Come away."

Still Henry stares at the tome behind the glass in much the way she has caught Julian look at it in the past and Linette sighs, strives for a patience she does not feel.

"Henry, please."

At last, he looks at her.

"Very well," he says, resigned. "But the answer is staring us in the face, Linette. I'm sure of it."

As a means of distracting him Linette decided upon a Welsh lesson, for there was precious little else to do now the weather had so spectacularly turned, and not willing to frustrate Henry with more folklore she gave him instead some questions to translate, questions one of the villagers might ask if they were ill. Now, with the rain lashing hard at the windowpanes, Linette waits for him to finish, listening to the scratch of nib on paper over the din.

He is slow in his translations; her attempts at distraction quite failed. He taps his foot, twists the quill fast between forefinger and thumb, staining his fingernails black with ink. At length Henry pushes the paper from him with a deep and heavy sigh.

"There," he says. "I've done my best."

Linette takes the paper, reads over his work. In only two lessons, the doctor has already mastered the Welsh alphabet and makes good progress with its pronunciation, only stumbling a little at double letters which trip over his tongue like a cough. As Merlin snores beneath their feet Linette reaches for Henry's dictionary, runs a determined finger down a page filled with c's.

"Here," she says, tapping a word halfway down the page. "You used this word where you could have used another."

"*Cartref.*" Henry looks at her to see if he has pronounced it correctly. Linette nods.

"It means 'home,' so you are not incorrect, but there are actually two other words for it."

"Of course there are," he says dryly. "Why?"

"It's to do with the context, and also whether the word is used as a noun or an adjective. But you will instinctively learn when to use the right one."

"I'll never remember it all."

"You will. Did you not say you had a mind suited to learning? One day it will become second nature. I'd wager in a year you'll be as fluent as I."

As they have been speaking Henry has outlined the C of *cartref* again and again until the ink is blurred onto the paper, a nebulous crescent moon. Linette bites her lip.

She understands his frustration for it matches hers, though likely in different ways.

This new discovery, that Julian is a member of a Hellfire club, disturbs her, but not so much as the more unsavory truth regarding her parents. She thinks once more of the portrait upstairs. When Linette was a girl she often looked up at it and admired her mother's beauty, the confidence that shone through the canvas, wondering how that woman could be so different from the one she knew. Now, her mother's expression—that playful smile—has taken on a new meaning.

What manner of woman had her mother been?

Linette rubs her aching temples, smothers a yawn. Her nights have been restless of late, and her fatigue has made her irritable, a state which she does not like. Indeed, it has been getting increasingly difficult to hide her emotions from Enaid, whose sharp eyes see far more than she lets on. The poor woman worries about her most dreadfully, but how can Linette tell her that her brother may have been murdered? It would break Enaid's already sore heart.

A heavy tap at the window makes her turn her head. Outside, the rain continues to fall persistently, and she listens to the lull of its beating force against the gravel drive. Many times over the years she would stop whatever she was doing and simply sit, and listen. Rain, of course, can be heard anywhere in the world, but Linette fancies that Welsh rain has a particular cadence to it, a freeing quality so wholly its own. It is this thought that sparks in her another.

"There is one more form of the word for 'home,'" she says, "but its meaning is complex. You won't find it in the dictionary."

"Oh?" Henry leans back, rests his quill on the table.

"*Hiraeth*."

"*Hiraeth*," he echoes, teasing the words across his tongue. He nods. "I like the sound. But why is it complex?"

Linette smiles, wistful.

"The word is more of a feeling. An emotion that ties you to the idea of home. It's a place in your heart, a feeling of rightness, a sense of belonging. It is what Plas Helyg is to me, what I suppose London must be to you."

He says nothing to this. In fact, he grows very still.

She wants to ask him about his childhood as a Foundling but dare not. He spoke of loneliness, once. Was it because he too feels that emotion? Linette wants to tell him she understands—understands so completely—but finds she cannot think of the words. Instead, she asks, "Do you miss London?" and that haunted look returns, the one he has worn so often since arriving here, and Linette regrets saying anything at all.

"Henry, what is it? Are you all right?"

He takes a little too long to answer.

"Yes, I'm all right."

"I'm not sure you are." Linette finds herself hesitating. "I have to ask you again. Why here? It's so strange that you should have left a grand city filled with opportunity, to have chosen Penhelyg of all places instead. When Julian received your letter—"

"My letter?"

His interruption is sharp, dark eyes narrowed, and Linette looks at him in confusion.

"Why, yes. You offered your services in response to an advertisement Julian posted on my behalf in one of your English newspapers."

He stares. "Linette. I did not offer my services."

"You did. He had your reply within the week."

She is shocked at how pale he has become. The rain—louder now—vies for attention with the carriage clock on the mantel as she waits for him to speak once more. Finally Henry breathes out, long and slow.

"I wrote no letter," he tells her firmly. "This position was offered to me. I had to take it. I had no choice."

Now it is Linette's turn to stare. Julian said that, out of all the applicants, Henry had been the best man to replace Dr. Evans. And now . . . now it appears Henry did not apply at all, that he has been, absurdly, sent here.

Julian has lied.

The rain lashes violently against the windowpane, an angry beat against glass that matches the fraught moods of those within.

"I don't understand," she says. "My cousin wrote to you?" Henry nods his head. Linette's pulse beats fast in her neck. "What do you mean, then, you had to take it? *Why* didn't you have any choice?"

His eyes close for a split-second. When he opens them again his brown gaze is shadowed, and for the longest time he is quiet. Then, when Linette starts to think he will not say anything at all Henry sighs, runs a hand through his hair.

"I suppose it's time I told you."

He crosses and uncrosses his legs, as if readying himself for the tale. Disturbed by the movement Merlin stretches, yawns wide.

"Back in December," Henry says quietly, "I was called into the governor's office and asked to examine a gentleman. My reputation, apparently, had preceded me—this man heard I was an accomplished surgeon, that I was renowned for successfully treating more complex cases. My skill with the scalpel was, in Guy's Hospital at least, unsurpassed. The man in question asked for me specifically."

Henry stops. Linette waits.

"He died on the operating table. It happens, in this line of work. Of course it does. Death is an accepted outcome of medicine; we trade in it every single day. But there was no reason why he should have died; his heart had been strong. I *still* don't understand it. He exhibited many of the common signs of a cancer—" he ticks them off on his hand—"loss of appetite and weight loss, fever and chills, tremors, nausea, vomiting, weakness, fatigue, abdominal pain, swelling! I made the decision to cut the canker out." Henry shakes his head. "I was told I'd misdiagnosed the patient. I suppose I must have. The kidney was, after all, clear of infection—there was no canker to remove. And if he'd been any ordinary gentleman, it would simply have been an unfortunate mistake."

Linette regards him evenly. "But?"

"But my patient, as it turns out, was a very important man. Not only was he a patron of the hospital, he was a viscount, a respected member of the *beau monde*. He held a seat in Parliament. The governor had assured his family I was the best person to treat him, that my reputation and skill were of the highest order, and so my failure was an embarrassment to the hospital. If reports were to publicly circulate that he had died within the walls of Guy's then the hospital would have lost its funding. Even had the family not insisted I be dismissed, the board would have done it anyway." He grimaces. "Their reputation was at stake, they told me, and I was in no position to argue. I thought I could secure a position elsewhere but despite their best efforts to keep the matter secret, news of my failure somehow reached other hospitals, because my attempts at finding another post were thwarted at every turn."

Henry's eyes narrow. "It is only when I received the letter offering me a position here that I felt hope. But now?" He clenches his fists on the table. "You say your cousin received a letter from me as a candidate to fill the post. But it was *Julian* who wrote to *me*!"

Linette can feel the frustration coming off him like mountain mist, can see he is striving to master himself, and she too must fight to keep her composure, but a sick sort of feeling slithers over her like an eel and tethers itself to her spine. If Julian has lied about this, what else has he lied about?

By heaven, what is going on?

As if in answer, Henry buries his head in his hands.

"This is too much."

Linette barely hears him, must lean in.

"Too much?"

"First the gatehouse, the shot in the woods. Then Dr. Evans, Dr. Beddoe. This. And . . ." He raises his head to look at her. "Linette, there's something else."

The eel writhes. What else, after everything they have already discovered, can there possibly be?

At this moment there is the sound of carriage wheels crunching noisily across the gravel drive outside, and together they look to the window just in time to see a gray stallion pull a phaeton into the stables, a dark-haired man at its helm.

Finally. Julian is home.

CHAPTER
TWENTY-ONE

Their procession to church is accomplished on the skirts of an unseasonably brisk breeze.

The rain that lashed the fields so vigorously the day before has abated but left in its wake sodden earth that sinks and squashes underfoot, and reluctantly Linette must cling to Julian's arm in an effort to keep her footing. On the surface Julian is everything patient and accommodating; he touches her elbow, guides her around muddy puddles, and the whole time Linette must pretend she does not mind.

But she does mind. All she has wanted to do is confront him, but Henry has advocated for silence; given his lies, and what they now know of his intimate connection to Dr. Beddoe, it may not help them to alert him to their investigation.

Even if they *had* decided to confront him, her cousin gave no opportunity. Julian was tired, he said (and indeed he *looked* tired—pale and gaunt, leaning heavily on his cane), and retired immediately to his room whereupon neither she nor Henry had seen hide nor hair of him until breakfast this morning. Henry he asked all manner of questions: how have you settled in, do you like your room, have the servants treated you well? He was shocked and outraged by the news of the gunshot, but though Henry had looked at her pointedly across the table he brushed the incident off as a hunting accident and Julian settled back into his seat, a look of grave contemplation on his face. Indeed, his behavior was beyond reproach.

And that—knowing what she does now—makes her all the more suspicious.

Linette and Julian lead Plas Helyg's party up the church path to where Mr. Dee waits beneath the arched stone doorway. He greets Linette with a polite nod, a perfunctory bow for Julian. On Henry, however, the reverend bestows a warm shake of the hand.

Plas Helyg's party enter the church, Julian's cane clicking on the stone floor, and there is a hush as people turn in their seats. Cold hard stares, that now familiar stab of hostile eyes. It was a surprise when Henry asked to attend the service, considering he has made it clear to her he is not a religious man. "Why?" Linette asked as she buttoned her coat at the door. "*You* have no obligation as I do," to which his only response was to say that he was not a coward. "But it will be in Welsh," she exclaimed, "you will not understand," and at this he leveled her with one of his intractable stares.

"I shall manage well enough."

As they walk down the aisle Linette tries to catch the gazes of some of the villagers, but none look to her; instead their attention is held completely by Julian and Henry. They have looked at Julian this way before, of course, and he has never batted an eye. But Henry . . . though she cannot see his face, Linette fancies his eyes would betray him if she looked into them. Truly, this hateful silence is deafening, could be cut clean with a scythe.

They slip into the box reserved for Plas Helyg—Linette nearest the wall, Julian in the middle, while Henry takes the aisle. The bench is cramped, a claustrophobic press, Julian's expensive London cologne cloying sickly in her nostrils. Linette turns her head so as to lessen the impact of the scent, and as she does, she catches Henry twisting in the pew. She thinks, at first, he is looking at her, but no; his gaze is focused on the space beyond her shoulder, the pew behind. Linette turns too, only to see Enaid, wrinkled hands clasped in her lap, head bowed in reverence.

Linette frowns. Why does Henry stare so? Perhaps, she reasons, turning back to the front as Reverend Dee ascends the pulpit, he wonders why she is here. In the bustle of the morning Linette clean forgot to tell him that on Sunday mornings her mother is dosed with laudanum and locked in her room.

Safe, where she can do no harm.

The vicar clears his throat, grips the pulpit with heavy fingers.

"My children," he intones, grave and heavy. "Today let us think on Jonah and the lessons his story might teach us." A bristle goes around the congregation in a rustle of breath and cloth. "God did speak to Jonah, calling him to go and cry against the city of Nineveh. Foolishly, Jonah thought he could flee the presence of God, but our Lord intended Nineveh to hear his warning! He wished Jonah to deliver that warning, and God punished him for his disobedience until he repented. Yet Jonah kept his resentment with him, wore it like a chattel, let it rot away at his heart. How could he bask in God's almighty love? How could he find peace?"

Next to her, Julian twists his gold signet ring. Linette watches the strange curling symbol on its face, once again wonders why he claimed it was the family crest. Such needless deception! Surely it would not matter if she knew of his club. It would have simply been one more thing to exclude her from, one more thing Julian cared about more than he did her, so why should it signify that he was part of some so-called Hellfire club at all?

Unless, of course, there was something specific he wanted to hide. . . .

A smell of damp permeates the Welsh stone, betraying a hint of stagnant moss. Though it is early morning the church is steeped in shadow; candles have been lit in the sconces, their flames throwing flickering shapes against the walls as they shiver in the draft, and in turn Linette shivers herself.

The Reverend Mr. Owain Dee drones on about the power of humility and forgiveness; a sermon, Linette realizes, in support of Henry. She turns in her seat, hopes to communicate this to him somehow, but as Linette angles her head to look past Julian's shoulder she sees that directly behind Henry sits Miss Carew, whispering intently into his ear. She hears the strains of English, realizes that the young woman is translating the sermon, and something twists in her gut. Linette did not miss the way Henry looked at Miss Carew that day in her cottage, the way his cheeks flushed pink or his words stuttered on his tongue. Nor can she blame him—Rowena Carew is a very pretty woman indeed—but it is Linette who is Henry's teacher, *Linette* who took the effort to help him understand the language of her people, and to see Miss Carew take her place . . . She cannot explain how she feels. Annoyance is too strong. Jealousy does not quite fit either, though an echo of it is there. A strange sense of abandonment grips her, a feeling of treading water at sea, and Linette presses her fingers into the soft leather of her prayer book, scolding herself internally. She is being irrational, she knows, and yet . . .

Yet.

A pew creaks as someone shifts on it. The vicar spreads his arms wide in a slow, reaching arc.

"Let your anger and resentment be dust before the face of the wind," he intones, voice heavy with accusation. "Let the angel of the Lord scatter these unjust thoughts. They are slippery like the snake of Eden, filled with corrupt darkness. Release them! Purge yourself of all such sinful thoughts, and let the good Lord pursue and vanquish them."

There is a hymn, a psalm. Linette fidgets, restless. To stand and not be moving, to hear the wind in the yew trees outside the window, it is all she can do not to fight her way down the nave to escape. When they sit once more, the reverend drones on and on (are his sermons usually so long?) and it irritates her that Miss Carew continues to whisper in Henry's ear, that Julian twists the ring between his clubbed fingers again and again and again. Linette clenches her jaw, focuses her gaze upon the trefoils above Mr. Dee's boxlike head.

It is a relief when the congregation kneels to pray. A hush descends from the rafters, whispers filling the pews like wasps. Linette herself stays silent, shifts her weight uncomfortably on the prayer cushion until, finally (at last!), the service is done.

As the villagers take their leave, the vicar waits at the open door. Ahead, Henry and Miss Carew are already saying their farewells. As she and Julian approach, Miss Carew leads Henry away leaving Mr. Dee free to converse, and in English Linette says, "It was very kind of you to consider Henry in your sermon today."

The reverend acknowledges this with a bow of his head.

"I'm glad my sermon met with your approval, my lady. I do not dare hope too soon, of course, but I feel in time a positive change will come. Dr. Talbot deserves a chance to prove himself, and God does not bestow upon us more than we can manage."

"To deliver such a sermon," Julian remarks, "you must be on agreeable terms?"

The vicar smiles. "He is a recent acquaintance, yes, but one I like very much. He's a man of sense. I like men of sense."

"Indeed? How gratifying."

A breeze pulls sharply at the air. Linette catches on it the dank but sweetish smell of bracken and sheep droppings.

"I plan to hold an intimate dinner in the coming days in

Dr. Talbot's honor," Julian continues. "The usual party are to attend, of course—Lord Pennant, Sir John, a few others. If you are so pleasantly acquainted, Mr. Dee, perhaps you would agree to dine with us, set our new doctor at ease among strangers?"

"It would be my pleasure," the vicar replies. "That is, if Lady Linette is agreeable?"

Beside Julian, however, Linette has gone very still. Another dinner, another evening of flowered insults delivered by her cousin's caustic friends. But what can she do? What can she say? Nothing, as always, except play her part.

"But of course, Mr. Dee," Linette says with a smile she hopes does not appear forced. "Henry will be glad of your company."

As the men discuss what days might suit the reverend best, Linette searches for Henry in the dwindling crowd. For a moment she does not see him, but then—over the head of one of the miners—she spots him standing at the lychgate with Miss Carew. Their heads are bowed together, intimate. Then, Henry hands Miss Carew a small glass vial. Linette squints. Not the one he found in the gatehouse; *this* vial is full, not empty. He says something more and Miss Carew nods, slips the bottle into her reticule before disappearing into the lane. Julian presses her elbow.

"Linette?"

Both men are looking at her.

"I'm sorry, what was it you said?" and her cousin purses his lips.

"I asked if Wednesday was convenient?"

"Oh, yes," Linette says faintly, "of course," and the reverend shifts his bulk beneath the arch.

"Then if you will excuse me. So much to do, and a sermon this evening as well. The Lord's work never ends."

The men bow. Linette curtsies. As they turn it is to find Henry approaching them, hands buried deep inside his pockets.

"Ah, Henry," Julian says. "Are you ready to return to the house? I'm keen to hear your thoughts on what we discussed before I left."

Henry goes very still. For a moment Linette does not understand, but when a look of unease crosses his face the answer suddenly clicks into place. After everything else, she has forgotten. What was it Henry told her?

Your cousin has asked me to take my professional measure of you.

"Very well," he says, and Linette can hear the deep reluctance in his voice.

"Splendid. Linette, my dear, I'm sure you can manage without Henry for an hour or two?"

Julian does not wait for an answer. Instead he turns on his heel, heads in the direction of the road.

"I'm sorry," Henry murmurs, as they follow behind.

"'Tis not your fault," she replies.

Her tone is subdued, but he does not reply. Linette licks her lips.

"What were you discussing just now with Miss Carew?"

His hesitation is obvious. "Nothing of consequence," he says, and avoiding her gaze he needlessly adjusts the rim of his hat.

Linette stares. Why, she wonders, should he lie about such a simple thing?

Suddenly, she does not want to go home. On the one hand she should stay close, perhaps find a way to listen to Henry and Julian's conversation unobserved. On the other, she does not want to be near either of them.

"Cousin," she calls, and the tall man turns. "I feel like walking home today."

"Walking?" Julian scorns. "In all this mud?"

"*Ie*, Cousin. A little peace."

Julian stares at her. She thinks for a moment he will object, but then he simply shrugs his shoulders, turns his head.

"As you please."

It is not the comment that stings but Henry's lack of reaction to it, and with a scowl Linette strides past them between the sinking gravestones of Penhelyg's dead, through the lychgate on the other side.

CHAPTER
TWENTY-TWO

The journey back up to Plas Helyg was not conducive to chatter. Julian's phaeton juddered and jolted up the woodland path, the servants' trap driven by the groundsman Dylan cluttering close behind, and together they produced an altogether noisy racket that left Henry's ears ringing. Now Lord Tresilian lounges back in his armchair before the fire, cigarillo in hand. He breathes it in deeply, seems impervious to the fact that it will do little good for his cough, and Henry watches the man blow smoke through his mouth in ever decreasing rings.

He looks sicker than when Henry last saw him—Julian's cheekbones stand out sharply from his skull, the dark circles under his eyes more pronounced. But his smile is as wide as it was the previous week, his black eyes beetle-bright.

"Come. Sit. We have much to discuss."

Indeed they do, Henry thinks as he takes the armchair opposite, but this is a situation in which he must practice restraint. When he first met Julian, he thought of him as nothing more than a rich eccentric, someone who had the best interests of his relatives at heart. But now . . . Henry glances at the bookcases on the back wall, the tome on its plinth that could answer so many questions. But would Julian, if asked? He has already been proven a liar. So, then, what to do? Watch and wait, as Francis would say. Watch and wait.

"Was your business in London productive, sir?"

The older man nods. "I've procured a few more artworks for my collection."

He gestures to a stack of paintings leaning against the curio cabinet, and Henry sees that one has already been unwrapped. It depicts a woman in deep sleep with her arms thrown below her, a demonic apelike creature crouched low on her chest.

"An unusual painting," Julian says, "is it not?" and Henry searches for a polite word but cannot find one, opts instead for honesty.

"Disturbing," he says, but the answer seems to satisfy his host.

"I saw this particular painting in the Royal Academy last year. *The Nightmare*, it's called." He tilts his head, gaze focused intently on the incubus before sliding to the horse's head on its left which until that second Henry had not noticed. "It caused quite the horrified stir, apparently. Nothing like it had been attempted before."

It makes Henry distinctly uncomfortable. Pointedly he turns his back on it, focuses on Julian once more.

"It must have been very expensive if you purchased it from the Academy."

"I'm sure it would have been, but this is not the original."

"A forgery then?"

Julian sucks on his cigarillo, a look of contemplation on his face.

"I prefer the word 'copy.' Quite a few of the pieces here have been purchased at a fraction of the price of the original. I use a dealer in Ludgate Street, you see. Unscrupulous character by all counts but he knows his stuff. But I did not ask you here to discuss my collection."

"No."

"No," Julian repeats. A pause. "Drink?"

Henry pulls his pocketwatch from his waistcoat. "It's ten minutes

242

past the hour of nine. In the morning," he adds meaningfully as if the point needs to be clarified but Julian smiles, holding a carafe of what Henry takes to be the expensive port.

"I know precisely what time it is."

Henry lets silence be his answer.

Lord Tresilian shrugs, pours himself a glass, cigarillo still smoking between his clubbed fingers. "Very well. But I hope you do not think less of me for indulging."

He replaces the stopper in the decanter, and as he does so his gold signet ring flashes in the firelight.

"Tell me, then," Julian says. "What do you make of our fair Linette?"

Henry licks his lips. "I have come to know Linette very well this past week."

Julian watches him over the rim of his glass.

"And?"

"And I do not feel her to be in any danger of inheriting her mother's—" he pauses, must consider how best to describe it, under these new circumstances—"malady. I think your concerns simply stem from her solitude here in Penhelyg for so many years, and, I hesitate to say, neglect?"

For Henry is sure now that contrary to Lord Tresilian's previous claim, no fondness for Linette induces him. There comes no reply to Henry's summation. He carries on.

"In short, I feel that Linette is merely a woman of strong beliefs who takes great pride in her role as mistress of Penhelyg. Indeed, I have a deep respect for her—I've never known a woman as enterprising as she is. You should be very proud of everything she has achieved here."

Some emotion darkens Julian's face. The fire cracks. He places his glass on the marquetry table between them.

243

"I see. Well. I confess myself relieved, then, on that score." Julian tosses the stub of his cigarillo into the fire, steeples his fingers together. "Neglect is a harsh word, Henry, but perhaps not completely undeserving. I confess, I never much liked children, and by the time Linette came of an age to be interesting . . . well, the damage, so to speak, was done." He smiles softly. "It's a comfort to know you have succeeded in gaining her trust and friendship where I could not. Still, I see now it is not appropriate for the pair of you to be so much in each other's company."

The last was said in a decidedly pointed tone, and the implication makes Henry sit up in his seat.

"Surely you do not think Linette and I have formed an attachment?"

Julian reaches for his glass again and takes a sip, swills the port around his mouth before swallowing, Adam's apple rising sharp above his cravat.

"You asked if my business was productive," he says, ignoring Henry's question. "While in London I also arranged for the repairs to the gatehouse. A ship follows mine at the port in Abermaw—I never do travel by road, far too slow and uncomfortable—and it should be here tomorrow. Work will begin as soon as the men arrive, and I'd like to see you established there before the week is out."

Henry's surprise at Julian's suspicion in regards to the nature of his and Linette's relationship pales in comparison to this unwanted news. He had not expected the repairs to be under way so speedily, and to leave Plas Helyg would be a risk. If Enaid Evans is as dangerous as he now suspects, then it would not be prudent to leave Linette and Lady Gwen alone.

Especially Gwen.

And of course, there is the matter of Julian, his dishonesty surrounding Henry's employment. He looks at the older man sitting opposite him, his harsh features, those black eyes that reveal nothing at all . . .

"I had not thought to quit Plas Helyg so soon," Henry says slowly. "I would not want your men to hurry with the gatehouse. I'd be quite content to stay here for the coming weeks while they carry out the repairs."

Julian shakes his head. "The men are fast workers; I employed them for that very reason. No, I think you'd be much more comfortable there. The sooner you remove to Dr. Evans's old haunt, the better."

If there was an ideal moment to bring up Dr. Evans's death and, indeed, the matter of his employment it is now, but instinctively Henry knows to hold his tongue.

Observation. Contemplation. Interrogation.

Watch and wait.

Henry strokes the pocketwatch that still rests in his hand, thumb scuffing over the filigree engravings, the H and T of his name. Julian gestures to it with his glass.

"A most unusual timepiece. Might I see it?"

Julian does not wait for permission, reaches across the Turkish rug, and Henry is obliged to unclip the watch from his waistcoat. As Lord Tresilian takes it, Henry's eyes drift once again to his little finger.

"If you don't mind me asking, that signet ring you wear—"

"Mm? What of it?"

His lordship is still examining the watch, its swirling filigree patterns on the dial, the engraved initials.

"Linette thought it was the Tresilian family crest, but I saw a similar ring on Dr. Beddoe, which I found odd since the symbol is also on that large book of yours in the cabinet."

Julian is silent a little too long. When he looks up it is in a way that makes Henry distinctly uneasy.

"You have a knack of noticing things others do not," he says, "but I suppose as a surgeon that is hardly surprising." A beat. "You're right, it's not a family crest."

"What is it, then?"

"What is it? Well now . . ." Julian grows thoughtful. "What would you say if I told you I'm part of a select gathering of people who subscribe to a more open philosophy of thinking?"

"A club."

He does not say the words that come next, though they echo loudly in his head: *Hellfire*.

"A club, yes."

Henry nods. Dares.

"It seems curious to form a club of political and economic interests so far away from Westminster."

Julian raises his dark eyebrows. "An acute knack indeed. I did not state the nature of the club, and yet . . ."

"Forgive me," Henry says, careful now. "I only meant that such clubs as I've heard of—back in London, that is—tend to be located where the influence of political power is at its strongest. Penhelyg, being so remote—"

"Location in this instance matters not. You see, members of our little group, being of similar mind, are therefore not restricted to London's social circles."

"But Dr. Beddoe is not in your social circle."

Here Julian shouts out a laugh.

"I did not think you so high-flown! It is not *social* status that counts in this case, but what *knowledge* one might bring to the table."

"And what knowledge does Dr. Beddoe bring?"

Julian stares. "That, my boy, is between me and him."

Henry tries to mask his frustration. He has become too eager, too fast. He must find a way to claw back the upper hand.

246

"I did not mean to pry, sir, but I confess myself intrigued. What philosophy of thinking do you prescribe to? Does it have anything to do with the theme of your library?"

Henry knows it does, of course, but he wants to see what Julian might confess to. Indeed, that man watches him now, index finger against his lip, as if deciding what information to share and what to hold back. At length he says, "Are you familiar with alchemy, Henry?"

"I understand the concept, yes."

"Then you will know that in the ancient world it was widely believed that if one were to invoke the powers of alchemy, it was possible to transmute all metals into gold."

Henry stares, not quite sure how to respond, and in the face of it Julian smiles.

"I speak of how something might transform from one state to another, how a man of lesser means might rise to a higher plane. Do you believe in transmutation?"

It takes Henry a moment for him to construct his next words.

"I believe we can better ourselves, certainly, but only through hard labour and learning. I do not think our state can be altered by spiritual influence."

Surely the man cannot believe in such nonsense? For all Julian Tresilian's failings, Henry took him for a man of sense. He thinks of Philip, Duke of Wharton, of Francis Dashwood's Monks. *They* merely flouted sacrilegious notions as a means for harmless entertainment, but this lays claim to something more serious. Henry glances down at Julian's ring. Was the strange curling symbol on the signet an icon linked to alchemy? Henry asks him outright. Julian inclines his dark head.

"The symbol is merely a sigil that we connect to," the older man replies smoothly. "That is all."

He had hoped for a more fruitful response, but for all Julian

Tresilian's earlier transparency, there is a measure of reserve in this last, and this lack of satisfying answer makes Henry bold.

"Might I see inside the book? I'd be very interested to know more."

"I'm afraid not," Julian replies, swift as knives. "The book is inordinately valuable, so cannot be handled."

"I see."

The older man smiles without warmth at Henry's obvious disappointment. Almost deliberately Julian runs a fingernail across the face of the pocketwatch, still sitting in his open palm, before handing it back.

"If you'll excuse me, I must ring for Powell. A dinner to arrange."

Henry blinks. "A dinner?"

"To welcome you to Penhelyg."

"Oh," Henry says, shaking his head. He cannot think of anything worse. "There really is no need."

"But there is," Julian says, the smile widening, splitting his face like a cut. "There most certainly is."

CHAPTER
TWENTY-THREE

She walks for hours.

Through the muddy fields, down across the salt marshes, past the Morgans' cottage, thence onto the beach. The tide is out, and Linette sits on the sand to remove her boots and woolen socks, presses her toes into the golden grains. A breeze has banked the shore and so she removes her hat too, lets the wind whip through her hair. Tying her bootlaces together Linette hangs them over her shoulder, begins to fill her hat with shells brought forth from the waves: rough winkles, button-like cowries, razor clams, tiny limpets, Chinamen's hats.

She likes the feel of them between her fingers, the hard specks of wet sand beneath her fingernails. To Linette it is a way to distance her mind from anything that serves to distress her, but no matter how many shells she collects, troubled thoughts niggle at the dark corners of her mind.

Henry has confused her—she thought they were able to tell each other anything. But he has somehow found another glass vial and confided with Rowena Carew, and when she asked him about it, he lied.

He lied.

The sun shifts behind a cloud. Her hat grows heavy.

Has she been mistaken in Henry? True, they have only known

each other a week (could he truly have only arrived seven days ago?), but in that time Linette has begun to consider him a friend. Yet, in truth, what does she *actually* know of him? A man from London with no family, disgraced from his profession for misdiagnosing a patient. A man with connections to Bow Street who has—and Linette is sure this is what they speak of together now—been instructed by her cousin to ascertain if she is mad like her mother. Is his claim that Dr. Evans was poisoned a ploy? For why *would* anyone murder a man so well loved? Henry suspects Dr. Beddoe because of the nature of the vial, and claims he has a signet ring bearing the same symbol as Julian's, but Linette has never actually *seen* the doctor's ring, has she? She simply took Henry's word for it. But then, Mr. Dee (so Henry says) confirmed a connection between the two men, and as a man of the cloth he would not lie.

So distracted is she, Linette almost misses the jellyfish beached on the sand. Its milky-quartz body lies bottom up, tendrils ribboning in the surf. She stops, looks further down the beach.

It is full of them. Large and small, like a blanket of gelatinous pebbles.

Linette bites her lip. Tomas has told her how jellyfish can be dangerous, their tentacles infused with poison. Would they still be a danger, dead? She is glad Merlin is not with her—he would not have hesitated to snuffle at their decaying bodies, and what would Linette do if he was hurt?

Time, then, to head back to Plas Helyg.

It takes her an hour to reach the track back to the salt marshes, but before she leaves the sanctuary of the beach Linette locates a rock pool. Ever so gently she tips her hat, lets the shells fall into its shallow depths, watches the tiny bristle-tails dash and dart as the shells settle at the bottom. Once she would have kept them—as a child she had collected shells in their hundreds—but when Enaid deemed her room too cluttered they were relegated to Geraint's glass-house where they were crushed into shards, his own little remedy for the slugs and snails.

Boot-clad once more, Linette ambles up toward the path leading to the village square. She has seen no one on her travels, nor should she; what with it being the day of rest, the villagers will be in the tavern enjoying their well-earned respite. Linette finds herself approaching it, pushing the wooden door open.

It is more a barn than a tavern—low-eaved, straw-littered floor. The smell of yeast fills the air and then the gradual lull of silence as the villagers look up from their drinks.

Linette comes here but rarely, and only then to order ale for Plas Helyg or the miners. It is not her place, Enaid once said, a fact she herself cannot deny, but today she feels rebellious and so she skirts about the small round tables to the bar at the far end, orders a glass of *cwrw*. Arthur Lloyd, the gray-haired tavern-keeper, places it before her with eyebrows raised.

"I'd be careful if I were you, milady. 'Tis awful strong."

She is conscious of the villagers' eyes upon her. There is Bronwen Lewis, holding her baby close to her chest; there too are the Griffiths, Catrin leaning heavily on her gout-ridden leg. The Parrys sit by the weakly lit hearth, their youngest playing with a wooden doll on the straw floor. Cai Jones sits in a far corner, cleaning his nails with his teeth, flanked by his parents. And there in the other corner sits Rhiannon Einion, dark gaze hard and unforgiving.

Linette takes a hesitant sip. Strong it is, but the ale has an agreeable smoky undertone and—suddenly conscious of a deep-seated thirst—Linette drinks fast.

The silence in the tavern is deafening. There is a feeling of restrained impetus, a knowing that something will break, and when Linette places the empty glass back on the counter, like storm clouds, it comes.

251

"You've not brought that Englishman with you, then."

The voice comes from behind. Taking a deep breath, Linette turns.

It is Gareth Griffiths who spoke, one of her merchant tenants. He stands with his wiry arms folded across his chest, and beneath his heavy black brows his eyes are iron.

"As you see."

"Find that surprising," he replies, ignoring the archness of her answer, "since it seems lately he's attached to your hip."

Linette stares. She has always shared a familiarity with her tenants not typical for a woman in her social position, but never—not once—has any of them spoken to her in so direct a manner.

"That's unfair," she says, looking from Gareth to the others who now, too, are rising from their seats.

"Kept right close to you the other day in the square, just like that dog of yours."

Linette feels a laugh bubble up in her throat. The ale *is* strong— already hazy spots are beginning to form behind her eyes.

"Dog is right," Rhiannon hisses from her corner. "A low-life English dog!"

The girl's words are echoed by nods and murmurs of agreement from the rest, and this time Linette does laugh.

"For pity's sake! Don't let your prejudices stand against reason."

Now Rhiannon shoots up from her chair; Erin clamps her arm, but the dark-haired girl pulls it away.

"I think I've a right to my prejudices!" she spits, and looks about the room, intent it seems on rallying support. "London scum. He's brought the Devil with him, just like the rest!"

Linette's *"No!"* is lost within the cheer that comes from the other corner of the tavern, and Cai pushes himself between Gareth and Rhodri, standing tall and proud on his damaged leg.

"You know yourself of the bad the English have done here. Lands taken, mines unsafe. Look what they did to Rhiannon's grandmother, all the rest!"

Linette swallows, thinks of everything Henry has revealed. *Hellfire*. Cai's lip curls.

"Your doctor's no better than any of 'em. Selfish, arrogant. He don't care. *You* don't care!"

There are shouts of agreement, vigorous nods, jeering applause. The ale has taken her now, and Linette feels tears brim hot and painful beneath her eyelids. She looks at them heart-raw. Have they turned on her now too?

"*I* don't care? That's an untruth, Cai Jones, and you know it!" Her hands begin to shake. "You cannot, *cannot* know just how much I've fought for Penhelyg over the years." The tears fall, and angrily she brushes them away. "Am I not a good mistress to you? Do I not treat you fairly? I can do no more than I already have."

"You can send him away," shouts Rhiannon.

"Get rid of him!" shouts another.

"Yes," cuts in Cai. "Were there no Welsh doctors to be found? What's so damn special about this one that he had to come all the way from London?"

The question momentarily silences her. What *is* so special about Henry Talbot, that Julian would orchestrate his arrival here in Penhelyg and lie about how he brought it about? Whatever she thinks of Henry now, there can be no denying his shock when he realized Julian had lied. In that, at least, he was innocent, and it is this knowledge that spurs her on.

"You have no notion how difficult it is to find a good physician in these parts!" Linette shouts back and the passion, the pain in her voice, shocks them into silence. "And not just a good physician, either, but one who is kind."

She thinks of him—not the Henry of today, the one who has made her doubt him, the one who has lied to her—but the one she has known this past week, the one she has grown to trust.

"Think of Dr. Beddoe, who barely lifted a finger for you after Dr. Evans died. Would you rather have him?"

The other villagers who stand close by look guiltily awkward, but both Rhiannon and Cai appear unmoved. Gareth clears his throat.

"Young Cai was wrong to say what he did," he says contritely. He pats the lad on the shoulder but Cai shrugs it off with a sneer. "There are many of us who've a lot of respect for you, milady, for all that you've done for us over the years. But bringing that doctor to Penhelyg . . . it was mighty wrong of you. Beddoe ain't no good, we know that, but surely there was someone else? Someone of our own kin who understands our needs and speaks the language?"

Bronwen's baby begins to cry, muffling the sounds of accord that spread through the tavern like pestilent fog. Linette lifts her chin.

"You dislike him, I know. You've made that painfully clear. But Dr. Talbot is here to stay whether you like it or not, and no amount of scaremongering will change that."

Rhodri screws his eyes in confusion. "Scaremongering?"

The time for the truth is now; the ale has made her brave.

"Which one of you demolished the gatehouse the day the doctor was due to arrive? Which of you tried to shoot him in the woods?"

Linette is met with blank stares.

"Come now," she snaps. "Which of you were responsible?"

The villagers look at each other, faces full of bewilderment. Even Cai and Rhiannon look perplexed, and as the people of Penhelyg begin to murmur among themselves and shake their heads, it dawns on Linette they do not know.

They have absolutely no idea what she is talking about.

CHAPTER
TWENTY-FOUR

Linette returned to Plas Helyg heart-worn and dizzy. Not wanting to speak with either Henry or Julian she retreated to her bedroom and slept through dinner, waking the next morning with a dry throat and pounding headache.

Enaid, of course, scolded her mercilessly when she discovered where she had been, but when Linette remained silent the old woman sank down on the bed beside her and stroked her tangled hair.

"What is it, *cariad*?"

"Nothing," Linette replied, voice muffled within her pillow. For what could she tell poor Enaid, without revealing the rest? The rest that, now, Linette doubts is even true? And so that day she stayed in her room, listening to the sounds of building work down at the gatehouse, the clanging bell of the front door as Plas Helyg received deliveries for Julian's dreaded welcome supper for Henry.

It was only when Julian sent for her for dinner that she ventured from her room, and even then she held her tongue. More than once Linette caught Henry watching her across the table, disturbed perhaps by her odd behavior, for she had never been short of words before. Despite her defense of Henry to the villagers, Linette's misgivings burned a hole in her throat whenever she looked at him. It had been a relief to escape to her bedroom once more and lock the door behind her, to hold Merlin close and bury her face in his wiry coat.

The next day is a beauty—the sun shines brightly like a jewel, no clouds mar the brilliant turquoise sky, and the birds sing merrily in their nests. The air is ripe with the smell of cut grass and the scent of fresh linen wends its way from the back of the house, where Angharad has hung the bedsheets to dry. Linette has taken breakfast in bed much to Enaid's continued concern. Now, however, she grows bored.

It is most unlike her to shirk her duties, but never has Linette felt quite so tormented as she does now. She has always been used to solitude, her days regimented, carefully ordered, her hours timed to precision so there would never be any instance for a maudlin thought in her head. But now? Now Linette's whole life has been upturned, and she does not know what to do about it.

At the foot of her bed Merlin yawns, stretches his long legs across the coverlet, oblivious to his mistress's torment. At the window Linette looks down onto Plas Helyg's drive, watches Dylan remove the weeds from the gravel as she teases her long hair into an untidy plait. Through the open window she can hear the faint sounds of woodsaws and hammers. Henry will be removing there within a few days, it seems.

Perhaps, she thinks, tying the end of her plait with a green ribbon, it is just as well. Linette's life can return to something more like normal. Or it will, when Julian has left for London. Linette frowns, calculates the days. It is, now, the second week of June; he usually stays no later than the end of the third. She heard his phaeton leave just past the hour of nine, the crunch of wheel on gravel waking her from a restless sleep. Julian rarely stays at Plas Helyg above a day or two, entertaining himself at the expense of Lord Pennant or Sir John. Sometimes she wonders why he bothers to come here at all.

Downstairs, the grandfather clock chimes the half-hour, making Merlin twitch.

"This is ridiculous," Linette mutters. She simply must snap out of this tiresome stupor, must apply herself to some sort of task before she runs herself quite mad. "I shall help Mrs. Phillips," she announces to Merlin, and the lurcher stares at her from the bed. "Oh, come now, you lazy brute." Linette tickles him beneath the chin. "I'll find you something to chew on."

She likes the kitchen. It is a place where she has always found some semblance of comfort. Linette loves the homely atmosphere of cooking, the calming smells from the array of herbs hanging from ceiling hooks, and the dish of buttermilk on the stone hearth meant to appease the *bwbachod*. When she was a child, Cook would pour her a glass of that buttermilk and find her a *cage bach* to nibble on, just as long as she did not get under anyone's feet. As Linette grew older and took on more responsibilities this happened less and less, but there were still occasions when she would come down to seek out a treat and settle down by the warmth of the range. This, though, is the first time in some months she has ventured to the kitchen, and Linette is surprised to find the servants' quarters so disordered—dirty linen piled high in baskets, tableware that Linette has never even seen before stacked along narrow sideboards flanking the stone corridors, all in various stages of cleaning. Soap-suds clash with the smell of cooking meat, making Merlin sneeze. When Linette appears in the kitchen itself it is to find Cadoc polishing a soup tureen, Mrs. Phillips elbow deep in dough, and Angharad battling to fold a large sheet beneath a brace of pheasants hanging from a hook, their once-bright spotted feathers now dull, necks hanging limply to the side. All three look at Linette in surprise when she appears on the threshold, and their eyes grow even wider when she announces why she is there.

"We couldn't possibly allow it, Miss Linette," Cook says, thin cheeks red with effort. "'Tis not proper."

"Nonsense," Linette says, rolling up her father's shirtsleeves. "Besides, I crave something to do."

Cook hesitates, looks at the table. On it are an array of bowls and plates, each filled with the raw ingredients of dishes yet to be made. Linette spies carrots, leeks and asparagus; a hare lies ready to be skinned, and next to it one of Plas Helyg's black hens.

"I don't know, miss. There's such an awful lot . . ."

"Surely I can do something to help things along? Grease pans, measure out ingredients—" she points at a bowl of peas still in their nobbly pods. "I can shell these, perhaps?"

Mrs. Phillips flushes with gratitude. "Well, miss, that would be mighty fine. His lordship, he's been so—" She cuts off, thin face souring. "It's a lot to do. I won't refuse your help if you've a mind to give it. Heaven knows Angharad is already run ragged."

"There, then," Linette says, pulling up a chair. "It all works out nicely, does it not? Cadoc, can we find something for Merlin? I promised him a treat."

"No, Cadoc can't," Mrs. Phillips says sharply, glaring at Merlin who sits at Linette's feet, tail wagging in anticipation. "Another of the hens has gone missing. Found out when Geraint dropped off that one—" and here she nods at the corpse on the table. "Feathers everywhere, apparently. No, miss, he's had quite enough treats for one day."

"Merlin," Linette scolds, and the lurcher looks up at her, all innocence. "How many times must you be told?"

The dog recognizes when he is in trouble, utters a small whine before slumping down on the flagstones, rests his chin on his paws, and with a sigh Linette draws the bowl of peas to her and sets to work.

Cadoc continues his polishing in grave silence, nor do Cook or Angharad say much beyond offering instructions, but this is a silence

Linette does not mind. It is a relief to be busy, to satisfy her restlessness with the shelling of peas. It is a comfort to dig her thumb into a pod, to hear the tinny *ping* of its bounty fall into the bowl like raindrops, and so each of them passes a companionable hour saying hardly anything at all. It is only when Enaid comes into the kitchen carrying a basket full of linen and looking thoroughly haggard that the peace is disturbed.

"That's the last of them," she says, hauling the basket onto a small table by the range. "All the beds stripped, all the rooms cleaned. Is her ladyship's lunch ready?" She notices Linette, then. "By heaven, child," she says, her surprise evident. "Why are you down here?"

"I'm helping," Linette says, raising aloft the skin of a carrot curling from its peeler. "I insisted."

Enaid raises a veined hand to her forehead with a sigh.

"His lordship will not be pleased if he finds out."

Pursing thin lips Mrs. Phillips wipes greasy hands on her apron, turns to prepare a tray.

"Well," Linette retorts, "his lordship need not find out if none of you tell him, will he? Besides, I am mistress here, he is not." She pauses. "I don't suppose you know where he's gone?"

Cadoc clears his throat. "To Abermaw. He has a meeting with Lord Pennant."

"Did he say when he'll be back?"

"Tomorrow, I believe."

Linette feels a quiet sense of relief. For tonight at least, she may have some peace. Except . . .

"Where is Dr. Talbot?"

"In his room, miss, last I saw."

It is Angharad who answered. She stands at the far end of the kitchen table, fingers slick with blood, the hare's pelt half-stripped in her hands.

259

"I took him his breakfast this morning. Reading medical books, he was—they were strewn all over his bed, barely had space to put down his tray."

Above them comes the clang of the doorbell. As one, they look to the beamed ceiling, then at each other.

"Another delivery, perhaps?"

Cook shakes her head. "No, miss. I have everything here."

The bell rings again.

"Maybe it's one of the men from the gatehouse."

"I already sent Aled down with a basket."

Linette looks at the servants. Enaid holds the cup and saucer in one hand, the teapot in the other; Cadoc's arms are full with a silver serving platter, half-polished. Mrs. Phillips is in the process of filling Lady Gwen's lunch tray and at the far end of the table Angharad brandishes her bloody knife above the hare. None are in a position to leave their stations. Linette wipes her hands on a cloth.

"I'll go."

It takes her a full minute to reach the vestibule in which the visitor pulls the bell again, and when Linette opens the door she means to scold them for their impatience, but when she sees who it is her words catch in her throat.

On the threshold stands Rowena Carew. She is dressed in a pretty walking dress, hair coiled neatly beneath a prim straw bonnet, and the sight of her is enough to ruin Linette's short-lived peace.

"Miss Tresilian," the young woman says quietly, amber eyes shadowed by the rim of her bonnet. "I am very sorry to disturb. But might I speak with Dr. Talbot?"

CHAPTER
TWENTY-FIVE

They take the woodland path up onto the lower reaches of Cwm Nant-col on foot. They do not say a word—have agreed not to speak until they are safely away from Plas Helyg—and this silence, though it is charged with anticipation of the news his companion carries, is calm, peaceful.

Nothing like the painful silence Henry shared last night with Linette. If *only* she had not seen him give the vial to Miss Carew! He had been on the cusp of telling Linette his suspicions when Julian arrived but he was thankful, in the end, of the interruption; Henry wanted to be absolutely sure before saying anything and causing distress. Of course, considering the deadly nightshade found in Dr. Evans's vial there could be no doubt of the matter, not really, and yet . . . Would Enaid Evans really have poisoned her own brother? Would she attempt the same with her mistress? The plausibility of it is untenable, but there can be no denying what he found. No, it had been best to keep silent. Still, it has been a trial. He knows Linette is confused by his behavior; Henry sees the distrust in her eyes, the hurt. Yet what could he do? What could be done?

Wherever possible he avoided both her and Julian—yesterday Henry had visited the apothecary in Criccieth to ascertain whether he recognized the vial, to which the Welshman stated (so Henry's dictionary revealed) that he did not. Dejected at this lack of progress, Henry has since confined himself to his room and trawled through old medical books to see if he could find any other explanation for Gwen's condition, something else to explain the fits, the aversion to light, the odd behavior that makes her say such strange things, but nothing provided a condition that accommodated all symptoms at once. His only course of action was to wait for Miss Carew to return with an answer.

And now, to Henry's intense relief, she has.

They continue up the woodland path. Leaves rustle above them, birds temper the air with their sweet song. At one point Miss Carew catches her boot on an exposed root, stumbles into him, and Henry takes her hand to steady her. It is small in his, fits the cushion of his palm perfectly. He feels bereft when she lets him go.

Soon the trees part, the fields stretch out before them, and Miss Carew veers to the right. It takes a few moments for Henry to realize that she is heading toward the stone structure on the far side of the valley—a cromlech, he remembers Linette calling it—set atop a gentle knoll.

It is large, larger than he anticipated from where he first saw it, and on their approach Henry looks at it with interest. Four stones lean against one another in a manner reminiscent of a cave; three of them are propped up to form makeshift walls and what serves as a ceiling is a long capstone mottled with moss and lichen.

"Let's sit here," Miss Carew says.

They sit just under the lip of the capstone, the grass acting like a cushion, and she brings her knees up to her chest, wraps her hands around her skirts, looks out across the valley with a wistful expression on her face.

As with each time he has seen her, Henry feels his pulse knock hard in his throat.

Her beauty really is unlike that of any woman he has seen before—those amber-brown eyes are little firelights, that flame-red hair molten silk. He even likes the sound of her name. *Rowena.*

The fields slope beneath them, lushly green after the recent rain. On the lower reaches are clouds of the same mustard-yellow flowers to be found in Lady Gwen's room, their vanilla scent strong against the warm breeze. In the distance Henry can see a rambling farm and beyond it, black cattle. A gull—or perhaps a buzzard or kestrel, for he can perceive only its shadow across the wide expanse of sky—soars aloft, arching across the clouds like a winged dancer before wending downward to the right, and as it does a cluster of stone huts snaps into view. Henry nods to them.

"Linette told me these were ancient settlements," he murmurs. "Can you imagine anyone living there? So desolate, so open to the elements. I can scarce picture it."

Miss Carew props her chin on her knees. "But people did live there once," she says quietly. "Not so ancient, either. Whole families, before Emyr Cadwalladr turned them out."

"Where did they go, do you think?"

Her nose creases, drawing attention to the pretty smattering of freckles on its bridge.

"Where they could."

Henry nods thoughtfully. "It must have been awful to see the fields sold off, one by one, wondering how long they had left."

Miss Carew says nothing, only picks at a blade of grass.

"Where are you from? Linette says you're not local to Penhelyg."

She hesitates. "I lived in the marches."

"Then how came you to be here?"

Again she hesitates, a little longer this time.

"I wanted more," she says softly.

Henry does not say what he thinks—that Penhelyg surely could

263

not offer more than the borderlands. Still, he thinks, picturing her little cottage, the table of herbs, Miss Carew has carved a life for herself here. She is useful to the villagers. Respected.

He was respected, once.

"I understand," Henry says, and he does—ambition, his brutal schoolmaster at the Foundling told him sternly, makes a man ripe for greatness, differentiates the wolves from the lambs. He never agreed with the analogy but Henry appreciated the sentiment, has lived by it for as long as he can remember. It is why he strove to rise so high at Guy's.

As if reading his thoughts she asks, "What was it like, practicing medicine in London?" And though the subject has been on his mind her question takes him by surprise.

"Different," he manages after a moment.

Miss Carew is looking at him now, eyes russet beneath the rim of her straw bonnet. "Progressive, I suppose?"

An image of the operating theater at Guy's pops into his head. Henry pictures the curving stalls filled with apprentices and rich patrons hungry for knowledge, how they absorbed his lectures like sponges.

"I taught."

"Really? How thrilling."

It feels like flattery. Henry likes it.

"It was," he says.

"Your parents must be very proud."

Henry tries not to think about the circumstances of his birth; what manner of person would abandon their child to somewhere so cold, so regimented, so devoid of affection? For a moment he is taken back to his boyhood, a time when he used to have night terrors and wet the bed. Each night he would wake, call for the ward nurse, and Henry remembers how she made light of his distress, scolding him for making her more work and disturbing the other boys, until, finally, the dreams stopped altogether.

"I don't have any parents," he says softly.

Miss Carew bites her lip. "Forgive me. I did not mean to—"

But Henry shakes his head. "I grew up in a place for children who had been abandoned. I may have had a roof over my head but there was no warmth there, no love. Just row on row of beds in a sterile room shared with other motherless boys." His mouth twists. "The nurses were stern, the schoolmasters sterner. We grew up on an appetite of gruel and scripture, structure and hard work. Every day regimented, every day the same. I was never more unhappy than I was there."

She turns her face away, for a long moment says nothing, staring down at the settlements as if hypnotized by them. Then she offers a small sad smile.

"I'm sorry."

"Whatever for?"

Miss Carew lifts her shoulders in a shrug. "It's only that it is a terrible thing, to have an unhappy childhood."

"Yours was unhappy?"

A beat. "Yes."

She looks so sad, so wistful. She truly is so very beautiful, Henry thinks, and until this moment he did not realise quite how much he yearned for her. A soft breeze loosens a long red curl from her bonnet, and with it, the scent of lavender. Very gently Henry leans over, tucks it back. He hears her breath hitch, sees the flutter of her dark eyelashes, and he cannot help doing what he does next. Henry cups her soft round cheek with the palm of his hand, draws her lips to his.

It is a soft kiss, quick, barely lasting above a few seconds, but in that instant he feels within him a deep and lustful longing. He wants to press her close, to have her kiss him back, but already she has pulled away.

"No," she whispers, pressing her fingers against the bow of her lips. "No."

Henry watches her, breathless with disappointment, his hand still on her cheek.

"Rowena, I—"

"Don't, Dr. Talbot."

She pushes his hand away, and he sees in its absence how the pillow of her cheek has spotted pink. Her eyes have shifted from brown to that rich amber he finds so fascinating and Henry thinks, then, she has never looked lovelier or more tempting.

"Please," he says, voice thick with passion. "Call me Henry."

"No. I cannot. I won't," Rowena says—and it *is* Rowena to him, for Miss Carew simply will not do—and looks determinedly away across the valley again.

Henry wills his body to calm itself. It is some moments before he can speak again.

"I'm sorry," he says. "That was wrong of me," and in reply Rowena lets out her breath.

"We barely know each other."

"No, I suppose we don't. I want us to, though. So very much."

Still she does not look at him. Will not, it seems.

"You've been very kind," Rowena says quietly, and Henry hears a tremble in her voice. "But what you want from me I cannot give."

"What is it you think I want from you?"

A little laugh escapes her. "What all men want."

His chest tightens at the implication. Has Rowena been with another man? Did he wrong her? Henry wants to tell her he is nothing like whoever it is she thinks of, to convince her she is safe with him, but Rowena is opening her reticule, is removing the glass vial he gave her from its depths, and the moment has passed.

Gravely she holds it between them. A spool of sunlight pierces the gray glass, casting her chin with delicate rainbows.

"You were right," Rowena says softly. "This is not laudanum."

It takes Henry a moment to compose himself, to apply himself to the change of subject. He lets out a calming breath, and she pulls the gold Turk's-head stopper from the bottle's neck.

"It's a clever concoction; it took me some time to identify the ingredients. I had to refer to my own stores and replicate it."

Rowena passes the bottle over, and Henry takes a sniff.

"Careful," she warns. "It works best by ingestion, but I cannot vouch for its potency when inhaled too deeply."

"What is it?"

"A mixture of herbs, all of them deadly taken in large quantities on their own. But the measure of oils extracted from each plant is just about safe if mixed with wine or water." Rowena replaces the stopper. "This is wine."

"What are the herbs?"

"Mandrake and valerian. Mugwort and henbane. The smallest touch of deadly nightshade but not to the potency of what was in Wynn Evans's vial."

Henry frowns at this. "Deadly nightshade I know, of course, but my knowledge of herbs is woolly at best. What do the others do?" and when Rowena tells him he swears. She nods in understanding.

"It's a risk to pair so many toxic plants together. I'm surprised Lady Gwen has not suffered more than she has. What prolonged effects such a tincture might cause, I do not know."

Henry does. Organ failure. Internal bleeding. Death. A slow death, but death all the same, and the thought leaves him cold.

"I need to put a stop to it."

Rowena shakes her head. "To remove the tincture so suddenly could do more harm than good."

"Yes."

"Then how will you do it?"

He sighs, runs his hand through his hair. "I do not know. But it isn't a simple task. There are many other factors to consider."

Henry considers them now.

First, there is the matter of Mrs. Evans. It is she who administers the tincture, she who guards Gwen Tresilian like a hawk. There is no question the old housekeeper knows she does not sedate her with laudanum (for if she knew, then why hide the bottles?) which raises further questions. Why? To what purpose?

Second, if Mrs. Evans is in possession of bottles identical to the one found in the gatehouse does that mean she, rather than Dr. Beddoe, played a part in her brother's death? Do the other servants know too? And what of Linette? How can it be possible that she has spent so many years unaware her mother is being drugged? It seems incomprehensible. So, then, has Linette lied to him all this time?

Then, thirdly, there is Dr. Evans himself.

Perhaps, as Reverend Dee suggested, the bottles *did* belong to the old doctor. If that was so he *must* have known what was in the vials given to Lady Gwen, and instructed his sister to administer their contents. But why? And if he did instruct such a thing, and the vials were indeed his own, then the one found in the gatehouse is not as suspicious as he once thought.

But then, what of the deadly nightshade within it?

Has Julian Tresilian known any of this? Surely he could not, for why bring him here as Lady Gwen's doctor when it was clear Henry would, in time, discover the truth? If such a thing was to be kept secret, then employing him was a reckless decision.

"Dr. Talbot?"

Rowena's voice is soft, tinged with concern, and Henry raises his head.

268

"I do not know," he says again, despairing, and a cricket chirps noisily in the grass.

"'Tis a difficult situation," Rowena murmurs. "I do understand. If I can help in any way . . ." The cricket ceases its song. She rises to her feet. "I should start back."

Henry stands too, moves to take her hands, then thinks better of it.

"Must you?" he asks, searching her face. "Aren't you lonely, living there all alone?"

Rowena sighs, looks out over the fields to the ruined cottages below. "Of course I am," she replies softly. "But I have to earn a living."

A thought flashes into his mind then, and Henry's stomach flips at the possibility of it.

"You could earn it with me. As my assistant. I'm not used to your traditional methods, but it is clear to me now I should adopt at least some of them if I am to get along here in Penhelyg. Your help, it would be appreciated. I can pay you handsomely from my own salary."

Rowena's eyes snap back to his. "Dr. Talbot, I—"

"The gatehouse will be ready soon," Henry says in a rush. "There's a spare room. It's yours, if you want it. Staying at the gatehouse would be far more convenient than living out here. Safer too."

"But—"

"If it's the impropriety of it you think of, I . . ."

He trails off. The gatehouse has only two bedrooms, no third to accommodate a companion. There is nothing that can counter that oversight, and as she looks up at him he curses inwardly. Why does he sound so desperate? It is foolish to act so, to ingratiate himself like this, but hell's teeth, he cannot help it!

"I want nothing from you," Rowena is saying now, "except one thing."

Henry swallows. "Anything," he answers, and gently she takes his arm.

"You may walk me back to Moelfre."

CHAPTER
TWENTY-SIX

After Henry left, Linette returned to the kitchen and peeled the last of the carrots. When she was done, she helped Angharad move the prepared foodstuffs into the cold store and covered them with muslin cloths so they would keep until the following evening, and found herself quite dismayed when Mrs. Phillips said after that there was nothing left for her to do.

"You've been a great help, Miss Linette," she said kindly, setting the hare into a pan of water, "but we can get on with the rest. Be off with you, now."

It is strange to be dismissed by one's own servants, strange for Linette to find herself so at a loss. She feels untethered, driven by despondency and anger. Alone now in the vestibule Linette childishly stamps her foot, and the sound reverberates through the stone and up into the vaulting ceiling. In response Merlin whines. Linette rubs her eyes. There is nothing else for it. What best keeps her distracted when her thoughts begin to overwhelm, as they so often do?

She retreats to her study, opens her ledger at its most recent page and looks down at its columns. Linette heaves a troubled sigh. Yes, the estate does well enough . . . just about. But in truth, the numbers filling those narrow columns should be far higher than they are.

*I did warn you about the risk of spending so much on your
tenants.*

It vexes Linette to admit Julian might be right. No matter how
much she resents his intrusions, he is a man of business. Thoughtfully she nibbles the end of her quill. Are there other ways around
this? *Could* she compromise? She will not lease the land to anyone
except Welsh tenants—Linette is quite set on that score—but pride
can only take her so far. Would it really be so very awful to open the
house up to visitors, to advertise Plas Helyg as an ancestral jewel of
Meirionydd? The mansion needs maintenance to be sure; how long
has her home sat neglected, the ballroom left in cobwebbed shadow,
its rooms dark and empty except for Linette, her mother and the servants? How long before Plas Helyg does indeed begin to founder? She
raises her head, stares at the other ledgers packed tightly on the
bookshelves opposite. The only way to know for sure is to look back,
to compare one year with the next.

It is a thankless job. It takes Linette nearly two hours to sift
through one ledger from last year alone. Tiredly she sits back in her
chair, twists her neck from one side to the other. Her shoulders ache,
her eyes feel dry in their sockets. Through the open window the
remaining black hens squawk. Merlin's ears flap and twitch.

"*Na*, Merlin," she sighs. "Have you not tortured them enough?"

Merlin looks up at her, cocks his head, and there comes then a
rumble, like the roll of distant thunder but louder, more resonant, and
Linette rises from her seat.

"What on earth . . . ?"

She rushes to the open window, looks out over the sill. The horses
shriek and buck in their stables and Rhys appears at the doors, a bag
of feed in his hand.

"What was that noise?" she calls out.

"Sounded like it came from the valley, miss," he replies, just as

271

Dylan and Aled appear over the rise of the footpath that leads down to the east of Plas Helyg's lands. They speak together in a tumble of tongues, gesticulating wildly, and Linette beckons them.

"What is it? What has happened?"

"We saw it, miss!" Dylan says in a rush, eyes round in his moon-like face. "We were chopping wood and saw it happen. The sky filled with a great dark cloud like dragon's breath!"

"A waterfall of dust," Aled adds, breathless with awe, and Dylan nods in agreement.

"For heaven's sake," Linette says in frustration, gripping the sill so hard her fingers sting. "Tell me what has *happened*?"

The two groundsmen look between each other, back at her.

"The mine, milady," Aled whispers. "There's been an explosion at the mine."

BRANCH III.

Like one, that on a lonely road
Doth walk in fear and dread,
And having once turn'd round, walks on
And turns no more his head :
Because he knows, a frightful fiend
Doth close behind him tread.

SAMUEL TAYLOR COLERIDGE
The Rime of the Ancyent Marinere (1798)

CHAPTER
TWENTY - SEVEN

The explosion came just as they reached Rowena's cottage, and Henry watched the smoke billow from the hillside of the mine with a rising sense of horror. By the time he and Rowena arrived at Plas Helyg it was all commotion; the servants' trap was being prepared, loaded with supplies—blankets, food and water, soap, spare clothes, anything that might help—and when Rowena agreed to stay behind and follow later in the cart, Henry and Linette rode ahead as fast as the horses would carry them.

Henry has never had to deal with a disaster such as this, but he already imagines what he will find—at best, superficial cuts and grazes, deeper lesions into flesh and muscle, broken bones; at worst, collapsed lungs, crushed skulls, miners trapped under mounds of earth and rubble, unable to catch their breath. He tries not to think of the miners he saw during his last visit; their legs wrapped in chains, dangling from the creviced ceiling, what such an almighty force of gravity might do to such a limb. . . .

The site is a swarm of activity, and Henry and Linette tie Gwydion and Pryderi as far away from the cavern entrance as possible to shield them from the cloying dust. As they walk to the top, the damage does not look so very bad—the cavern entrance is clear of rubble, and the miners, though dirty and bloodied, appear blessedly unharmed.

But that does not mean those below should be as lucky.

At least twenty miners have managed to emerge above ground, but Henry knows from his visit with Linette that he saw far more than that. For those he does see, he begins to catalogue injuries. Many possess cuts and grazes as Henry originally surmised, a man holds a dirty rag to his nose. One lad of no more than sixteen nurses an arm to his chest, holding it at a crooked angle. Nearby a donkey stands, swaying, bloody scratches on its bony knees. Henry shares a worried look with Linette, and she shakes her head in dismay.

"Where is Mr. Lambeth?"

A miner limps by, and Linette stretches out her arm to touch his. *"Hari, ble mae Mr. Lambeth?"* she asks, and with a grimace the man points over his shoulder before lumbering away.

The bewigged man is standing near a cart piled with felled tree trunks—Pennant's offering, Henry surmises—with his leather folder poised, pencil in his gloved hand. Lambeth does not notice their approach, so absorbed is he in his papers, but when Linette calls his name he looks up, and his already sour face shifts into an expression of deep annoyance.

"This is not a place for a woman."

"What happened?" Linette asks, ignoring the comment, and the agent looks between her and Henry, lips settling into a thin unpleasant line.

"There wasn't enough room to get the wood down to build the pulleys, so we set off some gunpowder in the smallest cavern to speed things along. It appears the site was not properly prepared, and the cavern collapsed."

Henry shifts his knapsack from one hand to the other. "How many still below?"

Lambeth levels him with a look. "You're here to offer your expertise, I see. Well, I'll not refuse your help though I would appreciate it if *she* does not interfere. As I said, this is no place for a woman."

"And this is no time for such nonsense," Linette snaps, and Lambeth's beetle-eyes grow wide. "I know the men, I can offer comfort. I have people from Plas Helyg coming with provisions. Believe me, I'm not here to be idle."

"Fine," he says, shutting the calfskin folder with irritable force. "Do as you will. But Lord Tresilian will not be pleased when he arrives."

"Damn my cousin! I'll do what I like."

"Don't you always?"

"How many are still below?" Henry cuts in, for he can see Linette's temper rising by the second and does not fancy seeing how far her viper's tongue might carry her this time.

"Thankfully the damage seems only to have centred in the smaller caverns," Lambeth replies. "They're the newest, where we were trying to expand. You'll be of no use down there, I promise you. Leave it to those more experienced in such matters. You can help with aiding those above ground while the others dig the rest out."

It is, then, as he feared. Through gritted teeth Henry repeats, "How many men, Mr. Lambeth?" and with a belligerent sigh the agent flips open the folder to a list of names, counts under his breath.

"I've accounted for forty-three. We're still missing seventeen."

The rest of the villagers appeared over the next few hours. For those who were injured, their presence was a comfort. For the rest they were a hindrance, disturbing the work of the other miners who were trying to focus on their rescue attempts, and an irritation to Lambeth who could not yet account for the missing. It was Linette who offered succor, Linette who deflected their hampering machinations, and her strength and patience were everything Henry needed—while she distracted worried wives and mothers, he could concentrate on treating the miners without suffering the fuss of their kin.

And they let him. They let him! He had been afraid at first that their stubborn pride and willful dislike would rule over their need for treatment, but the miners—perhaps seeing little choice in the matter—acquiesced to Henry's care without argument. He stitched cuts, set broken arms. One man (Henry had to bite down his anger) had lost a foot, the remains of a chain still wrapped around his leg. But he treated them, one after the other, and Henry felt a sense of deep elation, the closest he has felt to contentment since arriving in Penhelyg—*this* is what he is good at, *this* is where his talents can be tried, and it is a relief to find himself useful again in the only way he knows how. No, his operating table is not made of smooth polished wood, and no, he does not work in a semicircular room filled with benches of learned men. Henry works now in an open field where tall grasses rustle in the breeze and distant cows bellow, observed by people who cannot rightly fathom what they are seeing, but despite it all Henry is in his element. And the miners seem to recognize this, the speed and skill with which Henry works; often he receives a word of thanks, a clasp of the hand. They look him in the eye, not with distrust and hatred but with respect and gratitude.

Of course, the external injuries have been easier to deal with, and the more minor ones can be left in Rowena's capable hands. But, at length, those who have been recovered from deeper within the caverns are brought to him, and here Henry's skill has been tested. One boy came to him with what Henry suspected were broken ribs, a man of middling age with a burst eardrum. Once more Henry was obliged to refer to his Welsh dictionary and his translated notes so he might understand the internal pain of his patients. But, somehow, he has managed.

He has managed it all.

It is just when Henry is tying off a suture to a split elbow that an unconscious man is brought to the top of the line, carried by three of his fellow miners. Only when he is set down on the grass does Henry recognize him. This is Rhodri Jones, their guide from the other day. The man's sandy hair is matted with blood. Carefully Henry parts it to find the cause.

"Jesus," he mutters. The flesh is torn along the cranium, a flap of skin exposing the ghost-white of skull. The skull itself possesses a deep compression of fractures, shattered fragments of bone reminiscent of cracks in broken porcelain.

Henry tries to measure the mathematical certainty in his head. The collapse happened (he removes his pocketwatch) four and a half hours ago. It is likely Rhodri will have been unconscious all that time, and the longer someone maintains such a state, the worse the outcome is likely to be. Henry peers closer at the skull. While there is blood present from the flesh surrounding the tear, there is very little of it within the bone's hairline cracks, and that can mean only one thing: the blood is pooling beneath, building pressure on the brain, with no place to go.

The miners are looking at him expectantly. Henry runs a hand through his hair. He has only done one of these procedures before, on a soldier who suffered a fall from his horse.

It did not work. He died from fever three days later.

This injury, Henry knows immediately, is worse than that soldier's. Would such an operation even work?

"*Tada! Tada!*"

Cai Jones, pointed face filled with abject panic, is running across the field as fast as his limp will allow and inwardly Henry groans. So far he has been lucky—Linette has managed to keep the rest of the villagers at bay—but he should have known that at least one would slip through, and for it to be Cai seems like a cruel sort of injustice.

279

With a feeling of rising dread Henry watches him approach, only a little relieved to see Linette and Rowena close at the lad's heels.

"*Paid â chyffwrdd ag ef!*" he cries, flinging himself down on the ground next to his father. "*Paid â meiddio!*"

The tirade of words coming from Cai's mouth is too fast for Henry to interpret, but from the mixture of hate and fear on the boy's face the general meaning is clear. Linette, caught up now and breathing heavily, confirms it.

"He doesn't want you to touch him."

"If I don't," Henry says, "he will die."

Linette translates, but Cai shakes his head at her with such violence that Henry feels sorry for him. They argue for what seems like minutes, and all he can do is try to drown their harsh voices out. Instead Henry plans what to do and, decided, reaches for his knapsack. Cai pushes his hand away.

"*Mi fydd o'n ei ladd o!*" he cries, and Henry must rein in his patience.

"Don't be a bloody fool! Either I try and he dies or I try and he lives, but if I don't try at all his death is a certainty. Which will you choose?"

Something in Cai's face makes Henry suspect that the boy comprehends some of what he has said. Cai stares at him across the unconscious body of his father, lip trembling. His cheeks are wet with tears, his nose snotty and red, but then Rowena very gently takes him by the shoulders.

"*Gad iddo drio, Cai,*" she says softly. "*Dyna ei unig gyfle.*"

For a long fraught moment they stare at each other. Then, to Henry's intense relief, Cai nods.

"Right, then."

He reaches for his knapsack again, removes a small green case.

"What is that?" Linette asks.

She looks tired, weary. Her unruly blonde hair has fallen from its heavy plait, her shirt is smeared with dust. It occurs to him that she too has been working without relief, and Henry feels a wave of affinity run through him.

"A skull drill set."

He lifts the lid. Linette pales at the sight of the instruments resting within.

"What are you going to do?" she whispers.

"Trephination. I'm going to drill a hole through his head, release the pressure of blood building on the brain. If it works, Rhodri should wake up."

"*If* it works?"

"*Ie*," he says. "If."

He clears a space around him, sets the cylindrical instruments out on the grass, some clean cloths, needle, thread, then moves to kneel directly at the top of Rhodri's head.

"I need two people to hold him down, keep him steady."

Again, Linette translates. One of the other miners steps forward immediately, sinks to the ground on Rhodri's left side. Linette settles down on his right, and Henry looks at her in surprise.

"Are you sure?"

She smiles a little with some of her old wry humor. "Don't vex me, Henry."

"Then I hope you have a strong stomach."

"It's strong enough."

He is as fast as safety will allow. The small circular saw is placed above the compression fracture, and he twists with as much pressure he thinks the skull will stand without cracking further. It is the noise that is the worst, its harsh scrape and grind against bone. Linette shuts her eyes, turns her head away. Rowena presses her hand to her mouth. Someone, somewhere, vomits.

It is a hard task. At one point Henry fears he might lose his grip on the instrument, his hold on Rhodri's head. His upper lip beads with sweat at the strain of it and his palm becomes sticky, but he dare not ask for help lest his concentration slips. But it is Cai who recognizes this, Cai who holds his father's head with a calmness that belies his earlier panic. It is Cai who watches intently as Henry stays true and the saw eventually eases through the skull with a raw dull *snap*. Blood starts to pool around the circular line.

"Scalpel." He points at the instrument with his free hand. Cai passes it to Henry handle first, then takes the trepan saw from him and places it almost reverently on the ground. The air is filled with an unbearable tension, a tension that simmers through all those who watch.

If he were to slip now, if he does not exert the utmost care, then it will all be over.

Henry turns the scalpel between his fingers, poises its deadly point above Rhodri's skull. Then, very carefully, Henry prises away the disc of bone. Immediately the blood flows loose and ready, and Linette passes Henry a cloth to stem the deluge. It soaks through almost instantly, but when Henry lifts it he sees the hole is clean, tidy, the healthy pulse of pink brain-matter visible beneath. And then, then, Rhodri stirs between them.

There is a release of collected breath, a shout of laughter. Cai begins to cry.

"*Henry*," Linette whispers, her voice full of wonderment, but Henry will not bask in it. He knows how crucial these next steps are and so he stitches fast, cleans the blood from Rhodri's hair and scalp, bandages his head tight.

"Tell them," he says when he is done, "that they must keep him still on the way back down the hill as best they can. No jolting to the head, keep it cushioned. He must, *must*, be kept to his bed until I say he can leave it. Tell them to watch for signs of fever. I shall visit tomorrow."

Linette does as he asks, and Rhodri—gaining consciousness now—is slowly carried from the field, Cai trailing behind. At the gate the lad turns, stares at Henry as if he does not know what to make of it all. Henry wonders if he means to say something, to thank him perhaps, but then Lord Pennant's carriage clatters up the hill behind him stirring dust in the wake of its wheels, and the moment passes like a great hand over the face of the sun.

CHAPTER
TWENTY-EIGHT

"But how bad *is* it?"

At the cavern entrance Julian is flanked by Mr. Lambeth and Lord Pennant. Their voices—high-strung and urgent—carry on a breeze tinged with bracken and the faint stench of sulfur, and together Linette and Henry pick up pace.

"It's only the lower cavern," the agent stutters. "A setback to be sure, but—"

"How long will it take to clear the debris?"

Her cousin's voice snaps like a whip. Mr. Lambeth—whom Linette always took to be a belligerent, acerbic man—seems to quail in the face of it, and if the situation were not quite so fraught she would exact some pleasure in his discomfort.

"Some days," he says quietly. "Perhaps even weeks."

"*Weeks!* What do I pay you for, Lambeth?"

The agent pales further, flips uselessly through the leather folder he clasps close to his chest. "I don't . . . it's not . . . the gunpowder, you see—"

"Is the mine safe?" Lord Pennant intercedes in a more lucid tone. "Is the site secure beyond the damage to the lower cavern?"

"We don't know yet, the miners are still—"

Julian cuts him off sharply with a curse, stamps his cane, turns his face, and the expression on it makes Linette stumble. The anger is pure, unadulterated. Never has she seen him like this, with wildness in his black eyes, a shot of color spreading high on his cheeks like a claret stain, and when he marks Linette and Henry's approach he does not bother to shield his temper.

"Linette, what the hell are you doing here?"

"These are my tenants, Cousin. Of course I am here."

"But they are *my* workers. This is no place for you."

She opens her mouth to respond, but before she can do so Henry has placed a warning hand at the small of her back.

"If I may," he says, "the mines will not be safe for quite some time. It's impossible to carry out any further work until the site has settled. Aside from the danger of subsidence, the effects of dust on the lungs can be fatal. The miners cannot possibly work in such conditions. Mr. Lambeth should be able to tell you that."

At the mention of his name Mr. Lambeth takes a step back, as if he might be safer if he stood further away.

"With all due respect," her cousin replies tightly, "I shall defer to my agent's greater knowledge of the subject, not yours."

"Please," Henry says, and Linette can hear his impatience, "you do not understand."

"I understand perfectly. But the fact remains we cannot afford a delay. Not now, not when . . ." Julian appears to rein himself in, proffers an insincere smile. "Forgive me, Henry. But you cannot be expected to understand mining business."

Henry stares. "Surely the safety of your workers is more important than the demands of your pocketbook?"

Her cousin narrows his eyes, touches the signet ring on his finger. It is casually done, as if a subconscious gesture.

"You and Linette are more alike than I anticipated. Without the demands of my pocketbook, as you put it, my workers would not get paid."

"Without the workers," Henry counters, "neither will you."

Linette smirks, cannot help it. Lord Pennant clears his throat.

"Now now, Dr. Talbot, there's no need—"

"With all due respect, there is every need."

The placating smile that was drawn across the older man's lips sours. The curls of his brown wig wobble in the breeze.

"My dear doctor, you are attracting an unwelcome audience."

Together, Linette and Henry turn. The villagers are indeed beginning to gather—mothers, fathers, sisters, brothers. Linette spies Rhiannon Einion, Meredith Parry, Gareth Griffiths, Arthur Lloyd. They watch the group with a mixture of curiosity and anger, and she can imagine what ugly thoughts must be picking themselves apart in their heads. At that moment Miss Carew pushes her way to the front of them, and Julian's upper lip curls.

"If you insist on being here, Linette, move them along. They're only in the way."

"'Tis easier said than done, Cousin," she murmurs.

"They are in the way," he says again. "I want them gone. Now."

Black eyes meet gray-green. Neither Tresilian speaks; the air thrums with a tension that seems to stretch and ebb like the pull of waves on a rocky shoreline and Henry takes Linette's elbow, draws her close.

"I hate to say it," he murmurs in her ear, "but your cousin has a point. They cannot stay, they're only hindering progress. I still have miners to treat. Can you not direct them back down to the village? There's nothing they can do except wait."

In that instant Henry's words—so rational, so grounding—make Linette overwhelmingly tired and she sags against him, rubs her fingers over her eyes. They feel tight and dry with dust, and she is conscious now of a headache beginning to tease the roots of her tangled hair. Henry is right, of course, but it galls her to bow to Julian's demands no matter how justified they might be.

She looks between them—Julian, Lord Pennant, Mr. Lambeth. The agent seems less caustic now that he has been cowed by his superiors but the echo of disdain still lingers beneath his countenance, and with an expulsion of air Linette turns her back on them.

"Please," she calls to the growing crowd in Welsh. "Return to the village. Everything is in hand. I promise we're doing all we can."

"But what of my husband?" a voice calls out. "Where is Pedr?" another shouts. Linette can only offer words of condolence, words she knows mean nothing to the families of those still to be saved, but at length the people of Penhelyg soften, reluctantly begin to disperse. Henry offers his body as support to a limping miner with a nasty cut on his thigh, and it is as Linette is trying her best to steer Cerys Davies away from the cavern entrance that she hears a familiar word.

Sharply, Linette turns; Julian, Lord Pennant and Mr. Lambeth stand close together by the spoil heaps, heads bent in conversation.

"This is an omen, surely?" she hears Lord Pennant utter, low and urgent. "But we cannot bring it forward, the timing . . . it's not right. The solstice is not for another five days. We cannot act before then."

"No," Julian replies, "we shall continue as planned. But our success is of even more import now."

On the lower reaches of the path, Henry calls her name.

"Coming," Linette calls back, and the three men clamp their mouths, bestow on her a look of contempt. With a frown Linette presses Cerys to her, guides her down the uneven stone path with a sense of deepest unease.

Of what success did they speak? And why—more intriguing— would they say such a word? What part could it possibly play in their conversation? It is a word her mother has uttered a thousand times over the years, a word that Linette always considered to be part of her nonsensical ravings, nothing more.

Perhaps she was mistaken. It is perfectly possible. But Linette is sure—absolutely sure—that the strange word she heard uttered on the last lingering screech of a gull, was *Berith*.

CHAPTER
TWENTY-NINE

Late afternoon inched into night. By ten o'clock four more miners were recovered from the cavern, leaving another four yet to be found. The atmosphere had been solemn, the air filled with such fearful melancholy that Linette could almost taste it, and it was not until one in the morning that she and Henry returned to Plas Helyg. On Linette's invitation Miss Carew accompanied them—it was not right, Henry said, to let her walk up to Moelfre alone at such an hour—and after all she had done to assist them that day, Linette felt it uncharitable to refuse.

Sleep, though, was an elusive promise. Ink blue turned to steel gray as dawn crept up over the mountains, and the sun had barely risen as Linette and Henry made their way back up to the mine, the servants' trap in tow. Again Linette gave succor where she could, while Miss Carew tended to those possessing more superficial cuts and grazes. To her dismay Dr. Beddoe did not come, the letter Linette hastily wrote the day before pleading for help ignored, and Henry was, in the main, left to deal with the miners by himself.

At nine, young Alwyn—Arthur Lloyd's lad—was found. Cold and hungry, a broken rib, yet, miraculously, otherwise unscathed. It gave Linette hope the others would be found in no worse a condition.

But no such luck was to be had.

She and Miss Carew were serving refreshments the moment the shouts came some hours later. Heart in her mouth Linette had rushed to the cavern entrance where Henry was tying off a stitch on the knee of one of the donkeys. Below, the darkness within the tunnels flickered with candlelight, getting brighter and brighter as footsteps splashed noisily in puddles on the path. *"Doctor, dewch ar frys!"* called one of the men. *"Rydyn ni wedi dod o hyd iddyn nhw!"* shouted another, and Linette swallowed hard.

Doctor, come quickly. We have found them.

The wait for Henry to return was torturous. Minutes passed in which the premonition in the pit of her stomach clenched so painfully Linette felt sure she would soon be sick. Indeed, she almost was when the bodies were finally brought up on their meager pallets. All were covered with thick mine dust, could be mistaken for stone statues had it not been for the fact that Linette knew who they were.

The first body was a man of indeterminable age, whiskers caked with dried blood; his mouth fell oddly, teeth missing, tongue bitten near in half. The next was no more than a year or two older than Henry. Punctured lungs, he told her softly with a sad shake of the head, an agonizing way to die. But the last . . . a boy of thirteen. There was no question of what killed him; his skull had been crushed, an ugly pit in the left side of his head the size of a fist.

Pedr and Hywel. Afan.

One of the other miners covered the bodies with a blanket, wiped his eyes with the cuff of his dirty sleeve. For a long moment neither Henry nor Linette spoke, the horror of it all too poignant.

"Where were they found?" she managed at last.

"That final cavern," Henry replied, a haunted expression on his face, and Linette sucked in her breath.

Two men and a boy.

Two red, one blue.

Did Henry remember what he saw down there that day? Those strange flickering lights?

Both Linette and Henry tried to delay the welcome dinner that evening, but Julian would not hear of it. Their argument—that such a meal would be in bad taste under the circumstances—fell on deaf ears. *Would you have the servants' efforts go to waste?* her cousin lectured, and to that she had no answer. Now, standing in the vestibule to await their guests, Linette shifts uncomfortably from foot to foot.

Her skin itches, her ribs hurt. Linette sighs, twists her shoulder, tries to unpick the dress from her armpit. It is the pretty full-skirted affair of green silk that Julian gave her for her birthday, but she hates it—why suffer so, when she has the means to be comfortable in her father's old clothes? But Julian says he will not have it. Not tonight.

Tonight, he says, is special.

Next to her he is everything elegant, from his coiled black hair to his neat slippers, his formal suit of satin to the cloying cologne that sticks in Linette's nostrils. He appears completely at ease, embodies perfectly the lord of the manor, but then, Julian is in his element in formal situations. He dines with the upper echelons of society, drinks with politicians, the cream of the *beau monde*. He need not suffer people he does not like, nor need he wear a too-tight corset of whalebone and stockings that pinch behind his knees. It is just as Linette moves to prise the offending garment from her leg that Julian whips around sharply, his patience clearly at fray.

"Please stop fidgeting," he snaps.

"Forgive me, Cousin," Linette bites out. "But you know I am not used to wearing a dress."

He looks at her then, slides a considering gaze up and down her figure, before raising it to the full-bloomed gorse flower Enaid has placed in her pomaded hair.

"A pity, you know, considering you can look rather lovely when you make the effort." Julian pushes a finger beneath her chin to raise it, and Linette stiffens. "Yes," he murmurs. "A great pity indeed." He releases her then, looks toward the staircase. "Where's our guest of honor? I'll be most put out if he is late to his own dinner."

As if on cue Henry appears at the top of the stairs, Merlin at his heels. Tall and handsome in a simple yet elegant suit of fine black wool, Henry is concentrating on taking one step after the other so he might not trip, but halfway down he looks up. The polite smile on his face slips as he takes Linette in.

She feels embarrassed, ashamed. Henry has only ever seen her wearing old unflattering garments, garments in which Linette feels completely at ease, but this attire makes her feel like a trussed-up doll, a sham of herself. A fraudulent fool.

Henry comes to stand in front of them, bows stiffly in greeting.

"Good evening." He nods politely at Julian, then looks to Linette. For a moment he appears not to know what to say. "You look . . ." Henry ducks his head, catching himself. "Forgive me, Linette. I'm not used to seeing you like this."

"I was just saying so myself," Julian says. "Is she not a picture?"

"She is indeed," Henry replies softly.

Linette flushes in her discomfit. "Where is Miss Carew?" she asks to change the subject, and this time it is Henry who colors, a soft shot of pink staining the high plane of his cheekbones.

"She returned home to change," he says. "It was good of you, sir, to invite her."

Julian inclines his head. "Under the circumstances I felt it only proper. I'm not ignorant of the fact that she has been invaluable help to you both at the mine. Indeed, adding one more to the party was no hardship."

The doorbell jangles loudly on its pull.

"Ah!" Julian exclaims, taps his cane. "The first of our guests."

Over Merlin's shrill barks Linette's nerves tighten like harp strings. She is dreading tonight's enforced formality, the tedious company she knows she will keep, the condescension, the veiled insults. Cadoc, who has been waiting quietly beside the fire, steps forward to open the door.

"Sir John Selwyn, Lady Elizabeth Selwyn," he announces needlessly, and Julian moves forward to shake the former's hand.

"Ah, my good fellow, welcome. I'm very pleased to see you."

"A pleasure, a pleasure!" Sir John booms, crossing onto the flagstones, trailing gravel. "The roads are dry for which I am grateful. All that rain we had, I was sure the way would be flooded." He pushes his hat into Cadoc's waiting hands without a glance. "We feared we'd have to send our apologies, did we not, Liza?"

Lady Selwyn sweeps through into the vestibule, peeling finely embroidered traveling gloves from her fingers one by one, looking around her with a vague kind of interest.

"Yet here we are," she says as Julian bends to kiss her hand. "I hope we've not kept you waiting."

"Certainly not," Julian demurs. "You're the first to arrive."

"Capital, capital!" Sir John claps, squirrel eyes pin-bright.

He is a man of average height and average build, but there is something of the blathering dandy about him, Linette has always found, and tonight is no different—he is dressed in a suit of navy pinstripe, the elaborately embroidered waistcoat too tight for his paunch. Sir John wears a dove-gray coiled wig in the French style, silver buckles on his shoes, and is as far a cry from a Welsh country squire as he could possibly be. Presently, he is looking at Henry with an expression of abject fascination on his face.

"And this is Penhelyg's new doctor," he says, pumping Henry's hand with more force than is entirely necessary. "*What* a pleasure!"

Angharad appears behind them, divesting Lady Selwyn of her cloak and gloves, and as she does Sir John's gaze shifts to Linette, then back again.

"Do you know you're both *exactly* the same height?"

At her husband's side, Lady Selwyn's lips stretch into an insincere smile.

"Linette, my dear. How *charming* you look," she says, and Linette suppresses a sigh.

So, it begins.

Over the years she has learnt to play her part, to curtsy and smile and pretend Lady Selwyn's condescending comments do not bother her when they do; under Julian's watchful gaze Linette finds herself politely tilting her head in thanks without missing a beat.

Lady Selwyn feigns a gasp. "Oh! You have flowers in your hair. What are they?"

"Gorse, madam."

"How *quaint*! I," she says, tapping her own towering black hair that can be none other than a wig, "prefer something a little more regal. Citrine and diamonds, my dear. Are they not magnificent?"

Linette regards them. The jewels are pinned up high on the side of the wig, large baubles with dangling pear-shaped drops which—if Lady Selwyn were to move her head with any force—Linette is sure would fall off. The color of champagne and starlight, they match perfectly the mustard-gold silk of her dress, the shining needlework on its fine hem.

"Very beautiful, Lady Selwyn."

Linette's voice is flat, but the older woman's satisfaction is nevertheless apparent.

"A gift from my husband. He is always so unfailing generous."

Henry clears his throat. "You're very privileged indeed to receive such gifts, and I must say they suit you admirably. But if you'll forgive me, madam, I think flowers suit Linette far more than jewels ever could."

Lady Selwyn's satisfied smile slips from her lips. Then, quite unexpectedly, she trills with laughter.

"La! Oh, Sir Henry, you tease. Still, I shall not be offended."

"Indeed you shall not," her husband says, taking her hand.

He raises it to his lips. Linette sucks in her breath. Henry's gaze sharpens too on their clasped fingers, the gold rings that shine there. The pointed look shared between them is interrupted when the bell chimes again, a discordant jangle. When Cadoc opens the door once more it is to find Lord Pennant and his wife, Lady Anne, on the other side.

Pleasantries are exchanged. The butler distributes small glasses of wine from a gilt tray, and Henry is pulled from her side, leaving Linette to suffer the indignities of the older women. They attempt many times to draw her in with carefully aimed barbs and backhanded insults—*how clever you are to read so much, how patient you must be to converse with farmers*—but Linette simply cannot bring herself to pretend not to understand them. Instead she keeps her head low, acts meekly as Julian would wish her to, all the while striving to keep the boredom from her face. Both ladies know perfectly well that Linette does not share their interests or a knowledge of their social circle—indeed, they have ceased trying to include Linette in their discussions and moved on to news out of London: the scandal of an earl's inappropriate relationship with his niece, the imprisonment of a Haymarket theater manager for not paying his debts, the death of a much-respected viscount at the hands of a Borough "butcher" in December last year. . . . Linette watches them with a look that feigns a politeness she does not feel.

Neither woman can be much older than Gwen Tresilian, but each wears her age differently. Lady Pennant is a short, squat woman in an ill-fitting plum-colored dress who has allowed her penchant for sweetmeats to get the better of her; her teeth are bad, her skin is dry, the small scars left by a cluster of spots on her cheeks ill-disguised by the powder she wears. Lady Selwyn's skin is powderless; her face is smooth and pale, her age only apparent from the fine lines about her eyes and mouth and neck. Her paleness is accentuated by the black wig she wears, the rouge she has painted on her lips. She was, Linette remembers, attractive once in a darkly seductive way, but now she appears gaunt.

The doorbell rings again, and Cadoc admits the last of the party: Mr. Lambeth, Dr. Beddoe, and at their heels Miss Carew and the Reverend Mr. Owain Dee. A look of relief crosses Henry's face and Linette envies him in that moment, that he should have found friendship outside of Plas Helyg where she could not. Merlin, excitable with so many new people in his midst, trots over to Lady Pennant, tail wagging wildly, sniffs loudly at her skirts. That lady swings them almost violently out of the way, wrinkles her powdered nose in distaste.

"Can't this ghastly animal be removed? I have no wish to smell like dog at the dinner table."

Linette settles on Lady Pennant a scowl, curbs the desire to say it would make not one jot of difference, but Julian clicks his fingers, a short sharp *snap* that echoes loudly in the vestibule.

"Take it, Powell," her cousin says.

"Yes, sir."

Cadoc leans down, grasps the lurcher by the scruff of his neck.

Merlin looks soulfully at Linette, brown eyes large. Then the butler leads him away, and all the while the dog looks back at her and Henry until the door to the servants' quarters shuts behind him.

"Well, then," Julian says, a broad smile upon his pale face. "Now we're all here, shall we go through?"

CHAPTER THIRTY

It has been some time since Linette has seen the dining room look like this. Candles have been placed in every sconce on the wall so it seems as though the fading damask wallpaper glows from within, and the finest of Plas Helyg's porcelain has been laid out in all its splendor, the silverware shining brightly in the light of the setting sun that streams orange through the window. The table has been expanded to accommodate the extra guests, piled with so many dishes that the crisp white tablecloth can barely be seen underneath. As Linette enters on Julian's arm she must commend Mrs. Phillips's efforts. Carrot soup, leek pie, and a medley of vegetables are arranged at the head of the table, while at the other end sit plates of oyster loaves, stewed haddock, and potted lobster. In the middle are dishes of roast mutton, mumbled hare, and dotted between them all a selection of jams and jellies, pickles and preserves. The crowning dish, however, is one of Plas Helyg's hens—it has been placed on a bed of its silken black feathers, roasted skin glistening crisp and golden in the candlelight.

"Oh, Julian," Lady Pennant says, eyes bulging greedily, the curls of her full-bodied wig bobbing. It is an unusual colour of grizzle, with what appears to be an odd shade of cherry-red powdered on top. Behind her, Cadoc clears his throat.

"Do you wish me to serve the soup, my lord?"

"Yes," Julian replies—short, clipped. "Before it grows cold."

"Very good," comes the reply, and the butler proceeds to ladle the soup into their waiting bowls.

There are eleven seated at the table. At the head sits Julian, on his left Linette; next to her Mr. Dee, followed by Lady Selwyn, Lord Pennant and Mr. Lambeth. On Julian's right (sitting far too close for propriety) is Lady Pennant. Then comes Henry, with Miss Carew, Sir John and Dr. Beddoe taking the remaining seats.

Linette looks at the older doctor as he flicks his napkin across his lap. Would he really have killed Wynn Evans for money, as Henry intimated? He scarce looks as though he needs it. His wig is still crisply white with no signs of yellowing, and his gilt-buttoned coat expensively tailored. What need does he have for the living here at Penhelyg? Indeed, considering he did not attend to the miners when Linette requested his presence, Dr. Beddoe could scarce wish for it.

"A toast," her cousin says, raising his glass of wine. His guests follow suit, and Linette takes the opportunity then to mark their hands.

Each and every one of them—except for Reverend Dee and Miss Carew—wears a gold signet ring.

"I am most pleased to welcome our new doctor to Penhelyg," says Julian now, his tenor grave and resonant. "Your presence here has been long-desired, and I am sure you'll bring us all very good fortune indeed. To Henry."

"To Henry," the guests echo.

Henry dips his head awkwardly in appreciation. The others drink. Linette frowns into her glass. Something about the wording of the toast rankles, but why she cannot put her finger on.

Cadoc finishes serving the soup, leaves the room. The party dip their spoons.

"Penhelyg must be," Sir John says, leaning over his bowl to address Henry further down the table, "a great change from what you are used to in London."

Politely Henry turns his head. "Yes, a very great change."

"I understand you taught?"

"I did."

"And what was your specialism?"

"I taught many subjects, lecturing on how to set broken bones, amputate limbs. Remove tumors, that sort of thing." His voice wavers at the last, and Linette knows he is thinking of the patient he lost.

"Most impressive," Lord Pennant says.

"Most excellent, indeed," follows Sir John, and next to him, Dr. Beddoe sniffs loudly. With a chuckle his employer pats his shoulder. "But you are, like my own good doctor here, so I understand, acting as physician not just for Penhelyg but the household too?"

The air shifts; as one, the party look to the conspicuously empty chair at the far end of the table, and Linette braces herself for the inevitable words of false pity.

"How *is* dear Gwen?" Lord Pennant asks. He smiles, frog-like, rubs the bezel of his ring. "You know, Dr. Talbot, that she and Linette's father Hugh were dearest friends of ours. We used to all be very close."

Linette stills her spoon. A vision of fleshy bodies appears unbidden in her mind's eye. She swallows, turns her face.

"*Very* close," Lady Pennant adds. "It grieves me she never recovered from Hugh's loss. She was so full of spirit! So uncommonly beautiful. But she has lost her bloom—her mind quite, quite gone."

"Indeed, such a shame about poor Gwen," Lady Selwyn echoes, dipping her spoon into her bowl. "She did love a party. What larks we had together in London! I assume, doctor, you're doing all you can for her?"

Henry shares a brief look with Miss Carew. The exchange is fast,

300

bare above a second, and Linette would have missed it had she not been sitting opposite them. Again, her insides quail but this time for a different reason. Her grip tightens on her spoon. Is the secret they share to do with her *mother*?

"For now, yes," Henry says. "It is a complicated case."

"Complicated?"

"I'm afraid I cannot discuss the treatment of my patients. Discretion, you understand."

Lady Selwyn tilts her head. The jewels in her wig gleam. "But of course."

The group lapses into momentary silence, in which the only sounds are the *tinks* of spoon against bowl and loud unpleasant slurps.

Lady Pennant shifts in her seat, its spindle legs creaking.

"I've heard of some healing springs near Aberystwyth, much like those in Hampstead and Bath. Would *those* help her condition? I hear a great many positive things about the cure." She leans conspiratorially across the table at Lady Selwyn. "The Duchess of Devonshire took the waters last year, and I hear it has been to *great effect!*"

The women titter, and in the wake of it Miss Carew gives a small cough.

"If I may," she says quietly, "the waters do nothing for one's health except leave a sickly taste in the mouth."

Again, Dr. Beddoe sniffs.

"Now now, Miss Carew," he says. "This is not the place to share your outdated methods."

He looks about the table, a sneer etched across his face, and Miss Carew flinches as if struck. Henry's jaw tightens. If they were not in polite company, Linette is quite sure he would strike the man.

"I must say," says Henry with narrowed eyes, "Miss Carew's expertise has been extremely helpful these past two days up at the mine."

301

The barb does not go unnoticed by Linette, but Dr. Beddoe diligently keeps his gaze fixed upon his plate.

"Herbal remedies," Miss Carew says now, cheeks flushed, "cannot always compete with more modern treatments, but many plants have curative properties."

"Such as?" Mr. Lambeth, this.

She lowers her spoon.

"Such as chickweed. I used a salve containing it on the miners who had only mild cuts and grazes. It's very effective at reducing inflammation and itching."

"But surely it's all in the mind?"

"Not at all, Mr. Lambeth. I've used the treatment often and with great success." Here Miss Carew hesitates. "But I admit that there are those who do believe plants have a spiritual use."

"Oh?"

"Well, chickweed is also thought to aid in the strengthening of relationships and family bonds. Mistletoe is considered a promoter of good fortune, sage enhances spiritual awakening, dandelions cleanse away impurities, and garlic has been known to ward off bad spirits. Maybe these measures are all, as you say, in the mind, but people claim they work. Perhaps believing they work is all that matters."

Linette said something similar to Henry once. It is gratifying, she thinks, that there is at least one woman at this table she can share an opinion with.

"What of trees?" Mr. Dee says, clasping his hands together in an upside-down basket. "Do they hold the same power as plants? There are an awful lot of yew trees in the churchyard, you see; I've tried digging them up many times over the years—their roots are awfully bothersome and interfere with the graves. I always had the notion they were thwarting me on purpose. Does that have any significance?"

Miss Carew dabs her mouth with her napkin. "Yew is often referred to as the Immortal Tree, for they are steadfast and hard to kill, as you've found. They are synonymous with longevity and resurrection."

Henry is looking thoughtfully at Linette. "I've been told rowan is the tree of enchantment."

"That's correct."

"What of gorse?"

Linette stills, swallows the last of her soup. She raises her eyes to meet his. He stares right back.

"Gorse? It is a tree for protection, to guard against evil intentions." Miss Carew hesitates. "Some say it wards off demonic spirits."

The soup is finished. As if on cue Cadoc enters to clear the bowls, leaving the party to help themselves to the remaining dishes. Lady Pennant wastes no time in reaching for a slice of roast mutton as the door swings shut behind him.

"Demonic spirits," Julian murmurs, filling his wine glass to the top. "How interesting."

"But not to be taken lightly," says Mr. Dee. "The Devil and his demons are to be feared."

"Are they now?"

"Certainly. As God has angels do His bidding, so the Devil has demons to do his."

"Bidding?" Miss Carew asks.

"*Ie*," the reverend replies, blinking in earnest. "Demons are fallen angels with a mission to promote sin, induce temptations or frighten us, to do anything that will keep us away from the light of God. Demons torment people through possessing them or by provoking visions that induce them to sin with only the merest whisper. They tempt with promises of wealth and status, of bestowing the heart's greatest desires, and it depends on which demon one communes with as to the reward. As the Bible says, 'Be sober, be vigilant; because

303

your adversary the Devil, as a roaring lion, walketh about, seeking whom he may devour.'"

The light shifts in the room. Outside, the dusk casts purple patterns in the sky. Soon, the lengthening twilight will turn the sky as black as pitch. Julian lounges back in his chair, teases the folds of his cravat. Lady Pennant reaches for her fan, waves it so hard the curls of her wig ruffle.

"I suppose, vicar," Mr. Lambeth says, "a man such as yourself would take great heed in such things. But it is my opinion that the villagers here too often mix up their Christian beliefs with their own little folk tales. Leaving offerings for their mine creatures and painting their doors white, for instance. It is all too absurd." He turns to Henry with a sneer. "For a man of scientific principles, you must find such things abhorrent."

Henry spares Linette an apologetic glance. "I confess I set no store in them."

"You *are* familiar with them though?" Sir John asks, poised over a slice of oyster loaf.

"Linette had me read a book of Welsh folklore, sir. To aid in my understanding of the language."

"And you don't," Lady Selwyn ventures, "even in some small measure, believe the tales?"

"Not at all."

"What of the *tylwyth teg*?"

"Nonsense."

"The Lady of the Lake?"

"Ridiculous."

"Dragons?" Miss Carew whispers.

"The stuff of fairy tales," Henry replies softly, indulgent almost.

"And what of the *tolaeth*?" asks Lady Pennant, looking very much as if she is enjoying this absurd back-and-forth and here Henry hesitates, lowers his fork.

"What are the *tolaeth*?"

Linette's pulse thrums heavily in her neck.

"The *tolaeth* are omens of death," she provides softly. "There are many different kinds, but the most common are corpse candles."

Henry frowns. "Corpse candles?"

"If one were to see a candle flame suspended in mid-air," Linette explains, "then it means a death is imminent. It could be your own or someone else's, but if a *canwyll corph* is seen then the outcome is always the same. Someone is fated to die."

Henry shakes his head with a wry smile. "I'm sorry, Linette, but you know I cannot believe in any of it. Not fay folk, ladies of lakes or stone women. Or corpse candles."

The tips of Mr. Dee's fingers dance together as if he is composing a psalm in his head.

"My dear boy, just because you do not believe does not mean they are not real. I've seen a corpse candle myself."

Henry blinks. "You have?"

"Once, many years ago. Darkest red it was, a large flame that bobbed along the road before me as I journeyed home from the tavern. Three days later, my father died."

"The tavern?" Lady Pennant laughs. "Are you sure, vicar, you had not imbibed too much?"

"No indeed, madam, for I only ever partake of one cup of *cwrw*. I assure you, I still had my wits about me."

"Then you must have seen something else," Henry says. "Candle flames are not red."

"Neither are they blue or white, but a corpse candle is a very different thing."

Henry pales, goes very still.

"I do not understand."

Mr. Dee smiles patiently. "The color of the flame denotes the gender; red represents a man, white a woman, blue for a child. One for each impending death."

Henry looks then to Linette. *Two red, one blue.*

He knows, then, she thinks. Finally, he sees.

"Dr. Talbot?" Miss Carew asks. "Are you well?"

He does not look well. Linette wonders if he will admit to it, wonders if he will mention the bodies of Pedr, Hywel, and Afan. But Henry says nothing, instead forces a smile.

"Yes. Yes. It's just fascinating, that's all."

"Fascinating indeed," the reverend says. He takes a long sip of wine and licks his lips before continuing. "Magic could be considered a kind of science, as yet unexplained. We sometimes use stories of myth and legend to rationalize that which we do not understand— rainbows become a bridge to cross realms, earthquakes are put down to the thrashings of fighting beasts, the strange sounds of the forest are considered to be the hauntings of lost spirits. Such stories help us make sense of strange phenomena."

"Is that so?" Lady Pennant whispers, and Mr. Dee nods vigorously.

"Take Harlech, for instance. Some years ago a blue mist rose from the marshes causing a fire that destroyed the barns and the hayricks. Soon the grasslands withered, the crops failed. Some believed that mist to be ghost lights. There may well be a scientific explanation but such ancient stories persist in many forms. Heroes battling giants have become a metaphor for Christian saints besting the Devil, whereas in other cultures another belief might be held. But of course," the vicar adds, "they could still be as real as you or I. Science might not have anything to do with it at all."

The last of the sun disappears behind the towering trees outside, and the dining room shifts into flame-lit shadow. Julian coughs throat-ily into his napkin. This time, Linette is sure she sees blood on its white hem.

"I commend your thinking, vicar," he says, "that science and magic can be considered the same entity depending on the conviction of the individual, but as you know I subscribe to a different philosophy."

There comes upon the table then a shifting. It is a subtle thing, like when rain clouds edge across the skyline to stamp out the cumulus, and Linette finds herself holding her breath.

"I would not," her cousin continues, "ascribe rainbows to bridges or earthquakes to beasts, nor would I consider magic an unexplained science. I rather subscribe to the notion that science and arcane magic are two very real and separate things." Julian twists his ring. "As you're aware I've collected many books over the years that speak of ancient scientific arts and spiritual awakening, texts which offer a more nuanced and broader view of the world and its many mysteries. Henry and I spoke of it a few days ago, did we not?"

Linette looks sharply at him. He meets her gaze, does not look away, and again she is conscious of what secrets he keeps. What else is Linette not privy to? Henry offers a tight-lipped smile.

"You mentioned alchemy, but I did not realise you considered it to be magic."

"Nor do I. I consider alchemy a science. But if that science were to combine with the mystical knowledge the ancients held, well. Think what might be achieved. Such a powerful combination of the two has not yet been seen."

Mr. Dee frowns deeply at him. "Forgive me, my lord. I do not understand."

"Gold," Julian says softly, "is the world's most precious commodity, is it not?"

He gestures to a space behind him, at nothing in particular it

307

would seem, but Linette sucks in her breath, realizing in that instance precisely what he is referring to. A piece of stone stored within a glass cabinet, the shining yellow flecks that sparkle within it . . .

"Think of the possibilities. Slate to copper, copper to gold. The world at one's feet. This is why we must keep up our work in the mines, despite its dangers."

Linette stares. Expansion, investment; that is what Lord Pennant said. Is this what he meant? Julian is not looking for gold, then, but a fresh vein of copper. Copper to turn, somehow, *into* gold, and a fissure of fury spindles up her spine.

"My God, Cousin," Linette breathes. "Three people are dead, many others injured. Some have been maimed for life. Was that all for *this*?"

Her ribs hurt against the corset, chest tight in its laces. Julian merely regards her over his wine glass, his expression a perfect blank.

"I fear," he says softly, "that the conversation might be taking an unfortunate turn. Come, Linette," and here he smiles in that way of his she has grown to hate. "Let us not ruin this evening by quarreling. This is a night of celebration."

CHAPTER
THIRTY-ONE

It is just as well Cadoc and Angharad come to clear the plates at that moment, for if they had not Linette is quite sure her temper would have spilled itself over without restraint.

Beside her, Mr. Dee touches her arm.

"Are you all right, my lady?"

"Yes," Linette whispers.

"Are you sure?"

"Yes, vicar. I am well."

With a frown—for it is clear he does not believe her—Mr. Dee settles back into his seat, and clutching at her wine glass, Linette takes a steadying sip as the conversation steers into safer waters; Sir John shares his ambition of cultivating an Arab line of horses for the King's guards, which naturally leads on to how the Pennants' youngest son gets along under Horatio Nelson's captaincy. While Henry and Mr. Dee are able to engage with the discussion in a limited and markedly subdued manner, Linette contributes nothing at all.

Nor does Miss Carew.

As Linette pours herself another glass of wine, that woman catches her gaze across the platter of salmagundi, offers a shy smile. There is a gentle sympathy in Miss Carew's amber-brown eyes, but Linette— her resentment and anger still simmering so quietly beneath the calm mask she wears—does not have the energy to smile back. Instead she merely stares at Miss Carew until that sweet smile slips and she turns her face away to answer something Henry has asked, their heads bent together in quiet conference. He is gentlemanlike, attentive, looks at Miss Carew as if she were some rare and otherworldly being, or a crystal vase that might shatter at the smallest touch. With Miss Carew his face is more open, his voice lighter; he does not act on edge as if a blade presses into the soft hollow of his neck. With Miss Carew, Henry is a completely different man.

Jealousy—and it is jealousy, Linette acknowledges that now—twists in the pit of her stomach. Henry and Miss Carew share something in which she has no part; something more than friendship, something that hints of a feeling which Linette has never had the opportunity to feel with anyone, sheltered as she has always been. Not even that silly adolescent attraction she experienced with Tomas all those years ago comes close.

But, Linette remembers, as Henry whispers something in Miss Carew's shell-like ear, that is not the only thing they share.

Between them lies a secret.

What was the *other* vial he gave her that day in the churchyard?

So many unanswered questions, so many things left unsaid. That unaccounted-for vial, the one found at the gatehouse. Undoubtedly the two are connected. Linette steals a look down the table at Dr. Beddoe where he leans across his plate speaking with Mr. Lambeth. How can Henry sit so calmly at the same table as the man he considers responsible for Dr. Evans's murder? It is as if he no longer cares.

She does not understand.

Suddenly Linette feels sick, does not want to finish the wine, does not want to be here at this table at all. The conversation around them is an incessant buzz, a troubling distraction, and if it were not for her inability to focus, Linette might have noticed the dining-room door swinging slowly open sooner than she did but it is too late to warn them, too late to prevent her mother padding barefoot across the ornate rug as if in a dream.

The table falls silent, though the atmosphere is charged with anticipation. Across from her Henry stiffens in his seat; she sees in him the same concern that has clamped itself to her ribcage.

Why is she not locked in her room?

The tune Lady Gwen hums—the off-kilter Welsh melody Linette heard her attempt on the harp only days before—sounds sluggish, but then she stops midway on a minor note, and her mother surveys the room with a smile.

"Good evening."

Linette shuts her eyes in despair. Where on earth is Enaid?

"Gwenllian!" Lady Pennant, this, her teeth revealing themselves in an acerbic crescent moon.

"My dear," rejoins Sir John, half-rising from his seat, his coiled wig dipping dangerously close to a candle. His wife presses her hand to his paunch and he sits back down again, his squirrel eyes watching the new arrival eagerly without blinking.

Linette's mother observes them, bow-mouth parted.

"You're all here."

There is a beat. Julian lets out a low chuckle.

"My sweet lady, where else would we be?"

Her gaze moves to his. She reaches out, very gently strokes her fingers across the back of Julian's chair. The table watch. Lady Gwen breathes out. Then she moves left and does the same to Lady Pennant's chair, then the next, and the next, a languid counterclockwise caress.

"Look at you. In your finery. My friends."

She moves past her own empty chair. Linette thought her mother might attempt to sit but instead she carries on, coming to a stop behind Lady Selwyn, and touches the citrine jewels in that woman's towering wig.

"So pretty. Like mirrors. Like little gold mirrors."

Between the last four words she tapped each one of the gems in turn.

"Oh *yes!*" Lady Selwyn exclaims. "You liked your jewels, didn't you, Gwen? I remember that glorious amethyst necklace you used to wear. It cost Hugh a small fortune, did it not?"

Linette has never seen such a necklace. In fact, she realizes, Linette has never seen one item of jewelry in her mother's possession. Her mother seems to have no recollection of such a piece either. She stares blankly down at Lady Selwyn, and Julian in that moment coughs, a contemplative expression on his pale features.

The door opens once more. Cadoc steps through it holding a serving tray, seemingly with the intention to clear the empty tureens, but when he sees his mistress standing so waiflike behind Lady Selwyn's chair he freezes, turns a sharp gaze to Linette. It holds a question, a warning, and Linette heeds it.

"Fetch Enaid," she tells him. "Quickly."

"Oh, but must she leave?" Lady Pennant asks, teasing. "Look how *sweet* our darling Gwenllian looks! It will be fun, to have her here. All of us, together again."

It will not be fun, Linette wants to say, not when she knows that in this dreamlike state her mother could become violent at any moment. Nor does her mother look sweet—white hair hangs down her back in greasy ropes; the thin nightdress she wears is stained on her breast where she must have spilled her dinner. No, Gwen Tresilian does not look sweet or anything of the like, and as if to acknowledge this Lady Selwyn laughs.

"Pretty Gwen," she taunts, and unpins one of the citrines from her hair. "Would you like to play?"

Henry has stood now, and his cheeks betray the same anger Linette feels.

"Madam," he says tightly. "It would be best we return her ladyship to bed. Would you not agree, Lord Tresilian?"

But Julian simply lounges in his seat, watches as Linette's mother takes the citrine from Lady Selwyn's fingers and bends to kiss her cheek.

It is a strange image, to watch her mother's lips touch this woman whom she dislikes so intensely. The same image from before comes to Linette's mind then, unwanted, sickening—*There were rumours that their meetings were of a more . . . physical nature*—and she stamps it down, hard.

"Let her stay, if she wishes it," Julian says. "Would you like to stay, Gwen? See, there. She's enjoying herself. It would be a pity to deprive her."

Lord Pennant, in that moment, has his hand resting on her mother's bony hip, is caressing the curve of her skin through the thin material of her nightgown, his signet ring glinting with the movement. Her mother simply sways under his touch, eyes half-closed.

"My God," Linette whispers in revulsion. "You've no decency, no compassion." She looks to the others. "None of you do!"

"Don't be a spoilsport, Linette," Lord Pennant smiles. "No harm will come to her." But he removes his hand anyway, and like a doe Lady Gwen darts to the other side of the table, where Henry takes her gently in his arms.

"Come, my lady," he murmurs.

There are cries of displeasure from the table, and trembling with anger Linette pushes herself away from it in a rush of scraping chair and cutlery. Mr. Dee is rising too, Miss Carew with him, and all at once they stand.

"Mamma," Linette says, stern. "You're going back upstairs."

"No."

The authoritative way her mother says the word makes Linette stare. Lady Pennant claps her hands gleefully together.

"See! She does not want to go. Come now, have her stay here with us. We'll take very good care of her."

But there is something in Lady Anne's expression Linette does not like—a look of triumphant hunger, a cruel and taunting greed—and as Lady Selwyn begins to titter the others follow suit, Dr. Beddoe and Mr. Lambeth watching in amusement. Linette turns her back on them all.

"Mamma, do not argue."

"No. No!"

Above her mother's pale head, she meets Henry's gaze. His dark eyes are hard, angry, and an unspoken truth passes between them.

Her mother is not safe here.

At that moment Lady Gwen begins to sob. Not the soft cries of a genteel lady but the sobs of (and Linette hates to think it), a madwoman. Loud and guttural, her breath catching at each rise and fall of her chest. Indeed, the change in her is quite extraordinary.

Henry takes both her mother's hands in one of his, wraps his arm about her shoulders, attempts to steer her away.

"Open the door," he instructs.

Mr. Dee moves to obey, but before he can do so Lady Gwen attempts to fling herself from Henry's arms, striking Linette sharply across the chin; a sting explodes along her skull and with a shout she falls against the wainscoting, holding a hand to her face. From the floor she sees that it is to Julian that Lady Gwen reaches—but he merely stares at her without expression, black eyes like deep pools of tar.

"You will not take them," her mother sobs, voice rising, desperate and wild, and Linette rises unsteadily to her feet, hand still to her jaw, wary, heartsore. Miss Carew gently takes her arm.

"Mamma, please!"

In that moment the dining-room door flings open and Enaid rushes through it, the keys on her chatelaine jangling loudly in time to her gait.

"My lady! My lady!"

The old woman's appearance is enough, it seems, to make her mistress cease her sobs. Linette's mother's eyes roll to the back of her head—the whites frightening in their starkness—and as she faints into Henry's waiting arms, Lady Selwyn's citrine jewel falls to the floor where it lands on the rug with a dull and heavy *thump*.

CHAPTER
THIRTY-TWO

Henry takes the first flight of stairs two steps at a time, Gwen Tresilian—weighing no more than a child—lying limp in his arms. He is tired. He is body-weary and brain-worn, a condition which can easily be accounted for by the upheaval of the past few days but now, after the events of this evening, Henry feels as if he has been entirely stripped of all vigor. He longs to simply shut his eyes and sleep.

He hated that dinner, hated the fakery, the forced politeness. Julian had held it in his honor yet it felt like a mockery, an opportunity to show him off as some sort of jest that Henry was not part of. Still, he has become adept over the years at discoursing with entitled gentry; has he not dined with the governor of Guy's Hospital and his arrogant associates, endured the likes of many such as the Pennants and Selwyns, the coarser company of self-entitled men such as Beddoe and Lambeth, and pretended to look as if he enjoyed it?

Linette, however, made no such attempt; her frustration was clear to see on her face, simmering like water boiling within a covered pot, and once Julian confessed to his ludicrous scheme—*Slate to copper, copper to gold*—he expected Linette at any moment to let her anger at Julian and his guests spill over, that she might let her caustic tongue run wild. And perhaps she would have, if it had not been for Gwen Tresilian.

If tonight has taught him anything, it is that he can keep quiet no longer. Indeed, Henry did not mean to keep his silence for as long as he has. Enough is enough.

They form an odd procession. Mrs. Evans and Linette, Mr. Dee and Rowena, following him up the stairs like a ceremonial troupe. The housekeeper trails close at his heels, wringing her hands in anguish.

"Oh, be careful," she whispers. "My lady's never fainted before."

"Perhaps because you never gave her the opportunity?" Henry retorts.

"I don't understand," comes the reply in a voice wobbling with emotion. "I've always protected her."

"What an interesting way of putting it," he replies as they reach his patient's rooms. "I'd not class poisoning your charge as protection, but to each their own."

At this the housekeeper stops in her tracks. Behind her, Linette shoots Henry a look of alarm.

"What do you mean?"

He nods at the door. "Open it and I shall tell you."

The scent of gorse is pungent: vanilla and coconut, cloying sickly with the scent of beeswax. Protection, Rowena said. But, Henry thinks grimly, what exactly does it protect against? Demonic spirits? Or evil intentions?

He crosses the room, past the housekeeper's truckle bed, through into Gwen Tresilian's bedchamber where he lays her gently down on the coverlet. Immediately the old woman moves to join her mistress, but Henry raises the flat of his hand to stop her.

"Stay where you are, Mrs. Evans. I'm afraid you have some explaining to do."

The housekeeper watches him, eyes wide as moons. "No," she whispers. "I cannot."

"Enaid?" Linette asks, leaving her vigil in the doorway and

317

stepping further into the room. "What does Henry mean?" She looks between him and Mrs. Evans. "What is going on?"

The woman does not answer. Linette, Mr. Dee, and Rowena watch. Henry clears his throat.

"Aside from her general lack of speech, and the fits—as she demonstrated to spectacular effect just now—in the main, Lady Gwen appears to be in tolerable health. Even so, there can be no denying that all is not well with your mistress. You keep her locked away in these two rooms. She never comes downstairs to eat, except that once when Linette had her dine with us. The only time I've been privy to one of her daily walks about the house is when, a few days ago, I found her alone in the garden."

Something shifts in the housekeeper's face.

"I think we can all agree that Gwen Tresilian is barely present in her own mind. So it's interesting, is it not, that she and I had a perfectly sane conversation before Mr. Powell interrupted us."

"You never told me." Linette, this, staring at him across the dim room, confusion writ on her face.

"I'm telling you now." Henry looks again to the housekeeper. "What do you have to say about that, Mrs. Evans?"

The old woman hesitates. "It is true there are times she is more aware, shall we say, than others. Linette herself has told you that."

"Indeed. But when are those times? Perhaps," Henry says, eyes narrowing, "when the tincture you give her wears off?"

Linette looks then from Henry to Enaid.

"What tincture?"

"The tincture found in the vials she keeps in a box underneath the bed."

A beat. Linette stares. Henry clears his throat.

"Do you realize pupils widen when a person is drugged? Ordinarily this widening happens when the eye is subject to the dark. If you look at yourself in the mirror now, you'll see what I mean. The term," he continues, "is 'papillary response,' and it should not occur in daylight. Yet that day in the garden your mother's eyes were dilated even though we were outside in full sun. I confess I did not mark it fully at first . . . not until I saw the same papillary response in Mr. Dee last week."

At the doorway the vicar's face clears.

"Ah," he says. "That is why you left in such a hurry."

"It is. I should have marked it long before then but I never had the opportunity. Clever of you, Mrs. Evans, to keep the curtains drawn to disguise the fact."

Even though the light is dim in the bedchamber, Henry sees how pale Linette has become. She watches as Mrs. Evans reaches for the armchair by the bed and sinks down into it, puts her head in both hands.

But Henry will not feel pity.

"I returned to the house immediately, went directly to her rooms. Your mother, Linette, was unconscious."

"Unconscious?"

"Yes, for I cannot in good conscience say she was asleep. Thankfully Mrs. Evans was not there so I took my chance; I opened the curtains and tested my theory." Henry's lips thin. "There was no natural reaction to daylight—her eyes remained fully dilated. I searched the room, found under the bed a box of glass bottles, the contents of which I did not recognize. It was not laudanum. So I took one."

On the chair, Mrs. Evans's shoulders shudder in silent sobs. Henry bends down, reaches under the bed. There is a clatter of glass as he pulls the offending box from beneath. He places it onto the coverlet and removes one of the strange gray-glass vials, holds it up to the scant light.

"I gave it to Miss Carew so she might identify its contents."

Something shifts in Linette's expression, as if the pieces of a puzzle have slotted themselves into place.

"What's in it?" she whispers.

Henry beckons Rowena to speak.

"It was a mixture of things," she says softly. "A toxic combination of plants that present in the patient a variety of symptoms. Mugwort induces hysteria, henbane hallucinations and restlessness. They were countered by mandrake and valerian which act as a narcotic and sedative respectively, watered down with wine."

"Dear heaven," Mr. Dee says, looking pityingly at Lady Gwen lying on the bed.

"There is one other ingredient," Rowena adds quietly, and Linette gazes at her with frighteningly blank eyes.

"Yes?"

"Deadly nightshade."

Mr. Dee sucks in his breath. Linette still looks blank, as if she has been drugged herself.

"Like Dr. Evans," she whispers, and at this Mrs. Evans's head snaps up, her cheeks wet with tears.

"What?"

Shock is so clearly writ upon her face that Henry begins to doubt his earlier suspicions.

"Deadly nightshade," he repeats, "a plant which, in large quantities, can kill. I found an empty vial of it some days ago in the gatehouse."

Visibly, Mrs. Evans swallows. "You . . . you mean?"

"Your brother was murdered, madam, with a potent tincture of deadly nightshade found in a bottle identical to these."

She says nothing to this. Cannot, it seems.

"Did you kill him, Mrs. Evans?"

The old woman's mouth drops and a shaking takes over her, those pale eyes once again filling with tears.

"How dare you. I *loved* my brother. Loved him! He was my only—I could never—"

She breaks down again into gut-wrenching sobs, and with an admonishing look at Henry Mr. Dee moves to stand beside her and wraps his arm around the housekeeper's shaking shoulders.

No, Henry thinks, watching them. There can be no denying Mrs. Evans's reaction. Any suspicions he might have had about the part she played in her brother's death is immediately quenched.

It takes some moments for Mrs. Evans's sobs to quieten. When they do, Henry turns to Linette, who has not moved from her stance at the door.

"In your mother's case," he says softly, "the amount of nightshade used here is minimal, but just enough was added to produce some very telling effects: psychosis, convulsions, seizures."

The room now falls completely silent. The smell of gorse wafts gently about the room.

"Henry?"

Her voice is weak, whisper thin.

"Yes, Linette."

"Is my mother mad?"

"No," he answers. "In my professional opinion I believe she is, merely, *touched*. I think that in the past something traumatized her—whether that was your father's death or something else, or both—and she has not been allowed to mourn and move forward." Henry turns back to the housekeeper, face grave. "You've been drugging her, Mrs. Evans, have been for years. And in doing so your mistress has been stuck in a kind of limbo—her mind exists in an eternal fog that produces visions of things that are not real, so much so that she does not recognize what *is*. It's why, Linette, she often does not know who you are."

"Oh!" Mrs. Evans chokes. Blood has rushed into her pale cheeks

321

now. When she speaks again her voice is cracked. "You cannot know what it has cost me to give it to her, every day, for twenty-six years!"

"Twenty-six years, madam, is a long time. Do you have any idea what that can do to a body? Her organs will be failing. It will kill her, eventually."

"But I didn't know that, I swear! Please, you must understand. I had no choice!"

"Of course you did! Everyone has a choice."

Mrs. Evans presses her lips at this, turns her face away.

"Who concocts it? Your brother? Dr. Beddoe?"

"I don't know."

He stares. He did not expect that answer. To possess so many bottles of the tincture, Henry expected Mrs. Evans to at least know that.

"What do you mean, you don't know?"

"He never told me," the old woman whispers, a frail hand pressed to her chest as if to suppress her grief.

"Who never told you?"

"Lord Tresilian."

It does not shock him to hear the name. But Linette raises a hand to her throat, looks as though she is going to be sick, and Henry feels achingly sorry for her then, knows now too that Linette had no part in this either, no part in this at all.

"Mrs. Evans," he says, striving for a calm he does not feel. "What happened to Gwen Tresilian? Why has Julian ordered you to keep her drugged? Has it anything to do with his club?"

She looks panicked, like a rabbit poised to flee. Mr. Dee presses his hands flat together in prayer.

"My dear lady. Speak. Confess. The good Lord will hear you and offer his forgiveness. You need not be afraid."

But in that moment Linette utters a choking gasp, is looking at the housekeeper with an expression on her face that makes Henry suck in his breath. Never, not once, has he seen anyone look the way she does now, as if her heart has been so completely torn in two.

"All my life I've looked up to you," she whispers. "All my life. But you've lied to me from the very start. How could you? *How could you?*"

Finally, the old woman's face breaks.

"Linette, I—"

But it is too late. With a strangled cry Linette turns on her heel and leaves the room.

Henry confiscates the tinctures. Mrs. Evans makes no objection— indeed, the old woman is too emotionally exhausted to even exert herself to try—and so he promptly takes the bottles out into Plas Helyg's gardens and deposits their contents into an obliging flowerbed, keeping only a few back with the intention to wean Lady Gwen off them later. These he locks in his trunk, tucks the key into his pocket.

Rowena and Mr. Dee have sat with Mrs. Evans while Henry has been downstairs, and when he returns it is to find the housekeeper quiet and dry-eyed, hands clasped as the vicar leads her in prayer.

"You have to understand," Mrs. Evans says to Henry when they are done. "There were circumstances, circumstances beyond my control . . ."

"I'm sorry, madam," Henry tells her, firm and unmoving, "but no circumstance can be so damning that they can justify what you have done here." He gestures to Lady Gwen sleeping soundly on the bed. "You're slowly killing her, don't you see?"

"I swear," she whispers, "I didn't know what was in those bottles. His lordship told me it was a more potent mix of laudanum, something more stringent to keep her numb, that was all. That's the truth."

"Then I ask once more. Why?"

"Because my lady was so disturbed she was a danger to others and herself! Lord Tresilian told me that unless she was sedated she'd have to go to an asylum, and I could never live with myself if she were sent to one of those. I've heard such stories!"

Henry thinks of Bedlam, and his lips thin. He knows what stories she might have heard, does not wish to confirm them.

"And if my lady went to an asylum," she continues, "I'd have lost my position, and poor Linette . . ."

She begins to sob again. Henry sighs.

"The bottles, Mrs. Evans. Do you recall seeing them anywhere else?"

The housekeeper shakes her head.

"And you've no idea why one with more deadly contents might have been used to kill your brother?"

Her face crumples. "No," she whispers on the edge of another sob. "None."

They leave her then, for it seems there is nothing more to be said. In silence Rowena and Mr. Dee descend to the darkened corridor below and stop outside Henry's room, where all three look at each other gravely.

The strain of laughter wends its way up the stairs. The vicar shakes his head in disgust.

"It is a most distressing situation," he says. "I am shocked. Most shocked. When you told me of dear Wynn, I hoped you were mistaken. Indeed, I'd begun to convince myself of the fact these past few days. But now . . ."

Mr. Dee wipes his forehead with a handkerchief, setting his wig askew.

"What can be done?" Rowena asks. "With Lord Pennant as magistrate we have no one to go to."

Another peal of laughter trickles up the stairs, the sounds of merrymaking unmistakable. How can Julian and his friends continue to enjoy themselves after this? How can they be so callous?

"Mrs. Evans's explanation is sound," Henry says now, trying to keep his anger at bay. "What concerns me more is what part Julian Tresilian played in all of this. There must be a reason why he insisted Lady Gwen be prescribed with such a powerful mixture rather than laudanum alone. And there *must* be a link between the vials—Lady Gwen's and the one that contained the poison used to kill Dr. Evans."

"Dreadful business," the vicar mutters. "Ungodly business." He pauses, yawns deep. "If you don't object, I do not wish to stay in the room prepared for me here. I'd much prefer the safety of my own home."

"Are you sure? It's very late."

"And the walk will be a blessing, I can tell you."

Seeing that the reverend means not to be dissuaded, Henry bows his head. Mr. Dee smiles weakly, turns to Rowena.

"Are you staying tonight? I can walk you home, if you too prefer to leave."

"Thank you, but I shall stay."

Mr. Dee nods, turns to Henry, clasps his hand in his.

"Come and see me before long. I cannot fathom what to do next but something must be done, of that there is no doubt. In the meantime, I shall pray for you. Whether you believe in God or not, He believes in you."

With that he bids them goodnight. Henry and Rowena watch his ambling gait as he descends the stairs, until they are quite alone in the corridor.

The only light comes from the windows. The moon has moved to the other side of the house, but there is still enough of its gaze to prevent them being in complete darkness. Her face he beholds in snatches; Henry can see only the irises of Rowena's eyes stark against their whites, the Cupid's bow of her fine mouth, the paleness of that beautiful satin-smooth skin. . . .

"Rowena," he says to prevent his fancy running away with him. "I wanted to thank you."

"Thank me?"

"Your help at the mine, with the vials. If it weren't for you . . ."

Rowena ducks her head. "You need not thank me, Dr. Talbot."

"Henry," he says, taking her hand. "Please. Call me Henry."

She says nothing, but nor does she pull away, and he feels the first flurry of hope. They would do well together, she and him—Henry with his medical knowledge, Rowena with her herbs. A partnership, based on mutual respect and trust.

Love.

Could Rowena learn to love him? Could he be so lucky?

Rowena looks up at him now in the lowlight. For the briefest moment Henry wonders if she might refuse him as she did the other day, but then she gives a small shaky nod.

"All right. Henry."

He wants to draw her into an embrace and, yes, *yes*, to kiss her, feels sure that this time she would not rebuff him if he did. Instead, reluctantly, he lets her go, and Rowena steps back from him as if released from a trap.

"Goodnight."

"Goodnight, Rowena."

Their eyes linger on each other for what feels like endless seconds. Then Rowena turns and walks down the corridor, pale skirts swinging in the wake of her hurried steps.

CHAPTER
THIRTY-THREE

The old housekeeper does not try to thwart him when Henry knocks on Gwen Tresilian's door the next morning. Instead she leads him without a word into the bedroom.

His patient is only just stirring. Henry goes to the window and opens the curtains by half, then turns to the housekeeper who stands at the doorway twisting a soiled handkerchief between her withered hands.

"A glass of water, if you please, Mrs. Evans."

She has not slept, that much is clear. Her wrinkled face is haggard, white hair poking out from her mobcap at odd angles, eyes red-rimmed. Gravely he takes one of the saved vials from his pocket.

"I shall administer five drops of this into a glass of water for her to drink every morning. In a week I shall reduce it to four drops, then three, and so on and so forth. While I would of course prefer her ladyship did not have the tincture at all, it is safer to acclimatize her body slowly. Only time will tell how much damage has been done. In the meantime you can expect vomiting, cold sweats, shivering. Aches and pains, irritability." Henry glances at her. "I trust you'll be able to manage? She'll be quite trying the next couple of days. For safety, keep Lady Gwen in these rooms. No daily walks, for now. Supervision, always."

The old woman nods. Licks her lips.

"You think I'm wicked," she whispers.

Henry only blinks. "The water, Mrs. Evans."

Defeated, the housekeeper goes to the small table next to Gwen's bed and pours a glass from the carafe that sits there. She passes the glass to Henry with a tremor.

"I do not think you're wicked," he says finally, pouring the tincture in drop by drop. "But you're lucky the truth was discovered, before further damage could be done."

"And my brother? Do you know . . . ?"

"Not yet. I'm sorry."

Mrs. Evans does not respond. Henry places the glass on the table, props up the pillows behind her mistress's back.

"Good morning, my lady," he murmurs. "How do you feel?"

Lady Gwen swallows, looks up at him weakly from the bed.

"My head hurts."

Her voice is hoarse and papery. Henry takes out his pocketwatch, measures her pulse. Fast as to be expected, but not erratically so.

"Do you remember anything?"

Lady Gwen draws her eyebrows together as if trying, but then she sighs, shakes her head.

"Here," he says, handing her the water. "Drink this. All of it."

Diligently she drinks. When she is done Henry checks her pupils (still dilated) then instructs Mrs. Evans to ensure she takes a turn about the room three times that day and he will check on her later on. He leaves them then, and in the corridor knocks on Linette's door.

"Linette? Are you there?"

Within, there is silence, but in the strip of light shining beneath the closed door the shadow of Merlin sniffs at the gap.

"Linette?" he says again.

Nothing. Not even a muffled sob, just stark unnerving silence.

Henry sighs, moves on.

The dining room is already full, the table spread with Mrs. Phillips's best efforts of bread and cheeses, boiled eggs and cured ham, an impressive pound cake and a pot of steaming tea. Cadoc Powell keeps station at the sideboard, staring straight ahead without expression, waiting to be called upon. Julian's guests—despite the lateness of the hour they undoubtedly retired to bed, look surprisingly refreshed (except Lambeth, who is nodding off into his teacup)—and as Henry enters the room they all look up.

Rowena is not there.

"Ah, Henry," Julian says from his usual chair at the head of the table. He holds a cigarillo lazily between his clubbed fingers. "Good of you to join us. You were sorely missed after the excitement of last night. How is the patient?"

A titter of laughter travels around the table. Henry narrows his eyes.

"I'm surprised at your concern. I heard how little Lady Gwen's distress disturbed your merrymaking last night."

Neither Julian nor his companions have the good grace to look ashamed. Instead Julian spreads his hands with a smile.

"Well, it would have been a shame to let Gwen's little episode ruin the evening."

With something like amusement Sir John grunts into his egg, its yoke trailing down onto the tablecloth in a sickly yellow mess. His wife smirks in response. Powell shifts, the tic in his jaw the only telltale sign that he has heard.

Henry, however, does not bother to hide his disgust. He has known people like them in the past; caretakers in Bedlam, for instance, who took pleasure from bullying the inmates, or mocking any person who felt even a small ounce of sympathy for the poor wretches locked inside their cells, and if they had an audience then all the better. To

329

Henry's shame he did not say anything then. But he would be damned if he does not say something now.

"Personally, *sir*, I found your behavior last night unpardonable. You told me when we first met that you cared deeply for Lady Gwen, but now I have my doubts. For you all to treat her illness as some sort of parlor game was in very poor taste. You should be ashamed."

Julian raises the cigarillo to his lips, all the while not taking his dark eyes from Henry's. Then, slowly, he blows the smoke from his mouth, and Henry watches as ash falls like little fireflies onto the tablecloth.

"Well," Lord Tresilian says silkily. "Linette has clearly been a bad influence on you, exercising that sharp tongue of hers."

"On the contrary, my comments are based entirely on what I've witnessed since we met. Last night alone was enough for me to settle my opinion of you."

Powell looks at Henry then, his expression unreadable. He fancies he sees some spark of approval in the butler's eyes, but then Julian is speaking again and Henry cannot tell for sure.

"You disappoint me. Still, no matter, I'm not in the least bit offended. But I'll take this opportunity now to tell you the gatehouse will be finished today." Julian picks a flake of tobacco from his tongue. "I have a ship at Abermaw waiting to take the workers back to London and they'll be gone long before evening. So, considering your intense disapproval of me I shouldn't think you would have any objections to removing yourself there as soon as possible. Of course, I'm not a fiend. Tomorrow will suffice. That's enough time to prepare yourself, is it not?"

Henry looks between the men and women sitting at the table before his gaze settles on Julian. How mistaken he has been in him, and to leave Lady Gwen and Linette in the house with the man is a risk Henry does not want to take. Yet what can he do? he thinks, shifting uncomfortably under Julian's hard black-eyed stare.

330

"Very good," he bites out.

Reluctantly Henry moves to leave, keen to put as much distance between them as quickly as possible, but at the threshold of the dining room he remembers himself and turns back.

"The meal last night was held in my honor, so I thank you for that," Henry says without the politeness he would usually strive to show in other circumstances. "But I hope you will forgive that I have no wish to repeat the pleasure."

Julian, the Pennants and Selwyns, Beddoe and Lambeth say not one word. Henry ducks his head.

"I bid good morning to you all."

"The wound heals nicely," Henry says some hours later, folding the soiled muslin around his hand and putting it into his knapsack. "No need for a bandage now. Let the air get to it."

He had left Rhodri Jones until last, visiting his other patients whose houses were further afield, including Tomas Morgan who (Henry was gratified to find) is now fully recovered, having caught the young man unmooring his little fishing boat and pushing it out to sea. The rest mend in degrees—superficial cuts and bruises have been aided by Rowena's administrations while other more severe injuries require more time, but Henry is satisfied that each and every one of the miners will make a full recovery, even if they are not all as they once were.

He thinks, of course, of the man who lost a foot, another with an arm so crippled he will not be able to work in the mine again. Head wounds such as this one, however . . . well, that is something different entirely. And yet, Rhodri does remarkably well.

"I'm very pleased with your progress." Henry rises from the bed, looks down at his patient sternly. "But you mustn't exert yourself. It is far too soon."

Rhodri grimaces. "I've no intention of it." He glances at his wife—a gentle woman with a kindly smile. "It's nice to have a rest for a change."

Henry thinks he comprehends.

Their exchanges are achieved in stilted Welsh—disjointed on his part, his dictionary has been well thumbed this day—but the Joneses understand him tolerably well and he them.

"I shall come again in a day or two, unless you have need of me sooner? You'll find me at the gatehouse as of tomorrow."

"We will send word up, I can assure you," Mrs. Jones says. "Cai can go, can't you, Cai?"

They all look to him. The lad sits silently in the corner of the tightly cramped bedroom he shares with his parents, watching Henry's treatment of his father with curious eyes. But at his mother's words Cai blushes furiously and scarpers from the room like a scared rabbit. Mrs. Jones shakes her head.

"I'm sorry, doctor. He's been so anxious since his pa . . ."

"There's no need to apologize," Henry says, swinging the knapsack onto his back.

Before, the boy was so hateful; now the conflict he feels is writ clearly upon his face. Only last week Cai despised him, Henry is quite convinced. But now? To be so sure of something, only to have all one's beliefs scattered to the wind like dust, is a feeling Henry well understands.

Henry tips his hat in farewell, backs out into the narrow landing. At the bottom of the rickety stairs he reaches for the door, but then a shuffling behind him makes Henry pause.

"*Doctor?*"

Henry turns.

Cai stands at the threshold of a tiny room to the right, leaning his full weight on his good leg. He looks awkward, shamefaced.

"Thank you."

The words are said in English, and Henry can see how much effort they cost him. Cai flushes into his collar, will not quite meet Henry's eye. Then, taking Henry completely by surprise, the lad holds out his hand.

It is small and dirty, the nails bitten to the quick, but it is steady and determined, and very slowly Henry clasps it in his.

"A truce, then," Henry murmurs.

Cai screws his eyes in confusion, and Henry dismisses his last words with a shake of his head.

"*Croeso siŵr.*"

A look of relief crosses Cai's face. Then he pulls himself up the stairs back to his parents, and Henry leaves the cottage, smiling.

His good mood, however, does not last long. Visiting his patients has been a distraction, but soon Henry's niggling worries invade his thoughts like burrowing worms. He crosses the road, starts the incline through the woods.

He was mistaken in Enaid Evans, that much is clear. But her confession—that Julian Tresilian ordered her to drug Lady Gwen—places him firmly as a suspect for Wynn Evans's murder. But why? And how? Julian would certainly have no access to deadly nightshade, which means Elis Beddoe must still play a part in the scheme. Henry frowns, steps over the protruding root of a gnarly oak. It is the rings that link the two men. Are the Pennants and Selwyns also involved? And what of the land agent, Lambeth? Again and again, Henry pictures the curling symbol on the signets, the portrait . . . the book.

Before, Linette doubted its connection. Now, there is no denying it.

A sigil, Julian called it. *A sigil that we connect to.*

333

The answer, Henry is quite convinced of it, lies inside the book.

Midway up the woodland path he passes the departing carts of the workmen. Henry tips his hat, calls to them his thanks, and as they call back their replies he feels a sense of nostalgic melancholy sweep over him at the familiar sound of cockney.

Will he ever see London again? Does he even want to? Henry stops in his tracks a moment when he realizes he does not know the answer. Above him the leaves rustle on their branches, and Henry looks up into their artery-like spindles. Not even in the lush green parks of London could he have seen an array of trees like this. Somewhere a sheep bleats. He sighs, continues on.

Plas Helyg is quiet on his return. The vestibule is empty, dark in the absence of a fire, and Henry frowns.

"Hello?" he calls.

Nothing. No one. Not the servants, not Julian or his guests. He wonders where Rowena is. Where Linette is.

How she is.

He has always taken Linette as a woman of strength, but after hearing the truth about her mother, the part which both the housekeeper and her cousin played in Lady Gwen's illness . . . how strong can one be, after a revelation such as that?

In his own room Henry kneels at his trunk, unlocks it, takes from it the letter Julian sent him. It is crumpled, well read, folded and refolded countless times, far more than Henry can remember since receiving it all those weeks ago, for he has memorized every line and word but needlessly he opens it, reads again the first sentence indelibly printed in his mind's eye:

It has come to my attention that you are without position under circumstances most unfortunate. To ease such misfortune it would

*be my greatest pleasure to offer you the vacant post of physician in
Penhelyg, Meirionydd.*

Frowning, Henry closes the letter again, rubs his thumb over the wax
seal, the sigil imprinted into its crimson face.

Observation. Contemplation. Interrogation.

Watch and wait.

But the time now for watching and waiting is past. Nothing has
come from Francis Fielding's advice, certainly nothing concrete
enough to provide an answer to all the unanswered questions lingering still about Penhelyg like a pestilent curse. No, now is the time for
action and, decided, Henry leaves the bedroom and climbs the stairs
to Linette's, knocks sharply on her door.

"Linette? Are you there?"

Still, silence.

"Linette!"

The door to Lady Gwen's room opens. Henry turns, expecting to
see Mrs. Evans, but is surprised to find Cadoc Powell standing at the
threshold instead, Merlin pushing his snout between his legs.

"She's out, sir."

"Out?"

"Somewhere in the grounds, I suspect."

"And Miss Carew?"

"With her, I believe."

"Can you think where they might have gone?"

Merlin looks up at the butler, wags his tail against the back of the
older man's knees, and Powell opens the door wider.

"Take the dog," he says, and Henry swears for the briefest of
moments that Powell smiles. "He will lead you."

CHAPTER
THIRTY-FOUR

Julian's guests left at noon. Linette watched them from the small dragon window of her bedroom, half-hidden behind a curtain. She watched through a red stained-glass wing as the carriages were brought round from the stables, watched as farewells were exchanged during which Lady Anne leaned a little too close into Julian's polite embrace, the bodice of her traveling cambric straining hard against his waistcoat. Linette watched as he helped her into the Pennants' carriage, Lord Pennant pulling his squat figure up after her, and then Mr. Lambeth—clearly still foxed from whatever he imbibed after dinner—as he climbed up after him. Sir John entered his own carriage with ungainly movements, followed pertly by that hateful Dr. Beddoe, but Selwyn's wife was altogether more serene. She dipped her knees in a perfectly executed curtsy, allowed Julian to kiss and linger over her gloved hand. Then she placed it on the carriage's doorway, turned in the direction of the house, her gaze resting on the topmost window of Linette's bedroom. Too slow to hide, Linette met that cold gaze of Lady Selwyn's head on. Then, as if she still thought the whole matter a joke, the lady smiled in that sardonic way of hers which Linette has grown so thoroughly to loathe, and raised her hand in a small mocking wave.

Linette could only grip the curtain so hard that it pulled free from one of its rings. The sound caused a rook to burst upward from the slate overhang with a loud discordant *caw*, and the shock of it broke the moment. By the time Linette looked down to the drive again, Lady Selwyn had climbed into the carriage.

Within moments, all of them had gone.

Now, lying once more on her bed, Linette pinches her eyes shut and tries to stem the ache behind them. She has not slept. Could not. All she could think of was her mother, of Julian, of Enaid's betrayal. At one point Linette heard a soft knock on the door and Enaid's frail voice sound through the paneled wood, but she did not have the energy to respond.

It was simply all too much.

In the space of twelve hours everything she knew—or thought she knew—about her life has changed. Until now Linette assumed her mother's condition was hereditary, a canker present from birth; that she has been weak and fragile in both mind and body, always, but her father's death affected her so deeply there had been no recovering from it. Now, to learn Lady Gwen has been made this way and given tinctures to keep her so under Julian's orders, is something Linette cannot comprehend. And Enaid knew. *She knew!*

Linette turns over, presses her face into the pillow.

She could confront Julian, of course, ask him why he ordered her to do such a thing, but after dinner last night, what use would it be? It would simply garner more dismissals, more lies.

No, Linette would get nothing from him now.

She wonders where Henry is. When he knocked at her door earlier she was too wretched to respond. Perhaps, Linette thinks, he is with Miss Carew and the reverend.

Miss Rowena Carew. Mr. Owain Dee. Did Linette not deserve to know Henry's suspicions? Did she not have a right above them? Henry suspected long before the collapse at the mine, and evidently

337

his qualms were confirmed the day Miss Carew came to call upon him.

It was cruel, unfair. Can she truly trust no one?

Plas Helyg's old floorboards creak. A sharp breeze whips the air, making the trees outside sigh like forlorn maidens. Linette turns her face to the window, marks the mackerel sky. She should go and see her mother. She *longs* to see her mother, but Enaid will undoubtedly be with her and she cannot bear to see the housekeeper, not yet. But she cannot continue to lie here and let bitter thoughts drown her in wasted hours.

She simply must get out of this room!

A walk, Linette thinks as she dresses, and in consideration of the weather that looks wholly unfitting for June shrugs into one of her father's old hunting coats. She pulls on her worn walking boots, treads carelessly over the green silk gown she ripped from her body in anguish the night before. A sharp *crack* sounds as her heel presses down into a bone of the corset, and with a little smile of vindictive pleasure, Linette imagines it to be Julian's spine.

Linette follows the footpath down to the valley west of Plas Helyg's lands. On a low knoll she comes to a stop, sinks cross-legged onto the ground among slug trails that glisten on the grass like silken thread. The copper mine is a bank of ugly stone, but the distant mountains behind it are starkly green against the sky, and rippling clouds weave above Yr Wyddfa like spun wool. Linette takes a deep breath, closes her eyes, smells on the air that all too-familiar scent of gorse and grass, the sweet pungency of manure, a hint of salty sea.

But still her heart thumps so wildly she fears she might choke on it. All Linette has are questions. All she has are secrets, with no means of discovering the truth of them. They tumble over themselves like butterflies trapped in a bell jar—Julian, her mother, Enaid, Dr. Evans, Henry—so many of them, all with different-colored wings. For minutes she sits staring into the valley before lying down on the grassy knoll, the ground warm against her cheek, and at length her heart begins to slow to a calm, steady beat . . .

"Miss Tresilian?"

Linette opens her eyes, realizes with a start that the sun has moved far across the sky; there is a crispness in the air which denotes the afternoon's shift to early evening and, indeed, shadows have lengthened across the valley. Blearily Linette leans on her elbow, looks up to find Rowena Carew standing above her.

Unbidden, a lump forms in her throat. She feels the hot swell of tears at her eyelids and angrily brushes them away.

"Still here, I see," she mutters.

A pause. Awkward. Shy.

"Might I sit?"

"If you must."

The younger woman hesitates in the face of Linette's cold response, then gathers her skirts, settles down on the grass, leaving a polite distance between them. In silence they watch the clouds shift lazily across the sky.

"You disapprove of me," Miss Carew says eventually.

Linette picks at a blade of grass.

"In truth I do not know what to think of you. You've ingratiated yourself into my life and appear to know more of it than I do myself. Can you blame me for being wary?"

"I cannot," Miss Carew replies. "I should feel the same."

Linette nods, does not know what else to say. None of this, she grudgingly admits to herself, is Miss Carew's fault.

The sun appears from behind the great bank of cloud, piercing a patch of grass on the valley floor, and together they watch it—its single golden beam—until it disappears. Miss Carew tucks her chin under her knees.

"My mother died when I was a young girl. My father had suffered some misfortune, drove himself to drink." Miss Carew pauses. "He used to beat her. For years, my father ruled with his fist until she could stand it no longer."

Linette stares. "What happened?"

"She hanged herself."

"I . . . I'm so sorry."

"Yes," Miss Carew says, as if she had divulged nothing more interesting than the weather, "it was rather terrible. It's a dreadful thing for a child to grow up without a mother. But at least, in some way, you had someone to love you in the absence of yours."

Enaid's name hovers between them. Linette feels her stomach twist.

"She lied to me," Linette whispers. "Is that love?"

"Is it not?" Miss Carew counters, finally turning to look at her. "You and I both witnessed your mother's fit last night. She is clearly a danger when she's like that. I see that bruise on your jaw." Involuntarily Linette touches it. She has forgotten it is there. "Perhaps it isn't right to keep her this way," Miss Carew continues, "but I think your Enaid did what she did out of love. To protect your mother. To protect you. To help you both find some measure of peace."

Linette is silent a moment, her thoughts tangled like a fly caught in a web. *Some measure of peace.* Is that what she has here at Plas Helyg? Peace? It feels to her more like a kind of purgatory. As much as she loves her home, not once has Linette ever felt at peace in it.

Not once.

"The tincture she gives my mother," Linette says quietly. "Henry said it would have killed her eventually?"

A pause. "She need not take any more. Henry has confiscated them."

"But there is no telling how much damage has already been done, is there?"

Miss Carew hesitates again. "It's quite possible that your mother's life has been shortened as a consequence. All you can do is find a way to cherish what time you have left."

Linette sucks in her breath, the pain with it. What state will her mother be left in without the tincture keeping her bound? What manner of woman will remain? Linette is under no illusion that Gwen Tresilian will suddenly turn into a loving mother, that she will be, after such prolonged mistreatment, *normal*. Again she touches the bruise on her cheek. It is—and here, she fights down a hysterical laugh—the only time her mother has ever touched Linette of her own volition.

"I have something for that, if you'll permit?" Miss Carew reaches for a small reticule which hangs from her wrist. "I always carry some herbs with me. Just in case. Sit up."

Linette does as she is told while Miss Carew removes from her reticule a small hessian pouch, and from within that a selection of leaves. She watches as Miss Carew pinches her bottom lip with her one crooked incisor before selecting a limp one reminiscent of a miniature oak leaf. She crushes it between her fingers then looks at Linette, amber eyes bright in the low sun.

"May I?"

Linette nods. She leans in.

"Feverfew," Miss Carew murmurs. "Better of course mixed with the juices of ribwort and sage, but this will ease the tenderness for now."

Linette's eyes sting with tears. Such kindness, from a woman she barely knows. From a woman she has treated with such cool disdain.

They worked well together at the mine, she remembers, and

341

Linette was grateful for Miss Carew's calming presence. As the younger woman rubs the sap into Linette's skin with short and tender strokes, she remembers too how gentle Miss Carew had been administering to the miners' more superficial wounds, and she did not charge them a single penny for her troubles.

Yes, Miss Carew is kind. She cares about the villagers. *Truly* cares. If anything might commend a person to Linette, it is that. How lonely she must be, alone in her cottage up in the valley. Lonely, just like her.

All this time, Rowena Carew might have been a friend.

"Thank you," Linette whispers.

"You're welcome."

They are sitting so close their faces are only inches apart, Miss Carew's fingers lingering gently on her chin. The two women look at each other, gray-green meeting amber-brown. Linette's mouth grows dry. Her breath hitches. She can count every single freckle on Miss Carew's finely turned nose. . . .

Behind them there comes a loud bark and quickly Linette pulls away, confused at the wild fluttering of her pulse. She turns to see Merlin bounding from the trees, Henry following close behind.

"There you are," he says, relief evident on his tired face. "I've been looking for you."

CHAPTER
THIRTY-FIVE

It has been arranged to meet at the grandfather clock at the hour of two. They should, perhaps, have left it longer for there was no guarantee Julian would be abed, but when one is set upon a thing it is always best to act at the earliest opportunity.

And it must be tonight.

"Why must it?" Miss Carew had asked when they were taking a light supper of leftovers in the safety of Linette's study. "Can it not wait until Lord Tresilian is away? To sneak about while he sleeps so close, the risk of being caught . . . I'm not sure I can bear it."

It had been agreed she would stay at Plas Helyg again this night. An extra pair of eyes, Henry said, but as he took Miss Carew's hand in his, Linette suspected he merely wished to keep her close.

"If I am to remove to the gatehouse tomorrow then our options have been cut short; it would be better we discover as much as possible now while we still have the chance. Dr. Evans's murder, your mother's mental state—both of these things are linked by the vials. It was Beddoe who roused my suspicions in the first place, but now we know he is a member of a Hellfire club led by your cousin, and that Julian ordered your mother's sedation. These things, they are all connected, and the book is the answer, I'm sure of it. Besides, what does waiting achieve? We tried that, and nothing has come of it. No," said Henry firmly, "we've waited long enough."

Linette started to reply—with what exactly she did not know—but then a knock came at the door and there was no need.

"Come in."

It was Cadoc who opened the door, Angharad hovering behind him in the passageway.

"Are you finished here, Miss Linette?"

"Yes, Cadoc," Linette said, pushing her half-eaten leftovers of oyster loaf away from her, "we are finished."

"Can we fetch you anything else?" the butler asked as he and Angharad cleared the plates, and Linette managed a tight smile and a small shake of her head.

"No, thank you. That will be all."

Her hands full of plates, Angharad dipped her knees and departed, but the butler did not move. He watched them, dour face a careful blank, and Linette shifted uncomfortably in her seat. There was something suspicious about the way he watched them, for all that his face was devoid of expression, and she longed to know what he was thinking. Could *he* be trusted? Or was he, like Enaid, one of Julian's pawns?

"You may leave us now, Cadoc," Linette said softly, and the butler bowed his head.

"Very good."

But at the door he hesitated.

"You will forgive me for saying so," he said quietly, "but I feel you should speak to Mrs. Evans. She asks after you constantly. She is most distressed."

It was the first time—the first time in twenty-six years—that Cadoc Powell had ever spoken out of turn, and the shock of it together with the mention of Enaid made Linette's stomach clench.

"That will be all, Cadoc," she told him tightly.

A beat. Then, a pointed bow. He shut the study door behind him with a click that felt harsh and dangerously final.

When Linette turned back it was to find Henry and Miss Carew looking at her across the table. The latter politely turned her face. The former cleared his throat.

"Have you not spoken to Mrs. Evans at *all*?"

Linette sniffed, rose from her seat, crossed to the window where it was open a little in its casement. The smell of jasmine whispered through the gap, and Linette took a deep calming breath of it.

"No, I have not."

Behind her, Henry sighed.

"Linette. While I feel she has acted terribly I do not, on reflection, think Mrs. Evans meant to cause intentional harm. Don't you think you are being, perhaps, a little cruel?"

Linette turned, stared at him aghast.

"Cruel?"

"She is upset," he said simply. "When I saw her this morning she looked—"

"I don't wish to hear it, Henry."

"Don't you think she might explain more to you? I'm still a stranger to her, but you. . . . If you asked her, I'm sure—"

"No, Henry."

"But—"

"Please!" Linette snapped, raising her hand. "I'm not ready. Don't force me to do something I do not wish to."

He watched her, troubled. "All right," he said eventually. "But you cannot ignore her for ever."

Linette turned away again, could not look at him, stared instead at her reflection in the windowpane. Her face was drawn, eyes like black holes, and she did not like what she saw.

From the moment Linette locked herself in her bedroom, sleep became an elusive dream. Instead she listened to the grandfather clock below strike its hour of eleven, then twelve. At half past, a wind outside picked up in a restless moan. At one o'clock Linette thought she heard the sound of vomiting come from her mother's bedroom, but over the wild rustling of trees she could not be sure. Then, as soon as the grandfather clock struck its sonorous chimes to the appointed hour, Linette slipped from her bedroom, silent as a wraith.

She is the first to arrive on the landing below. While she waits Linette watches the clock's galleon tip back and forth in time to the heavy *clunk* of turning cogs.

Back and forth. Back and forth. Back and forth.

It is mesmeric, calming. And she needs that calm now, needs something to stem the beat of nerves in her chest.

There comes a soft footfall above. Linette freezes, preparing to take flight lest it should be Cadoc or Enaid or, heaven forbid, Julian himself, but then Henry and Miss Carew turn the corner of the stairwell. Like her, both are fully dressed. Henry holds a green box—his surgical tools, Linette remembers—in one hand.

"Are you ready?" he asks, and Linette nods, though she is not. Together, their party of three descend the stairs to the vestibule, steal as quietly as they can across the flagstones, into the corridor leading to Julian's study.

"I shall wait here," Miss Carew says. "Keep watch."

"Are you sure?" Henry asks, and visibly she swallows.

"I'd be no use to you even if I did go in with you. I'd be watching the door the whole time anyway and could not concentrate. Please," she says, stronger now. "I would much rather do this."

"All right, if you're sure. Linette?"

She nods, closes her hand over the study's doorknob, and sighs with relief as the brass ball turns smoothly in her hand.

The study is dark—the light of the moon does not reach here—and smells of beeswax, the sickly hint of Julian's London cologne. Outside, the trees bend in the wind, moaning on their trunks. The shadows of leaves skitter across the wallpaper, like hundreds of hands reaching for them as Henry and Linette cross the room to the bookshelves.

"Here," Henry whispers, "take this." He passes her the instrument box, unclips its clasp, opens the lid, selects a long thin tool from its velvet casing. "I hope it isn't hard to pick."

On Julian's desk sits a candle. Linette reaches into her pocket, removes a tinderbox. She strikes the spark, lowers it to the candle's taper, and light blooms briefly before the flame dims and settles. Linette holds it out so Henry can see, and as he commits himself to the task she stares at the tomes behind their glass casings.

Again, the books send a shudder down her spine. In the darkness of the room they look even more distasteful. She reads their titles with a deep sense of foreboding:

Compendium Rarissimum Totius, Clavis Inferni, Histoire des Diables de Loudun, Lemegeton Clavicula Salomonis, Epistolae Theosophicae. . . .

The lock clicks. Henry removes the instrument, places the green case on the desk. Then, very carefully, he removes the tome from its stand. The edge knocks against the piece of stone, and it wobbles slightly before falling still, its gold flecks flashing in the candlelight.

"Christ," he bites out, laying it down upon Julian's desk, "it's heavy," and for a long moment Linette and Henry simply stare at the book, transfixed. Before, it was merely a dusty antique to gaze upon from behind glass, but now it is within her grasp she is fearful of it. Hesitantly she puts her hand out to touch the symbol on its cover—hard, rough, reminiscent of leather but not, with odd raised edges that remind her of rope—and Linette brings her hand back as if burned.

It feels like no book she has ever touched before.

Henry opens it. The spine creaks.

The first page is blank. Henry turns it, and there comes then a crinkling sound not unlike that of old parchment. Like the first, the next two pages are also blank but on the fourth are a set of ornate words, written in Julian's tight cursive. Together Henry and Linette lean to read them, and Linette sucks in her breath.

Property of The Order of Berith

And underneath that:

Clavis Umbrarum

Magus Goetia

"Berith," Henry breathes.

Berith.

That word. The word her mother has said so many times over the years, a word that Linette has taken no heed of until she heard Lord Pennant say it that day at the mine.

"*Clavis umbrarum*," she murmurs after a moment. "What do you suppose that means?"

Henry shakes his head. "I'm not sure."

"Well, what of *magus goetia*? Is it Latin?"

"I think so, yes, but as I told you before, my Latin is rusty."

Henry turns the pages. Many of them are filled with tightly packed writing but some are crammed with bizarre images. Circles containing strange symbols similar to the one on the book's cover; lines made up of triangles and angular shapes, some projecting tiny crosses, some odd little swirls and dots. On one page there is drawn the diagram of a hand, its fingertips adorned by similar shapes, its palm a blazing sun. The wrist shows an eye set within a star, staring unnervingly up at her.

Linette glances back again at the occult books, their crumbling spines tightly packed on their shelves, then back down again, a suspicion starting to take shape at the back of her mind. She thinks of the stories Enaid used to tell her as a child, tales of the old traditions. But, Linette thinks, biting her lip, this *cannot* be what she thinks this book is. Surely such things do not exist? As if in answer the wind sighs against the windowpane, and she must suppress a shudder.

Henry turns another page. This one has more text but on the opposite page there is another image, far more disturbing than the rest. It shows another circle, but within it a skull is placed atop a small plinth, and lying in front of it a dagger colored yellow to represent gold. Henry stares down at it with a frown.

"Did your mother not mention a golden blade?"

"Yes," she says faintly.

He turns another page. More text. He turns another. Line after line of it.

"This book is completely handwritten," he says after a moment. "Nothing is printed."

Henry is right, she acknowledges grimly as he turns the pages, again and again until, finally, he stops. The candle Linette holds flickers, casting Henry's face into shadow as he looks at what nestles between the pages.

Linette stares, reaches for it with a shaking hand. She brings it up to the candle flame, twists the calamus between forefinger and thumb. It is an old feather, dull, with little of the rainbow sheen she knows should be there, but she knows it all the same, would recognize one of those feathers anywhere.

It is the feather of a black hen.

One of Plas Helyg's hens.

"Look," Henry says. He points then to the page beneath the feather.

It shows another circle, a circle filled with more symbols. Standing in the middle of it is a naked man, his body covered with those very same patterns. He holds in one hand a golden blade, and at his feet there lies a black hen, blood pooling from its neck.

Guiltily Linette thinks of Merlin. That poor dog. Blamed all these years for something he did not do!

"This is more than a club for the rich," Henry whispers. "This is ritualistic." He presses her elbow. "Look at the writing."

Henry points at the line of text at the top of the page and in shock Linette stares down at it, unable to fathom what she is seeing:

HOATH, REDAR, GANABEL, BERITH

"Mamma's words," she whispers.

Henry nods. "These aren't Latin, though."

"How do you know?"

"They just don't sound Latin. They don't follow the same rhythm."

"What are they then?"

"I don't know. But have you not noticed?"

"Noticed?

"This isn't ink."

Swallowing, Linette brings the candle closer to the page. He is right. The writing is not black, but brown. A faded shade of—

"Red," she breathes. "It's red. You mean . . ."

"Blood," Henry confirms grimly. "This book is written in blood. And there's something else."

Linette stares at him. "What more can there *possibly* be?"

"The paper."

Henry trails off, runs his hand across the page. Linette places her own hand on the parchment beside his, rubs the pads of her fingertips against the grain. It feels soft, leathery, almost like . . .

Revulsion turns itself in her stomach.

"Skin. It feels like skin."

"Yes."

They look at each other. Henry shakes his head in wonder.

"What *is* this?" he asks, and Linette shuts her eyes, suspicions now confirmed.

It can only *be* one thing, something she has only ever read about in her book of folklore, or heard from stories Enaid told her long ago.

"A grimoire," Linette answers, opening her eyes once more. "A book of magic, compiled by whoever it belongs to. It includes methods of crafting talismans and amulets, instructions for casting spells." She licks her lips. "It tells how to invoke otherworldly beings such as angels, spirits, deities. And . . ."

"And what?"

"Demons."

Henry says nothing. Fearfully Linette runs her fingers across the page.

"Witches would make their grimoires from what they called virgin parchment. It is made from the skin of a young goat, stretched and dried out to make paper. Then the pages are blessed and sewn into a book."

His face is hard in the candlelight as he looks down at the feather Linette had put down on the desk, the book, its strange symbols. Then he attempts a half-hearted smile.

"You know," Henry says quietly, "that I do not believe in witches or grimoires or magic. It is clear, however, that Julian does." His fingers hover over the image, the bleeding hen. "The Order of Berith," he murmurs. "That, then, is what his Hellfire club is called. It *sounds* cultish, and there's no denying this book is ritualistic in nature. But to what purpose?"

Tiredly he turns the page to reveal the symbol from the cover of the book drawn on the page beneath. Under that, English words. Together, she and Henry bend forward to read:

Whosoever breaks a covenant with Almighty Berith
will be devoured by a beast of darkness, and that sinner's soul
shall belong completely unto Him.

"Covenant," Henry murmurs. "An agreement. And look . . . the sigil is slightly different. Berith," he reads, tilting his head at the letters spaced out within the symbol's disc. "Berith is a person, then?"

"Or a demon."

The words sits between them a moment. Outside, the tree branches sway, rustling their leaves.

"Look," Linette whispers, "there's more."

To ensure salvation the bargain must be struck with the sacrifice
of one's own ancestral lifeblood, the bond of two united.

"Bond of two united. . . ." Henry repeats under his breath, and with a frustrated sigh Linette moves the candle from one hand to the other.

"It makes no sense, no sense at all!"

"Not yet, perhaps," he murmurs. "But it obviously means something. What are these?" Henry points to a series of strange symbols set below the last line of text:

Linette shakes her head. They look similar to all the other symbols scattered within the book. With a sigh Henry turns the next page but it is blank, as is the next and the next.

There is nothing else.

Henry rubs a tired hand across his face, goes back to the page of English handwriting.

"Let's find something to copy this down with," he says. "It's all we can do."

He opens the drawer, bends to search it. Stills.

"What's wrong?"

He does not answer, pulls something out, something long and thin, wrapped in black silk. Very slowly Henry begins to unwrap it, revealing the point of a gold dagger. . . .

He lets the silk drop, holds it between them like a talisman. Linette raises the candle, and in the gutter of the flame the dagger almost appears to glow. The symbol, the symbol of Berith, is carved into the blade, and both she and Henry look at it, mesmerized.

"It's the dagger from the portrait," he murmurs.

Suddenly, Miss Carew's head pokes around the door.

"Hurry!" she hisses, urgent. "Someone is coming!"

Henry swears, and Linette pushes the black feather back between those awful pages. Then she looks down at the one in front of her and makes a choice.

Linette takes the dagger from Henry's grasp, slices the page from the book. He stares at her aghast.

"Are you trying to get us caught?"

"Do you have another idea?"

She pushes the page into her pocket and Henry swears again, rewraps the dagger with hurried movements, places it back in the drawer.

"*Beth wyt ti'n ei wneud i lawr yma?*"

Linette and Henry freeze. That is Cadoc Powell's voice.

That is Cadoc Powell's hand pushing the study door open; that is Cadoc Powell holding a candelabrum aloft, standing there in his nightshirt, wig dangerously askew. His eyes go from Linette, to Henry, to the book on Julian's desk, then back again.

"You should not be here," the butler says finally. His voice is measured, carefully devoid of emotion. "It is best you all go back to bed."

Behind him Miss Carew hovers in the hallway, eyes wide. Linette draws herself up, determined not to show her own fear that has clamped itself to her ribcage with sharp tenacious claws.

"Exactly where we were going," Linette replies, trying to hide the wobble in her voice. Next to her, Henry very slowly closes the book, replaces it in the cabinet, shuts the door. "We're finished here, aren't we, Henry?"

She does not wait for him to answer. Linette sweeps around the desk as if she has every right to be there and crosses the study floor.

"Step aside, Cadoc," she says.

But Cadoc does not step aside. Instead, he stares at her. His expression is impenetrable, and desperately Linette keeps her face the same, hopes he cannot hear the pounding of her heart. Then, finally, Cadoc lets her and Henry pass to join Miss Carew in the corridor.

They do not look behind them as they retreat, but Linette can feel the butler's piercing gaze at their backs like knives, and outside, the wind in the trees cries a soulful warning.

CHAPTER
THIRTY-SIX

It does not take Henry long to pack his belongings for he brought very little with him to begin with. The medical books from Guy's have been returned to his trunk, the unused vials of Lady Gwen's poisonous tincture kept safely wrapped above those, his box of surgical implements laid carefully on top. Angharad has already left his laundered clothes in a folded pile on a chair, so little effort is required to fill his portmanteau once again. It is all done within minutes.

Three items of luggage: the trunk, the portmanteau, the knapsack. As Henry ties his cravat he looks at them set down by the bedroom door, and briefly feels sadness that this is all he has to show for his life, that it is so very little.

This will be the second time he has moved in as many months. He had not wanted to come here and yet, now, Henry does not wish to leave. He feels duty-bound to Lady Gwen, to Linette, for last night something shifted, like a chess piece moved across a board. He thinks of Julian's grisly grimoire, what they found within it. Strange symbols, ritualistic circles. The feather of a black hen. He hears the word Linette uttered, teasing the back of his skull, tries to deny it but cannot.

Demons.

It was always said that the Hellfire clubs of Wharton and Dashwood's day danced with the idea of Satanic rituals, but that had only ever been rumor, conjecture; Julian and his club, this so-called Order of Berith . . . did they really believe they could summon a demon? It was madness, pure madness, but what irritates Henry more than anything else is that after all he and Linette have discovered they still do not have any sure answers. What actually happened to Gwen Tresilian? Why has Julian kept her drugged all these years? Henry dips his hand into his pocket, presses his thumb into the shell he finds there, worries the dulled spikes with his thumbnail. With a frown he pictures the gold dagger they found in Julian's desk. Linette told him her mother had spoken of a golden blade. Could it be she saw it in use? What else did she say? *Wings. Beating. Poor, poor thing!* Was it the hen she spoke of? And, of course, that strange chant he heard her utter at dinner: *Hoath, Redar, Ganabel, Berith.* So many things Lady Gwen has said now make perfect sense. Is it possible that the cult did something to her?

And what, if anything, does Dr. Evans's death have to do with any of it? Did he die as part of some ritual?

Henry does not know what to think. What he does know is that demons do not exist, any more than hounds of hell and everything else he has heard of since he came to Penhelyg. Whatever Julian is playing at, well, that is all it is. Play. A game. The Order of Berith is nothing more than a chance for him and his friends to exercise their sordid fantasies away from the prying eyes of London's *beau monde*.

What is to be done though? Henry thinks of the page Linette took, the only clue remaining to them. That page is the key. They must, however, be careful. He and Linette might have come closer to discovering the truth of Plas Helyg's past, but they are not the only ones to know it.

Cadoc Powell caught them. He caught them, but said nothing.

And it is that very act—that lack of confrontation—which makes Henry distinctly uneasy. One more person not to trust. And to leave Linette at Plas Helyg alone does not sit well with him at all.

Yet what choice does he have? It is clear Julian wants Henry out of the way. Which means there is a reason, a reason Henry cannot know until he *does* leave. No, he will quit Plas Helyg today as instructed and become a willing player in this game of which he does not know the rules.

But first, he must see Gwen Tresilian.

He finds her hunched over the chamber pot, Mrs. Evans holding back the heavy white plait of her hair. The stench of vomit fills the room, and Henry goes to the window, flings it open wide. Leaves scatter across the lawn below, casualties from the wind the night before.

"Come, my lady," the old woman murmurs. "Back into bed."

Henry watches as she helps her mistress under the covers. She is unsteady on her feet, bends to grip the bedsheets as if they were a lifeline, her spine poking from beneath her nightdress like the scales of a reptile he saw once at the British Museum.

"Has she been eating, Mrs. Evans?" he asks, removing the vial of tincture from his pocket.

"Middling," the housekeeper replies. "She doesn't have much of an appetite at the moment."

"Even so," he says, pouring water from the carafe into its accompanying glass, "make sure she eats something. The sickness will pass in time, but she needs to eat to conserve her strength."

He looks at his patient now, marks how very ill she looks.

"It's still early days," Henry says to her. "I promise, this *will* pass."

Lady Gwen watches as Henry pours the drops into the glass of water, and when he holds it to her she shakes her head.

"No."

"Yes."

"I can't."

"You will."

They stare at each other for a long moment, and Henry is gratified to see more green in her eyes than black.

"Drink up, milady. I shan't take no for an answer."

Reluctantly she takes the glass, drinks it down. She coughs at the last swallow and then, in a petulant way that reminds Henry of Linette, flings the glass back at him, sinks into her pillows, plucks at the coverlet.

"Enaid tells me you're to leave Plas Helyg today."

Her voice is hoarse, weak. But when she looks at him, her gaze is strong.

"Only as far as the gatehouse," he tells her. "You'll still see me every morning until I deem it unnecessary."

"I see."

Lady Gwen looks away through the window, at the towering trees outside. She sighs, says nothing else. Henry sits down on the edge of the bed.

"Do you know why I'm doing this?"

On the other side of the bed Mrs. Evans sinks down in the armchair, gently takes her mistress' hand, but Lady Gwen snatches it away.

"I'm a grown woman, Enaid. Please stop mollycoddling me like a child!"

A shot of hurt splits the old woman's face and she draws her hand back, tucks it away into her apron. Despite his earlier frustrations at the housekeeper, Henry feels now a deepening sympathy for her. To be shunned by not one but two of her charges is a cruel hand indeed.

"Do you know," Henry says again, turning his attention back to Lady Gwen, "why I am doing this?"

His patient shrugs. "I'm sick," she says simply.

"But do you know *why* you're sick?"

A shadow passes across her face. A memory? Or confusion?

With a sigh Henry removes his pocketwatch, gently clasps Lady Gwen's wrist to take her pulse. As he does her gaze drifts downward, her eyes widen, staring down at the watch, and Henry is sure this time a memory ghosts her face when her irises darken from green to gray.

By the time Henry comes downstairs his belongings have already been brought to the vestibule and Julian stands beside them, waiting.

"Good morning, Henry," he says, as pleasantly as if they were old friends. "I see you're packed promptly as agreed. Very good."

Henry ducks his head in an effort to hide the look of dislike he knows has crossed his face. "I would not presume to disobey you, my lord."

"Would you not?" Julian's voice is laced with amusement, as if he recognizes the lie. "Well, that is most gratifying."

He clicks his fingers at Powell who comes forward from the shadow of the stairwell, Julian's cane and cocked hat in hand, and as he passes them to his master the butler's eyes meet Henry's. Has Powell told Julian what he saw last night?

"I am to Lord Pennant's on mining business," Julian says now, placing the hat on his head. "Plenty to do, much to arrange. The accident set us back some weeks, as I'm sure you can imagine."

At that moment Linette appears at the top of the stairs. Henry inclines his head, as much to greet her as to reply to her cousin.

"If all goes as planned, then I expect we shall make good progress in due course. Not all is lost."

Outside, the sound of wheels over gravel. Linette comes to stand beside Henry as Julian crosses the vestibule, pulls open Plas Helyg's wide doors, steps out onto the drive. With an effort he pulls himself into his phaeton; Rhys hands up the whip. Then Julian flicks the reins and turns his dapple gray horse down the driveway, and Linette watches her cousin go, frowning deeply.

"Are you really going to leave today?" she asks.

"I am."

"Henry—" Linette begins, and he turns to her with a smile.

"But I never said at what time, did I?"

Rowena joins them in Linette's study, where the latter flattens the page out in the middle of the table.

In the cold light of day it does not seem quite so sinister—the text merely looks like brown ink, the "paper" like old parchment. If Henry did not know better, it could merely be an aged diary entry filled with neat handwriting and itinerant doodles.

"What do they mean, do you suppose?"

It is Rowena who has spoken, and together all three of them stare down at the page.

"The whole book had symbols in it like this," Linette murmurs. "Much of it is written in a foreign language except for Julian's words here."

"Some of it is Latin," Henry adds, "I can see that much. But these symbols . . . these I don't recognize."

Rowena hovers her finger over them. "Hebrew, perhaps?"

"Hebrew or Latin," Linette retorts, "that hardly makes a difference if none of us can speak it."

She leans over the page to rest on her elbows, looks closer.

"There has to be a way to translate it. Was there a dictionary in Julian's bookcase? I don't remember seeing one."

"Nor I," Henry says, and in response she sighs.

It is heavy, drawn out. Linette's eyes widen.

"Henry, *look*."

"What?"

Linette picks up the page, holds it between them.

"When I sighed just . . ."

She puts her face close, sighs once more, and to Henry's amazement a series of letters appears beneath the symbols.

"Christ," he mutters, taking the page from her.

Letters have appeared beneath a few of the central symbols: an N, an O, a P, a Q. Francis Fielding had mentioned this once—steganography he called it, a way of hiding messages within an object.

Blood could not do this. Julian must have used a special kind of ink.

"These aren't symbols," Linette whispers. "This is an alphabet."

"Quick," Henry says, moving toward the fireplace. "We must light the fire."

It takes some minutes to produce a decent flame, but soon the fire is roaring, and very carefully Henry leans into the grate, holding the page above the flames.

"Be careful," Rowena whispers, but there is no need; already the fire is doing its job, and soon the letters appear beneath their corresponding symbols, clear now as day:

A B C D E F G H I

K L M N O P Q R S T V

X Y Z ɑ

"Get paper, quill," Henry tells Linette, but she does not need telling twice. Already she has pulled her desk drawers open, laying paper and ink next to the torn page, diligently dips the nib.

He watches as Linette makes fast work of the symbols, their corresponding letters, and when she has finished neither of them speak for some moments. Henry tries to deny what is before them, tries to convince himself Linette has mistranslated, that what he sees is nothing more than a trick of the eye.

"This can't be right," he finally manages.

Linette too is staring at the page before them, looking as shocked as he feels.

LINETTE

HENRY

Their names. The symbols spell out her and Henry's names.

"Why would Julian have written our names in the grimoire?" Linette whispers.

With a shaking finger Henry pulls Linette's translation toward him. This cannot be possible. *It cannot be possible!*

"Our names," Linette cries as if he cannot see. "These are our names!"

But he does see. He sees and is just as baffled as she is, looks between the pages in confusion. Linette chews her lip.

"You said the grimoire was ritualistic, did you not?" she asks, and Henry nods, lowers his eyes once more to read the passage below their names:

To ensure salvation the bargain must be struck with the sacrifice of one's own ancestral lifeblood, the bond of two united.

It means nothing to him. He continues to stare at the page, the strange lines of Julian's handwriting turning themselves over in his mind: Ensure salvation. Bargain struck. Sacrifice. Ancestral blood. Two united. The answer is there, but Henry cannot see it. What, *what*, is he missing?

Next to him Linette is reading the passage too, mouthing the words under her breath. Three times she does this until she falls silent, eyes following the words now rather than her tongue. Then, suddenly, she draws in her breath.

"No."

"Linette?"

But she has started to shake her head in dismay.

"No," she whispers again. "How? *How?*"

"Linette, what is it?"

"It can't be. It can't."

"*What?*"

She reaches for one of the chairs at the table and sits down, weakly looks up at him, scarce able, it seems, to form the words.

"Think of your childhood, Henry," Linette whispers. "You were a Foundling, yes? You never knew your parents. The watch. Your token. What was supposed to happen to it?"

A creeping cold spindles itself up his limbs like needles.

"It . . . it was for when my parents came to claim me. To identify me. But no one came."

"Perhaps they did, and you didn't realize. *Julian* claimed you, when he brought you here. Ancestral lifeblood. The bond of two united. Don't you see?"

Henry stares. Gently, Linette puts her hand on his.

"Your name," she says softly, "is not Talbot. It is Tresilian. Henry Tresilian."

For a long moment he is silent, scarce able to fathom it. This is madness, he thinks, it makes no sense, *should* make no sense and yet, somehow . . .

"We're related?" His voice sounds wooden, far off. "I'm Julian's son?"

"You must be."

"But," Rowena cuts in, who until that moment has stood quietly, too shocked it seemed to speak, "this is all conjecture, surely? You're finding ways to tie the threads, and yet there's no way of really knowing."

Linette turns to look at her.

"Yes, there is."

"There is?"

"The Bible," she says simply. "The family Bible, in the cabinet upstairs."

Very slowly Henry raises his head to the ceiling, as if he might somehow look through Plas Helyg's ancient bones up to the floor above. The women follow suit.

"We must look inside," Henry swallows. "It's the only way to know for sure."

With something like her old strength Linette rises from her chair and crosses the room, reaches for the bell-pull by the door, its emerald sash.

"What are you doing?"

"Cadoc," she says. "He has the key."

She tugs the pull. Within moments Powell appears at the study door.

The butler looks between them, his stern gaze going from Linette, to Henry, to Rowena and back again.

"What is it you need?"

"We need you to unlock the cabinet upstairs," Linette says. "Now."

Henry watches the butler insert a small key into the curio cabinet. It is stiff in the lock and takes him a second or two to make the key turn before it gives with a dull *thunk*, to lift the glass lid. Instantly the smell of camphor rises, mixed with a faint aroma of must, a sure sign the Bible has not been opened for years.

As one Henry and Linette step forward.

The Bible sits grandly in the middle of the blue velvet bottom, an unopened promise. Henry has given it little mind since coming here—only the portrait above claimed his attention—but here it is in front of him, ready to confirm Linette's wild claim, and a part of Henry now does not want to know the truth.

The Bible is truly beautiful. Though very like Julian's grimoire, it does not hold the same sinister air; ornate patterns—ivy, he sees now—curl prettily around the holy cross, framed by brass filigree corners, held shut by handsome clasps, and Linette reaches down to unclip them from the pins that holds them in place.

With infinite care, she turns the cover. The family tree stares up at them from the first page, a sea of names inked into its coiling willow branches. Generations of Cadwalladrs trickle down from the top in looping copperplate, but Henry pays them no mind; he looks only to those at the bottom of the page, scarce able to believe what he is seeing:

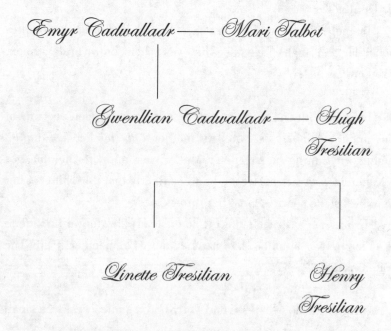

He is too shocked to speak, too shocked to do anything. Even Cadoc Powell seems at a loss for words—he is staring hard at the Bible, a muscle working in his jaw. It is Linette who lets out her breath, Linette who reaches into the cabinet, though it is not to the Bible that her hand goes but to one of the small locks of hair either side of it. She hovers a finger against the blonde, then in turn the brown.

"I always thought they were from my parents," she whispers, and finally Henry finds his voice.

"When was your birthday, Linette?"

She licks her lips.

"The day you arrived."

A beat. "And mine."

He has never marked his birthdate. A scrap of paper handed over with the pocketwatch, a worthless piece of information that always meant nothing to him.

Until now.

"I'm not *Julian*'s son," Henry says, the truth of it barely comprehensible. "I'm Hugh's." He raises his eyes to hers, brown to gray-green. "You are my sister."

"Twins."

Henry and Linette spin around. Standing in the open doorway of the upper chambers is Linette's mother—*his* mother—crumpled nightgown trailing on the floor. Mrs. Evans supports her meager weight, clasping her mistress's hand so tightly that the whites of her knuckles stand sharp against her thin skin.

"Twins," she says again, taking an unsteady step forward. "Linette is older by two minutes. I remember now. I remember it all. The watch, you see . . ."

Beside him, Linette stills.

"Mamma?" she whispers, and Lady Gwen smiles weakly, a small sorrowful smile that makes a lump form in Henry's throat.

"It is time you both knew the truth."

BRANCH IV.

I must have your soul ;
Must have it mine, and mine forever.

MATTHEW LEWIS
The Monk: A Romance (1796)

CHAPTER
THIRTY-SEVEN

"I hated Penhelyg."

Gwen Tresilian is seated now on the narrow ottoman beneath the window in the corridor, thin and waiflike in her cotton nightgown, hair coiling like rope to her waist. She looks frighteningly wan, seems scarce able to put one word after the other.

"My mother—your grandmother—died in childbirth. With no siblings all I had for company was my father and Enaid." Her face splits into a rueful smile. "I'm sorry to say I was a resentful child. I had no friends, nothing to entertain me. I felt trapped. Soon I became precocious, in severe need of discipline which no one had the will to give."

The smile fades into a troubled frown.

"My father, Emyr, never remarried. He took to drink and gambling, spent weeks on end away in the city. I was jealous of that, begged him to take me with him but he never did. I think he considered children as nuisances. To be seen but only briefly, and never *ever* heard. Then, one day, he began inviting his English friends back here to Plas Helyg."

She stops. The corridor is silent but for the muted churn of the grandfather clock on the landing below them, the galleon's tipping axis.

"The things I witnessed as a child," Lady Gwen whispers, "things

I know now I never should have seen!" She shakes her head. "My father did not wish me to have any dealings with his friends, but they were new to me and exciting; when everyone was abed, I would sneak downstairs. Oh, I must have been very wicked not to have been disgusted or afraid, but I confess I found your grandfather's sordid gatherings intriguing. I'd look through keyholes and listen at doors until I became too tired and cold to keep vigil." Her face darkens. "There were names for gatherings such as Emyr Cadwalladr's, I later learned."

"Hellfire clubs," Henry says, and her mother—*their* mother— gives a resigned nod.

"These ones called themselves the Order. They would gather here once every few months, usually at the turning of the season. Solstice or equinox, without fail they would come. To begin with they merely drank and gambled, conducted silly little ceremonies that bordered on the ridiculous. Sometimes a whore or two would join the party, and you can imagine what happened when they did. But then, when I was sixteen, they started to bring girls from the village to the house."

At this Enaid ducks her head, but not before Linette has seen the shame writ upon her face. She knew this too, then.

"There have always been rumors," Miss Carew ventures quietly from her station at the cabinet. "The Einions . . ."

"Ah yes, the Einions." A pause. Pale fingers knead cotton. "Often the girls were enticed away on the promise of money or some favor to their families, then used in whatever way my father and his friends saw fit. All of them, all at once. Old flesh on young. Who knows how many children he and his fellow Hellfires fathered? Still, many returned to their homes relatively unscathed. Until, that is, Heledd Einion."

"What happened?" Linette asks, cutting across Henry's "Go on," and Lady Gwen sighs deeply. It is a sigh filled with sadness and regret, disgust binding the two.

"Heledd Einion was a great beauty. She was already married with children of her own, but from what I saw she was willing enough to partake in the Order's games. Not like the others. They were shy, unsure. But Heledd . . . Heledd relished in it. I've never been quite sure at what point things went wrong. I remember ropes, blindfolds. I remember her being eager until she wasn't, that one minute Heledd was alive and the next she was not."

Their mother grimaces, coughs into her hand.

"I only saw what happened in that moment, none of what came after. It was only later I heard her naked corpse had been found on the road beneath the willow trees. The village of course was in uproar, fighting fit for blood. But Lord Pennant—who was a very young man then, one of the Order and newly appointed as the district's magistrate—turned a blind eye. Nothing was done. The villagers had no means for recourse, and being so remote what could be done if the law refused to stand by their side?"

Their mother closes her eyes, rests her head back against the window-pane. Even from her stance at the cabinet, Linette can see the sheen of sweat on her brow, her pulse pounding hard in her neck.

How much of the tincture still runs through her veins?

"It put a stop to Emyr's amusements," Lady Gwen says weakly. "The Order did not come to Plas Helyg again. My father went back to his resentful moods, his prolonged absences, began to gamble Plas Helyg away stone by stone. I became angry. Obstinate. How could I stay here and watch him destroy this place and let me rot along with it? I *missed* the Order. I'd been given a taste of life, you see. I longed for adventure, anything that would take me away from the monotonous existence of Penhelyg. When Father finally took me to London I threw myself into the Season, became the most disgraceful flirt. I was young and foolish, I see that now, but at the time I would do anything to win someone's hand, anything to escape."

Linette stares, unsure what to feel. Her mother is not the woman she thought she was. The knowledge that she was once part of Julian's own club, the implications of it, this is something that has niggled at the back of Linette's mind for days, a distasteful truth she has tried so hard to ignore, but there is no ignoring any of it now. Her mother is revealing herself, piece by sordid piece. . . .

"When Father lost the slate mine to Julian in a game of cards," she continues, "it made him desperate to secure me a match. Thankfully Julian's elder cousin Hugh had enough money to buy Plas Helyg six times over which of course was all that mattered to my father, and I was married off before the Season was finished." Lady Gwen shivers, wraps the shawl tight about her bony shoulders. "I remember those to be the happiest months of my life. I moved to Hugh's townhouse in London, found the excitement I'd always craved. Hugh was all I could have wanted in a husband: handsome, passionate, amusing, with a talent for intelligent conversation. He showed me what life could be like, all the pleasures it afforded. Everything I had missed living here in Penhelyg he returned to me threefold. We grew to love each other. Then . . ."

"Then?"

Lady Gwen sighs at Henry's question.

"Julian created his own club."

She waits for her children to say something more, but when they do not she lifts her chin in a gesture of defiance, and Linette braces herself for the fall.

"It transpired that my father had spoken to Julian of the Order. I suppose, after what happened to Heledd, I should have been opposed to joining it but here—finally—was a chance to experience everything I had only fantasized about."

Their mother bites her bottom lip, chews at a dry flake of skin.

"Continue," Henry says softly. "Please."

Enaid takes her mistress's hand, squeezes it, and this action propels her on.

"Julian rented rooms in Covent Garden where we would meet every week. We played cards and drank beyond what was proper and danced until dawn. We . . . we also indulged in things polite society frowned upon. I enjoyed such attentions, enjoyed the thrill. It felt revolutionary. Finally, after so many stagnated years, I felt *free*."

Linette's stomach churns. She shuts her eyes against the image but opens them again when the dark canvas of her eyelids only makes it worse.

"What changed?" she whispers, and Lady Gwen raises her eyes to hers.

"Father died. We returned to Plas Helyg. Hugh began restoring the estate. Julian went traveling in Europe, and we did not see him again for over a year. But when he came back, he was different. He was excited in a way we had never seen him before, spoke of a great power that would bring us luck and fortune."

Henry frowns. "A great power?"

"He spoke of talismanic magic, the lore of Solomon, ancient rites of passage. We dismissed it all at first as one of Julian's fantastical ideas, for he'd spouted off many of them during those days in London. All those books he collected! But then he proposed we rename the club the Order of Berith, and hold our gatherings here in Penhelyg. The London Hellfire clubs, you see, were coming under scrutiny; Francis Dashwood's Friars had already been forced to move to Medmenham Abbey to ensure their privacy. Julian too wanted somewhere remote, like in Emyr's day. Hugh was disinclined to allow it, but I must admit I had begun to grow restless. Hugh was in his element here restoring the house and lands, but I longed for the excitement I'd left behind. So he agreed. However, he had conditions—no village girls, and the mansion itself could not be used. London, he said, was one thing, but Plas Helyg was our home and he wanted to keep the gatherings here separate."

"Then where did you go?" asks Henry, and at this she offers a weak smile.

"There are tunnels under this house," Lady Gwen replies softly. "They lead to underground caverns where Cadwalladr ancestors used to store smuggled goods. We let Julian use them. And all went well, at first. It was as things ever were, except Julian brought more cere-monial elements to the evenings. Elaborate costumes, ritualistic tools, that kind of thing. To me it was just a game, but it soon became clear how seriously Julian took it. He was obsessed with a book he had begun to curate on his travels. A grimoire. *The Shadow Key*, he called it. The symbol on its front—"

"Berith," Linette provides.

Lady Gwen shivers and shuts her eyes, as if the very name has made her cold.

"Yes. Berith. A Canaanite demon of the old world. It is said that he could turn all metals into gold, ensure riches and power for those who worshipped him. Julian bred black hens," she continues, "started to use them during the ceremonies as blood sacrifices. And as much as that sickened me, there can be no denying we all became rich beyond anything we could have imagined. Julian expanded across the valley, and the mines started to yield copper ore. One day Julian's workers found a piece of gold, and he became convinced Berith was behind it."

At this Linette sucks in her breath. *Slate to copper, copper to gold.* When she shares a look with Henry, his mouth twists into a sneer.

"Did you believe it?"

"I didn't know what to believe," their mother says, "nor did I care. I was happy, happier than I could ever have expected to be, except for one thing. Hugh and I had been married for nearly four years by then, but we had struggled to conceive. Yet not long after Julian introduced the sacrificial ceremonies . . ." Her mouth twists. "Our joy, however, was short-lived. It was as if it were Julian's triumph, not ours. He said that my pregnancy was proof anything could be achieved as long as Berith was on our side. His vehemence disturbed us. It frightened me. Hugh and I decided it was best to bow out of the Order after that."

The chain of the cabinet begins to shake. Cadoc—who has until this moment stood so silent Linette has forgotten he is there—very carefully lowers the lid. He is looking at his mistress now with an expression Linette has never seen him wear before; a look of pity mixed with something else. Is that bewilderment she sees on his sallow face?

"We could have refused Julian access from then on," her mother continues, "but at that point—aside from those poor hens—he had done nothing particular to cause concern. It was all talk, that's what we thought. The club too had dwindled by then to a select few; the Pennants and Selwyns, others of their more immediate acquaintance, people in London whom Julian cultivated in order to enrich his financial and political partnerships, and so Hugh and I did not mind that they came to Penhelyg just as long as they kept themselves to themselves."

Their mother falls silent a moment. A flash of pain in her gray-green eyes.

"Hugh and I went to London before the birth. You weren't due for another few weeks, and I was desperate for some distraction. Away from Julian, the Order. Plas Helyg. Even Enaid." Lady Gwen dips her head, squeezes the old woman's hand. "She had begun to smother me, in those last months. I craved the freedom I used to have, just one last time, before the baby came. But some days later Julian followed, tried again to convince us of Berith's power. We argued, for hours it seems, and the distress of it . . ." She swallows. "Later that night I went into labor. Dr. Beddoe was called—"

"Beddoe?" Henry interrupts, sharp, and Lady Gwen nods.

"He ran a practice in London at the time. It's how we all met. But yes, it was Elis who attended me, and when Julian saw you both he claimed it to be a miracle. Twins, he said, one boy, one girl, the surest sign that Berith had blessed us. He kept referring to an old archaic quote he'd found; something about bonds and unions, claimed the demon wanted you for his own. Julian said that if we were to make you both a sacrifice, Berith would ensure our fortunes for the rest of our lives."

Again Linette looks at the locks of hair from the cabinet. She looks at the darker curl. Henry's. Her brother.

Her twin.

That is why Linette became so attached to him so quickly, recognized in him a kindred spirit, a shared affinity. The same stubbornness, the same temper. She and Henry were made of the same cloth, though their resemblance is a shifting thing; Linette takes after Gwen, Henry after Hugh and in turn, Julian. All those times his expression stirred in her a feeling of recognition! She glances up at the portrait of her parents, of Julian beside them. Hugh and Julian look so similar. No wonder she recognized Henry, deep down.

"Hugh would not stand for it," Lady Gwen continues tiredly. "He ordered Elis from the house, Julian too when he became aggressive. That very night your father visited other members of the Order, men he trusted—a Bow Street official and a member of the High Court Justice—explaining what had happened, begging them to arrest Julian. But it did no good."

"No good?" Henry, this.

She shakes her head.

"They refused to help—they were loyal to Julian and saw Berith as a way of advancing themselves, no matter the means. Men of power, they hold it all. If those of high office can turn a blind eye to such monstrosities, what could be done? We had no choice but to take matters into our own hands. It was the idea of twins that obsessed Julian, and if it was essential to his cause that you should be kept together. . . ."

"So you separated us."

Lady Gwen nods.

"It was a terrible choice to make, which one of you to lose, but in the end it was obvious. A boy would get along better in the world than a girl. A boy could make a life for himself. A safe life. There was no guarantee Linette could do the same. So I gave Hugh all my jewels to be put in trust with the Foundling Hospital so that when you came of age a suitable education could be paid for. Hugh left the pocketwatch as a token, in the hope we could be reunited in time."

Henry removes the silver watch from his pocket and places it into the palm of his hand, the initials H T facing up, then looks down at the locks of hair in the cabinet. Watching him, Lady Gwen's mouth twists. She looks ragged now, as if the confession has spent her strength. She sits back against the windowsill, leans her fair head against the glass.

"Early the next morning, we began the journey back to Plas Helyg. We knew we had perhaps six hours before Julian discovered us gone. And when he did . . ." She takes a shuddering breath. "He caught up with us a day later. He tried to flag us down, but Hugh pushed the horses harder. It had been raining, Julian would not . . . the carriage . . ."

Lady Gwen presses a shaking hand to her eyes. Beneath his breath Linette hears Cadoc swear, and she turns to him, wide-eyed. He is leaning now against the wall, looking monstrous pale. When he catches her looking, the butler shakes his head in dismay.

"I was ill when your parents left for London. I'd caught cold during a hunting party, and Lord Hugh insisted I stay behind. When Julian turned up at the door of Plas Helyg with a screaming baby and her ladyship insensible, saying my master had been involved in an accident . . ." He shakes his head. "*O'r nefoedd*, I wish I'd been there. I could have stopped this, I could have—"

"Done nothing," Lady Gwen cuts in. "There is nothing you could have done that we had not already."

"I could have shot him."

A tired smile passes her lips. "No, Cadoc. I am glad you were not there. If you'd been a part of Henry's escape you would have been in danger from Julian. And who else could have protected Linette?"

He has nothing to say to that, it seems. It is Enaid who breaks the silence, and she looks at both Linette and Henry, watery-eyed.

"After the accident, my lady was in such distress that I had trouble making sense of anything she said. She kept repeating the word *Berith*, over and over. It seemed she had gone mad with grief. When Julian arranged for a special tincture to calm her I thought it was to ease her pain, but I see now it was to loosen her tongue, desperate to find Sir Henry. When it became clear the tincture only muddled her mind further I think Julian must have realized it was better this way—anything she said regarding his plans would be considered mere ravings. Oh, but I should have known! I should have known!"

Lady Gwen sighs, lowers her hand.

"You could not have, Enaid," she says softly. "Besides, I welcomed oblivion. I *wanted* to forget. I did not want to think about any of it. I was dependent on the tincture, in the end."

"But what of Dr. Evans?" Linette asks. "Surely he knew Mamma was being drugged?"

"Yes," Enaid sighs, "he knew, could never understand why Julian insisted upon it. Surely, he said, it was better for my lady to grieve her husband rather than pretend none of it had happened at all? I agreed, but when she lashed out at him in one of her fits we finally accepted it was the kindest treatment."

She lapses into silence. Below them, the grandfather clock ticks. Henry swallows, Adam's apple hard at his throat.

"When did you remember all this?"

He addresses their mother, but it is Enaid who answers.

"Only this very morning. After you left, my lady asked about your pocketwatch. I told her you were a Foundling, and it all seemed to come flooding back. The birthmark she saw that night; she recognized you then, although she did not know it. Imagine my shock when she told me the truth!"

Silence again. Only the clock speaks, a solemn knock as the galleon swings back and forth, back and forth, back and forth . . .

"Julian Tresilian is a fiend," Cadoc murmurs. "All these years, wasted. I've cursed every single day that his lordship was lost to us."

"Hugh is not lost."

The words are said so softly Linette scarce hears them, and they each look to Lady Gwen once more, sitting so pale and wan on the fraying ottoman.

"He stands here, in front of us, in his son. My Henry. My dear Henry. Come home, at last."

CHAPTER
THIRTY-EIGHT

In the small cottage across from Penhelyg Church, the Reverend Mr. Owain Dee pours nettle tea from a steaming stoneware pot. Henry—sitting at the small table overlooking the mine, its hillside blotched with the eddies of spoil-heaps—clasps his mug quietly between his hands in grave contemplation.

"I confess, I cannot think what to say to you," the vicar says finally, placing the teapot in the center of the table. "You, a Tresilian!"

Henry lifts his mug to his mouth, tests the temperature with his tongue. Rests it down again.

"I don't . . ." Henry stops. Can hardly find the words.

He still feels shock, disbelief, unable to fathom the truth of what he has been told; in the space of a few hours his life has turned on its axis, the past he thought he knew blurred like watercolor on wet canvas.

Henry Talbot is, in fact, Henry Tresilian, not a Foundling at all. He has a mother. He has a sister, a twin. But as strange and wondrous as all that is Henry has not forgotten the means of how he discovered it, that there are ultimately more sinister dealings at play.

Lady Gwen—his mother, he corrects himself—said the reason why he had been sent away was because Julian had meant to kill him, planned to sacrifice both himself and Linette as part of some bizarre ritual. It is, Henry sees now, why Dr. Evans is dead, to get him out of the way—Julian deliberately orchestrated Henry's return, which can mean only one thing:

He intends to finish what he started.

"I didn't know who else to speak to," Henry tells the reverend now, gripping his mug tight, the warmth of hot nettle seeping into his palms. "I don't know what to do. Lord Pennant is magistrate, but he is also part of the Order. He'll do nothing, just like he did with Heledd Einion."

Mr. Dee sets down his tea.

"Even if you were to report to an honest magistrate, what you have told me is so far beyond the realms of reality that any court of law would easily throw it out. Hearsay, conjecture. You'd be accused of libel. Besides some cryptic notes in a spell book and the claims of Lady Tresilian who—I am sorry to add, but the truth of it is necessary to my argument—has long been considered a woman of unstable nature, you do not have any concrete proof. With your birth being unregistered . . . well, do you not see the quandary? A name in a Bible could easily be added at a later date. Ultimately, you are accusing men of the peerage. Julian Tresilian has the ear of high office, and with the support of Lord Pennant and Sir John Selwyn he is formidable, unlikely to be doubted. If one has money, then the law can be bent without a second thought."

Henry sits forward in his seat. "You understand the import of what I say though, don't you? Julian arranged for me to return to Penhelyg. Somehow he tracked me down, and now that I am here he means to finish what he began all those years ago. Linette and I are in danger."

"So you keep saying." The vicar looks down at the torn skin of parchment Henry brought with him, Julian's untidy scrawl. "'To ensure salvation the bargain must be struck with the sacrifice of one's own ancestral lifeblood, the bond of two united,'" he recites. "Of course it is troubling."

"It's more than that! Lady Gwen said that Julian had promised a vast fortune if we were sacrificed. His wording, it is most particular. 'Ancestral lifeblood': a relation. 'Two united': twins. That much is clear. The only thing I don't understand is the first part of the passage. 'To ensure salvation.' Salvation from what?"

The reverend taps his finger on the rim of his mug. "What did the other pages in the grimoire say?"

Henry sighs. "It was all written in a language I did not understand."

"Hebrew or Theban perhaps. Lady Tresilian spoke of Solomonic magic; those are the most likely to be used in such ancient texts. Hebrew is a Semitic language, familiar only to one native to the Levant, or, of course, an experienced scholar such as Julian. As for Theban . . . well, it is less a language and more a writing system, specifically a cipher of the Latin script. That is why it appears here as an alphabet. Interesting," Mr. Dee adds, pointing at the two lines of Latin, "that Julian should use full Latin here. '*Clavis umbrarum.*' '*Magus goetia.*' Perhaps he required something easy to pronounce. Theban text, and Hebrew for that matter, are very difficult to read. They don't, you see, have quite the same nuance."

Henry takes a sip of his tea, ignores the tart burn.

"Can you assist me with the Latin?" He taps the two lines the vicar just referred to. "What do they mean?"

Mr. Dee wets his lips.

"Well, the word '*magus*' could be used to describe a magician, a sorcerer, a member of a spiritual caste. Even a priest. But in this context, together with the second word '*goetia*,' I believe it simply means magic. '*Goetia*' refers to the evocation of demons or evil spirits. So, in literal terms, '*magus goetia*' loosely translates as the Magic of Demons."

"And '*Clavis umbrarum*'?"

"Hmm." His expression shifts into one of deep contemplation. After a moment he says, "Let us break it down. The word '*clavis*' means key, which as you know refers to an instrument with which to open a lock. '*Umbrarum*' translates to something like 'of the shadows.'" The vicar looks pensive. "A strange mix. Let me see. Yes. Key can also symbolize the key to mastering a talent, and shadows . . ." A beat. "Did you know that the word 'shadow' in Latin actually has multiple meanings? It can mean shadow, yes, but also shade, ghost . . . or demon. I think, then, the literal translation of '*Clavis umbrarum*' is this—the key to summoning demons."

Henry stares down at the parchment, remembers his mother's words.

"The Shadow Key," he murmurs.

"Yes, that's a fair translation." The reverend lets the words sit between them a moment. "In regards to your other question, the salvation Julian Tresilian refers to . . ." He turns the page around so Henry can look at it upright, taps the first of Julian's notes:

Whosoever breaks a covenant with Almighty Berith will be devoured by a beast of darkness, and that sinner's soul shall belong completely unto Him.

"It is quite obvious," he says. "If Julian does not complete the sacrifice—if he breaks his promise to Berith—then he will die himself and lose his soul."

The reverend says this with such seriousness that Henry cannot quite manage to hide his contempt.

"Surely you do not think Berith is real?"

"Surely, after everything you have seen and heard since coming to Penhelyg, you cannot be so sure he is not?"

Henry hesitates. He thinks of the lights in the cavern, those so-called corpse candles down in the mine before the accident, admits that there at least he has no explanation. *Two red, one blue.* Red for a man, blue for a child. He pictures the cold bodies of Pedr, Hywel, and Afan. No, he has no explanation, but there *must* be one.

"How can you believe in God," Henry asks, "yet also believe in these ridiculous superstitions?"

"Because, my dear boy, they are all connected! Myth and religion go hand in hand; to believe in one you simply *must* believe in the other. Besides, many legends, such as our Lady of the Lake, speak to a more rational sense of us. They are life lessons—" here he slaps his palm with the edge of his fingers—"thou shalt not steal, thou shalt not kill . . . or, in that unlucky man's case, do the lady physical harm. If one ignores these lessons there is always a cost, and all of it reinforces our belief in the supernatural, the spiritual and the afterlife. The same person who believes in the *tylwyth teg* also marks the door of their home to ward off the Devil."

Henry shakes his head. Mr. Dee smiles kindly.

"I understand your cynicism, I truly do. For a man of science such as yourself it is to be expected. But think, Dr. Talbot—Tresilian!—of the most important debates of our age. Could the Devil be dethroned by reason and Man be liberated from superstition by science? Even if one were to find a persuasive argument in favor of such a claim, it still would not be considered! The problem is that the existence of God is ingrained into our very being, and not even the greatest scientific minds such as Isaac Newton could dispute His existence." At Henry's look of mild surprise the vicar says, "Oh yes, I read widely during my training! Indeed, Newton saw God as the masterful creator of all, believed that all which has been discovered in the name of science was created by God in the first place. And if God exists so too does the Devil, for one cannot exist without the other."

Henry pushes his mug away. "I respect your faith, I do, but I cannot be persuaded to believe in the existence of either. Lady Gwen . . . my mother . . . she told me once that within each of us there lies a devil, and I have never heard a truer word spoken. We are all capable of doing terrible things. The Devil doesn't have anything to do with it. Julian acts from his own wickedness, no one else's."

"Are you so sure? Indeed, we are all capable of acts of evil. But why? The Devil comes to us in pleasing shapes, so it is no wonder we lesser beings are often led astray. But Lucifer rarely takes it upon himself to do the leading. As I said before—God has angels to do his bidding, the Devil has demons to do his."

"Demons like Berith."

"Yes, like Berith." He takes another sip of tea, swirls the liquid in his mouth, seems to ponder his next words deeply before continuing. "I admit, I'm not familiar with the name, but there are many within the Devil's circle that are not directly mentioned in the Bible. Of course, considering the connection to Solomonic magic, a demon such as Berith would not be referred to explicitly in the scriptures anyway."

"No?"

Mr. Dee shakes his head. "Remember I said '*goetia*' referred to the evocation of evil spirits? Goetic spirits are the demons associated specifically with black magic, those summoned by King Solomon to build his temple." He hesitates. "My memory is hazy, of course. My orders were conducted many years ago now, but I seem to remember these demons are named in the first section of a seventeenth-century grimoire called *Lemegeton Clavicula Salomonis*—or, if you wish for the English—the Lesser Keys of Solomon."

"Yes," Henry says, remembering its aging spine. "Julian owns such a book."

Sagely, the vicar nods.

"Originally called the Spirits of the Seals, they're also known as the seventy-two Princes of the Hierarchy of Hell. The *Lemegeton* differs from other goetic texts because entities are compelled into obedience with the promise of a sacrifice, rather than asked for simple favors without some means of return. This Berith is likely one of them."

"The promise of a sacrifice," Henry echoes. "And, according to Julian, Linette and I are that sacrifice."

The vicar taps his mug. There is nothing more to say, it seems. Henry rubs his eyes.

"Look, what do you suggest I do? Whether this Berith is real or not the fact remains that Julian *does* believe, and means us harm. If he thinks his own life is at risk then that makes him all the more dangerous."

"Indeed, you are quite right." Mr. Dee considers a moment. "I'm afraid that all I can suggest is for you and Linette to rally. Never go anywhere alone, ensure safety in numbers. If it will make you feel better then by all means write to Bow Street. I might be wrong—your Mr. Fielding may take your claims seriously and endeavor to take action."

"Is there no one closer? Where is the next magistrate?"

"I'm afraid I do not know. There is a county sheriff—a Robert Evans of Bodweni—I believe, but Bala is near sixty miles away."

Sixty miles. Such a distance might as well be London, for all the good it will do.

Henry sighs. It is growing late. Out of the window he can see the sun beginning its slow trajectory across the sky, a glowing sphere of molten gold. He looks at his pocketwatch (his father's pocketwatch)—a little after seven—and stands, holds out his hand for the reverend to shake.

"Thank you, Mr. Dee."

"I'm sorry I cannot be of further help," he says. "It is most distressing, most distressing indeed."

Henry pushes his chair back under the table, retrieves the torn page of the grimoire from its top and folds it away into his pocket. It is just as he is turning in the direction of the door that his attention is caught once more by the spectacular wall of lovespoons. He crosses the small sitting room, looks at them hanging on their individual hooks. What was it Mr. Dee told him they were? *Tokens of love*. His gaze goes to the spoon he picked from the wall the first day he came here, the one made up of intricate knots intertwining a heart and, decided, Henry turns to the vicar.

"May I purchase one?"

Mr. Dee looks surprised, but then he reaches out to the wall and plucks the lovespoon Henry points at from its hook.

"This is a lovely one," he says, gazing down at it. "Took over a week. These knots, you see, mighty fiddly. Am I right in thinking this is for Miss Carew?" Henry colors. The vicar nods knowingly. "You are welcome to it, but may I impart some advice?"

"Of course."

"Be mindful of a pretty face."

Henry drops a coin into the reverend's waiting palm. "I think I'm old enough to know what I am doing, Mr. Dee."

"I'm sure you are," comes the reply, and when the vicar passes him the lovespoon Henry clasps it tight between both hands.

CHAPTER
THIRTY-NINE

On his return from the vicar's cottage he wrote to Francis as Mr. Dee suggested, but as to the good it will do, Henry has little confidence. What the reverend said is true—what has occurred here is too far beyond the realms of reality. Still, Henry thought as he passed the letter to Cadoc Powell, it is worth a try. Francis surely cannot dismiss his claim so readily, not after all he has done for him in the past.

"So," Linette says now, staring at Henry across her bowl of uneaten soup. "Mr. Dee can suggest nothing?"

A light supper has been served for Henry, Linette, and Rowena, but after the events of the day neither one of them is in the mood to eat, and the tureen of soup Mrs. Phillips has concocted from the last of the leftovers sits growing cold on the dining-room table.

"What *can* he suggest? He too thinks that very little can be done."

"Well, we cannot sit here and let them all think they can get away with this!" Linette pushes her bowl away from her with such force that the soup splashes over the rim onto the tablecloth. "Everything Julian has done, everything he means to do. . . . It is diabolical."

Next to Henry, Rowena presses her napkin to her mouth, pushes her own bowl away with more care. "I feel ill," she says.

Henry takes her hand. Linette sighs her frustration.

"Perhaps while we await a reply from your Mr. Fielding we could write our depositions. At the very least, then, we'll have a record of what has occurred. Anything is better than this. Would that help us, do you think?"

"It might."

What Henry does not say, is that he suspects this task too will do little good. You'd be accused of libel, Mr. Dee told him. *Hearsay, conjecture.* Besides, after what Lady Gwen told them, can Bow Street even be trusted? A Bow Street official, she said. Still, writing down their accounts of the matter is a better use of their time than wallowing in this state of limbo they have now found themselves in, waiting for something to happen.

Waiting for Julian to act.

Henry shudders. Ritual sacrifice. Ancestral blood. Twins. *The bond of two united.* It is still too much for him to comprehend. For pity's sake, how did Julian even expect to carry out the deed? And, of more concern at this juncture, where *is* Julian? At Lord Pennant's, would be the obvious answer. Are they preparing, perhaps? He thinks of the others—Pennant's wife, the Selwyns, Beddoe, and Lambeth. There are other things, of course, they could be doing. Henry curls his lip in distaste.

Cadoc Powell, who has just now entered to clear the bowls, is looking at the near-full tureen, their barely touched bowls.

"Are you not hungry?" he asks. "It is not Mrs. Phillips's best offering, I confess, but—"

"It's not the cooking," Linette assures, managing a smile. "Under the circumstances we just cannot eat. Please, send our apologies."

"Of course. I quite understand." Powell dips his head, replaces the lid of the tureen. "Can I get you anything else? A glass of wine, perhaps?" He looks between them. Henry, Linette, and Rowena shake their heads. "Then I shall leave you to your thoughts."

"I don't want to be left to my thoughts," Rowena murmurs, when the door closes behind him. "My thoughts frighten me."

"I am not frightened," Linette shoots back. "I am angry. I'm so angry I could kill Julian myself."

The words—said with such bitter hatred—do not shock Henry, but they make him feel uneasy all the same. He sees the darkling look in Linette's gray-green eyes, a look of dangerous intent. As if to acknowledge her anger the candles flicker in their candelabra, the light of their flames flashing reflections in the silver tureen like fiery tongues. The mantel clock ticks. Henry glances at it. A quarter to ten.

"It is late," he says. "It will do us little good torturing ourselves like this. I say we go to bed, make a fresh start of it in the morning."

In agreement Linette rises from her seat. Merlin, who has been sleeping beneath her feet, scrambles up with her, wagging his tail. He is, Henry thinks wryly, the only happy creature in the room.

In the vestibule Linette looks at Henry, at Rowena clutching her carpet bag, the meager belongings she brought with her to Plas Helyg for these past two nights.

"Why don't you both stay here? Julian will never know. Besides, the reverend did advise—"

"Safety in numbers," Henry says softly, "I know. But my things are down at the gatehouse now."

"And I need to get home," Rowena says softly. "Forgive me, but I'd feel safer there than here."

Linette purses her lips. He lays a hand on her arm.

"Please do not worry. I shall walk Rowena home and then I'll lock myself in the gatehouse. I shall be perfectly all right. It's you I worry for. Will *you* be all right, alone?"

"I won't be alone. Mamma and Enaid are only down the corridor. Cadoc will be downstairs." She glances at the lurcher pressing his lean body against her legs. "If it makes you feel any better, I shall keep Merlin with me and lock the door."

"It would."

"Very well." Linette nods over his shoulder. "Go on, then. Miss Carew is waiting."

He turns. Rowena stands just outside on the gravel drive, tilting her face to the sky. Her hair is piled prettily atop her head and in the purpling dusk it looks the most delicious shade of auburn. Henry presses the lovespoon in his coat pocket, closer to his heart.

"Yes," he says. "Yes, she is."

When he turns back it is to find Linette watching Rowena too. There is something strangely haunting about her expression now, a lost expression that makes her look heart-achingly young. When she notices him looking Linette swallows, forces a smile.

"Goodnight, Henry." A pause. "Brother."

Brother. The word makes his chest tighten. So strange to hear her say it, so strange to know that this strong stubborn woman before him is his own flesh and blood. His sister. His twin. He takes Linette's hands, clasps them in both of his.

"It's hard to believe, isn't it?"

Linette says nothing, does not seem able to. Taken by a sudden surge of affection Henry draws her close, folds her in an awkward embrace. For a long moment she stands stiffly in the circle of his arms until little by little Linette softens, lets herself sink into him. It lasts mere seconds; he feels the shudder of a sob in the tilt of her shoulders and as if ashamed of her weakness Linette pulls away from him, shuts Plas Helyg's heavy doors, leaving Henry and Rowena alone in the dying light.

He is not sure when the decision was made, if it was in the moment Linette shut the door or when Henry pulled Plas Helyg's creaking gates apart, but at the end of the driveway both he and Rowena ignored the turn-off into Cwm Nantcol and instead took the path down to the gatehouse.

In silence they walk, the only sound an owl on the hunt, the whisper of leaves in the trees. He should lead her back up through the woods, out into the valley toward Moelfre, but he cannot quite force himself to do it. Rowena is here, alone, beside him willingly, their fingertips grazing softly together, the air between them charged and full of promise. When he puts the key into the gatehouse's lock, Henry must remind himself to breathe.

It is a different place. Even in the dark he can see the gatehouse is neat and tidy, tastefully furnished. The smell of fresh wood and paint lingers on the air, mellowed by the polish of beeswax. Rowena places the carpet bag on the floor beside a small table at the bottom of the stairs. On it, a candle has been left in its holder next to a tinderbox, and Henry lights it. His reflection surfaces in the new mirror in front of him, and in the dim light his eyes look hollowed out. Behind him, Rowena presses a yawn into her hand.

"You're tired," he says pointlessly. "I should have taken you home."

"I *am* tired. But I . . ." She watches him. "It felt wrong, somehow, to leave you after everything. I cannot even begin to understand how you must be feeling. Your mother, Julian . . ."

Something twists in his gut.

"I'm not quite sure I know myself," he tells her reflection. "Linette is angry, but I feel nothing except confusion and . . ." Henry tries to name what he feels. "Loss, I suppose."

"Loss?"

"For a life that was never mine, the life that was and that I can never get back. The life I could have lived if not for Julian."

She nods. "I can appreciate that, to mourn a life that should have been yours. To be denied it."

He turns from the mirror, hesitantly closes the gap between them. "Rowena?"

"Yes, Henry?"

The sound of his name on her lips thrills him. Before his courage deserts him he takes the lovespoon from his pocket, shyly holds it out to her.

"I brought this for you. It's only a small token, but I wanted to show you . . . to say . . ."

His nerves trip over his tongue and he cannot finish, but Rowena is reaching for the spoon now, is taking it almost reverently. He hears the little flutter of breath in her throat as she turns it over in her hands, runs her fingernail over the knots, the small heart set at the top.

"It is lovely," she whispers.

"I . . . I hoped you might like it."

A pause. "No one has given me a gift before."

"No one?"

"Not ever."

"Well, then." He feels himself flush. "I'm glad to be the first." Still she does not look at him, is as quiet as the woods outside, and for one terrifying moment he thinks he has offended her. "Rowena? Rowena, I—"

She is kissing him.

It is not like their first kiss, that fleeting moment of abandon he felt, the swift disappointment of her refusal. This kiss is freely given, laced with a passion that Henry could not have imagined ever coming from her, and he kisses her back fiercely, imprinting all his longing and lust into it. When she pulls away, he is panting.

"Rowena . . ." With his free hand he cups her cheek.

"Come," she says, and heart pounding Henry lets her lead him up the stairs, his hand lingering on the banister in the wake of hers, Rowena's fingertips a hair's breadth away. At the top she crosses the landing into the room meant for him, takes the candle he holds, puts it down on the table beside the bed, the lovespoon with it. He watches her, already hard with need, but when she returns to him and begins to unfasten his breeches he wills himself to still her hands.

"We don't have to do this," he says thickly. "I said I'd never force you and I meant it."

"You're not forcing me."

She kisses him again, this time softer, gentler, and Henry knows in that instant he is incapable of refusing. Together, they sink onto the bed.

Her skin is satin-soft, her body pliant. She smells of lavender. Curling his fingers into Rowena's thick hair he kisses the curve of neck where it meets shoulder, her cheek, her temple, her nose, her lips once again, drinking deep as if she were elixir. She rises into him, clutches his shoulders, nails digging in, and as Rowena sighs against his mouth Henry's passion tips itself over, and he cries out her name in the dark.

CHAPTER FORTY

At that very moment Linette stands in front of her mother's door, listening to the strains of harp music wend its way beneath. No discordant notes, no strange mixture of minors and majors. This is a melody she knows, and knows well. "*Hiraeth am Feirion.*" Enaid sang it to her as a girl, the pretty ballad of a homesick sailor, and the memory of it has Linette rooted to the spot. She has been standing here these past five minutes, unable to rouse the courage to knock for she knows Enaid will answer, and Linette is ashamed of herself for having treated her so cruelly.

I had just cause, she thinks, curling her hand into a fist. The hurt she felt at Enaid's betrayal ran sharp and deep, a physical pain that tore at her lungs and has buried itself there these past days, burrowing further and further like a worm. But the clarity of enlightenment has instilled in her an all-encompassing guilt; Linette thinks of how Enaid cared for her as a child, when she read to her the old Welsh legends at bedtime, mended her wounds whenever she fell and scuffed her knees, the times she patiently teased the knots from her wild and tangled hair. In her heart Linette should have known the old woman would not have lied to her unless she had cause, but instead of trying to understand she had punished Enaid in the only way she knew how: with silence, shunning her at every turn. Linette had treated Enaid just as badly as Julian had treated her, and worse too for she knew that Enaid truly loved her, and now a hate courses through Linette's veins like liquid fire; she was not lying earlier when she said she could kill Julian. Indeed, she can think of nothing that would give her greater pleasure.

Linette shuts her eyes, tries to calm herself, raps hard on the door before her courage deserts her completely. When Enaid opens it the old woman's eyes fill with tears, and Linette's guilt surges to the fore once more. The harp music stops.

"May I come in?"

"Of course," Enaid whispers, holding the door open wider. "Of course."

Nervously, Linette steps over the threshold. The canopy of yellow gorse has wilted now, the petals shrinking into brown. As she passes, Linette raises her hand to touch a branch nestled in a vase. Protection, that is what Enaid used the plant for, she had never lied about that; no wonder she kept the plant so close, trying to press the flowers onto Linette at every opportunity.

She feels a lump form in her throat. That is all Enaid has ever tried to do. Protect her, protect her mother, and Linette turns in the threshold of the bedroom, the last of her reserve dissolving like ice in hot water. There is so much she meant to say, so much she feels needs to be said, but in that moment Linette realizes there is only one thing she can say that actually really matters.

"Oh, Enaid," she whispers. "Can you forgive me for being such a beast?"

The old woman's wrinkled face breaks. With a cry she comes closer, tenderly kisses Linette on the cheek.

"My sweet, sweet girl. It is I who must ask your forgiveness. Do I have it?"

"Of course you do," Linette whispers, holding Enaid close. She smells of soapsuds and rosewater, all the things she found such comfort in as a little girl. "Of course you do."

"And what of me, Linette?" a voice asks softly behind them. "Can you ever forgive me?"

The two women release each other, and heart pounding Linette steps into the bedroom. Gwen Tresilian gazes up at her from where she sits at the harp, twisting her thin fingers in the tassels of her shawl.

"Mamma . . ."

Her mother offers a watery smile, her swallow visible in the hollow of her throat.

"I'm sorry," she whispers, and the pain Linette hears in her mother's voice sets her heart beating faster. "I'm sorry for all the times I never recognized you, for all the pain you have endured these long years. To have suffered so cruelly . . . Enaid has told me all." Her mother shakes her head sadly, the neat plait of her white hair lying limply on her breast. "This is not what I wanted for you, I hope you know that. I never thought it would come to this when we made that terrible choice. I'm so sorry," she says again. "So very, very sorry."

It is a relief to hear the words, words that until that moment Linette had not realized she longed to hear. She looks at her mother, the mother she has never truly known and one day might; in the lowlight Lady Gwen does not appear quite so gaunt, so ill—her features are softened, her skin infused with golden light, and in the curve of her sad smile Linette sees the shadow of the lively beautiful creature she once had been. When her mother holds out a shaking hand, Linette takes it without thinking twice.

"Look at you." She is gazing at her daughter with unmistakable pride, squeezes Linette's fingers tight. "I see the ghost of your father in your face," Lady Gwen says softly. "Your strength, your passion. Everything I loved about him lives, still, in you."

Her mother's voice breaks then, and all of a sudden it is too much for Linette to bear. The last of her defenses crumple, the lump in her throat dissolves, the tears come hot and fast, and with a sob she sinks to her knees. Linette rests her head on her mother's lap, craving the closeness she was always, always denied. It is a shock to feel her mother's hand on her hair, the gentle touch of someone who loves her, and Linette cries and cries until she has no more tears to shed.

Later, Linette sits at her dressing table. She meant to go straight to bed for she was tired in both body and mind, but she simply could not settle. Instead she took her writing implements from her study and brought them back upstairs, where she has been penning her deposition for the last half-hour.

She reads it with a rising sense of dissatisfaction. After much thought Linette decided to commit her entire history to paper before relating the circumstances of the last few days in minute detail, but reading her words back now she realizes she sounds like the madwoman Julian always pretended she was. What court of law would believe such wild claims? Blood rites and rituals, sacred circles, demons called Berith, and names written in an alphabet whose language she does not even know? Even the parts describing Julian's cold treatment of her over the years reads like nothing more than the complaints of a spoiled child who does not know her place.

Linette places the quill back into its inkwell, puts her head in her hands.

She sits like that for several minutes, until, at length, a dark thought begins to invade her mind like malicious wasps.

I *could* kill him, the wasps say, and Linette presses her fingers hard into her temples. It would be no less than he deserved, a fitting payment for the life he took from her, from her mother, from Henry. From her father. *A life for a life.* Slowly the shadow of a plan begins to swirl in her mind and Linette lets it take shape, feels a sense of rightness envelope her. Yes, the wasps whisper, it is only right. Cwm Nantcol could hide a body well enough, especially if she were to bury it in the lower reaches of Moelfre where the land is mostly bog. A body could sink very easily if she were to weigh it down.

No one would ever know.

There is a clatter of wheel, the crunch of gravel. Linette lifts her head. Merlin rolls over on the bed where he has been stretched out snoring, ears twitching at the sound, and with a strange sense of inevitability Linette rises from the dressing table. Wrapping her dressing gown about her shoulders she goes to the window, pushes the curtain along its rail, and when she sees who it is her anger rises once again to choke her.

As she thought. It is Julian.

Gripping the curtain Linette watches him steer the dapple gray to the side of Plas Helyg in the direction of the stables. He was not supposed to be back until tomorrow, she thinks, that is what he told them. But then Julian Tresilian is a liar, and always has been.

It comes as naturally to him as breathing.

Linette lets the curtain drop.

I could kill him.

The words are loud in her mind now, and they do not belong to the wasps. They belong wholly to her.

I can kill him.

I will *kill him.*

Ever so quietly Linette leaves her bedroom, shuts the door softly behind her. She pads barefoot along the threadbare carpet, down the corridor, down the stairs to the landing below. At the grandfather clock she stops, the pendulum clunking loudly in its mighty casement, slow and measured, back and forth, a deep and resonant lullaby.

Waits.

It is some minutes before Julian lets himself in. From the shadow of the stairs Linette watches him cross the vestibule, but instead of disappearing through to the west wing he approaches the ancient fireplace. Her cousin reaches up, places his hand upon the sconce fixed into the stone. Linette grips the balustrade tight, watches with astonishment as Julian pulls the sconce down. In that moment there comes the rumbling of stone; the hearth draws back, slides away to reveal an opening.

But.

Julian does not go through the doorway the sconce has revealed. Instead he turns, crosses the vestibule again to the west wing, disappears through the door, and Linette is left frozen with a dawning realization.

There are tunnels under this house.

And he has just opened one of them.

She hovers with indecision. Confront him now? Or follow him through the tunnel when he returns and see where he goes? Heart in her mouth she moves out from her hiding place, descends the stairs. At the bottom—resolve hardening like iron—she follows her cousin into the west wing.

Candlelight slithers beneath his study door. She can hear movement, rustling, a creak. Without making a sound, Linette pushes the door open.

Julian stands behind his desk, the grimoire in his hands. He looks up; their eyes meet. He does not appear surprised to see her. Indeed, he simply laughs.

"Cousin," he says. His voice is hoarse. He looks even sicker than he did the other night—his face pale and drawn, dark crescent moons beneath his eyes.

"Julian."

Her cousin places the book back down on his desk, almost tenderly strokes the curve of Berith's circle.

"I saw the light in your window. I knew you'd come down." Julian tilts his head. "The Devil is in you," he remarks. "I can see him in your face."

There is no point in drawing it out, no point wasting her breath with lies. Better to be honest, to say precisely what it is she intends to do.

"I know everything."

He stares at her across the desk. Then he smiles, cold and hard and taunting.

"I know you do."

She blinks, not expecting that, for how *can* he know? But, no matter. It changes nothing.

"You won't get away with it," Linette tells him, stepping into the room. "I'm not afraid. All of you—Lord Pennant, Sir John—you will pay for what you've done, but I shall see to it that you pay first."

He laughs, a cold laugh that sends frosty needles down her spine. "And how do you propose to do that, Linette?"

She steps closer. All she needs is the ceremonial dagger. All she needs is to bury the blade in his heart and watch him bleed onto the rug. . . .

"No one will believe you," Julian says now, smooth as silk. "No one will take your claims seriously."

The amusement leaves his face, as if someone has flicked a lever. His dark eyes narrow as Linette takes another step forward. He coughs into his hand, and when he lowers it she sees the glint of blood on his palm.

"They'll put you away. As mad as poor Gwen Tresilian, they'll say."

Linette nods. "They can say it, but it won't be true. However, I had no intention of telling anyone."

403

Julian watches her. He opens a drawer in the desk—not the one Linette wants open but another—and brings from it a familiar glass vial. Almost tenderly he places it on the table.

"You don't plan on doing anything stupid do you, Linette?"

"What I plan," she says quietly, "is one of the most intelligent things I think I shall ever do."

Her cousin lifts one side of his mouth, dips his hand into the inner pocket of his coat and brings out a handkerchief. Slowly, he wipes the blood from his hand.

"Your arrogance has always amazed me," Julian says. "You know so little of the world and yet you think you know better than anyone how to live in it." Casually he removes the gold stopper from the vial, tips a few drops from it onto the bloodied handkerchief. "Of course, you do not know better. You never have."

Linette looks at that handkerchief, resting now in his cupped hand. She needs to reach the desk, needs to get hold of that knife, but Julian does not move, stands so quietly, so still, and for the first time since leaving her bedroom Linette feels the smallest flicker of doubt.

"What do you mean to do?" she asks.

"If you know everything, you need not ask."

"Not that," Linette says. She nods to the handkerchief. "That."

Julian's smile is the most genuine one she has ever seen him give her. It is sinister, wicked, and Linette realizes then that she has been too hasty, should have found another way, and in the split-second she decides to run he moves from the desk so fast that she does not even get a chance; within seconds he has her in his grasp. Linette struggles against him but despite the anger that propelled her—despite the fear that has replaced it—Julian is stronger, is pressing the handkerchief to her nose and mouth.

The last thing she sees is the grimoire, the raised symbol of Berith on its cover, before her vision turns black.

CHAPTER
FORTY-ONE

He wakes to the unmistakable smell of sulfur and a room as black as pitch. His mouth is dry as quarry stones, his teeth pitted against the rough plane of his tongue, and Henry blinks wide-eyed into the dark.

Something is wrong.

Henry does not know how he knows, cannot explain this feeling of surety. The room is cold, the noxious smell of sulfur so strong he must sit up and cough, and it is in that moment he realizes the bed is empty.

"Rowena?"

Nothing.

"Rowena!"

"I'm here."

With relief he turns in the direction of her voice. She is silhouetted in the frame of the door, looking out onto the landing. Rowena wears only her shift, red hair spilling down her back in long flowing curls.

"What is it?"

She half-turns, beckons him. "Can't you hear?" Her voice carries on it the edge of fear. "Someone is downstairs. I . . . I think I can hear voices."

Henry swears, fumbles on the floor for his breeches and pulls them on, searches for his boots, his shirt, joins Rowena at the door. Like a frightened child she leans into him, and Henry puts his arm around her shoulders.

"Listen," she whispers.

There *are* voices, or what he thinks are voices, but the sound has a strange undulating rhythm to it, a cadence not wholly natural.

Not wholly natural.

His stomach lurches. Henry knows instinctively what those voices are, knows exactly to whom those voices belong: Julian Tresilian. The Order.

It is the sound of chanting.

Henry tries to think. The candle burned down hours ago, and he left the tinderbox downstairs. There are no weapons in the bedroom, nothing to defend themselves with. And yet he cannot ignore it. Will not ignore it.

Something must be done.

"Go up to the house," Henry says, putting on his boots, his shirt. "Get Powell to send for help."

"I'm staying with you."

"You're damn well not."

"I *am*," Rowena insists, looking up at him. In the dim light from the landing window her eyes are large, her heart-shaped face set, and in frustration Henry sighs.

"You're growing as stubborn as Linette. Very well. But stay behind me at all times. If you have to run then do not hesitate, get as far away from here as you can, do you understand?"

Rowena nods. "I understand," she says, and Henry takes her small hand in his.

They cross the landing, make their way slowly down the stairs. The treads do not creak and for that he is thankful, but it occurs to him when they reach the bottom that it does not matter how much noise they make; Julian has called to them deliberately, has made sure Henry has heard.

But how?

Henry opens the door of the gatehouse, wonders if perhaps they are outside, but the path lies empty. What he does mark is that the sky is not the pitch black of night but a lighter shade of indigo, already turning itself over to morning. Within the deep canopy of trees he hears an owl screech. What time is it? Henry wonders. Three? Four?

Behind him, Rowena sucks in her breath. "Look."

"What?" Henry asks, turning away, and she points in the direction of the sitting room.

It is exactly how it was earlier that evening—not one piece of furniture out of place, nothing to raise alarm; except for a strange light at the far end of the room. Henry moves closer, toward the library door standing ajar, and slowly pushes it fully open.

A door is set within the bookshelves. Beyond it, a passageway lit brightly with thick pillar candles set in ornamental sconces, row upon row of them leading down to the end.

"Rowena," he says quietly, gathering her close. "Promise to keep behind me. Do you promise?"

"I promise."

He looks at her. Her face is frightened-pale, those amber eyes muted beneath the dark fan of her lashes, but Henry is not afraid. The anger he did not feel before—the anger that belonged so completely to Linette—begins to spiral in the pit of his stomach, a righteous tug of injustice pulling on his insides. That Julian would dare do this, that he would lure Henry to him in this childish way, is beyond reprehensible. Did he truly believe that he could get away with it?

At the bottom of the staircase there is a rush of air, that putrid smell of sulfur mixing with the dankness of earth and wet stone.

Henry grips the iron banister. Another passage stands before them running in a different direction, lined with torches attached to intricately wrought braziers, rust thickly cloaking the filigree shapes. The chanting is much louder now, as if carried along on their echo; Henry can hear words repeated in a language he does not understand. What was it Mr. Dee said? Hebrew, Theban?

Gripping Rowena's small hand, Henry continues on.

It is cold. So cold, Henry can see his breath cloud in the air before him. At one point the dirt floor rises upward, down, then up again. Behind him Rowena stumbles; he stops, must press against the damp wall to steady her. It is only as he is turning to continue, only when he wipes his wet hand against his thigh, that there is another rush of sulfur-infused air, and Henry realizes where they are. Underground, yes. That much is obvious. But not just any place underground. They are somewhere very specific.

"Of course," he mutters, and Rowena presses his fingers between hers.

"What is it?"

"We're in the mines."

Henry remembers the blocked-off tunnels when he visited the mine that first time, thinks of why the mines are so close to the house in the first place; the Order could not meet in Plas Helyg itself, they needed somewhere else, somewhere private. Somewhere hidden, yet easily accessible.

There are tunnels under this house.

"Henry," Rowena whispers. "Look."

Ahead of them is a cavernous entryway, glowing eerily orange. On the cusp of that dreadful sulfuric odor Henry detects another smell, the sweet and woody scent of frankincense.

"Come on. And remember, Rowena—when I tell you to run you do it."

She nods but does not answer. Taking a deep breath, Henry continues on to the end of the passage.

It is as they draw closer that Henry glimpses through the arched entrance a pair of stone pillars, what he thinks might be—bizarrely—a strangely shaped throne. The chanting is monstrous loud now, compounded by the echoes that fill the cavern like an unholy choir, and just as he and Rowena reach the arch, a figure steps into view.

Despite his earlier resolve, Henry feels his chest tighten with unease.

The figure before them wears a crimson floor-length hooded cloak, its golden embroidery glistening in the lowlight. Whoever it is has their back to him, but Henry sees clearly what the person holds in each hand, and it is this that has given him pause.

In the left hand, the limp body of a black hen held by its clawed feet. In the right, the ceremonial dagger, its tip dripping a glistening red.

Henry realizes then that he recognizes the words, those words repeated over and over, again and again, in a sibilant haunting chant:

Hoath, Redar, Ganabel, Berith. Hoath, Redar, Ganabel, Berith . . .

Enough, he thinks. Enough now.

Henry steps into the room. The chanting stops. As one, the Order turn to greet him.

He is in what looks to be a temple. Two pillars stand at the far end flanking the throne Henry glimpsed just moments before. They appear to be of natural formation, as if belonging to the mountain itself rather than a man-made creation, but the throne has carved into it symbols from Julian's grimoire. A black curtain hangs behind it and above, suspended from chains in the ceiling hangs a large sigil of Berith made from pure gold. Torches are set high into the walls which are, strangely, patterned with lush green moss. At the sound of trickling water Henry realizes why; a stream runs along the length of the room, and from the direction of the flow he deduces it must be the same one that runs along the back of the gatehouse.

All this Henry takes in within the space of a few seconds, for his attention is soon drawn to the circle set within the middle of the room and those standing around it, hand in hand.

He is looking upon the same image from the grimoire, brought to life with frightening accuracy. In what looks like blood, a circle has been drawn upon the stone floor, a circle filled with those same strange symbols. At the top a skull has been placed, just as the image in *The Shadow Key* depicted, but one thing is different: lying in the middle of the circle is a body, and Henry feels the first stab of true fear run through him like a sword.

It is Linette who lies in the circle, her skin as pale as death.

"Welcome, Henry," a voice says softly. "We have been waiting for you."

Pulling his gaze away from Linette, Henry looks into the faces of the Order one by one: Lord Pennant. Lady Anne. Sir John Selwyn. Lady Selwyn. Matthew Lambeth. Elis Beddoe . . . and, of course, Julian Tresilian.

"Rowena," Henry whispers. "Run now. Go to Plas Helyg, fetch Powell."

"Oh no," Julian says, a hoarse catch in his throat. "Our little hedgewitch stays here."

Henry senses rather than sees Rowena press herself against the stone wall. Julian smiles.

"Your sister is still alive, by the way," he adds conversationally. He places the dead hen at the foot of the circle, the south to the skull's north, and as he moves Henry realizes Julian is wearing an elaborate headdress made of ivory and feathers, and an ornate costume beneath the cloak. In the spaces where his flesh shows he sees that his skin too is marked with those strange archaic symbols. Henry swallows, glances at the others forming the outer circle, and sees that they are clothed and marked the same way.

"What have you done to her?"

"A little sedative," Julian answers, tapping the tip of the bloodied blade against the cushion of his palm. "She'll wake soon enough. We need you both awake, when Berith comes."

Henry shakes his head. "You're mad." He looks to the rest. "You all are."

Beneath her hood Lady Pennant gives a little laugh. "*Dear* Sir Henry! You cannot be more wrong."

"Can't I?" he shoots back, his anger returning. "You believe in something that doesn't exist. All this—" Henry gestures to the pillars, the throne, the skull, all of it—"is just a way to play make-believe. It's all in your heads."

The Order of Berith chuckle, an irritating laugh that echoes round the circle like the fall of a domino line, and Henry clenches his fists. Seeing it, Julian shakes his head with amusement.

"I felt as you did, once. But then I discovered my books and the world opened up to me, blessed me in ways I never thought possible." He steps forward, a look of urgency on his face. "But it *was* possible, Henry! The things I've seen! The treasures I've possessed, the pleasures I've tasted! All because of this." He gestures to *The Shadow Key* set open on a stone lectern, Berith's sigil carved on its base. "I brought the secrets of Solomon home, persuaded others of their merits. So many riches we've received! As long as we honored Berith, our wealth was secure."

"Your wealth?" Henry shoots back. In turn he looks from Lord

Pennant to Sir John, back again to Julian. "It came from slaves in Jamaica, from shipbuilding and horses, from the yield of Welsh mines, not from *this*." Henry gestures at the hen bleeding into the circle, staining the hem of Linette's nightgown red.

"But you are wrong, Henry! What more proof could there have been of Berith's magic than you yourself?" Julian's words are strangled now on the edge of a cough. "You and Linette," the robed man continues, glancing at her prostrate body in the circle, "were a miracle. Gwen and Hugh could not have children until we evoked Berith's power."

He does cough now, a violent expulsion into his hand, and Henry marks the blood that fills the palm, blood which Julian shakes onto the stone floor. Henry shakes his head in disgust.

"They could not conceive for other reasons that have nothing to do with your so-called demon. Sometimes such matters take time. Believe me, as a man of medicine I should know. It was a coincidence, nothing more."

Julian turns, his cloak whispering on the stone floor, begins to pace.

"That is just what your father said. Coincidence. But it was Berith who brought you into this world and it is Berith who will take you from it." He stops, smiles again. "Your mother's attempt to save you was all for naught. Despite her best efforts, we found you at last."

Henry hesitates. "How *did* you find me?"

"With difficulty," Julian replies softly. "I searched London high and low for you, paid handsomely for others to do the same, but it wasn't until a year later I discovered you'd been taken to the Foundling Hospital. A lot of beggars sleep near the gates—some coins loosened one of their tongues, described your father perfectly. Of course, by then, I had no way of knowing which child you were. Names are changed, origins kept secret, the infants taken to the country until

412

they reach the age of four. I thought my name and pocketbook would work in my favor but it seems they had already been warned someone might come. I had no idea what token was left, if any. So there you stayed. The only thing I had to go on was your birthmark."

He points at the purple stain on Henry's collarbone, peeking through from the open neck of his shirt.

"Of course, with it being hidden you would be impossible to find unless I searched every boy in London. Impractical to do such a thing, but I did discover that all Foundlings are taught a trade, packed off as apprentices at the age of fourteen. I tried to find you that way— tracked down all manner of tradesmen: tailors, bookbinders, printers, goldsmiths, had all their lads checked for a mark. Nothing. The years slipped by. Our London friends found their homes in debtors' prisons or early graves. The mines ceased adequate yield; the money dried up. Pennant's slaves and ships, John's horses. It wasn't enough. We needed more. And then . . ."

Julian raises his bloodied hand.

"The canker is deep-rooted, as I told you. The growth spread slowly but steadily until it was clear that only divine intervention could save me." The older man nods, as if to assure himself of the fact. "This was Berith's punishment for not fulfilling my promise to him. I was at my wits' end until providence led me to you, when I happened to attend a lecture on lesions in the brain last summer. You demonstrated on a live patient, do you recall?"

Something shifts in Henry's mind.

"You asked a question about the temporal lobe, its effects on memory. . . ."

"You do recall! I wasn't sure you did."

"I hadn't until just now."

Julian looks pleased.

"It was your resemblance to my cousin that made me take notice

413

of you, and when you timed the patient's pulse with the pocket watch—Hugh's watch, I'd know it anywhere—it all began to fall into place. It made sense then why I could not find you; Foundlings are not typically trained in the medical field. A university education costs money. Clearly your parents made a provision for you right from the start. Of course, I still could not be sure. My eyes could have been playing tricks on me. I *wanted* you to be Henry Tresilian. I could easily have deluded myself that you were, even if you were not. But then . . ." Julian lets out his breath with a satisfied sigh. "Then you removed your cravat, and I saw the birthmark. I have given thanks to Berith every day since that it was hot in that theater, otherwise you'd never have done it. Bodies packed in like sardines on the benches, every seat taken. You were a popular man, Henry. Respected. Such a pity your downfall had to be so severe."

Something in the way he says this. Henry stares.

"The patient I lost. What part did you play?"

Julian nods sagely. "It took a lot of planning. Baverstock was a fool of a man with a penchant for cards and drink. We had met at Almack's some months before over a game of whist. He spent money like water, did not seem to care or was too old to notice that he kept losing it all to me. During the weeks after I found you, I slowly began to spike his wine with a little concoction that would make him ill, the ingredients of which would mimic the symptoms of cancer. And all the while I held his confidence. I encouraged him to seek out the renowned surgeon Henry Talbot of Guy's Hospital, who I myself saw operate on a patient close to death with such skill and finesse that there could be no doubt at all that doctor could not cure *him*."

Within the circle, Linette stirs.

"I made sure the viscount took a particularly strong draught the morning of the surgery. To calm his nerves, I said. His death was inevitable, as was your dismissal from Guy's, for that too I ensured—the governor was easy to bribe. A Hellfire man, with secrets best kept inside our close-knit circles. All I had to do after that was make sure no one would engage you. Your letters were intercepted. So many letters!" Julian *tsks*. "For four months you tried, Henry—I almost felt sorry for you. When I knew you must have exhausted all avenues, made sure you would have no choice but to accept, I sent the letter offering you the position in Penhelyg. All that remained was the destruction of the gatehouse."

Henry stares. "*You* did that?"

The Order chuckle in unison. Sir John Selwyn bows his head. "That was one of us, yes."

His wife smiles, lips cracked dry beneath the rouge. "It was my idea. You couldn't possibly stay in the gatehouse—how else could you be expected to form a connection with Linette if you were not living under the same roof?"

"It has been a pleasure to watch, I must say." Lord Pennant, this. "To see you become so close, after all these years. At dinner it was clear just how much you meant to each other."

"And you *do* mean a lot to each other, don't you?" Lady Pennant's voice is as cloying as treacle. "The bond between twins is supposedly very strong. It will make the sacrifice to Berith all the more potent."

The Order nod in unison, and Henry must look away. Through all of Julian's speech Henry has tried his best to keep his anger subdued, but he can feel it bubbling up again in his throat, hot and ready to burst.

"You killed Dr. Evans."

"Ah yes," Julian muses, as if he has forgotten the man even existed. "Dear old Wynn Evans. Well, you could not come to Plas Helyg while he still lived, could you? He near burst his heart running away in fear. The nightshade soon finished him off."

A small groan escapes Linette's lips. Once more, Julian smiles.

"Of course, all Dr. Evans saw was one of our smaller rituals. The hens have only ever been an interlude, a mockery of what should have been given all those years before. You and Linette." He presses the dagger against his palm. "Berith gave us time, on the promise that we would one day bring you both to him. The blood spilt over the years has been enough to keep us ticking along, but as I said the money started to dwindle and my illness . . ." He shakes his head. "When the mine collapsed, we knew we had run out of time."

Julian coughs again, a heaving gurgled effort. Beddoe and Lambeth step from the circle. The Pennants and Selwyns start up their chant once more:

Hoath, Redar, Ganabel, Berith.

"We've waited a long time, Henry."

Julian takes a step toward him, Beddoe and Lambeth moving in from both sides.

"And it's time our debt to Berith is paid."

CHAPTER
FORTY-TWO

Lights waver beneath her eyelids, orange eddies dancing on a black canvas. Her throat is sore, her ears filled with the sound of bees. She can smell incense, the noxious scent of sulfur that curls within her nostrils. She is cold. When she turns her head to the side it hurts, even though the motion has only been slight.

Hoath, Redar, Ganabel, Berith.

Not bees. With difficulty Linette opens her eyes.

The staring holes of a skull look back at her and with a cry she jolts up. She barely registers the strange temple-like room she is in, instead feels a sense of panic as she looks at the robed figures above her, their hands joined together to form a circle. Linette stares at Lady Selwyn, eyes closed in abandon, her pinched lips moving in passionate chant, then the hands unclasp, and Henry is thrown in beside her.

"Henry!" she cries as the circle of figures rejoin, larger now with the addition of Dr. Beddoe and Mr. Lambeth. Henry takes the hand she holds out, pulls her up to stand beside him and she wobbles, shocked at her lack of balance. Dark spots pattern her vision, the after-effects of whatever Julian drugged her with.

"Are you all right?" Henry murmurs.

She nods, opens her mouth to reassure him, but he does not look at Linette. Instead his eyes are darting beyond the circle as if looking for someone, and suddenly Linette sees her—Miss Carew—pressed against the wall as if frozen in fear. But then her view is obscured by Julian, who has stepped up to a large stone lectern. She can see the pages of his grimoire fluttering in the cold breeze, the ceremonial dagger resting by its side.

"Where are we?"

"The mine," Henry whispers back, and it becomes clear to her— the towering stone walls, the cathedral-like ceiling. The cold. The wet ground beneath her. The smell of sulfur.

Linette swallows. Almost lovingly Julian turns a page of the grimoire, raises his arms to the air as if in prayer.

"Thee I invoke, the Boneless one, who dwellest in the Void Place of the Spirit! At this most sacred solstice we offer you the souls of my own kin, the blood of twins, as pledged to you years afore."

Her cousin's voice echoes through the large chamber. The torches flicker in their sconces, beating a deadly pulse against the stone walls. Beside her, Henry shakes his head.

"He's mad. All of them are."

As if in reply the circle of robed figures raise their clasped hands, their painted arms creating a fleshy barrier.

Hoath, Redar, Ganabel, Berith!

"In return," Julian intones over the din, "you will grant us riches on this earth, renewed health and vigor, and when our time to pass the veil arrives, you, Almighty Berith, will bestow upon us the greatest seats beside your unholy lord and master."

Linette stares. Henry is right. Julian *is* mad, and it is clear there can be no dissuading him from his course. She looks at the ceremonial blade. If she can only finish what she intended! If only she can reach it! Pressing Henry's hand she flings herself at Sir John, tries to break the barrier of the Order's arms but they stand fast, continue their sonorous chant:

Hoath, Redar, Ganabel, Berith!

"Hear me!" Julian cries, his arms once more held aloft. "Hear our call!"

Suddenly the torches dim, dipping the temple into an eerie semi-dark. The smell of sulfur grows stronger now, as if it comes from directly beneath her, and Linette lowers her eyes, looks at the dead hen at her feet and swallows.

Surely not, she thinks. It cannot be possible.

Hoath, Redar, Ganabel, Berith!

She clutches Henry's hand tighter, slips her free one into the pocket of her dressing gown, reaches for the sprig of gorse Enaid gave her. "I know you do not believe in its protective powers," the old woman had said, but Linette crushes the needle-like stem in her fist and does not care that it hurts.

There is a rumble deep within the cavern. The chanting grows louder. Fearfully Linette watches Lady Pennant, Mr. Lambeth, Dr. Beddoe, the rest, and she realizes then that they no longer look like themselves; there is a wildness about them now, a cruel and maniacal presence as if they have been transformed, each one of them in the throes of those terrible words:

Hoath, Redar, Ganabel, Berith!

At the lectern Julian throws off the cloak, revealing his elaborate robes beneath.

The portrait, Linette thinks. It is the costume from the portrait!

"Hear us!" Julian shouts now into the din. "Hear us, Almighty Berith! I invoke thee! *I invoke thee!*"

It seems impossible that the torches should go out, but in that moment the temple is plunged into darkness. Only the candles from the passageway highlight the room, the Order in their circle and Julian, Julian who has stepped down from the lectern, walking toward them with slow and measured steps.

419

"Henry," Linette whispers, her fear now as sure as breath. *"Henry!"*

There is another rumble. A knock. Stone on stone. Something else. Something that cannot be described, only, somehow, felt—there is a hunger to it, a dark and savage hunger that resonates in the hollow of Linette's chest like liquid fire. The fine hairs on her arms stand up, her breath catches in her throat. And sulfur, that dreadful stench of sulfur, so strong it makes her nostrils burn!

"Keep hold of my hand, Linette," Henry tells her, voice urgent, and within it she can hear his own fear reflected back at her. "When I run you follow. Don't look back, do not let go of my hand, do you hear me?"

Hoath, Redar, Ganabel, Berith!

The circle parts then. Julian steps into it, the ceremonial dagger held high in his hand.

"I surrender you both in the name of Almighty Berith," he whispers. His dark eyes are frenzied in his pale face, and Linette stares at him in horror. "May this sacrifice which we find it proper to offer unto you be agreeable and pleasing unto your desires. May you be ready to obey us."

His dark eyes are captured in shadow, his face a *cythraul* taunt.

"Berith!" he cries. "Do my work!" and Julian raises the dagger high.

The rumble comes again. This time it is louder, deafening in its intensity. It is a sound heavy and resonant that reverberates right down to the soles of Linette's feet and makes Julian pause, makes the Order's chants dwindle, for *this* time it does not come from within the circle.

It comes from outside. It comes from above.

"What is it?" Linette hears Lady Pennant cry. "What is it?"

Something falls from the stone ceiling, clatters at their feet. The hard clout of a stone hits Linette's shoulder and she cries out. Another clatter to her left, another deafening rumble. There is a sharp exhale, a grunt, as it happens again and again, until, suddenly, like rain, the cavernous ceiling above them begins to fall, and the Order start to scream.

"It's the mine!" Henry shouts over the din. "Linette we must move, we must—"

A larger rock falls to her right. She feels the rush of air, hears the thud of stone on flesh, the sharp cry of pain. Lady Selwyn, is it? It makes Linette jump—she lets go of Henry's hand, and in her panic she loses him in the dark.

The stench of sulfur is so strong! Desperately she holds on to the branch of gorse, looks for the candlelit passage, a safe path toward it. But, no good. The cavern is collapsing, hunks of stone bar the way. Another rock falls in a shower of dust and Linette recognizes the voice of Mr. Lambeth as he cries out for help.

With no way forward Linette spins, retreats further back into the temple, but she can barely see; all she can do is hear. The screams around her are high and desperate, the sound of collapsing stone hard and quaking, and Linette gasps back her tears.

"Henry!"

"Linette!"

Suddenly a hand clamps onto her, clubbed fingertips pressing hard into her wrist. Linette can feel his sour breath on her face.

"You won't escape me," Julian rasps. "You won't escape him!"

"*No!*" As hard as she can Linette thrusts him from her, and in that terrible moment she hears the deafening rumble of stone, the sickening crunch of bone, Julian's strangled scream of pain. "Julian," she whispers, and for the briefest moment her fear gives way to shock as she glimpses the flash of a gold ring on outstretched fingers, reaching, reaching, reaching . . .

"*Henry!*" Linette cries. "*Where are you?!*"

They find each other by accident, a fumbled clash in the dark.

"The passage is blocked," she sobs into his shoulder. "We need to find another way out."

"There must be one," he answers with panting breath. "How did *you* get here?"

Plas Helyg's fireplace flashes into her mind's eye, but then there is another crash of stone, an answering scream. Henry presses Linette's hand.

"Rowena." Like Linette he sounds desperate, frightened. "Where is Rowena?"

"I don't know!"

"Rowena?" Henry spins around, dragging Linette with him, staring blindly into the darkness. *"Rowena!"* he shouts, and suddenly Miss Carew is upon them, pulling at their sleeves.

"This way," she says, and Henry cries out in relief. "I've found a way out."

Miss Carew leads them to the stone throne. Linette hears the faint rush of silk, realizes the curtain she saw behind it was a doorway itself, and they find themselves now in a narrow tunnel. It is even darker here, darker than the cavern they have just left. Behind her the mine continues its devastating collapse and Linette can feel the repercussions beneath her feet. On they go, the only sounds the rumbling cavern behind her, the scuff of dirt, the heave of their panicked breath.

The tunnel smells of drier earth now, the scent of Plas Helyg's woodland in spring when Penhelyg's fauna grows anew. Linette wonders how deeply underground they are as Henry pulls her behind him, and as the beating of her heart settles into a steadier pulse she finds herself wondering too about the people they have left behind. Has anyone found a way out? But the screams she heard were too terrible, the sounds of falling rock too final.

None of this, none of it, seems real.

The tunnel has narrowed, the ceiling becomes lower. There is silence behind them now, and a sob catches harshly in Linette's throat.

A cold sort of damp fills the air. Minutes have begun to stretch, leaving Linette with the feeling they are running further and further from help. Surely they should have reached the house by now? But this is a darkness deeper than any dark Linette has ever known. She bites her lip, concentrates on the echo of Henry's boots.

The echo of Henry's boots . . .

They are not, then, treading on earth any longer. They are treading on stone. Plas Helyg, at last!

"Here!" comes Miss Carew's voice from the front. "There's a door."

A door? That's not right. There was no door through the fireplace, only an open tunnel. But Linette hears the groan of hinges; a dim skein of light appears in front of her, and as the door opens wider that light floods the tunnel like a balm. She squints—it hurts her eyes—and a rush of cold fills her with ice.

"My God," Henry says.

"What?" Linette whispers. "*What?*" and he pulls her through. She gasps.

They are in the Cadwalladr crypt.

Linette has come here only once before. When she was a child Enaid tried to press upon her the importance of honoring the dead, but the crypt frightened her so much that she made the housekeeper promise never to take her there again. She remembers well the high windows shaped like arrow slits, the monolithic tombs carved with Celtic ropes and holy crosses, the newer one that belonged to her father, the angel that adorned the tomb's lid like a sentinel.

Henry lets go of Linette's hand.

"Well done, Rowena," he murmurs, kissing her cheek. He strides then between the tombs, toward the large double doors of the crypt.

For a split second Linette fears they will be locked, but Henry pushes his weight against them and they open with a groan, their hinges screaming with the effort of old iron over stone.

Together, they step through.

Dawn has already crept upon the forest like a welcoming blanket; the morning is fresh and filled with the scent of the woods, and in its air is the promise of summer heat. Linette breathes it in, relief washing over her like a wave . . .

. . . but then she feels a cold sharpness at her throat.

"We must get as much distance between us and the crypt as we can," Henry throws over his shoulder. He is rushing across the clearing, heading toward the gully of willow trees on the other side as if they are a beacon.

"Henry," Linette calls hoarsely.

"We'll go to Mr. Dee," he continues, breathless with the effort of it. "He's closer."

"Henry?"

Halfway across the clearing now. Soon he won't hear her.

"You can both stay there while I go to the village, get Ivor to send for help. We must—"

"*Henry!*"

"What? What is it?"

He spins around. Stares. Linette sees his reaction, sees the sequence of expressions pass his face almost too fast to name them: shock, disbelief, hurt, and then a horror that turns his eyes opaque.

For at the steps of the crypt Rowena Carew has Linette pinioned in a cruel embrace, the ceremonial dagger pressed into the hollow of her throat.

CHAPTER
FORTY-THREE

Henry stares. Dismay and dread spindle down his spine like cold fingertips on his vertebrae.

"I don't understand."

Rowena smiles but there is no warmth in it. The woman who stands before him now is a creature filled with malice—it exudes from her like a miasma, her face no longer beautiful but as hard and cruel as Julian's had ever been.

"I don't understand," he says again.

"No," she replies, "I dare say you don't. But you will."

Realization dawns.

"You were one of them."

"Yes."

"You used me."

"And you made it so easy," Rowena says softly. "I knew the minute you looked at me you wouldn't be able to resist. Few men can. All I had to do was smile prettily and act the innocent, and you fell over yourself to become my protector."

He *did* fall over himself, acted like a lovesick fool whenever she was near, all clarity of thought swept away by a pair of exceptional amber eyes.

"But how?" His voice cracks. "How could you be involved with them?"

"Easily," Rowena says, as if she were proud of it. "Julian, you see, made me an irresistible offer."

Henry swallows, a coil of jealousy tightening in his gut.

"What were you to him?"

"A pawn. Just as he was mine."

Her voice is hard as granite, and as she stares coldly at him something else clicks into place.

"You destroyed the gatehouse."

"I did."

"You made the tincture that killed the viscount and Dr. Evans."

"Right again."

"And it was you who drugged Gwen."

"Your mother. Yes." Again, she presses the knife. Linette gasps as a bead of blood appears at her throat. "Not to begin with, of course. For years Julian used Dr. Beddoe's weaker concoctions—ill-made tinctures that Gwen's body had started to reject. That's what comes from using a quack, I suppose. No wonder he lost his fancy practice in London. He was found out, eventually, as all his type are in the end, and fled to Criccieth under Sir John's protection. But three years ago, Julian found me."

Henry says nothing. Cannot.

"It was quite by chance, really," she continues. "Julian had been visiting a local landowner who was to pay a handsome fee for a large shipment of slate. He lived in a manor house on the outskirts of the town I lived in at the time. The man's wife had fallen ill with a fever and the local physician was held up elsewhere so Julian—to ingratiate himself, I suppose—asked for someone who might help. He was directed to my door. I accompanied him back to the house, sat up all night with the lady, and the next day he escorted me home. But Julian

426

took a fancy to me just as you did, and the money he promised was more than I'd ever see in one year. So for the month he stayed at the manor, I became his mistress."

All the while Rowena has been speaking Henry has tried to distance himself from the pain he felt at that initial blow, forced himself to focus on the dagger pressed against Linette's neck. Linette is taller than Rowena by some inches, and though Rowena is holding her at an awkward angle she wields the knife with confidence; there is no way at all Linette could make a move without falling victim to it. But at Rowena's last words Henry's concentration is lost, and he looks into her hard face in the growing light.

"Mistress?"

"I had no qualms about it, either. By then it was a way of life for me. I'd learnt to suffer the touch of a man since I was a little girl."

Henry swallows, sick at the thought of it.

"I'm so sorry."

"Are you?" She shrugs. "Well, perhaps you are. But what you feel does not matter to me. It never has."

It is a hurtful boast. Henry stamps it down.

"How came you to be here?"

Rowena's eyes narrow. "He's an arrogant man, Julian Tresilian. After he'd had his fill, he liked to tell me of his excursions abroad, his illicit little club. I didn't listen at first. To me he was just another man eager to hear the sound of his own voice. But then he said a name, a name I had grown to hate with everything in me since the very day I was born."

"What name?"

"Emyr Cadwalladr."

Linette stiffens in Rowena's grasp. "My grandfather? I don't understand."

"Then let me make it clear."

The tenor of Rowena's voice has lowered into something dangerous. She twists the knife. The blood that has blossomed at Linette's throat runs down her neck in a crimson trail that starts to soak into the collar of her nightgown.

"My mother was one of the women Cadwalladr's Hellfire club seduced. He promised her a great deal of money to play a willing part. But he lied, and Emyr wanted rid of her after the Order had their fun. Ours, you see, was one of the families that lived on Plas Helyg's lands." Rowena looks at him across the blade. "You remember, don't you, the ruins we saw that day in the valley?"

Henry pictures them, the roofless dilapidated cottages, their crumbling walls.

"I remember."

"There," she says. "We lived there. I was not born then, but my father never let us forget our history. My parents, together with my brothers and sisters, were forced out into penury. No provision was made for us—your grandfather simply sold the land to pay his debts and didn't give a damn what happened to those left homeless." Her grip slackens on the knife before it tightens once more. "They had nowhere to go. My siblings died one by one either from cold or starvation or from the beatings—and my father, being such a hot-blooded man, made sure to replace them. He used my mother like a breeding mare, and she—who I remember as such a weak pathetic woman—had no spirit to stop him.

"Eventually my parents found their way to the marches and to charity, such as it was. A hovel in a town which cared little who we were or what we'd been, only whether we could pay the board. And each year there was another child and each year one died, and each year my father beat my mother until her will simply gave out. She hanged herself from the rafters in their bedroom while my father was out drinking. It was me who found her."

Something clouds in Rowena's face before it clears again.

"On my mother's death it was up to me to find work; I became an apothecary's apprentice, learnt my poisons young. But it did not matter, it made no difference, for nothing really changed and every day—*every single day*—my father would speak of wicked Emyr Cadwalladr who robbed him of his livelihood and used his wife like a whore. How it was Cadwalladr's fault he beat his children, how it was Cadwalladr's fault he raped his wife. That it was Cadwalladr's fault he did the same to me."

Henry watches her, the pity in his chest ripe and painful. He wants to cry for her. But Rowena . . . Rowena sheds no tears. Her eyes are dry as bone.

"It was also Cadwalladr's fault I was driven to poison my father. I'd learned my trade well, knew exactly what to give dear old Pa that would not arouse suspicion. Later it was said he drank himself to death for he always did like his liquor, liked it enough to favor it above the rent." She pauses, lost it seems in memory. "And for a while I was free of him. For a while I managed to get along. But then I met Julian. Can you understand what it was I felt when he told me who he was? Can you?"

"I'm so sorry, Rowena. I am sorry for it all."

"Sorry means nothing," she spits. "It changes *nothing*."

"I know," Henry says. "But I'm sorry all the same."

There is a space of silence between them. Henry can see Linette's pulse pounding in her neck. The blade is pressed against her jugular vein, he realizes.

If only he could reach the knife!

"What happened then?"

Rowena regards him a moment. "I knew Julian was a man of ambition, he made no secret of that. I knew he had a scheme of some sort. So I took a risk. I told him about myself: where I was from, how I'd lived, what I had been forced to do. I told him I wanted revenge. I wanted the Cadwalladrs dead, every single one of them."

Again she twists the knife.

"This pleased him. It *excited* him. He asked me about my knowledge of herbs. I said I knew every plant and what each was capable of, good and bad. He asked me to concoct something that would turn the sanest woman mad without killing her. A test, he said. So I did what he asked, tried it out on the landowner's wife, to spectacular effect."

Henry risks a step closer. "And then?"

"He told me what he planned. How one day the heir of Plas Helyg would be found and that he and his sister would die. He'd make it look as though their mother—in her madness—had done it. After that, Gwen too could die at the hands of the decrepit housekeeper. An extra dose of deadly nightshade to tip her over the edge." Rowena sneers. "The old lady had been drugging her mistress for years, after all, no one could deny it. She'd find herself at the gallows before the month was out."

A cry of anger rips from Linette's throat, and she squirms in Rowena's unforgiving hold.

"Linette, don't!" Henry warns, and Rowena twists the arm she holds behind Linette's back, presses the point of the dagger into her neck until she stills. Linette looks at Henry, eyes large and pleading.

"Rowena," he tries, "stop. Please. You don't have to do this."

A warm breeze cuts through the clearing, making her red curls dance. Was it really only a few hours ago he had buried his fingers in them?

"After their deaths," Rowena says, as if she had never been interrupted, "Plas Helyg would be Julian's in its entirety. The last of the Cadwalladrs, gone. And I said I would give him everything he wanted,

I would do everything he asked of me just as long as I could be witness to it when the time came. So he brought me back here."

"What of the Order?"

She shrugs. "A means to an end. They thought they owed their wealth to their silly little club." She scoffs. "I never believed in Berith, but I had no way of gaining access to you if I did not participate. I played my part. And then, Henry, when you finally arrived, all I had to do was make you trust me. Make you *both* trust me. When you came to me that day in the cottage, you put me on the spot; I had no choice but to tell you the truth. But when I told Julian what you were about he thought it was funny. There you both were, believing you were solving crimes together, while *we* simply bided our time until the solstice. We knew you could never find any real proof. All I had to do was lead you to the temple when the time came." Rowena's face darkens. "But everything went wrong, didn't it? The wrong people are dead. And my revenge is not yet complete."

Again, Linette strains against the blade.

"We've done nothing to you," she hisses. "Nothing. We don't deserve this!"

"Nor did I deserve any of what I suffered, but here we are." Rowena turns her head to Linette's cheek. "It is enough you are a Cadwalladr, enough you lived on Plas Helyg's lands while I endured the cruelties of poverty and abuse."

There is a rustle in the trees. A stick cracks in the undergrowth and Rowena scans the woodland over Henry's shoulder. He watches her, dare not turn to see for himself—his focus is entirely on Linette and the dagger. One small movement and it could all be over . . .

"I am not ignorant," Rowena says now, looking at Henry again, "that both of you have been mistreated. But neither of you can begin to compare your childhood with mine and you know it. You have never had to go cold or hungry. You've never slept in hedgerows, or

431

traveled miles on foot in all weathers. You have never been beaten until your skin bruised black. You have never suffered the roughness of a man's touch against a dirt floor. You have never—"

All of a sudden a dark shape bounds from the trees at breakneck speed, ears pressed low against its skull. It runs straight across the clearing, long legs traversing the space in seconds; its teeth are bared with intent, and it is aiming right for them.

"Merlin!" Henry shouts. "*Paid!* Don't!"

It happens all too fast; he has no means to stop it. With a snarl Merlin flings himself at Rowena.

"No! *No!*"

But it is too late. The dagger leaves Linette's neck and finds the dog, and with a yelp Merlin falls to the forest floor with a hard and sickening thud.

CHAPTER
FORTY-FOUR

"No!" Linette cries again as Merlin shudders on the ground. She flings herself down beside him, cradles his head in her lap and the lurcher whimpers, looks up at her with pain-filled eyes. The wound is bad; a horrific fur-matted tear from Merlin's thigh to just beneath his belly. Blood pools the earth. Henry shrugs off his shirt.

"Here," he says. He bunches the material together in a tight wad, presses it onto the wound. "Hold it down, try to stem the bleeding."

"It will do little good," Miss Carew says from above them. The gold knife drips, beads of blood shining like rubies in the sunlight. "He'll be dead soon, and so will you."

Linette looks up at her with all the loathing that has built within her chest since the moment she woke in the mine. Nothing can stop it—it is as sure as the sun rising above the cavern wall.

"If you wanted us dead," she cries, "then you should have done it the moment we got out of the crypt! You've missed your chance."

Miss Carew's amber eyes flash with anger. Henry rises, holds out a calming hand.

"Linette's right. There's only one of you and two of us. Do you honestly think we can't overpower you, now we know what you mean to do?"

Some of the smugness fades from Miss Carew's face. The knife wobbles between her bloodied fingers.

"Rowena," Henry says, hoarse with emotion. "You don't have to do this. It doesn't have to be this way."

"Yes, Henry. I'm afraid it does."

Linette watches her in the glow of the morning sun. Miss Carew's red hair is a halo of fire, her eyes like garnets lit from within. A sunbeam shines on the golden knife, glinting sharply bright along its vicious blade, the grooves of Berith's symbol, and in that moment she lunges. Linette screams.

Miss Carew is quick, there can be no denying that, but Henry is quicker. The blade just misses his shoulder and he takes her roughly by the wrists, as if warding off a battering ram. They struggle against each other, a tangle of limbs. Miss Carew kicks at Henry's knees, screeches at him with wild fury, hair flying in a mass of tangled fiery curls—as mad as Gwen Tresilian ever was during one of her terrible fits—and Miss Carew will not relinquish the knife. For such a small woman it is incredible how much strength she has in her.

Desperately Linette looks down at Merlin. Henry's shirt is nearly soaked through; her own hands are caked with blood. She should let the dog go, let nature take its course, for she knows, knows, there is nothing she can do for him now.

Her tears are hot against her eyelids; a strangled cry rips from her throat.

"Merlin," she whispers. "*Mae'n ddrwg gen i,*" and ignoring the pain wrenching at her heart Linette rushes to stand. She means to pull Miss Carew away from Henry, means to drag her from him with all the strength she can muster but then, *then*, a gunshot tears through the morning sky.

The sound of it echoes through the cavern, ricochets loudly off the stone walls. A flock of birds burst from the trees with a deafening explosion of wings. It takes Linette a moment to realize what has happened, to realize the struggle above her has stopped.

She turns her head to look.

Henry stands, breathing heavily, a splatter of red spanning the plane of his cheek, staring at the ground. Linette lowers her eyes.

On the woodland floor lies Rowena Carew, red hair fanned about her like water, a bullet lodged into the side of her skull.

"Stay there!" a voice shouts from above. A man stands on the edge of the cavern wall, his body caught in sharp relief against the sun. "I'm coming down."

The figure disappears, leaving a patch of blue summer sky.

She hears Henry take a breath. It is a strange, strangled sort of noise and Linette looks to him in alarm. He is staring at Miss Carew where she lies barely three feet from her, eyes round with shock, the ceremonial dagger still clutched in her bloodied hand.

"Henry," Linette manages weakly. "Are you all right?"

He swallows hard. His hands clench and unclench. Then, finally, "Yes," he says faintly. "I'm all right."

Linette does not think he sounds all right at all, but before she can say anything Cadoc Powell appears between the willows, Plas Helyg's ornate flintlock pistol in his hand.

He rushes toward them across the clearing, past the Cadwalladr crypt. His clothes are rumpled, he wears no wig. The butler looks as though he has spent the night sleeping rough. Linette has never seen him like this her entire life.

"You've had us in a state, Miss Linette," he says when he reaches them. "Mrs. Evans went to wish you goodnight but you weren't in your bed. We heard the mine collapse, found the tunnel through the fireplace." Cadoc looks grave.

"Did you go through?"

"*Do*, to a point. The tunnel is blocked. The one in the gatehouse

435

too. I sent the dog on, knew he'd be able to sniff you out. . . ." He tucks the pistol into his trousers. "I followed his tracks, heard the struggle. Got here as soon as I could."

Cadoc kneels down, strokes the lurcher's ear.

"Ah, look what you've done to yourself. Couldn't wait for me, could you, boy?" With a sigh he looks up at Henry, the blood on his cheek. "Is that hers or yours?"

Henry is staring at him with searching eyes.

"It was you who shot at me in the woods," he says quietly.

Cadoc rises with a grimace. "I'm afraid so. When Julian told you to keep an eye on Miss Linette . . . well, I didn't know what manner of man you were. I feared you'd agree with him that her mind was unsound like her mother's." He shakes his head. "It was a warning shot, that was all. I hoped it would scare you off back to London."

"You could have hit me."

"I wouldn't have. I was Hugh Tresilian's hunting partner back in the day. Best aim in all of Meirionydd. Didn't work though, did it? Stubborn as your father ever was."

Emotion twists Henry's face. He turns away.

The butler clears his throat, looks at Merlin with regret.

"Let us get back to the house. He'll not last much longer."

The lurcher stirs then but it is a feeble movement; his breath is shallow, hardly there at all. Linette strokes his blood-matted fur.

"Henry . . ." she whispers. "We need to get him home."

For a long moment Henry says nothing. He is staring still at Rowena Carew's corpse as if he might will breath back into her.

"Henry," Linette says again, and this time he comes to himself, looks down at Merlin on the forest floor.

"Yes," he says, "yes," and Henry takes Merlin gently in his arms.

Meirionydd
Autumn 1784

Gwna dda dros ddrwg, uffern ni'th ddwg
Repay evil with good, and hell will not claim you

WELSH PROVERB

October suits Penhelyg well.

The trees have marked the month russet and gold, the woodland awash in rich honeyed colors. Along the forest floor pine cones have begun their seasonal drop and acorns litter the path, brown glossy bodies peeking from within their capstone cases. One has fallen loose from its cupule and Henry bends to retrieve it, presses it into the palm of his hand a moment to feel its grounding warmth before tossing it into the dying bracken of the bank. A rabbit bounds from the ferns, and on the path ahead Merlin's ears prick up as he watches it dart deeper into the undergrowth, white tail bobbing.

He does not chase it. Instead Merlin sits back on his haunches, twists his fine head around to look at Henry as if asking permission. Henry smiles, scratches the wiry fur between the lurcher's ears.

"Not today, old boy."

Merlin licks Henry's hand, thunks his long tail, appears almost to grin.

His wound was wide and deep. By the time Henry had carried the dog back to Plas Helyg he himself was soaked with blood and Merlin barely breathed. Linette proved to be a worthy surgeon's assistant; she did not so much as flinch as she held the torn flesh and pelt together so Henry could stitch it shut. It took twelve sutures, six tightly bound bandages and a splint before the job was done, before he could begin to process everything that had happened all those hours before.

Henry had grown up without family, had the freedom to make his own way in the world; his professional success was all his own doing, no one else's. Still, it was galling to discover his life had already been mapped out for him. The fact that Julian was the reason such measures needed to be taken at all, Henry still struggles to accept. If not for him, Hugh Tresilian would still be alive, and to treat his cousin's wife with cruelty and Linette with such contempt was truly wicked. And then, for Julian to have robbed Henry of a career he loved and to contrive so carefully to bring him to Penhelyg to satisfy the demands of a demon that cannot possibly ever have existed . . .

Henry's grip tightens on the walking staff he carries, the rough bark of oak grazing the soft pad of his thumb.

Even now he cannot explain what he saw that night, why the torches went out all at once or why the cavern collapsed at the very climax of Julian's ritualistic words, for nothing in particular had set those rocks falling. Some believed, it was later said, that it was the doing of the *bwca* or *coblynau*; others simply believed that the mines had been worked too fiercely and the collapse was inevitable, especially so soon after the last.

Yet.

Henry thinks of that overpowering stench of sulfur, the unearthly growl he heard just before the rocks began to fall.

Whosoever breaks a covenant with Almighty Berith will be devoured by a beast of darkness, and that sinner's soul shall belong completely unto Him.

Was this "beast of darkness" the mine? Berith himself? Could it all really have been the demon's doing? Logic dictates it cannot be so, but though Henry will never be able to relinquish his reliance on science he now no longer turns his nose up at the old superstitions.

Some things simply cannot be explained by logic alone.

But it is over now. Life in Penhelyg has begun to find some semblance of normalcy. For Enaid, for Cadoc, for the rest of the servants at Plas Helyg, Julian Tresilian's death came as a relief, as if a dark veil had been lifted from the old Welsh stones and the mansion could once more breathe. For Lady Gwen and Linette especially, Julian's death was a longed-for release, a chance for them both to finally heal.

As the last lingering remnants of Rowena's tinctures wore off, his mother became (according to Enaid), more like her old self and grieved for her husband, for the lost years. She will always be weak—the toxic herbs did their damage and did it well—and only time will tell how far her health can sustain her. But she accepts it all with a grace and dignity that Henry did not expect, and Lady Gwen's good nature softened Linette in turn, the frustrations and bitterness she felt for so long fading as the relationship between the three of them blossomed and grew. The path to recovery is a lengthy one, but it is now free of obstacles and pitfalls.

The way ahead is clear.

Henry sighs, pats the lurcher's neck. Merlin's recovery is taking much longer. Over a year later the poor thing still experiences painful twinges in the muscles of his thigh which Henry must patiently massage out, and it is clear the dog will always walk with a limp. Merlin's hunting days are over.

"*Tyrd*," Henry says gently. "Come along."

Merlin tosses his nose, sniffs the autumn air, rises carefully, begins a slow plod toward Plas Helyg. Henry follows close behind.

News of the mine collapse traveled fast along the coast and beyond; perhaps it was the deaths of so many gentry that fanned the tale and prompted Francis Fielding to come directly to Penhelyg rather than send a reply to Henry's hastily written letter. The Bow Street man listened to Henry and Linette's story and the testimonies of their mother, Cadoc and Enaid, and the Reverend Mr. Owain Dee with quiet contemplation, but though he did not dismiss their wild claims he could not support them either. "What's done is done," he said, a line simply drawn underneath the matter. Still, Henry is sure that had it not been for his prior relationship with the Runner the aftermath might not have been quite so neat; the ownership of the mine was transferred back to the Plas Helyg estate and Julian's own personal riches handed over to Linette, all without dispute. A neat job, Francis assured, no questions asked.

And so it was.

The tunnels were cleared, the bodies retrieved. Julian was buried in the Cadwalladr tomb beside his cousin much to Linette's chagrin, but tradition meant she could not object. The Pennants and Selwyns were returned to their families, Mr. Lambeth transported back to Dolgellau, Dr. Beddoe taken across the estuary to Criccieth. As for Rowena, Henry and Mr. Dee buried her before anyone could see the bullet wound and question why it was there. She lies now within the cromlech where he first kissed her, and he hopes she rests peacefully in the lands in which her kin once lived.

Rowena. Henry's stomach twists. That thick flame-red hair, those round amber eyes he thought so innocent. He remembers Mr. Dee's words all those months ago—*Be mindful of a pretty face*—and grimaces. Henry thought the reverend had been warning against the temptations of the flesh, espousing Christian morals, but now he is not so sure.

Perhaps he truly has the ear of God.

The gates of Plas Helyg come into view. Merlin wags his tail at the sight, and Henry finds himself smiling at the lurcher's excitement to reach home.

Home.

It took Henry a long time to fall in love with Wales—to truly fall in love—but it had, it seemed, been creeping upon him in degrees from the very start. He did not expect to warm to Penhelyg so completely,

442

especially after all that had happened, but as the weeks passed and the villagers finally accepted him as one of their own, a sense of belonging washed over him. No longer did Henry crave the bustle of London or the cold dark halls of Guy's Hospital, not even after Francis secured him his pardon. No longer did Henry feel bitterness or regret over what he had lost, or resent the wildness of the Welsh countryside and its quietness, its changeling weather. He did not realize his heart had lost itself to this place until, one evening late in August, he left the Morgans' cottage and caught sight of the sunset across the sea.

The sky was shot with flames that dipped into gradient shades of mauve and indigo; the clouds whispered across the purpling water like skeins of cotton with seagulls dancing in their wake, and across the water the proud mountains stood silhouetted against the gold-spun sky.

Henry had never seen anything more breathtaking in his entire life.

Linette knew—as only a twin can—the moment he arrived back at the house. As she took one look at his face something changed in hers, and Linette reached out to cup his cheek.

"You will stay."

"Yes."

"You are home."

"I am."

She smiled then in a way she never had before. It was a smile free of the reserve that had always darkened it, a smile of true happiness.

"Mamma will be pleased," she said and Henry smiled back, teasing almost.

"But are you?"

Linette cuffed his cheek lightly with her knuckles, gray-green eyes sparkling.

"*Ydw*. Brother. Besides, if you left, who else would I argue with?"

Now Henry grins at the memory, digs his thumb harder into the crook of his staff.

Of course, it meant he must think of the future. *Really* think of it. It soon became clear that despite his acceptance that Wales was now his home, Plas Helyg was too large for him. Henry had grown up in confined spaces—the claustrophobic quarters of the Foundling, the narrow halls of hospitals, the compact rooms of lodging houses—and while he did not want to return to those restrictive measures, he did not feel comfortable within the mansion's cavernous walls either. He could never act like a Tresilian lord (even if the title was his birthright), would never manage the estate as Linette did (he was perfectly content to leave such matters in her more than capable hands). So, despite its sordid history, despite Linette's most strenuous objections, Henry chose to remove permanently to the gatehouse.

"But why?" she demanded. "You belong here. Plas Helyg is your home as well as mine!"

But the villagers did not know that, would never know that (for how could it possibly be explained?) and he was, after all, still their doctor. He needed somewhere that suited his status, Henry explained to Linette, somewhere the villagers would feel comfortable coming to if they ever felt the need.

Somewhere an assistant could live, as well.

Henry considered offering the role to one of his old students in London, for there were many who would fill the position admirably. But then he remembered Cai's careful interest at the mine, and then at his father's bedside; the cramped room he shared with his parents, the independence he might crave. Why *not* one of Penhelyg's own? It made perfect sense. Still, he had been surprised when Cai agreed, even more surprised that he took to his training so easily. Their relationship is still a tenuous thing; Cai's wilfulness is just as strong as it ever was, and Henry's patience with him sometimes lacking, but they manage well enough together. Henry speaks more than passable Welsh now, and time will only strengthen the bond between student and teacher.

It had taken time for Linette to accept Henry's removal to the gatehouse. She had argued with him, lectured him, but none of it did any good—his mind was set. It was their mother, in the end, who convinced her to see reason.

"Henry is a free spirit, *cariad*, just as you are. Would you listen to him, if matters were the other way around?"

Of course Linette would not.

Henry pushes Plas Helyg's gates open. They no longer squeak—Cadoc takes his new post as estate manager very seriously indeed—and Merlin, tongue lolling, ambles through. Up ahead there is a trickle of laughter. Henry picks up pace, gravel crunching loudly beneath the heels of his walking boots, and follows the sound to the side of the house.

There, across the pond, arm in arm, walk Linette and Lady Tresilian. His sister no longer dresses in their father's old clothes but has instead ordered her own masculine pieces from an Aberystwyth tailor, looking every inch the lord of the manor much to Enaid's growing despair. Indeed, she is as far from being "a lady" as she ever was; now that Julian and Mr. Lambeth are dead the mines are her sole responsibility and Linette has taken to the task like a duck to water—the copper mines have been closed and the slate reopened, with stringent safety measures employed and new equipment to ease the workload. Penhelyg's miners are content. Still, it was a lot for Linette to take upon herself, despite her obstinate insistence that she could cope. Promoting Cadoc had been Henry's idea to alleviate the pressure of managing both the estate and the mines, and Lady Gwen insisted on reclaiming the running of the house; next year they will open Plas Helyg's grounds to the public one day a week, and there is much still to prepare in readiness.

Henry looks to his mother. Her white hair is pinned high on her head, her slim figure dressed exquisitely in a gown of pale lilac. She looks nothing like the haunted wraith Henry met the year before. She is happy and—for now—healthy. A bright and shining star.

With pride he watches them, his mother and sister. Both strong women, stronger than he will ever be, stronger than anyone he has ever known, and Henry releases a contented sigh, raises his gaze to the horizon. Beyond the wide expanse of willow trees the edges of the clouds are trimmed with pink light, the woodland on the far side of Cwm Nantcol retreated into deepening shadow. The autumn air is as soft and warm as gentle breath, and thin glints of sunshine have shifted behind the fountain, making the spring of water soaring from its base a beam of gleaming gold.

Linette sees him. Waves. He waves back. His mother smiles brightly and beckons him. All is as it should be, Henry thinks as he approaches, Merlin still at his side. Even so, there is something that he can never tell them, for Henry will not ruin their hard-fought peace.

He is happy at the gatehouse. He made the right choice to remove there, he knows that. The tunnels to the mines have been sealed and there is no way in or out. At Enaid's behest the Order's temple has been stripped bare, blessed with holy water and cleansed with the smoke of burnt rowan, scattered with the protective flowers of dandelion, garlic and gorse. But sometimes—just sometimes—when he is lying in bed at night, when the sea air wends its way sharply over the salt marshes and up through the forests of Penhelyg like a sigh, Henry is sure, is absolutely positive, he can smell the distinct and pungent scent of sulfur.

AUTHOR'S NOTE

I was still living in the Midlands when I started working on *The Shadow Key*, and every time I sat down to write I was drawn back to the beauty of the Welsh countryside, felt acutely the call for "home," my own form of *hiraeth*.

The word *hiraeth* has no direct English translation but has been likened to homesickness, to longing, yearning, nostalgia and wistfulness, an earnest desire for the Wales of the past. Although not Welsh myself, my links to Wales go way back—childhood summer holidays were spent caravanning along the Cambrian coast or on the mountains overlooking Cadair Idris. In my late teens my mother moved to northwest Wales, and it was inevitable after that I should attend university an hour and a half away in Aberystwyth, so my connection to the area has always been an intrinsic state of mind. *The Shadow Key*, then, is my love letter to Wales but also a nod to its not always bright and beautiful heritage, for during my research I came to understand the country's culture in an entirely different way. As such this novel became, without my quite meaning it to, a study of Wales's social history through a Georgian lens.

There was a long-held assumption in the eighteenth century that Wales was a backward place of stagnant traditions, a view encouraged with the dissemination of Welsh culture through English landowners who attempted to "tame" their tenants. Many estates falling to wrack and ruin were purchased by Englishmen who spent most of their time absent from them, only using the properties as their summer retreats, but insisted that they were overhauled without much thought to the consequences for the tenants. It left a lot of bad feeling in the air, especially as communication continued to be a barrier—the English generally made no effort to speak Welsh, and attempts to enforce their own language on the Welsh people were not well received. *Hope and Heartbreak: A Social History of Wales and the Welsh, 1776–1871* by Russell Davies, *Welsh Gothic* by Jane Aaron, and *The Remaking of Wales in the Eighteenth Century* edited by Trevor Herbert and Gareth Elwyn Jones, were all invaluable to me in conveying Wales's social history to the page.

Despite the English's best efforts, the spirit of the Welsh could not be dampened, and this is evident in their many myths and legends. Anyone who has lived in Wales and walked the woodland lanes and majestic mountains, who has experienced its haunting strangeness and rugged beauty, cannot avoid the country's folkloric heritage. Wales is called "Land of Dragons" for a reason, and *The Shadow Key* is an amalgamation of all these things—borrowed, placed, replaced—set in one of the country's most atmospheric regions: Snowdonia. Here you will find stories of King Arthur and his knights, fearful lake monsters, loyal hounds, mighty giants, and fay folk both pure and mischievous, many of which I've attempted to include in the novel. However, to my regret, many were also left out. A sin eater was included in original drafts but later discarded. The *gwyllgi* (a Black Shuck–like creature), the *Mari Llwyd*, phantom funerals and cursing wells were also relegated to the cutting-room floor. In short, there was just too much source material to choose from and the cultural records were too varied—I simply couldn't include everything I wanted to! For those curious about the myths and legends of Wales, I recommend the following texts: *The Mabinogion* (the Oxford World's Classic edition translated by Sioned Davies is best); *Supernatural Wales* by Alvin Nicholas; *A Relation of Apparitions of Spirits in the Principality of*

Wales by Edmund Jones (an interesting account from 1780); *British Goblins: Welsh Folk-Lore, Fairy Mythology, Legends and Traditions* by Wirt Sikes; *Welsh Monsters & Mythical Beasts* by C. C. J. Ellis; *The Welsh Fairy Book* by W. Jenkyn Thomas; *Rumours and Oddities from North Wales* by Meirion Hughes and Wayne Evans; and *When the Devil Roamed Wales* by Jane Pugh.

Speaking of the Devil, religion and the occult often go hand in hand. The Welsh at that time were a very religious people, and as much as they believed in the *tylwyth teg* they also believed in Satan and his minions. While the eighteenth century was considered the "age of reason"—a period when many began to rely on logic due to the progression of science—the old ways could never be fully relinquished. Those who worshipped the Christian faith believed in all the basic creeds of Christianity such as the Holy Trinity and the concept of heaven and hell, but the advent of the Grand Tour allowed members of the aristocracy to broaden their understanding of other cultures and religious beliefs. As a result, these beliefs were adopted and adapted, and no better example of this habit can be found than within the "Hellfire" clubs of the period (for further reading see *The Hell-Fire Clubs: Sex, Satanism and Secret Societies* by Evelyn Lord).

The most famous Hellfire Club was referred to as the "Monks of Medmenham Abbey" founded circa 1755 by Francis Dashwood, 11th Baron le Despencer, where members would dress in exotic costumes and partake in acts of drunkenness and debauchery. Many clubs of this nature existed during the eighteenth century, and rumor had it that some even included Devil worship, so Julian's sordid history is not completely beyond the realm of reality. For any young and impressionable aristocrat who went on the Tour, it was very possible they might encounter ancient books on the occult and become fascinated by them to the point of obsession. These occult books are varied, disturbing and obscure, often compiled from other compiled works that came before them. Most are written in Latin, German, Italian, or French. For someone who doesn't have much of a head for languages I've had to rely on translated editions, of which there is a very limited catalog. However, the English versions I did manage to acquire are no less obscure—they're extremely fantastical with very little "practical" information of use. So, instead of pulling my hair out to make the occult lore fit the novel, I chose (in the tradition of such books and, indeed, of the aristocrats who adopted them) to create my own lore by compiling elements of the texts into Julian's grimoire, and I plead creative license to any experts on Solomonic magic; this is, after all, a work of fiction. For reference, the texts I referred to were *The Magus, or, Celestial Intelligencer* (the 1801 work of self-acclaimed occultist Francis Barrett), the original *Three Books of Occult Philosophy* by Heinrich Cornelius Agrippa, *Grimorium Verum* translated and edited by Joseph H. Peterson, *Touch Me Not: A Most Rare Compendium of the Whole Magical Art* edited by Hereward Tilton and Merlin Cox, and *The Greater and Lesser Keys of Solomon the King* translated by S. L. MacGregor Mathers and edited by Aleister Crowley. The following texts were also used: *Encyclopedia of Demons in World Religions and Cultures* by Theresa Bane, *Solomon's Secret Arts: The Occult in the Age of Enlightenment* by Paul Kléber Monod, as well as the websites Holy Books and Estoric Archives.

For more general insights into Welsh history, *Wales: Epic Views of a Small Country* by Jan Morris was a brilliant resource. I also found *The Rural Poor in Eighteenth-Century Wales* by David W. Howell, *The Foundations of Modern Wales 1642–1780* by Geraint H. Jenkins, and *The Agrarian History of England & Wales Volume VI, 1750–1850* edited by G. E. Mingay—more specifically the chapter titled "Landownership and Estate Management" written by J. V. Beckett—particularly useful for the running of Plas Helyg and its lands. However, in 1783 Meirionydd was extremely rustic with little "civilization" to be found. Established towns in the vicinity of the novel were few and far between—Criccieth, Harlech, Barmouth (described here as the traditional Abermaw) and Dolgellau were the only settlements of note, and even those had limited means in comparison to those found in rural England. This made navigating the immediate area somewhat tricky, and so some more obscure texts were necessary for research purposes. The official "landscape" of the novel was taken from the English translation of *The Gestiana* by Alltud Efion (edited by Richard Walwyn), and Walwyn's own account of the area titled *A Little History of Borth-y-Gest*, both originally published in the nineteenth century. Many of the scenic descriptions in the novel were inspired by the writings of the naturalist Thomas Pennant, whose *A Tour in Wales* and *Journey to Snowdon,* published in 1778 and 1781 across various volumes, was extremely helpful in picturing an eighteenth-century Wales, together with the anecdotes compiled by David Lloyd Owen in *A Wider Wales: Travellers' Tales 1610–1831.* The rest was taken from my familiarity of the area and, of course, my whimsical imagination. Any errors in the geographical history are—it goes without saying—entirely mine, and sometimes deliberate; the landmarks noted within the novel are all authentic in some shape or form but "borrowed" from various places, and Plas Helyg, its grounds, and the village of Penhelyg are purely fictional.

My final note is on medicine in Wales—*Physick and the Family: Health, Medicine and Care in Wales, 1600–1750* by Alun Withey was a prime source of valuable information, and gave some excellent insights into Welsh medicine, its practices, and the attitudes toward them. For medicinal herbs I drew specifically on the lore set down by the Physicians of Myddfai (who, incidentally, are linked to the Lady of the Lake legend) using the excellent *Welsh Herbal Medicine* by David Hoffmann as reference. *Botanical Curses and Poisons: The*

Shadow-Lives of Plants by Fez Inkwright was also an enlightening text and one I recommend to anyone interested in the history of herbal toxins.

I moved to Wales permanently in the autumn of 2021. This is where, one year later—after three missed deadlines and over 100K of discarded words—I finally finished a first draft of *The Shadow Key*, and the day I typed the last word I took a very long walk in the valley of Cwm Nantcol. It was freezing cold but the ground was dry, the sky was clear, the sunset one of the best I've ever seen, and looking out across the distant sea I felt a deep sense of relief and contentment.

Like Henry, I knew that I was home.

ACKNOWLEDGMENTS

The county of Gwynedd (Meirionydd) is a bit of a blind spot in terms of eighteenth-century records, so finding out more particular details about the area was extremely tricky. Thankfully Aberystwyth University's Department of History and Welsh History has many wonderful experts on the subject, and I am grateful to Dr. David Jones and Professor Phillipp Schofield for directing me toward the texts on Welsh estate management and agriculture. Special thanks in particular go to Dr. Eryn White who took the time to chat to me in detail about Welsh religion in the area and clear up a few more specific queries I had. Thanks also to the staff at Porthmadog's Maritime Museum for introducing me to Richard Walwyn's writings; a big thank you as well to Robin Lovatt for the many instances I reached out for his advice on translations, and to Miriam Williams for checking and correcting my imperfect Welsh (it goes without saying any errors that remain are solely my own, with apologies). I'd also like to express my appreciation to everyone at Tŷ Newydd for their continued support and providing their writing retreat cottage, Nant, just when I needed it. Thank you too to Amanda Bevan and Charlotte Smith of the National Archives, who clarified some shadowy areas of family law and the loopholes of mental illness when it came to matters of inheritance, and Laura Shepherd-Robinson for putting us in contact.

It truly takes a very big team to make a novel into something tangible. Thank you to Rachel Neely and Kiya Evans at Mushens Entertainment for their insightful comments on one of the early drafts and especially to my agent Juliet Mushens who—aside from *always* being right—has far more confidence in me and my writing than I do. I will forever remember her telling me to "stop being mean to yourself" and shall try my best to take her words of wisdom on board every time I'm hit with self-doubt. Massive thanks go to my editor, Liz Foley, who had a lot (*a lot*) of work cut out for her when editing this novel but steered me clear with the patience of a saint, once again understanding better than I did just exactly what I was trying to do. Thanks too to Mary Chamberlain for her eagle eyes, and the amazing team at Harvill Secker and Vintage for all their hard work in every area of the publication journey, thanks I echo to all my wonderful publishers overseas. Thank you also to my cover designer Micaela Alcaino for creating yet another stunning UK cover, and her all-round enthusiasm for the novel. The fear of producing another book after the success of a debut is crippling (second-novel syndrome is very real!), and I can't express how grateful I am that my publishing team thought *The Shadow Key* a worthy follow-up. As with *Pandora* they put 100 percent behind its journey from raw manuscript to physical book, and I couldn't be more thrilled with the results.

Writing is often a lonely business and it's always appreciated when I hear a word of encouragement. Thank you to my fellow authors Elodie Harper and Jennifer Saint for being altogether the loveliest women I could share a publishing journey with, and Liz Hyder for her gentle words of wisdom. Also to my friends Daniel Bassett, Chris Blackborow, Hayley Clarke, Heddwen Creaney and Glen Howell, Alison and Adrian Eynon, Beth and Mike Jennings, Barry Lambe, Meghan Mazella, and many others (who, if I named them all here, would risk stretching the acknowledgements into a novella) for always being unfailing in their support, Sarah and David Lobjoit for being on hand with the bubbly and laughter whenever I needed it, and of course my dearest thanks to my mum, Sally, who was my crutch during the times I felt afraid of failing. Thank you all.

ABOUT THE AUTHOR

SUSAN STOKES-CHAPMAN is a writer based in North Wales. She grew up in the Georgian city of Lichfield, before spending four years in the town of Aberystwyth and graduating with a BA in education and English literature and an MA in creative writing. Her debut novel, *Pandora*, was an instant number-one bestseller in the UK, was short-listed for the Lucy Cavendish Fiction Prize and Goldsboro Glass Bell Award, and long-listed for the Bath Novel Award.